MW01701634

Those Who Broke the World

Derek Ward-Colston

Edited by Laura DeMarse

For all those I love;

the ones moved on and the ones still here.

99

Nothing brings a family closer together than tragedy. Tragedy forces loved ones into each other's arms, so they may be comforted in their darkest hour. They shed tears and suffer through the pain until the despair is bearable again. The average family feels tragedy together so that they may heal together. Unfortunately, for those with evil in the deepest part of their souls, this peaceful unity is nothing but temporary. Soon their true nature returns to conquer all that is good and force them to push their loved ones away.

*****

The town of Loveland was the perfect American small town, placed snugly between two mountains. A small river cuts along the bottom of the northmost mountain, the cool refreshing crystal-clear water that families swim and fish in during the warm summer months. Forests run along up and down both the rock giants that sit and watch the small town filled with modest houses with well-kept lawns and pristine white picket fences. The town of Loveland really was perfect. The mayor, Jim Staylers, knows the birthday of everyone in his town, even gets them a little gift.

The milk in the fridge of every house in the town comes fresh from a local family farm that lies just past the trees on the outskirts of town. This is the same place where the butcher gets the meat he sells in his shop each morning. This was the kind of paradise everyone secretly wants to be a part of.

Of course, every perfect town has that perfect family and the Brooks were just that by all outward appearances. The Brooks family was the most loved and respected family in Loveland; Winston and Elizabeth had a perfect marriage and two beautiful, healthy children.

Winston Brooks was the local proprietor of the family-owned General Store, which is his namesake Brooks Family General Store. He was an impressive man to gaze upon, the black-haired man with green eyes stood at 6 '2" with 250 pounds of pure, lean muscle. The few gray hairs haphazardly hidden in his neatly trimmed beard were the only thing that hinted at his true age. Mr. Brooks always wore a suit and tie to work; he believed that a publicly admired man such as himself should always dress distinguishably. He also believed that an owner of a general store should make it his business to create a personal connection to all the patrons that entered his store, knowing everything he needed to know about his fellow community members.

He knew Harry Gunderson liked a special dark roast coffee bean that he had grown a taste for while studying abroad in Spain, and Winston made sure he had some in stock when Harry would come into the store at the end of each month. When Mr. and Mrs. Feildstein came in on Monday morning to buy eggs and flour for their bakery, Winston would always give them the finest ingredients they needed for a full week of baking. Every Friday, children would run to the Brooks Family General Store after school to get candy and sweets with their weekly allowances and Mr. Brooks would make sure to have a wide variety of fun, exciting candies.

The way Winston Brooks ran his shop made him the most influential man in town. Every man, woman, and even a few kids from time to time would go to Winston for advice and bits of wisdom. If you ever need anything, then you just go down to The Brooks Family General Store because good old reliable Winston will always be there to help. That was a fact in the town of Loveland.

While Winston was a metaphorical father of the town of Loveland, his wife Elizabeth was regarded as the mother of this tiny community. Her chestnut hair and emerald eyes paired perfectly with her beautiful, ear-to-ear smile that made the day of all who beheld it. She was by far the most beautiful woman in the entire town. Every woman in town worshiped her in hopes that she would reveal to them the secret to looking so effortlessly beautiful all the time.

However, it was not just her magnificent beauty that drove others to jealousy; she was also an incredibly smart graduate of a major university. Elizabeth proudly ran the town book club; she even hosted the meetings in her perfect two-story house.

Her home was also a source of envy for her neighbors. The stunning residence made of pristine dark red bricks sat behind an outstanding garden full of healthy, brightly-colored flowers. There was absolutely no sign of weeds or sickly plants. The garden mocked the Brooks' guests with its beauty as they made their way to the front door. Of course, the envy did not stop once the guests entered through the doorway. Smells of fresh baked goods and sights of clean, organized rooms made all who found themselves in the walls of the house ponder how Elizabeth Brooks had the time to create this perfect life.

Every member in the town loved her cooking. Whenever there was a town potluck or community picnic, Elizabeth's dish would always disappear first, especially if the dish was her award-winning apple pie. Neighbors would beg, plead, and even bribe her for one of her delicious one-of-kind pies.

The Brooks were the most beloved and respected couple in all of Loveland, with deep, personal relationships with each of their neighbors. To their friends throughout the town, it appeared as though Elizabeth and Winston were not only a perfect couple, but wonderfully perfect parents to two lucky children as well.

Lillian was the oldest of the two Brooks siblings and was accurately nicknamed "the Loveland prodigy." The 17-year-old girl was as beautiful as she was smart, proven by the fact that she aced every class she had ever taken throughout her school years. It was a safe bet to assume that the brilliant chestnut-haired girl would be off to an prestigious Ivy University in a couple short years.

However, her brain was not the only thing the townsfolk of Loveland took note of; Lillian was a stunning young woman. Her piercing, icy-blue eyes and soft round face had all the boys her age — and a few happily married men, too — gawking over her. Of course, Lillian had no interest in finding love so early in her life, and thus made no attempts to get a boyfriend. That didn't stop her male classmates from trying of course. When Lillian worked the counters at the General Store, the store would be filled with a constant stream of young boys who decided to help their parents out and take care of the family shopping for the week. Most would stare from afar till she glanced their way; they always had a grand plan or flawless pick up line that they would use while checking out that they believed would make this perfect girl fall madly in love with them. The plans never worked. Every interaction ended the same way, with Lillian telling her desperate suitors that her priorities were school and family, and once she had a law degree from an Ivy League college (she never named which school she wanted to get accepted to because she thought that would be bragging), she would have time for love. This response caused most of the boys who sought her affection to cease any further attempts at romance; a couple persisted, however, and asked her out on a date. This annoyed her a little, but she remained polite and told the boys she simply had no time for dates. This was by no means a lie. Lillian spent most of her free time outside of school working in the general store, helping her mother bake, studying for her classes, volunteering around town, or helping her younger brother with his homework.

The youngest Brooks was the most peculiar and easiest forgotten member of the clan. Jamie Dean — who preferred to be called JD, but only his sister actually called him that — was average in every sense of the word. The green-eyed boy was not the brightest, best looking, or biggest 14-year-old, and when compared to the rest of his family, he seemed like an adopted outcast.

The boy with black hair had very few friends at school as he was a very shy, introverted kid. The few "friends" he did have only ever talked about how hot they thought his mom and sister were, which made JD very uncomfortable. JD would not hang out with any of his "friends" outside of school; he spent most of his time in the Family General Store. He helped his father restock shelves or sweep the floors. He worked around 20 hours a week in the store, but never saw a dime from his father. He received no allowance or pay because his father believed that his son should work for a valid reason like how it helped the family. "No man should work for money alone," his father would always remark anytime his son talked about getting paid for his labor. JD only brought up once that he felt it was unfair that his older sister was paid handsomely for her time in the shop because it upset his father greatly. "Life is not fair; the sooner you learn that the better." JD feared his father when he got intense like that.

*****

It was fall. The leaves turned colors of orange, dark red, and brown, and a few leaves had already started to fall to the ground. With each passing day, the weather got colder and at night neighbors would meet up to gossip and drink around fires, enjoying the spoils of the season. On this Saturday, the skies were cloudless and the wind gently blew the few leaves that had already reached the ground. JD and Lily were enjoying the day by walking along the outskirts of the town near the forest. Lily had blown off her own friends to hang out with her brother because he seemed sadder than usual at breakfast. She knew that a nature walk would brighten his day, but the frown had yet to leave his face. "What's wrong, JD?" Lily inquired softly while she stopped to lean back against a tree. "You seem quiet today, like you're not your usual self. Is something wrong?"

He forced a fake chuckle; over the years he had learned to be stoic in his appearance. He buried the thoughts that disturbed him or made him sad because he noticed it made others uncomfortable. It was not easy and some days it was harder to hide his sorrow, especially from his sister. "I'm fine, really," he lied, and Lily was well aware it was a lie.

She just looked at him. When they were younger, JD would run into her room at night and cry into her arms while he sobbed through the memories of his nightmare. Until one night their father intercepted him on his way to his sister's room, and gave JD a long, stern speech about how 'a man must hide his tears for tears are a sign of weakness and weakness is not a quality found in a powerful man.' Ever since then, JD bottled his emotions up, hiding them from the rest of the world. "Alright," Lillian started. She wanted to press and force her brother to open up, but feared that he would storm off feeling betrayed. "but if there is something wrong, you know you can always talk to me, right?"

"Of course I do," he responded, flashing a smile of genuine love and happiness. His sister was his favorite person in his life. They continued to walk along the edge of the forest making unimportant small talk and stupid jokes as they strolled along. They kept walking until they got to the area where the river, forest, and mountains met. The locals referred to it as God's Point, because it was a beautiful sight of fun and enjoyment all year round. All the local kids would play here over the summer months, but it was avoided during the fall because the rocks became really slippery. The two young children decided to climb the rocks anyway.

Only one Brooks child returned home that day.

*****

The weeks following the accident, everything was dark and dreary. The sun didn't shine for weeks as rains fell from the skies, as if God was crying over how the world was doomed now that its brightest child was no longer there to fix its problems. Every town member grieved the loss at God's Point as if they had lost their own child. The school even closed down for a couple days to allow teachers and students the chance to grieve properly. A tragedy like this is rare in this small town, and when they do happen, they hit hard. The flags outside the town hall flew at half-mast for months. A couple stores even closed down in response to the loss, but one store never closed — the Brooks Family General Store. Despite their loss, Mr. and Mrs. Brooks stood tall for their neighbors. Winston was behind the counter to help anyone who walked through that door get the stuff they needed to get through this troubling time. While her husband worked in the store, Elizabeth ran grief counseling sessions in the gym of the local high school so people could grieve and help each other grow and move on. The whole town was in a state of disbelief. They just could not believe it. Lillian Brooks was dead.

On that horrid, world changing day, it was just the two siblings. No one else was around to see what happened and JD was so traumatized from the loss of Lily that he could not bring himself to talk about the events. It did not take long for rumors to spread throughout the town like a plague. The town talked and gossip until they all agreed on one thing: JD killed his sister. If mob justice had prevailed, then the members of the town would have united to throw the young boy down a deep, dark hole for the rest of eternity. Luckily for JD, Sheriff Clint Harrison was a morally driven man of the law. While he agreed with the town that the young boy had a hand in his sister's death, Sheriff Harrison had no way to prove that the boy did it. As much as he hated it, he had to officially rule it as an accident.

Eventually, even the 14-year-old boy's mother and father blamed him for their daughter's untimely departure. Winston Brooks started drinking heavily in the days following his loss, and each night he would drink more and more. He was angry at the world for taking his sweet innocent angel, but he did not blame his son until he overheard a conversation between Mrs. Johnson and Ms. Beard. They both believed the young boy killed his sister in a fit of jealousy. That night, his drunken anger changed from the world to his own flesh and blood.

It was in the middle of December — just 13 days before Christmas — the night hell surfaced on earth. The drunken, vengeful Winston Brooks staggered up the stairs and forced himself into JD's room. The boy sat in a deep depression, looking out his window watching the gray, gloomy snow fall to the earth. He jumped to his feet when his father burst into his room. JD was caught off guard when Winston Brooks struck him to the ground. While he lay there on the ground, JD's father spewed his hate onto the boy.

"You took her from me!" Winston slurred as he drove his foot into the boy's gut. "Why, you little bastard?! Why?!"

Wails of bloody agony filled the house. For the next 20 minutes, JD was beaten within an inch of his life, all while his mother sat at the kitchen table in shock from the loss of her daughter. Winston and Elizabeth Brooks put on a show of acceptance to look strong for the community, but once the ivory colored door of their two-story home closed, they changed. Winston Brooks drank his whisky by the bottle each night till he either passed out, or beat his son and then passed out. He would get invited out to the local bar on main street by his friends, but he would turn them away with the excuse that his family needed him each night. And in a sense, he was right, as his wife became a statue when she arrived home. She would sit down in the living room or at the kitchen table and just stare off into space. No sounds could divert her glassy eyes from the nothingness that grabbed her attention - screams, phone calls, and even Sheriff Harrison knocking at the front door fell on deaf ears.

"Winston? Elizabeth? It's me, Clint. I was just stopping by to make sure you guys were okay. Some neighbors heard crying and

I wanted to make sure everyone was alright." The calls from outside stopped Winston Brooks mid-strike. He looked down at his bloody victim – whose wails were now no more than painful whimpers. Winston Brooks rose to his feet and composed himself so he could get the door without raising suspicion.

"Clint!" Winston Brooks exclaimed in a deviously joyful tone. "What brings you out to my house in such terrible weather? And at such a late hour!"

"Well, umm, some folks heard screams coming from your house, Winston." He pointed off into the storm to the nearest houses that were still a decent distance away. "I was just concerned; figured I would stop by just to make sure everyone's safe and okay."

"Well, I thank you for doing your job, Clint, but it's just Jamie crying about losing his sister. This tragedy has been the hardest on him. He was so close to her. Elizabeth and I think it's best to just let him cry it out... so he can get closure. Ya know?"

A smile appeared on the face of the middle-aged Sheriff. Clint had known Winston Brooks his entire life and never once had a bad encounter with him. Realizing how ridiculous his visit was, he bid his old friend a good night. Winston Brooks remained in the doorway as he watched the Sheriff get into his car and started the engine. Once the car disappeared into the white blur, Winston Brooks removed the fake grin from his face and returned to his house. He checked in his son's room to make sure that he was still alive before he continued onto bed.

The next day, the shell of Elizabeth Brooks cleaned the blood from her son and sent him on his way to school with the warning to sit in the back of the classroom and to hide his wounds and bruises from his teachers and classmates. JD walked two and a half miles in four feet of snow with the events of the previous night running through his head, not fully understanding why it all happened.

He sat in the back of the classroom with his sweatshirt hood up to hide his face. JD didn't have to try very hard to hide his wounds from his classmates, for they all just ignored him as they had everyday since the rumors started. It wasn't until his last class that his teacher, Miss. April, noticed the swelling and faint bruises in the boy's face while she passed back the homework from the previous week. She pulled the young boy aside at the end of class and that's when she noticed the boy's black eye and fat lip. "Jamie! Did you get into a fight before school today?" Miss. April asked.

"No," he replied, looking at the ground.

"Jamie, do not lie to me. I understand that this is a difficult time for all of us, but starting fights is no way to..."

"I didn't start a fight with anybody," JD snapped at his teacher. Miss. April was taken aback by the sudden outburst of rage from the scrawny boy before her.

Miss. April had to check her emotions. "I do not care who started it. You cannot get into fights with your classmates." She was starting to become very annoyed with JD.

"I didn't get into a fight with any of my classmates," the boy replied.

Miss. April was quickly losing her patience with JD. "Alright Jamie, if you didn't get into a fight with anyone, then what happened? How did you get these bruises?" She stared at the boy, demanding an answer to please her.

JD decided to trust his teacher and told her the perpetrator of his beatings. All Miss. April could think of as she heard her student's tale was her crush on his father. For years, the teacher had yearned from afar for Winston Brooks, and hearing JD speak so poorly of his father upset her. Just as JD finished his tale of abuse, Miss. April slapped him across the face, sending him to the ground. "You little shit! How dare you make up those lies about your father?" Miss. April came around her desk and kicked JD in the gut while he lay on the ground.

Springing to his feet, he ran out of the classroom as quickly as he could to escape the wrath of his screaming teacher. He sprinted into the snow coatless, having left his winter coat and backpack behind. JD ran until he collapsed into the snow from pain. After a few moments of lying in the cold, white snow, JD stood to walk home slowly. He was indifferent to the cold that surrounded him, as a fire of pure hate towards the world filled his heart. It burned so violently it blackened and charred his soul in black flame.

*****

The next four years, JD only cared about surviving. He faced inconsistent beating from his father and no help from his mother. He learned to hide his black eyes, bruises, and cuts that he received from his one-sided skirmishes. JD wanted to make sure no one knew what was happening to him because he could not trust anyone in the town. Every single person in the town of Loveland worshiped his parents as gods that could do no wrong, and any person who muttered otherwise was a heretic who was subjected to violent mob justice. It was four years of hell.

*****

JD decided he had enough the morning of his 18th birthday. He would get revenge against his parents; he would be reborn in their blood. He entered the kitchen to find his mother sitting at the kitchen table, still wearing the same clothes and vacant stare she wore last night. Elizebeth Brooks paid no attention to her son as he grabbed a knife from a drawer and joined his mother at the table. JD fiddled with the knife as he watched his father enter the kitchen, still hungover from the previous night's drinking. Winston Brooks turned his back to his son and wife to pour himself a morning drink of whisky. Just as he took his first sip, JD stood and swung the knife at his father, slicing his left arm and drawing blood. Winston Brooks let out a yell of pain as he let his glass fall to the floor with a crash. JD was caught off guard when his father struck him with a sucker punch to the jaw. JD fell back, crashing into the fridge and tumbling to the ground. His knife flew from his hand and stuck into the wall behind him. Elizabeth Brooks did not move a muscle as her husband whaled into JD. Winston Brooks grabbed his bottle of whisky and poured it over his son — almost all of it went into his son's mouth. Once it was empty, Winston Brooks spiked the bottle at his son, breaking it over his head. He then walked calmly over to the knife stuck in the wall; Winston Brooks was going to kill his son once and for all. As blood poured from his face, JD jumped to his feet and ran out of the house, and into the forest, his father's vile curses chasing his retreat.

JD ran until he collapsed from exhaustion. The alcohol in his system and blood streaming from his forehead wore him down just as he reached the place where it all started: God's Point. JD cried.

He sobbed into the river. Then he heard a smooth, hypnotizing voice call out from behind him, "What's got ya down kid?"

JD jerked around to find himself staring up at a well-dressed, tall stranger, in a slick black suit with a bright red tie. He was well groomed, his black beard fresh and neatly trimmed, his midnight colored hair flowing backwards on his head. JD stared into his crystal blue eyes that swirled like a storm and felt calm. The Stranger's gaze was comforting and his grin was mischievous and fun.

"Who are you?" JD asked while wiping tears from his face.

"The man who will make your wildest dreams come true. I have been watching you for some time and now I am here to help you." As The Stranger spoke, JD could see flickers of silver in his mouth. "You can call me your savior for all I care. I am here to give you what you desire most in the world."

JD just stared at The Stranger, trying to process what was going on.

"Damn it boy, get on your feet. You are better than this. Honestly, it disgusts me to see you wallowing in the dirt," he barked at the boy on the ground.

JD rose to his feet, anger in his green eyes, “I know who you are!”

The well dressed Stranger was caught off guard by JD’s fire. “Is that so? Do tell, who am I?”

“You're the Devil. You make deals for souls.” JD gritted his teeth. “I’ll make a deal with you. You change the past so that she never dies, and you can have my soul."

The Stranger smiled, “Changing history is no simple feat. I would need more than one twisted, black soul."

"How many would you need? How many souls?"

The mysterious Stranger thought for a moment. "The real question is, how many souls is your sister's life worth to you?"

"100," JD responded without hesitation.

"Then for 100 souls, I'll change the past." He said with a crooked grin and a shake of JD's hand. "Now, let's go kid. There is work to be done."

*****

It had been over six years since the day JD made a deal that changed his life. He sat dressed in a black suit and tie on a train headed towards the city of New Maris. The now 23-year-old man gazed out the window next to him. In his hands, he held a small, black notebook that could easily fit in his pocket. JD opened it and reread the first page. They were rules he designed in his last six years of training with The Stranger. JD considered the rules to be essential to his plan. They included:

- No killing around the place you live
- No killing people of power
- No killing during the day
- Always wear gloves

- Go to different spots of the city each night
- Keep a low profile
- Favor those who will not be missed

He broke his gaze with the window, turning his attention to the other passengers on the train. The passengers did not look human — he did not see them as people, anyway. Numbers filled the train, walked the aisles, and interacted with each other. Sitting across from him was a number named Adam Carlisle, who greeted JD when he first sat down, but had since sat in silence. JD tried not to look at the middle-aged man in the gray suit because every time he did, he saw deadly slashes marked out on him like a paint by number picture.

"Lovely day, isn't it?" Adam spoke, pulling JD from the darkness of his own thoughts. Adam had blonde, shaggy hair and the patches of blonde whiskers on his chin and cheeks made it obvious that he had not shaved in a couple days. He was dressed in a gray suit that was not cheap, but was not expensive either. They made small talk for the rest of the train ride.

The conversation was dull and pointless, until Adam asked the only meaningful question JD cared to answer truthfully: "So, what brings you to the city? Business? Pleasure?" He emphasized the last question in a suggestive and joking manner.

"Reinventing myself. I wanted a change of scenery that was different from the small-town vibe. I've always felt more comfortable in the background." He was cautious not to reveal much about his hometown. He wanted to forget that hell hole as soon as he could. "I'm starting over with just my suit and bag."

Adam admired JD's honesty. "Well, if you need work, my pops runs a butcher shop in North Park. He's getting up there in age and could use a shop hand and I can't be there every day for him. We have an extra room too, I'm sure my old man wouldn't mind you renting it out."

The offer was sincere, but seemed too convenient. JD looked around the train car for any familiar faces among the unknown masses.

"Do you have any experience in a butcher shop?" Adam asked, bringing JD's attention back to the conversation. "It can be pretty gory work if you're not used to it."

A small grin emerged on JD's face. "Gore is no problem. I used to help the local butcher clean his shop back home. I have no problem with blood." His speech faded as flashbacks bombarded his senses.

"Perfect! We can head over to the shop when we get to the station."

After they reached the New Maris station, the two men took a cab over to where 8th and Juddson Avenue meet. JD introduced himself to Adam's father and owner of the shop, Gareth Carlisle. He had greasy, black, thinning hair slicked back against his tan head and bad teeth that could be seen across a crowded room as they seemed to defy the laws of physics with how they jolted in all directions. Gareth explained the jobs and duties that JD would complete around the shop. JD even learned a little more about how Adam, Gareth's only son, had done those jobs before he left for college. After hearing the extent of his obligations, JD gladly took the job and headed upstairs to the unoccupied guest room to settle in.

The room had one white dresser, one twin sized bed, one mirror on the wall by the door, and a window that looked out onto Juddson Avenue. After he finished unpacking, he took out his notebook and a golden square shaped object that was about the size of his hand. He read over his guidelines of his mission while he fiddled with the golden object. Then he pressed the center of the object and it began to change. Parts began moving and it unfolded into a six-inch blade with a golden handle. The knife was given to him by The Stranger before he embarked on the beginning of his mission. The weight and balance of the blade and its ability to transform made it easy to conceal on his person. He pressed down onto the cap of the handle, the blade returning to its square shape. He placed the object and his notebook back into his suit jacket, grabbed a pair of black gloves, and headed out for the night.

*****

His first three victims were homeless. It was a dark, damp, moonless night and they were crowded around a fire under a bridge on the east side of town. The orange glow illuminated their dirty and torn rags that were draped over their bodies, but none of the surrounding area could be seen. The homeless trio stared into the fire because it was more comforting than looking out into the black abyss. JD felt bad for adding to the suffering, but he knew their deaths would not bring unwanted attention. Once he was certain he was alone with his prey, JD emerged and slashed the throat of the nearest homeless person. Before the blood of the first victim could hit the ground, JD leaped and cut the next throat. The third victim tried to run, making a mad dash into the shadows, but JD turned and threw his blade into the back of the frightened runner. He walked over to the last victim to retrieve his blade and return it to its more concealable version. He then began to check the three homeless people for any form of ID, the last of the victims was an older woman.

Only the first man had any ID, an old military ID. His name was LT. Fredrick Rotolo. He looked upon the dimly lit dirt and blood covered face of the man, and memorized his face while he wrote down his name. 'What a shame,' he thought. 'What kind of monstrous society would leave veterans to rot on the streets?" JD then memorized the faces of the other two victims; he wrote down 'John Doe 1' and 'Jane Doe 2' along with where they had been slain. They may have been nameless, but they would not die in vain. None of them would.

*****

By the end of his first month in New Maris, JD had reached 37 victims. Of the names in his notebook, 30 were homeless — a majority of which were male. He hated killing the poor men and women who lived in cardboard houses. These poor souls had been through enough in life, and he felt a strange form of guilt from taking their lives — even if he was ending the misery of their mortal life. The only benefit to killing the people living on the street was that no one cared. When the police came across the bloody crime scenes, they would just shrug their shoulders and move along. The men and women who protected the city had more pressing issues to attend to than "finding the random joe who dropped a bum."

The other seven lives, whose names were trapped in his black leather notebook, belonged to random strangers who passed by the wrong dark alley at the wrong time. The cops, once again, posed no threat to him. Random corpses lying in their own blood — missing all their fancy watches, jewelry, and money — were assumed to have been put there by slash happy muggers or desperate hobos. JD took their valuables for that very reason; he left credit cards and IDs, but took cash, watches, and jewelry. He kept the green and threw the shiny stuff into the sewers. This kept the cops focused on the well-known pickpockets and muggers rather than trying to find a killer on the loose.

JD kept killing. Animals during the day, humans at night. He claimed 45, then he claimed 50. JD had just killed his 52nd person. Connor Irvin Meeuwe was a 28-year-old male immigrant attending the university in the eastern part of New Maris. JD stared into his blood, letting the guilt wash over him. He felt like he was taking on a part of the souls he claimed; with each kill, his own soul felt heavier. Then he saw her. He gazed out from his dark alley and looked upon innocence. The fantasy of a perfect soul sat alone underneath the luminescent glow of the street lamps while she waited for the bus to take her wherever she needed to go. Mesmerized, he slowly emerged from the shadowy alley with every intent of learning everything he could about her, but once he emerged from the darkness the moonlight showed his true self. The bright red sins that stained his gloves and sleeves forced him back into the safety of the shadows. He ran away.

For the next three weeks, JD returned to observe the bus stop, always returning at the same time, but never seeing her. Winter started to present itself; each night seemed colder and darker than those that came before. He sat on the bench one night feeling the cold scratch at his face, hoping that she would appear from the darkness to free him. JD was lost in his own mind, trying to understand why he cared so much about this complete stranger.

He did not even notice her sit down. "Hi!" Her sweet voice filled his ears, and for a moment, he felt like he was sitting on a beach with sand between his toes and the warm sun on his face. She was even more stunning up close, her mahogany brown hair pulled back into a messy bun. She had an outstanding face with beautiful dark brown eyes. Her eyes pierced into the soul of men, shining a light of admiration onto the parts of themselves that were worth loving. She had one of those smiles that could turn any bad mood for the better, an infectious, glowing smile impossible to ignore. A smile that chipped away at the darkness until only two pure and joyful grins remained. Maddie was her name.

JD returned her greeting and they talked, laughed, and enjoyed each other's company on that harsh, cold night. The bus never arrived — though even if it did come Maddie would not have gotten on. She suggested they head to a small nearby café where they spent the next few hours. When the coffee shop closed, they spent the rest of the night walking around a local park. They talked about everything and anything they wanted. The only bad part of their night was when they had to say goodbye as the sun rose on a new day.

Over the coming weeks they spent as much time together as they could. As they peacefully lay in JD's bed one morning, he felt as if the weight of all those souls that burdened him had been lifted, all thanks to the beauty beside him, whose face glowed with the heavenly golden rays of the sun. He had not killed anyone since the first night he met her.

*****

The butcher shop that JD worked at was not usually busy, which gave him plenty of time to tend and clean the shop by himself. He had grown a fondness for isolation. JD would start each morning by preparing and cutting the meat for the day, a task that often reminded him of the lost faces he had slain. He would wait around the shop for the few daily customers to visit throughout the day, contemplating his bloody sins and reminding himself that their deaths are not meaningless. Everytime he thought of the dark deeds that weighed on his soul, Maddie would materialize in his thoughts. He thought about her laugh, her bright red lips, and the warm fuzzy feeling he got when he stared into her rich brown eyes. When she entered his mind, all guilt, fear, and pain faded from his life. JD's favorite days were the ones where she visited for lunch. On those days, he had no dark thoughts, only hope.

One day he was hanging in the stockroom waiting for his love to stop in for the day when he heard a familiar voice call to him.

"Hey kid, long time no see."

JD turned to find The Stranger standing in the doorway of the stockroom.

"Look, I hate to be that guy, but you're a little behind on your monthly quota." The deep voice chuckled. The Stranger smiled at him with a tooth filled grin and he was wearing a dark red suit that looked like it was made out of the pig and cattle blood JD had washed down the drain earlier that morning.

"What? No kind words for an old friend? Look, I'm here to remind you why you came here in the first place, and honestly, I never thought I would have to. I thought that pitch black soul of yours would carry you to the finish line all by its lonesome. I mean she is cute and all..."

"If you hurt her, I swear I will track you to the end of the Earth to kill you."

The Stranger just laughed at the cleaver-wielding man who had interrupted him with a threat.

"Don't get ahead of yourself kid, even if you could kill me, then how do you expect to get your sister back? Kill me and all those poor innocent people you slaughtered will have died for nothing. Besides, I have no interest in hurting that girl. I just want what I was promised."

JD continued to look on, weapon at the ready. Even if it meant losing his chance at bringing back his sister, he would kill this devious, dealmaking mystery man to protect Maddie.

The Stranger looked on with a sly grin. He was fully aware of what this man was capable of and he had no doubt that JD would put up one hell of a contest, but he knew his advantage would help him in a brawl.

"I promise her safety. Just don't delay any longer." He remarked as his grin faded before he turned and walked out the front door of the butcher shop.

A few hours later, Maddie stopped by the shop for dinner. All JD could think about was her safety. That night, he took the lives of four more people.

*****

Over the next week, JD went out to collect lives every night. The 65th person that JD killed was the youngest person he had killed, a 19-year-old prostitute named Bessie Veck. He looked upon the girl with a frown on her face, but a smile on her throat and could not help but see signs of the woman he loved in her eyes. JD threw up. After a few moments, he collected himself. He wrote down the poor girl's name and where she was slain without looking back at her face. Then he left to go meet Maddie across town for dinner. He didn't want to be late and then have to lie about why he was late. Lying to her was like hurting a kitten: inhumane and impossible not to hate himself for such an immoral act.

This became the life of JD. After working at the butcher's shop till four pm, he would try to fit in a quick murder or two before he would meet Maddie. He made sure to be extra careful when he took a life as Maddie hated the sight of blood. When she would stop by the shop, she would either stay in the kitchen where they prepared their own food or would go right up to JD's room to wait. This meant he had to make sure he had no red stains — animal or human — on his clothes. He did not want to cause her distress.

He also had to be careful of the police. Now that bodies were dropping in larger quantities, all with the injuries from the same knife, the police presence around the city had increased. If he got caught before he finished his mission, not only would his love be heartbroken and utterly destroyed when she finds out about his bloody secret, but he would also never see Lily again. Getting arrested was not an option.

He continued killing whenever he got a chance. He continued making love to Maddie whenever he got a chance. He would stain his soul with the dark red blood of his prey and then lay in bed while deep in Maddie's embrace and the stains seemed to wash away in her light.

He killed and killed, reaching 75, 85 and 90 names in his book of death. Then one day he was enjoying a beautiful dinner with Maddie when she said something that caused all color in his face to fade.

"Did you hear about the serial killer in the news? They are calling him the Shadow Slasher. They think he's killed between 60 to 80 people all around the city." She said between bites of grilled chicken. "Crazy isn't it? Makes me feel scared to go out at night. It's a good thing that you walk me back to my place every night."

JD quickly changed the subject to something else.

After dinner, JD walked Maddie back to her apartment on East 20th Street. They passed by a dark alleyway and Maddie once again brought up her fears of the monster terrorizing the city. "It's just crazy to think that someone could be waiting in the shadows to try to kill me."

JD started to scream internally. "Don't worry," he said with false calmness. "You have no need to worry about that psychopath as long as I'm next to you. I would never let anyone or anything hurt you."

They reached her apartment shortly after and JD gave her a hug and a kiss before heading out into the shadows towards his home.

All he could think about while he walked home in the pitch-black darkness was the increased difficulty of his mission. Maddie did not want him to head home that night; she feared for his safety, though she had no reason to. She begged him to stay the night and love her till morning and, in all honesty, JD would have loved nothing better than to spend the night in her arms. But there was too much on his mind, so he made up some bullshit excuse about having to finish inventory to justify his denial of her proposal. It broke his heart to lie to her innocent face, causing tears to roll down his cheeks as he walked on that brisk, cold night. One thought pounded in his head over and over. He was going to break her heart and he was certain that it was an unavoidable consequence.

*****

When JD reached the butcher shop, he flipped on the local news. The anchor woman was reporting breaking news on the Shadow Slasher, giving her viewers a spot on description of what JD looks like. He paced back and forth in the TV room, whispering incoherent babbling while he tried to comprehend why everything was falling apart so suddenly, just when he was so close to completion. Then the answer to his questions appeared at the door.

"Hey yah champ, you seem upset. I'm guessing you've seen my handiwork." The silver-tongued Stranger said with a smile.

"You did this?" JD screamed, spit flying from his mouth. "Why would you tell them about me?"

The slick dressed Stranger's grin got more arrogant, "I wanted a little more excitement. It just seemed too easy for you. I trained you too well over those six years. I blame myself. The police were completely lost and had no idea what they were doing. So, I left some anonymous tips to the authorities and the media." The Stranger chuckled, but the anger did not fade from JD's eyes.

"I suggest you hurry up and get those last 10 souls for me. If I had to guess, I'd say you got about a week to get them... give or take six days. Depends how long it takes them to find the letter with your name in it."

JD reached inside his suit pocket, felt the object in his hand, and pushed the center.

"Oh and don't worry, if you get to triple digits, I'll take care of the cops for you," The Stranger said with a wink.

Once he finished talking, JD pulled out his knife and charged at The Stranger with a scream, but the black haired man just fluidly dodged the attack before throwing JD across the room. When JD looked up, the Stranger was gone.

JD filled the room with the sounds of obscenities and anger. All the shouting caused Mr. Carlisle to check up on his live-in employee.

"Gosh, boy, what's got you all in a stir? It's not lady trouble, is it? Cause I really like that Maddie girl."

JD collected himself and quickly hid the blade from the sight of the man that he had grown quite fond of over the last couple of months. "No, I just found out I was betrayed by someone I thought was on my side."

Mr. Carlisle eyed JD for a moment before shrugging and wishing his employee a goodnight.

*****

The following night, JD went out to collect the last ten names he needed to be free of this deal with a backstabbing Stranger. The first two were homeless, both female. He walked up with urgency, slitting the throat of the first woman and then stabbing the second in the heart. He continued on in the night leaving their bodies out in the streets. JD turned the corner and found a shopkeeper who was locking his doors for the night. JD slipped behind him and slit his throat with one easy stroke before continuing on as he scribbled the names into his notebook as he searched for his next victim. He needed seven more names. He found 3 homeless men sleeping in an open-face tent. JD sneaked up and carefully plunged his knife into the heart of the first man, being cautious as not to wake the easy prey that still slept. He killed the next two men in the same way. JD walked on from the three dead and found two prostitutes on a poorly-lit street corner. He sliced the first girl's throat and reached for the second girl, but missed her by inches and she took off down the street. JD threw the bleeding body of the first girl to the ground and chased after the frightened women. He chased her down an alleyway, threw her against the wall, covered her mouth with his left hand, and plunged his knife into her gut 3 times. He let go of her mouth and delivered a quick final slash to her throat. Only two to go. JD exited the alley and saw a man stumble his way out of a bar by himself. The determined killer followed the man — who was drunkenly oblivious to the man with a bloody knife in his hand — into an alleyway. He drove the knife into the back of the drunk man three times before he heard the wail of sirens behind him. JD turned to see two armed figures emerging from the ocean of red and blue that filled the night sky.

"Freeze! Put down the knife," the officer closest to him shouted.

"No, no, no, not yet. I'm not done yet. I'm so close." JD screamed as he swung the bloody knife at the officer.

The man dodged the attack and tackled JD onto the ground. JD noticed the officer's face and his blue, storm-like eyes; it was The Stranger. He screamed in anger as he was handcuffed.

"You bastard, I'll kill you. I was so close." JD's screams turned to tears as he was taken in by the police.

*****

The interrogation room was gray, damp, and reeked of sweaty, middle-aged men. As soon as Detective David Appleton walked into the room, JD confessed to everything — except the parts about him believing he made a deal with the devil. He figured lying about the lives he had claimed was pointless at this point. He was caught with blood on his blade and a list of every victim that he had slayed. Once it was all said and done, Appleton looked at him with utter disgust.

"Can I ask you a favor?" JD asked in a calm voice. "Can I write a note to someone that I care deeply about?" Tears began to fall from his face.

Most people would have spit in his face and denied his request on the spot, but detective Appleton saw remorse in the green eyes of the murderer before him.

Without saying a word, Appleton rose and retrieved a pen and paper. He agreed to let JD write his letter as long as the detective read it after it was done to make sure it wasn't a call to action for a copycat killer. JD understood and accepted the terms. He began to pen an apology letter to Maddie. He told her that she was the only thing in this world that he truly loved and he was sorry for what he had done because it caused her pain. He told her that he would have never hurt a soul if he knew it would cause her to suffer. He promised her that she was never in danger. He explained his past. He poured the only good he had left in his soul into the letter. A letter she would never read.

*****

He sat alone in a holding cell. The number 99 repeated over and over in his head. Then he heard an officer walking towards him.

"Hey yah kid, how ya holding up," the familiar voice said with a chuckle.

JD did not bother to look over; he continued to glare at the gray wall across from him.

"Seems you got yourself into a little bit of a jam. Need me to help you out?"

"Why did you stop me?" he asked The Stranger. "You could never bring Lily back, right?" The Stranger did not respond to his question and for JD that was answer enough. "You're not the devil, are you?" JD said in a monotone voice.

The Stranger smiled. "Not the one you're thinking of, but I can still make a deal to get you on the other side of these bars."

"I'm done with your deals," JD replied as he rose and walked over to the sink and mirror in his cell. He stared at the blue-eyed Stranger in the mirror, then drove his head into the mirror.

The Stranger's grin disappeared into a concerned frown as he watched blood drip from the cracked glass. "Stop, what are you doing?! Somebody bring me the keys to open this cell!" He shouted down the hall to the other officers.

The Stranger looked back at JD, blood gushing from his forehead. JD's reflection was grinning at the bastard that had betrayed him. He looked into the Stranger's swirling blue eyes through the cracked glass and whispered, "100."

The Stranger grabbed at the cell doors and then ripped them open with moderate ease. He ran at JD, but it was too late. JD drove his head into the mirror one final time and collapsed on the ground into a pool of his own blood. The Stranger stared down at the smiling, dead face of JD.

The other two cops arrived at the cell.

"Holy shit, what the hell happened?" one of the officer's asked.

The Stranger did not respond; he just walked out of the cell past the officers. That was the last time anyone in the precinct saw the man who watched JD Brooks die.

Zombre

The undead have not walked the Earth for hundreds of years. A feared and unstoppable power that few can control and fewer understand. Yet, despite the absence, the curse of the undead has returned with no suitable explanation of how or why. The undead walks the Earth again.

*****

It was a chilly morning, just like any other of November. The firstborn son of Eric and Melinda Ombre, Zachary, was born two days earlier on a brisk Halloween morning. After a short stay in the hospital, the married couple was returning home with their newborn son. They pulled into the driveway and noticed a large, mysterious package sitting on their front porch. The package was addressed to Zachary, but the return address had been damaged. Mr. Ombre assumed the package was from a family friend or distant relative and opened it. Inside the brown box was an old ornamental black chest with gold accents. His curiosity heightened and then turned to pure horror as he opened the chest to find an ornate, 16 inch, curved Roman Sica. The blade had two silver decorative snakes that curled around the handle and came to end next to a silver skull with a purple gem in one eye and a green gem in another that capped the handle.

Mr. Ombre could not believe that someone would send this to his newborn son. He was disgusted and threw the blade back in the box. He was tempted to just throw it out but had problems with the neighborhood kids going through the trash, so Zachary's father decided to hide the blade deep into the attic and forget all about it. It was not found for 18 years.

*****

It was the morning of Zachary's 18th birthday and the now legal adult was snooping around the attic trying to find his birthday present. The blue-eyed, brown-haired boy just wanted to know what his parents had gotten him and knew the attic was their secret hiding spot. Zachary moved a box labeled kitchen and saw an ornamental black and gold chest up against the wall. He moved some more boxes and pulled the small chest free from its hiding place. Curiosity took over and young Ombre opened the box to find a beautifully ornamental sword. Zachary knew there was no way in hell his parents would get him a sword for his 18th birthday, so he figured it must be some sort of forgotten family heirloom or wall decoration that got thrown in the attic. Zachary took the blade and returned the chest to its hiding spot. He brought the blade into his room and stuffed it into his duffle bag. He wanted to show it off to his friend who lived a couple of neighborhoods over. He said goodbye to his parents and left for his friend's house.

After hours of Zachary and his friend messing around with the weapon, Zachary returned home so he would not miss his birthday dinner. Night had fallen and the streets were flooded with people and children dressed in all types of costumes. He decided to avoid the busy streets and took a back way across the railroad tracks that would drop him off near his house.

In the dark of the night, Zachary did not see the figure appear until he was right in front of him. "Give us your wallet...and empty your bag," the man sternly commanded. Zachary took a couple of steps back and was about to sprint in the opposite direction when he heard another large man appear behind him and blocked his only chance of escape. Then Zachary remembered what he had in his duffle bag.

"I don't want any trouble guys. I'm just trying to get home," he said as fear trembled in his breath.

"Then do as we say. Empty the bag," the first man repeated, this time revealing a small, yet very sharp-looking knife.

"It's just clothes," Zachary lied as he undid the zipper and reached inside. Zach felt the handle of the blade and gripped it tightly. He pulled the small sword out from the duffle bag and pointed it at the large man in front of him. The blade seemed to glow as the moonlight hit the shiny, untainted steel. The large man took a couple of steps back and Zachery smiled with confidence. "That's what I thou..." He was interrupted by a loud bang that came from behind him.

Pain was all Zachary could feel. He dropped to his knees and began to cough up blood. Both men just laughed at him as they watched him finish collapsing onto the railroad tracks. A final tear rolled down Zachary's cheek as he closed his eyes for what he thought was the final time. All of a sudden, the blade glowed a bright, ghostly green.

Zachary's eyes shot open and glowed the same color as the blade. Slowly, the boy stood up from the ground, much to the disbelief of the two men. They watched as his bullet wound glowed and began to heal. "What... t-the... hell," stuttered the man who shot Zachary point-blank into the back. Zachary turned and stared at him with a blank expression. The man panicked and fired two more times at the boy with glowing green eyes. Both bullets struck Zachary in the chest, but he was unfazed by being shot this time. The holes glowed and began to heal just like the wound that had killed him. Zachary raised the blade and swung it at the gun of the man, clipping his hand and sending the gun flying off into a patch of tall grass. He was about to attack the gunman a second time when the first man charged and stabbed him in the back with his knife. Zachary responded by elbowing him in the face, causing the man to leave his knife in Zachary's back. Zachary quickly delivered a lethal strike to the first man. The first man fell back onto the ground dead, a purple smoke-like light glowed from his wound and traveled to Zachary's blade. Zachary turned his attention back to the gunman who looked on in pure horror at Zachary Ombre. He glowed green and purple as the light seemed to swirl around him and his weapon. He was about to strike the man who killed him when he heard police sirens wail in the distance. Zachary was pulled from his trance and the lights dissipated. He quickly grabbed his duffle bag and ran off in the direction of his house, leaving the gunman and his dead friend behind in the dark alley.

From that day forward, Zachary didn't feel like himself. He felt duller, his blue eye color had faded and become gray, and he no longer dreamed at night. He felt incomplete, like something was gone and it would never return. Two weeks after the incident by the railroad tracks, Zachary ran away from home. He did not feel human anymore and felt reminded of it every time he was around his parents and friends. The day he left hurt Zachary more than getting shot.

*****

Zachary looked out of his small studio apartment window and watched the late summer sunrise over the coastal city of San Gywnn. San Gywnn was built into the side of a mountain that overlooked the Pacific ocean. The warm climate city had 4 main burroughs: Hillcrest, Lowerside, Historical District, and Wharfway. Large commercial buildings and fancy restaurants climbed the mountain of Hillcrest. Lowerside sat in the shadow of Hillcrest; it was home to most of the city's residents, with each building being the same height as its neighbors'. To the west of Lowerside was Wharfway, where all the piers, beaches, and shipping companies resided. Then there was the Historical District, where the first patrons of San Gwynn settled. The buildings there were older, with many old churches and historical landmarks.

For the past six years, Zachary had been living in the Lowerside, fighting crime under the alias Zombre, a nickname his father used to call him. He had originally come to San Gywnn to hide amongst the concrete and steel, blending in and avoiding attention. However, one night while he sat on his bed watching TV, fate forced his hand. He heard a woman calling for help in the alley. Zachary looked out of his window and saw an older woman fighting for her purse with an attacker. No one came to help her. The panicked woman reminded Zachary of his mother. He felt Compelled to help her. He grabbed his blade and a hat he brought with him to hide his eyes and flew down the fire escape. This was the creation of the Zombre persona. He scared away the mugger, but before he could ask the woman if she was alright, she was running down the street in fear. Zachary tried to make that a one time occurrence, but after reading about all the muggings and robberies in the Lowerside, Zachary felt as though he had to do something to help those in need. After all, not everyone had a blade that would keep them from dying.

Overtime, Zachary switched out the hat for an old-school hockey mask to hide his face better and always dressed in black nylon and polyester pants and a blank white t-shirt when he went out to fight crime. He did not want someone to recognize him or get a picture of his face. The last thing he needed was his family learning about what he was doing. Zachary stopped countless muggings, robberies, and murders over the years and all without any combat training. He was a complete amateur, relying heavily on the mystical blade. Over the six years, Zachary had been shot 13 times, broken 15 bones, stabbed every other night, and lost his entire left arm once. Each time he was injured, he healed to perfect health again. Zachary did his best to save as many people as possible and had not taken another life of a human since the night at the train tracks. Even though he was in some sort of strange trance, he still could not forgive himself for what he did.

Since Zachary did not kill any of his victims, it left many witnesses to talk about the masked crime fighter. The local papers gave him all sorts of names like "zombie hero", "undead warrior", and "the master of death". Zachary tried to tell criminals that his name was Zombre, but most of the time they were unconscious or too focused on the knife wounds on their arms, legs, and hands. But all the news coverage brought unwanted attention.

Zachary had just returned from another night of patrolling for crime and the whole night he felt like he was being followed. As Zombre, he stayed in the shadows and moved through the city by sticking to alleyways and rooftop jumping. That night Zombre kept catching glances of at least three people in gray and black robes following him all over San Gywnn, but when he tried to confront his stalkers, there was no one around. It was around six in the morning when he felt like he finally lost them, which was perfect because had to be at work at 7:30 am.

*****

Zachary worked as an assistant manager at a local burger and fry shop. One of the benefits of dying was being able to function on very little sleep which allowed Zachary to work a 12-hour shift, then fight crime all night as Zombre with just a one-hour nap between his two "jobs".

It was around midday and Zachary was dealing with a very entitled, annoying customer during their lunch rush when he noticed three people in black and gray suits walk in and sit down at an empty table without ordering at the counter. His attention was all on them, when he was rudely interrupted. "Hey, are you listening to me? I asked for a burger with no pickles and that's not what I got. I waited 30 minutes and you guys got my order wrong and now you seem distracted. I am a customer sir. Are you braindead or something?"

Zachary wanted to respond to her comment with 'No, I'm dead dead' but instead he just apologized and offered to get her a new burger without pickles. The lady seemed to ignore his offer to fix her situation and just kept complaining about her wrong order. Zachary just let her complain while he continued to size up the three ominous-looking men. He was trying to see what the pin on their lapels was when the lady called him back to her again. "Excuse me. I'm trying to tell you how much of an inconvenience this was for me! I've wasted an hour now."

"That's on you. I offered to fix it an hour ago," Zachary replied with a shrug. A side-effect of his powers was he struggled with controlling his facial expressions. The lady scoffed in disgust and stomped off shouting how she will never come back. He hated customers some days. Zachary looked over to the table where the mysterious suited men were sitting previously, but they had left. Zachary knew something weird was going on.

*****

That night after Zachary's shift ended, he changed into his Zombre outfit to patrol around the city looking for his stalkers. An advantage of Zachary's powers was a near-perfect physical form. He could function on less than four hours of sleep, healed quickly, was rarely sore, had insane endurance, a perfect immune system, and crazy fast reaction time. Those bonuses almost made up for the fact that the 24-year-old still looked 18. Zachary also struggled with concealing, showing, and even just feeling his emotions. Most days he felt more like Zombre than Zachary.

Zombre felt himself being followed shortly after he started his patrol of San Gwynn. He decided to enter a poorly-lit alleyway and let his stalkers confront him, but it was not his stalkers that entered the alley. Instead, five scruffy-looking men with knives, chains, and metal baseball bats stood there staring at Zombre. "Well, you are definitely not who I was expecting. Who are you?" Zombre asked.

The man in the middle with the long, heavy metal chain smiled at Zombre. "We're the guys who were hired to kill you. You must have pissed off the wrong people because they paid us some pretty big money to kill the 'Undead Hero' that the papers keep going on about," the man explained in a menacing, deep voice.

"I see," Zombre responded, "You didn't happen to get a name did you?"

The man with the chain frowned. "Get him," he commanded his boys. Just then, the man on the far right charged at Zombre. He was carrying a silver metal baseball bat. He swung at Zombre, who ducked just in time to avoid a blow to the head. Zombre then delivered a quick strike to the man's shin causing him to jump back a bit as he screamed from the pain. The baseball bat assailant recovered and took another swing at Zombre. Zombre raised his blade just in time to catch the bat, causing sparks to fly from the clashing of the metals.

Zombre pushed back the man who attacked him with the bat but was unable to react to another attack from a second man with long black hair and a small knife. The long-haired man cut Zombre on the left arm. He winced in pain. Zombre then noticed that the attack left the long-haired man exposed. Zombre wasted no time. He struck the other man in the face with a sucker punch, breaking the nose of the long-haired attacker. Zombre grabbed the long-haired man by his jacket as he began to fall away from him and tossed him towards a dumpster. The long-haired man went headfirst into the grime-covered metal and was knocked unconscious.

"Can I ask again who hired you? I honestly don't have the faintest idea," Zombre asked the obvious leader of the group as he rushed towards him. Zombre was so focused on the leader that he did not notice the baseball bat man had snuck up behind him. He hit him across the back causing Zombre to yell out in pain, then the leader swung his large metal chain down at Zombre, catching the top of his forehead and cracking his hockey mask and his skull. Zombre collapsed hard to the ground as blood gushed from head.

The leader started laughing. "See I told you he wasn't unkillable." He laughed with his men, prematurely celebrating their victory.

Zombre slowly stood to his feet, much to the shock of his attackers. The cut on his arm, the wound on his forehead, and eyes began to glow green as the blade started to heal his injuries. They may not have killed him, but they did hurt him. "I got this," a shorter man with brass knuckles said as he charged at Zombre.

This time, Zombre went on the offensive and swung backhanded with his blade at the shorter man, who not only dodged his attack, but also delivered a nasty right hook into Zombre's left shoulder. The short man was quick and landed many hits on Zombre, sticking him in the face, chest, and gut. The short man ultimately backed Zombre up against a wall. The short man leaned back for a big hit and went in for a major right hook, but Zombre lifted his blade up so the brass knuckles hit the broad side of the sword. Zombre was able to deflect the attack away and slid past the shorter man so that he was now behind him. Now that the short man was between Zombre and the brick wall, Zombre grabbed the back of his head with his left hand and slammed his attacker into the wall, disorienting the shorter man.

Zombre turned and immediately stepped back as the man with the baseball bat returned to take another swing at him. He missed his intended target and instead struck his friend in the back of the neck with great force, knocking the short man with brass knuckles unconscious as his head once again slammed into the wall.

The man with the metal baseball bat was so distracted by his mistake that it left him open for an attack.

Zombre swung and cut the top of his left thigh. The pain was so great it caused him to drop his bat as his hands moved to cover the fresh wound. Zombre finished him off by punching him square in the face with the butt of his sword. Blood flew out of his broken nose as the man fell backwards, unconscious.

"Now," Zombre said to his two remaining attackers. "Can we just stop for a minute to talk about all this?"

A big man in a black vest with no visible weapon looked at him with a fiery expression. "I'll kill you!" he yelled as he charged at full speed towards Zombre.

Zombre stood there for just a moment before jumping out of the way at the last possible second. The big man was moving too fast to slow down. He slipped on the blood of his friends and collided head first into the brick wall with enough force to knock himself out. He collapsed to the ground with the other two unconscious thugs.

"Oh shit, that worked," Zombre said, amazed that his plan worked the way it did. With three goons knocked out on his left and a fourth passed out by the dumpster on the right, all that was left was Zombre and the leader of this gang of hired goons. "Now do you want to come clean and tell me who hired you?" Zombre asked as his eyes returned to gray as he was now fully healed.

The leader just gritted his teeth and began swinging his chain in the air. Zombre shrugged and approached the leader. The leader swung high and missed, then swung again and missed, then he swung towards Zombre's left side. This time he hit his target. His chain wrapped around Zombre's left arm, breaking it in two places as it wrapped itself around. Zombre pulled the chain towards him and delivered an overhead strike to the chain with his blade. The chain broke free from the leader's grip, much to the disbelief of the man who had just been disarmed.

The leader took a couple of steps back before trying to run for the opening of the alleyway behind him. Zombre thought quickly and threw the chain that had been wrapped around his arm at the leader's feet. This caused the escaping man to fall flat on his face. He spun onto his back just in time for Zombre to grab him by the collar of his shirt. Zombre pulled him to his feet and held his blade to the leader's throat. "Last chance. Tell me who hired you," Zombre bluffed.

The man looked at Zombre with terrified eyes. "Okay, okay. I don't know who, but I can tell you where I was supposed to bring your body. It was a church on..." The leader was interrupted by a loud bang, then Zombre felt a sharp pain in his chest and the leader's face went expressionless as he coughed blood up onto Zombre's cracked mask. Zombre let the man go and he fell to the ground, dead. A single gunshot wound in the center of the leader's chest. Zombre felt his chest and felt the bullet fall out of his body as his blade healed him with a ghostly green light. After he was fully healed, the blade and Zombre's eyes started to glow purple, so the sword could collect a piece of the soul of the leader of the gang who had just been shot and killed.

Zombre looked across the street, the only place the bullet could have come from and thought he saw movement in the window of an abandoned building. Zombre raced across the street, but by the time he got there, no one was there. The only evidence of a shooter was a single shell casing, left sitting upright on the window sill and Zombre felt it was not left there by accident.

Zombre wanted to stay behind and wait for one of the four unconscious goons to wake up so he could interrogate them, but the sound of a gunshot attracted the attention of the police. As the cops came to pick up the unconscious assailants and their dead leader, Zombre disappeared into the night and returned to his home. On his journey back to his apartment, Zombre did not have any feelings of being followed and the news mentioned nothing of the men picked up in the alleyway or their dead leader. Zombre hoped that whatever it was, it was over. He was wrong.

*****

Zachary was sitting in his reclining chair watching TV on a Sunday, the only day that he took off from both work and crime-fighting, when he heard a knock at the door. Zachary was caught off guard for a moment. He did not have any friends who would just stop by unannounced. In fact, he did not have any friends in the city. Zachary figured it was probably one of his neighbors. "Mr. Harwas? Do you need something?" He walked over to the door, opened it, and was immediately met with a large fist to the eye socket. He fell to the ground unconscious.

Zachary woke up a couple of hours later in his kitchen tied to a wooden chair. "What the?" He mumbled to himself as he looked around the kitchen. His eye stung real bad and he could see his blade and mask were sitting just a couple of feet away from him on his kitchen table. He could only be healed by the blade's magic if he was physically touching the sword.

Also at the table was a big, fat, tall man with a brown, upkept beard and short brown hair. He had a large scar between his left eye and ear. Zacahry could only see his left side because he was watching the TV that was still on in the other room. The large man was wearing a gray and black suit similar to the ones he saw the other day at his work and now that he was up close, Zachary could tell they were very expensive. The big man turned and the two made eye contact. Zachary was surprised such an intimidatingly large man had such soft blue eyes. "Hey, he's awake," the bearded man shouted in a French accent.

"Ah, wonderful!" a French voice called out from around the corner in his living/bedroom.

The TV turned off and Zachary heard his bed squeak as someone got off of it. "Ah man, I just changed my sheets too." Zachary said. His joke was ignored by the large man sitting next to him.

Around the corner walked a short man with short black hair in a similar suit as the big man. A third man, who was very skinny and lanky, walked next to the short man, making it a total of three captores in Zachary's apartment. "It is a pleasure to meet you, Mr. Ombre," the short man said with a cocky smile.

Zachary looked at the short man quizzically, "Well colored me embarrassed, you know who I am but I haven't a clue who you are."

The man just laughed. "Our names don't matter as much as who we represent. We are the worshipers and disciples of the great

Arios Pearl," he said with dramatic grandeur, pausing to allow Zachary to react to the name, but his face showed no reaction. "Have you not heard of the glory of Arios Pearl? He is the most powerful of the old world gods! What a disappointing state the American public school system is in," he said to his associates.

"While all this is very interesting," Zachary interjected before the man with the French accent could go on a zealous rant, "I really don't see what it has to do with me."

The Frenchman looked back at him annoyed, "Well you see, Mr. Ombre, the great Arios Pearl was betrayed before he could complete the transformation that would have made him unstoppable. He could have made this world a beautiful place, but tiny, insignificant men feared his greatness and his vision for the future. But now, thanks to your magnificent ability, you can help us bring in the era of Arios Pearl."

"Yeah, thank you for the offer, but I'm gonna pass. No offense or anything, but you guys sound crazy," Zachary said with a laugh. The Frenchman started laughing and the two other henchmen in the room laughed with him. Then the short Frenchman suddenly struck Zachary in the face. Zachary and the chair fell to the ground, blood dripping from his mouth.

The big bearded man walked over, grabbed the bleeding boy, and set him back upright. The big man then patted Zachary on the shoulder before returning to his original position. The short Frenchman leaned in close to Zachary, allowing Zachary to smell the alcohol on his breath. "We don't need you, Mr. Ombre," he explained, "that blade is what's powerful, not you. We wanted you to join us because Arios Pearl is the future and you deserved a chance to serve him willingly as one of his champions, but now I see that you are just a worthless idiot who lucked upon the greatest gift imaginable." His comment angered Zachary, this fool had no idea what price the blade carried. "So, one last chance. Accept our offer to join the great Arios Pearl, or die, painfully."

"Well, if those are my only two options, I guess the choice is simple." He said before slamming his forehead into the Frenchman's nose, breaking it and causing blood to gush from his nostrils. Zachary then jumped in the air and landed on his backside, causing his cheaply made wooden chair to shatter. Zachary leaped to his feet in an attempt to grab his blade, but the skinniest of the three cult members jumped forward and kicked Zachary in the chest, sending him flying back. He slammed his head into the fridge with a thud, dazing himself slightly. The man who had just kicked him grabbed Zachary's blade and made a break for the fire exit outside his window. The biggest of the three men stepped forward in between Zachary and the short Frenchman as he cursed at his injury.

Zachary got back up and was about to face off against the big, bearded man with the scar when there was an unexpected knock at the door. The three remaining men in the room all stopped and looked towards the door. "Hey Zach, you're making a lot of noise. Everything okay there?" It was his next-door neighbor, Mr. Harwas, who was an older gentleman that lived alone.

"Oh, I'm fine, Mr. Harwas. I'm just watching a war movie marathon and I tripped into the fridge. Nothing to worry about," Zachary lied, hoping to prevent his unwanted guests from involving his innocent neighbors. "I should warn you that you might hear some more loud noises. I'm currently dealing with a pest problem," Zach said with gritted teeth as he wiped blood from his face with the back of his hand while staring down the bearded brute in front of him.

"I have a few extra rat traps if you need them," Mr. Harwas offered.

"Thanks, but I think I have everything I need," Zachary replied.

"Ah, very well. Good luck then," Mr. Harwas said as he walked back to his room. With the interruption now passed, the German man swung his right fist at Zachary's head, which he ducked to dodge. However, he had no luck evading the left fist which struck him in the jaw, spraying blood from his mouth all over his kitchen wall. The giant man then kicked Zachary in the chest and sent him flying backward into his fridge again. Luckily for Zachary, he had gotten the wind knocked out of him, which caused him to suddenly collapse to the floor and thus evade a direct blow to his face. The large, French goon punched his fist into the metal door of the refrigerator and a heavily bleeding Zachary escaped through his legs.

Zachary stood and reoriented himself just in time for his large attacker to strike him with one of his cheaply-made, wooden chairs, breaking it over his head. Zachary stumbled back against the bloodless wall of his small kitchen. The bearded brute then grabbed him by the throat with his left hand and lifted Zachary with ease. The large Frenchman — who looked like he had not been in a fight with the exception of Zachary's blood on his hands and clothes — punched Zachary once in the side and then once in the face. Zachary panicked and spat blood into his attacker's blue eyes, causing the bearded man to release his hold on Zachary's throat. The bloody and beaten Zachary fell to his knees, then put all his strength into a blow below the belt. The big man yelled out a slur in French before crumbling to the ground.

"We don't have time to waste on this insignificant nothing," the short Frenchman yelled as he raised a black pistol with a silencer and shot Zachary at point-blank range. "Now come on. We don't want to miss the revival of the great Arios Pearl!" Those were the last words Zachary heard before he passed out on his kitchen floor.

Everything was dark and empty. Zachary used to have colorful and vibrant dreams when he was a child, but all that ended after he died, the first time. When he was shot at the train tracks, his world went blank and darkness consumed everything. Then the darkness was overtaken by a green light and he awoke from the darkness. But every night since, his sleep was filled with darkness again. Perpetually empty.

Zachary's eyes shot open and blood spewed from his mouth as he coughed in pain. He slowly stood up, trying to focus on anything but his injuries. He had a mind-splitting headache, bruised ribs, a broken left forearm, and internal bleeding. Of course, that's not including the bullet lodged high in his left shoulder. His mind was clouded, but not from the pain. What clouded his mind was craving for what was taken from him. Zachary began to enter a trance brought on by his separation from his sword and as he went deeper into the daze the feeling of pain began to vanish. All thoughts of pain faded, leaving only his desire to reclaim the blade. Zachary was able to grab and put on a spare, unbroken mask before his mind was completely lost into a zombie-like state. Zombre stumbled out the front door of his apartment building and down the street. The blade called to him and he followed that call.

As a mindless creature of the night, Zombre stumbled down the streets towards the Historical District. He did not care about the glares and sideways glances that were focused his way by the ordinary people that all filled the streets that night. Most of them assumed he was doing some weird zombie walk. Others assumed he was just a kid acting that way for an internet video, none considered that he had entered a zombie-like state in order to hunt down the blade his body craves.

The closer Zombre got to the blade, the more his mind started to return. One by one, his thoughts returned bringing with them a clearer mind. He noticed he was heading north, deeper into the city. With each step he took closer to the blade, the more in control he felt. He stopped at the rusty, black front gates of a medium-sized, gothic-style church with a worn-down graveyard off to the side.

Zombre felt as though the fog had faded and he could once again think fully; he knew that his blade was inside this house of worship. He opened the creaky gates, stepped inside, and immediately fell to the ground as the pain returned. Once again his head pounded, his ribs ached, and the bullet hole in his shoulder stung like hell. Zombre forced himself to his feet, fighting the pain so he could reclaim what was taken from him. Zombre walked up to the front of the church and stopped just before the front steps.

Zombre looked up towards the large, ornate, wooden doors and decided it was probably not the best idea to burst through the front door and right into the middle of some ancient cult ritual. As blood began to drip down from the bottom of his mask, he decided to head around the side of the church to find a side door. He found a door near the back of the church that was unlocked and snuck inside. Zombre could hear chanting emanating from the main sanctuary, but he could not make out the words that were being said. He crept up to a closed door and cracked it open so he could see what was happening. Through the crack, Zombre could see numerous men and women dressed in gray and black hooded cloaks along the edges of the room chanting under their breath in a language that Zombre did not recognize. In the middle of the room were two men wearing red and white robes with two medium-sized, bottles filled with stones and sand hanging around their necks on a black rope. Between these two men was a marble island that held his blade. Zombre considered making a mad dash for his knife but doubted he could reach the middle of the room before being stopped by the other zealots. He instead gently closed the door and began to look for another way he could get to the center of the room without going through every member of the cult unarmed. Zombre found a small, winding staircase that led up to a mezzanine. He snuck up the stairs and found the mezzanine empty. From there, Zombre was able to get a perfect view of the dealings below him.

From his new vantage point, Zombre could see the entire layout of the church below. He looked over to the altar and surrounded by candles were bones: large almost inhuman-sized bones laid out in the shape of a human skeleton. The hands had sharp claws, the skull looked a mix of a cow's skull with the horns of a gazelle and sharp teeth of a tiger, and the whole skeleton looked larger and taller than any human who had ever lived. He stared at the bones with frightful curiosity and wondered if that was Arios Pearl.

Zombre was pulled away from his grim realization when the cult members started chanting louder. The two men in the middle began to call out in a strange dialect and the bottles around their necks began to glow a ghostly green. He looked on from above as his blade began to glow the same shade of green and start to levitate above the marble slab. With each foot it rose into the air, the chanting from the zealots became louder. Zachary moved back away from the edge to avoid being seen. The blade reached its peak and the green light leaked down to the skeleton. The bones began to rattle and shake as the green light engulfed them. Zombre could only watch on in horror as muscles, veins, and ghostly white skin began to wrap around the bones. The eyelids of the beast shot open to reveal deadly red eyes. It clamored to its feet and let out a monstrous roar that echoed through the church and silenced the chanting. The beast stood at its full height of 10 feet tall, closed its eyes, and basked in the green light as its worshipers dropped to their knees.

Zachary knew he had to do something drastic and fast. He stood and took a couple of steps back. He closed his eyes, took a deep breath through the pain, and then ran as fast as he could towards the ledge. Each step he took sent shock waves of agony through his body. He reached the edge and prayed that he had enough strength left in his body. Zombre was lucky that the beating he had received had left his legs relatively unharmed and allowed him to leap with just enough power; he flew through the air and reached out for his blade. He felt the handle hit his hand and he gripped with all his might as he began to plummet towards the ground. With the sword out of position, it stopped healing Arios Pearl and everyone just watched as Zombre hit the pews with a loud crack. "What is going on?" Arios Pearl asked his followers as he took monstrous steps towards the spot where Zombre had landed. He had been resurrected enough to talk and exist, but was nowhere near his full strength.

The green light that had surrounded Arios Pearl now surrounded Zombre. All the pain, bruises, broken bones, and his bullet hole healed within moments. Then Zombre stood and stared down the monstrous self-proclaimed god. "I hope you don't mind that I dropped in. I'd love to stay longer, but I got what I came for and I must be on my way," Zombre snarled as he tightened his grip on his blade.

"Kill him and bring me the blade," Arios Pearl commanded as he sat on his altar, sending his followers into a mad frenzy towards Zombre. "With that damn shield around the planet, I need that sword to regain the rest of my strength."

The hooded Zealots ran at him with weapons drawn and he was ready to take them when he noticed something different. He could see the weaknesses of the men and women rushing towards him. The first cult member that reached Zombre had a bad knee, he could see the cracks in her bones and the tears in her cartilage. Zombre kicked her bad knee and felt it shatter under his foot. She yelled in pain and fell forward leaving her open to attack. He punched her in the face with the same hand that held his blade, knocking his attacker unconscious.

Zombre looked for the next attack when someone jumped onto his back. They began to stab at him, hitting him in the head, neck, and shoulders with a dagger. He reached up and grabbed the cult member and threw him to the ground, but then was hit by the blade of another attacker. Zombre did not want to kill these people, but he was getting outmatched and overwhelmed. He faced fatal blow after fatal blow, trying his best to take out his enemies without taking their lives, but then something came over him. Not anger or desperation, but apathy. He began to slice at his enemies, not caring where his attacks landed. Purple light began to leak out of those that fell to the ground dead as the green light continued to heal Zombre's injuries. His left eye glowed purple and his right eye green.

A medium-sized man with a neatly trimmed beard ran at Zombre. He could not see any major weaknesses, so he just swung at the man's chest, slicing it open. Then he heard familiar heavy footsteps behind him. He quickly turned and swung overhand, catching the neck of his assailant and decapitating him. The head flew past and Zombre confirmed it was the head of the Frenchman who had wailed on him at his apartment. He had gotten the last laugh.

He looked for his next opponent when he felt severe pain in his back. Zombre turned and slashed as the person who had just stabbed him and just barely got him in the chest. The blow he dealt was fatal. Zombre fought like a madman, exchanging deadly blows with his numerous attackers as auras of green and purple light surrounded him. The zealots' attacks slowly walked him back into a trap. The attacks stopped as Zombre found himself in the shadow of the monstrous Arios Pearl.

Arios Pearl looked down at the blood-stained intruder before him and chuckled deeply. "Such tenacity, strength and courage. A true warrior of legend. You have proven yourself worthy of sacrifice to the great Arios Pearl," he boomed in a deep, eerie, and echoey voice. He turned his attention from Zombre to the remainder of his followers. "Whoever brings his head to my feet shall win my favor."

Zombre scoffed loudly as the semicircle of zealots began to creep in. "Must not be all that powerful if you can't even smite me yourself," he ridiculed the self-proclaimed god.

Anger filled the face of Arios Pearl and he held up his right hand to halt his worshipers. "HOW DARE YOU CHALLENGE ME!" Arios Pearl screamed as he rose from his altar and stepped forward toward the armed man who ridiculed his power. "NOW YOU SHALL ENDURE THE FULL WRATH OF ARIOS PEARL!" He screamed as his followers began to back away and run from the incoming attacks. Zombre leaped to his left and just barely avoided Arios Pearl's large fist as it crashed down from above and through the floorboards.

Zombre got up from the hardwood floor and stared down his 10-foot-tall attacker. Arios Pearl snarled as he swiped at Zombre, catching him in the stomach and chest with his claws. Zombre flew backward and landed hard on his back as blood sprayed onto the floor. Zombre had suffered many fatal strikes, but these wounds stung as no others had before. They burned like they had been splashed with some kind of acid or poison. His power still healed him, but his abdomen continued to burn as he rose back to his feet. Zombre tightened his grip on his blade and charged at Arios Pearl.

He swung his green-glowing blade at the ancient giant, blocking a backhand strike from Arios Pearl. Steel clashed with bone claws as Zombre was forced backward from the strength of his opponent. He tried to recover as quickly as he could but was unable to dodge the overhand closed-fist blow that broke his shoulder blade on impact. He was laying on the ground when Arios Pearl stomped on his head.

The ancient monstrosity turned to address his devout followers now that his challenger lay on the church floor with his skull split open. "Let the reign of Arios Pearl resume!" he announced, sending the mass of zealots into a roar of cheers and applause. His moment of triumph was ruined by a sight he noticed in the corner of his eyes. Arios Pearl turned back to the bloody mess to see him stand back up on his feet.

Zombre's mask had shattered from the previous blow that he was dealt. Blood dripped down from the top of his head as he glared at the self-proclaimed deity. The act of defiance of not succumbing to the might of Arios Pearl sent the power-hungry cult leader into a furious rage. He had been challenged enough by this relentless undead nuisance.

"WHY WON'T YOU STAY DEAD?!" Arios Pearl roared as his hand began to glow red. Arios Pearl knew he was not at full strength yet and did not want to use up what little power he currently had, but he was getting annoyed with Zombre's persistence. He reached back and threw a ball of red hot energy towards Zombre. The ball landed right at his feet and exploded, sending Zombre and debris flying through the air. He soared through the air and slammed against the stonewall of the church before crumbling back down to the ground. Arios Pearl was determined to make sure that his opponent was down for good. Arios Pearl lumbered towards Zombre, but Zombre was not willing to give in to the monster that was revived because of his blade. He stood and immediately ducked to avoid another ball of energy that came flying towards him. The attack crashed into the wall above him, creating a giant hole and sending debris down onto him. Arios Pearl fired two more attacks, both of which missed their target and created massive amounts of smoke. Zombre used the cover of the smoke to charge at Arios Pearl. He swung his blade and caught the monstrous, self-proclaimed god in the left arm. Arios Pearl let out a painful roar. He grabbed Zombre by the back of the neck and threw the undead hero off to the side towards the marble stairs that rested below the altar that once held Arios Pearl's bones.

Zombre once again got to his feet and looked upon the furious monstrosity that sought to destroy him. He had no reason for fighting other than he felt it was his obligation. The blade which gives him his powers is what this thing used to return from the dead. He was powerful, crazy, and Zombre knew that if he did not stop him then a lot of people would die and those lives would be on him. So he kept attacking over and over, suffering painful blow after painful blow, until he defeated Arios Pearl or died for the final time.

Zombre's entire body ached and burned as he recovered from another attack that failed to kill him. He was being dealt more injuries than his power could recover from, causing his blood to spill freely and his internal organs to be exposed to the outside world. Even pieces of his brain could be seen through missing pieces of his skull that had yet to heal. Zombre knew his body could not handle much more. His power was the only thing keeping him alive. He was missing fingers, chunks of flesh, and looked like he had just crawled out of a grave. His mind was blank except for one goal, kill Arios Pearl. It was in this state of depravity that Zombre noticed a weakness in Arios Pearl that one of his more recent strikes had exposed. A vein that ran along the back of the artificial god's right leg glowed like a beacon to Zombre. He charged for one final time at the pissed-off god, but instead of attempting a strike, dropped to his knees and slid through the legs of the confused Arios Pearl. Zombre spun and sliced the exposed vein. Arios Pearl crumbled in pain as his blood spewed out of his leg. Zombre jumped to his feet and raised his blade above his head and used the remainder of his strength to decapitate Arios Pearl. The head of the vile monster fell to the ground as the few remaining followers looked on in disbelief.

Arios Pearl's body began to glow and crack as the energy that he was made of became increasingly unstable. Zombre ran and hid behind the first row of pews as Arios Pearl's body exploded in a bright light of energy. Zombre's ears rang from the blast and debris fell all around him. Zombre took a moment to collect himself and heal before looking up from behind his cover to see if any religious zealots remained in the church. When he was certain the coast was clear, Zombre got up to swiftly head to the exit.

As he was about to leave, Zombre looked over at the charred pile of bones and noticed the skull of Arios Pearl laying nearby in large pieces. The only thing that was not burned was the faceplate of Arios Pearl's skull. He grabbed it before he left. He figured if those cult nutjobs could not find all the pieces then they could not bring back their psycho leader. He walked out of the church into the dead of night and headed home to sleep for a long time.

*****

Over the next couple of weeks, Zachary returned to his nightly crime fighting while keeping a close eye on the news to see if there were any references to the incident at the church, but was surprised when he saw no mention of what had happened. He walked past the church one day and was shocked to see it had been torn down and in its place a construction site for some generic research laboratory building.

Zachary was happy that he had not encountered any more of those crazy cult members. He thought about hiding or burying the faceplate of Arios Pearl's skull, but was afraid someone might discover it by accident. Zachary decided to wear it as his facemask instead. The sharp tooth, monstrous skull was more intimidating than a store-bought hockey mask. Zackary hoped that the whole event was behind him, but his encounter with Arios Pearl was only bringing him more unwanted attention.

The House

Trauma never disappears. While the physical wounds will heal as scars and bruises fade with time, the mental toll remains. It comes and goes in waves as it hides in the recesses of the mind, until a sudden reminder of what was lost or the terrible things that happened. The struggle to heal is an ongoing fight that never ends.

*****

Deep in the wooded swamps just outside the southern city of New Vida, there was a house known as the Rising Sun: a mansion with a back alley notoriety for satisfying the deepest, darkest desires of anyone who entered through its grand mahogany doors. Men and women could gamble, screw, or drink their hearts away at any hour of the day. The man who oversaw it all was the proprietor, Dennis "Baldur" Vandale, who had been gifted the underground casino from a powerful friend. The regulars referred to the 42-year-old man as Baldur in reference to the Norse deity, who was god of joy and purity — the latter a joke of irony. The man with short, spiky black hair and ice blue eyes got the nickname because of his god-complex and his regular position standing on the indoor balcony outside his third floor office and looking upon his domain of sin and pleasure, basking in the sights and sounds of people letting off steam and enjoying themselves, for a price of course.

It was like any other Tuesday morning in May, Dennis watched the late-night crowd of deviants slowly getting replaced by the early-morning sinners who wanted to get in a little fun before work. This would be the beginning of the end for the Rising Sun.

*****

Light from the morning sun broke through the window onto the face of the now 23-year-old Jennifer "Jenni" Clarkson. The short, young woman had blonde hair with subtle hints of brown streaked throughout her wavy locks; her emerald eyes with flickers of gold stared aimlessly at the blank wall besides her. Jenni wore black spandex shorts and a white, partially torn t-shirt. She layed on stained sheets like a ragdoll that had been through unimaginable hell over the last two weeks. She was forced into a life of prostitution by someone she thought was the love of her life to pay off gambling debts he owed Baldur.

They were visiting from the city of Stargellsburgh. It was a vacation to bring them closer as a couple, but her boyfriend Anthony had other motives when he suggested New Vida. Jenni was excited for the trip and looking forward to experiencing the vibrant culture of the city she had never been to before. However, she never got the chance. On the first day they arrived, Anthony lured her here under the guise that it was a fun, secret haunt that only the locals know of. When they finally got there, Jenni was drugged and hauled off to work off Anthony's sizable debt as an involuntary sex worker. For two weeks, she suffered while he galavanted around the city unharmed and carefree.

The door to the small room creaked open and Jenni's heart sank into a deep pit of fear and sorrow while she prepared to be violated again. A soft voice called out to her; she recognized it as the "House Mother" who went by the code name Neaera. Neaera is the one who oversees all of the sex workers: both those there involuntarily paying off debts and those there working of their own free will. The brown-haired woman worked under a fake name to protect her from some of their dangerous and creepy clientele. "Happy birthday, dear. As long as you are not requested, you get the day off." She said it so casually and sweetly, like she was not the one who sent men and women into her room to destroy the few bits of humanity that remained inside her soul. Neaera knew it was her birthday from the license Jenni had on her when she was taken.

As the older woman closed the door, Jenni's heart filled with anger, her fists with wrath, and her mind with thoughts of vengeance. She decided right then and there, as the sun shone down on her bruised face, that she would not die here; she would be free once again and she would have her revenge on the people who trapped her there. Her 23rd birthday gift to herself would be their deaths.

It was ten in the morning when Neaera heard a commotion coming from down the hall. She grabbed her blood-stained "perspective adjuster": a wooden, 2-foot paddle. She figured she would have to remind someone of the house rules — either for one of the involuntary girls putting up a fight that a client cannot handle themselves or a patron who was taking it a tad too far with their abuse fantasy. "I'll be right back," she said to the two men who guarded the entrance to the basement. Baldur liked to refer to his enforcers as his Garrison of Angels.

As Neaera got closer, she realized the situation was more pressing than she previously thought. The brown-haired woman kicked open the door to see one of the unwilling working-girls on the bed in a blood-soaked hysteria while an unrecognizable, smashed-face john lay on the wood floor. The sight made Neaera gag. That is when Jenni jumped out the closet with a primal scream of wrath, tackling Neaera to the ground. "GUARDS!" Neaera yelled out as she struggled with Jenni.

The blood-soaked girl on the bed shrieked and bolted for the hall, running out of the room as Jenni and Neaera rolled on the ground fighting for control of the wooden paddle. Jenni was able to pry it from the house mother's hands and began beating her over the head until the brown-haired woman was begging for mercy through blood-soaked teeth. "Please, stop, please. I was good to you! Why are you doing this?"

"DIE!" was the last word Neaera heard before the final blow. Jenni jumped to her feet, ready to run for her freedom when the two guards finally entered the room. They grabbed her before she could defend herself. One hit her in the jaw, causing her to bleed in the mouth. They pulled her from the room, kicking and screaming bloody murder. As their hands, wrapped around her malnourished arms, dragged her through the hall, Jenni noticed what happened to the other woman who had fled from the room previously. She laid, crumbled on the floor, a stain of her blood sliding down the wall. After she bolted from the room, she ran into the guards who shoved her so hard into the wall that it killed her. As Jenni stared at the dead girl's partially opened eyes, she lost her will to fight. All Jenni could think about was how the poor girl deserved better than this. They all did.

Jenni was carried upstairs via a less public entrance, gagged, and tied to a chair in Baldur's office. "Ah, is this the little troublemaker?" Bladur asked as he entered the office behind her. The semi-casually dressed man wearing a gray collared shirt and blue jeans walked over to a private bar that had a small gas grill next to it. Above the drink station was a 300-year-old katana mounted on the wall. "Do you know how much your little stunt is going to hurt my business? I have to find a new Neaera to replace the one you killed and the replacement is going to want more money since the previous was killed after one of the girls went ape-shit psycho murderer," he paused to take a sip of his gin and tonic, "And I have to deal with the clusterfuck that comes with the girl you killed mid-performance. She was paying off someone else's debt too, ya know. Not to mention what the consumer will think. They will want discounts and assurances that this won't happen again. It will take weeks to charge the going rate again, if not a full month." He took another sip of his drink and turned to face her. His blue eyes were ice cold. His jaw had a slight red glow from a fresh shave. He ran his hand through his spiky hair as he walked between the front of his desk and Jenni before he leaned against the red oak work surface. "Why did you do this? You are here to pay off a debt, not prove the power of women or show how much of a badass you are." He pulled the gag out of her mouth to let her speak for her actions.

"I'm going to fucking kill you, you sick son-of-a-bitch," Jenni spat as she struggled, trying to free herself from the ropes that held her to the chair. Baldur just laughed. She raised her voice to a scream. "You think I'm kidding? I'm going to tear your fucking balls off and shove them down your throat!" Baldur was the first to violate her. It was his standard practice to be the one who welcomes the "repayment girls" to the Rising Sun.

"Oh, I believe you would, sweetcheeks. I sincerely believe that everything inside you wants to kill me, but — and maybe you're too dumb to realize this — I'm not the one tied to a fucking chair." He smirked and Jenni spit blood onto his shirt. This got his attention, causing him to leap to his feet. "Now what the fuck was that for?! This is an expensive shirt! Oh, and look you got your blood on the carpet, that's not going to come out easily." Jenni responded by spitting more blood onto the carpet.

Baldur walked over and backhanded Jenni on her face with his right hand. The blonde looked back at him, her angered expression unwavering. "You hit like a wimp," she replied as she spit more of her blood and saliva mixture onto the floor.

The blue-eyed man shook his head. "Honestly, bitch, read the room. You are not worth my fucking time. No money or piece of ass is worth this level of crazy," he said before slamming back the last of his drink.

"Then why don't you kill me? Or better yet, untie me and we will see who the bitch really is," Jenni snarled as she once again fought against the restraints.

A grin appeared on Baldur's face as he laughed. "She has got some fire in her, you hear her Mike?" he asked one of his goons before sighing and looking back at the blonde woman. "I would, baby doll, but like I said...Not. Worth. My. Time." He forcibly patted her right cheek twice. "But don't worry, my angels will take extra good care of you. Have fun playing with the gators in the swamp."

"I'll kill you."

"Bitch, you can't kill a god," he whispered to her before looking up at the two men who brought Jenni to his office. "Carry out my will and smite her," he commanded.

Jenni screamed as the two men reapplied her gag and added a blindfold to try and terrify her as much as possible in her final moments. They carried her downstairs to an unmarked black van that was parked behind the mansion.

*****

Jenni's hands were bound in front of her in the back of the van, bouncing and landing hard onto the metal floor with each bump from the uneven, dirt road. After 30 minutes, the vehicle stopped and the two men exited from the front seat. Jenni heard the backdoor open. She tried to kick blindly at her captor, but he grabbed her by the legs, pulled her from the van, and tossed her onto the road below. She was then dragged around the vehicle to the edge of the swamp.

Jenni could smell bad gumbo and cheap scotch from the breath of the man who leaned in close to her. "I want to see the fear in those pretty eyes, sweetcheeks." He burped and slurred. As her blindfold was removed, a flash of white light gave way to the ugly sight of a crooked, yellowed smile of the shorter obese man before her. There was a look of joy in his blood-lusting eyes.

The other of her two captors was a tall, skinny man with a patchy goatee wearing knock-off alligator boots and a thick gold chain. He was leaning against the driver's side of the van smoking. "Will you hurry up, ya dumbass? I don't want to be out here any longer than I have to. Stupid swamp water is gonna ruin my shoes," the skinny man chirped in a southern accent in between drags of his cigarette.

The larger man turned back to his partner and started a lengthy argument of pointless bickering. Jenni did not care to listen. She looked to the sky and out into the beautiful swamps that surrounded New Vida. The serenity of nature was something she always enjoyed when she would visit the large parks of Stargellsburgh. Tears rolled down her black and blue cheeks as she thought of her mother and sister back home. She did not fear dying; she feared not getting to say goodbye to those who would miss her when she was gone. That is when she noticed the white berries of mistletoe in the trees. She had forgotten that a strand of it grew in the swamps of Louisiana. The sight of it reminded her of a story that her late father used to tell her, a story of mistletoe killing a god that everyone thought was immortal. The name of that god escaped her, but she reached out and grabbed the berries from a low hanging branch.

The closest goon to her waved his gun back and forth in the air while he continued to whine about the things his partner does that annoy him. When the matte black glock was down near the large man's waist, Jenni sprung forward and grabbed it — her aggressiveness startled her overweight captor and knocked him to the ground after he lost his balance on the loose mud of the swamp. The skinny man — also stunned by the sudden fight in the believed-to-be-broken victim — tried to draw his gun, but fumbled to get it free from his waistband. Jenni fired a bullet that tore into his left eye. He fell lifeless to the ground. Without a moment of hesitation, Jenni turned the pistol onto the man who lay on his back in the mud. He stared up at her with shock and horror draped over his face. "You should see the fear in your eyes," Jenni joked in a monotone, steady voice. One bullet later and she was free from her captors.

As the blonde woman drove away from the two bodies in the swamp, she thought of what she would do next. She had a pistol with 11 bullets, a handful of mistletoe, and a soul craving revenge.

*****

Night arrived at the same time that Jenni reached downtown New Vida. She sat in the black, mud-covered van across the street from the hotel her boyfriend — or more accurately ex-boyfriend — and her were staying at before he traded her life away to pay off his debt. The blonde knew that he would not have moved on from this hotel. She had booked the stay in her name and on her credit car. There is no reason that cheap bastard was not just extending the trip knowing he would never have to pay it off.

Her suspicions were confirmed when she saw the sleaze-ball walk out the front door. He was dressed in a white, untucked button-up shirt with a matching black tuxedo coat and pants. Jenni rubbed the handle of the pistol. She considered hunting him down and disposing of him in the alley like the trash he was, but a chaotic bachelor party turned a corner and in the mix of black and white she lost track of Anthony.

Jenni stepped out of the van and crossed the street, entering the hotel. She wrapped a food-stained, cotton, zip-up jacket that she found in the back of the van around herself allowing her to conceal the gun. The smell of the lobby — a generic cleaning solution with hints of chlorine from the pool area — was a welcomed paradise to her senses. The last two weeks had been nonstop unbearable smells that she wished to never experience again. Jenni walked over to the front desk where a black-haired woman in a white shirt with a green vest stood. The employee seemed shocked at the dirt-covered, bruised, battle-tested woman that stood before her. "Hello, can I help you, ma'am?" she asked in a Creole accent while her hand was on the phone so she could quickly call security. Jenni read the woman's name tag before responding.

"I hope so, Amanda," Jenni began. "I was out for a jog when I fell and lost my phone and wallet in a storm drain. I was wondering if you could make me a new room key? Room 122, Jennifer Clarkson."

The hotel worker took her hand off the phone and pulled up the information on the requested room. The name matched, but to be certain she checked the copy of the license that was scanned when the guests checked in. Jenni's wholesome, smiling face popped onto the screen, giving the black-haired employee confidence in the dirt-covered woman's story. "I am so sorry that happened to you, Miss. Clarkson," the woman behind the desk said as she began to print off a new key card. "Let me get that for you so you can get back into your room."

"Thank you so much, Amanda," Jenni replied as she was handed the flat piece of blue plastic.

The hotel worker smiled, "Of course! Let me know if you need anything else."

"I will," the blonde woman lied as she walked towards the elevator. The metal door closed as she let out a sigh as she leaned against the cool steel back wall. Jenni was exhausted. The short ride ended and she walked over to the hotel room. The electronic lock clicked after Jenni tapped the key and for the first time since she entered the building, she worried if the room would actually be empty. Her ex could have snuck back in or left a guest in the room. She gripped the gun in her jacket pocket as she slowly opened the door. Jenni walked into the dark, messy room. The door closed behind her and she removed the pistol from its hiding spot just in case she needed it, but there was no one else in the room.

Jenni turned on the light and looked upon the disaster of clothes and trash that covered the bed, floor, and furniture. Her old suitcase was open in the corner: ransacked. She walked over and looked through it. Half of her possessions were missing. Anything of value — like her designer clothes, handbags, and jewelry — sold to fund Anthony's gambling urges. Jenni grabbed a clean shirt, pair of pants, and underwear; the first bra she grabbed was not hers and she tossed it away in disgust.

Jenni had many dreams of hot showers while held captive. Those that were there willingly were allowed to come and go as they pleased, given liberties like fresh food and hot showers whenever they desired or needed. The women who were working odd debts — either their own or on behalf of others — were excluded from such autonomy. The involuntary were given small portions of stale, leftover food and only allowed to clean themselves with cold water that was sprayed on them with a hose while supervised. It was hell.

Steam filled the bathroom, fogging the mirror. In her blurred reflection, Jenni almost seemed normal to herself again, but when she wiped away the condensation with her left hand, she was reminded of her suffering with each bruise on her body. She placed the pistol on the back of the toilet and stepped into the shower.

The hot water burned in a good way, cleansing off the dirt and grime. However, no peace was found in the shower. With each noise from the hall, Jenni reached for the gun in panic, aiming it at the bathroom door as she hid behind the plastic curtain until she was certain there was no threat. Jenni wished more than anything that she could turn the water hot enough to wash away the poisoned memories and bruises of the last two weeks down the drain with the filthy water.

The blonde turned off the water and stepped out of the shower. She dried herself off with the last clean towel and dressed in the freshest clothing she had dawned since the day her freedom was taken away.

After clearing empty Thai food containers and a pair of beer-soaked pants from the black rolling desk chair, Jenni took a seat at the room's desk to wait for Anthony to return to serve his death sentence. She placed the pistol on the wooden surface and picked up the hotel phone. She dialed and listened to the line ring. Even though it was just the answering machine, the sweet sound of her mother's voice brought tears to her eyes. "Hi, you've reached The Clarkson's residence. We are not home right now, but if you leave a message, I will call back as soon as I am able. Thank you!"

The robotic beep sounded and the blonde woman cleared her throat to speak. "Hi mom, it's Jenni. I'm sure you've been wondering where I've been," she began as tears rolled down her face, but the words started getting caught in her throat as the challenge of telling her mom what she had been through seemed impossible. "Just...I hope to be coming home soon, okay? I just need to take care of one thing first. I love you, mom. Tell April I love her, too." April was her little sister who was seven years younger than her. Jenni hung up the phone. What she was unaware of was Anthony had been texting her mom from her phone. Telling her family that they decided to stay in New Vida. Whenever her mom or sister would try to call Jenni, it went unanswered and then Anthony would reply with only text messages. Her mother did go to the police, but they told her they could not do anything since Jenni was an adult and there was no proof that anything illegal or untoward had occurred.

Her soft sobs echoed off the aqua-colored walls, but a loud-talking group in the hall pulled her from her sorrow and back to her mission. Jenni grabbed the pistol and pointed it at the door, her vision blurred from her tears. The voices — which she could now tell were female voices — became quieter after they passed her door and got on the elevator. Jenni lowered her hand and set the gun back down.

The blonde wiped her eyes and noticed something strange in the trash bin. The boredom of waiting for her prey would have led her to investigate it soon enough. On top of a greasy foil burger wrapper from a fast food joint down the street was a business card with the day's date written in pen. Jenni inspected it further. The business card was for a place called King's Toy Store across town and under the handwritten date was the time: 11 pm. The blonde checked the digital clock on the desk; it was 10:44. The only other thing on the card was the business' strange slogan: 'A check for a King me.'

Jenni contemplated her next move. She could wait here, but she had no idea when Anthony would return, or if he would be alone. Plus, killing her ex-boyfriend in the hotel room that was rented in her name would almost guarantee she goes to jail, and he had cost her enough of her freedom already. Jenni decided to hunt him down. She grabbed one of her own sweatshirts so she could conceal the handgun without having to put back on the disgusting stained one. She packed the few clothes she still had left into her suitcase to bring with her. Luckily, her makeup remained untouched. She caked her bruises with concealer. Jenni smiled as she looked in the mirror at her almost-normal complexion. Jenni left the room with determination in her eyes. Little did she know, the hotel phone rang moments after she closed the door and walked towards the elevator. It was her mother returning her call.

On her way out of the hotel, Jenni stopped by the front desk again. "Hi, Amanada. May I ask you a question?"

The black-haired employee smiled, "Of course, ma'am!" she responded in her Creole accent.

"How long do the room keys work after I check out?" Jenni asked.

"They are deactivated as soon as you check out," Amanda explained.

Jenni smiled, "Perfect. I would like to check out now then." The blonde figured if her sleazy ex survived the night at least he would not be able to mooch free housing on her dime.

Amanda smiled. "Let me take care of that for you."

"Thank you," Jenni replied. "Oh, and just throw away anything you find in the room. Everything I left behind is garbage."

*****

Jenni pulled into the parking lot of King's Toy Store around 11:35 and turned the engine off. The business looked closed save for the numerous expensive cars in the parking lot. The green-eyed woman exited the vehicle and walked towards the entrance, the pistol in her back waistband. Jenni peered through the dark windows and tried the front door, but it was locked. She decided to check for a rear entrance. A single flood light illuminated a wooden door that was sandwiched between two green dumpsters. She walked over and noticed there was a smaller flap with an iron grate just above eye level on the wood. Jenni knocked.

The small flap opened and a pair of brown eyes looked down at her through the iron grate. "Password?" he asked in a deep, deep voice.

Jenni paused for a moment. 'Password?? What the fuck could that be?' her inner thoughts panicked. Then the green-eyed woman remembered the weird slogan on the card she found in the hotel room and figured it was worth a shot. "A check for a king me."

The small flap slammed closed, and for a moment Jenni thought her guess was incorrect. Then a loud metallic, scraping sound could be heard as the door unlocked. The blonde woman walked inside and immediately saw two large, bald, physically intimidating men dressed in all black suits with no neckties. They both had Mac 10s strapped around their shoulders, resting on their hips. "You're a little late if you're looking to get in on the games." This was the same intense voice that spoke through the small flap before. He wore a single diamond earring in his left ear.

"I'm here to meet my boyfriend." Jenni half lied, figuring the full truth would bring trouble. "He said he would be here, but he has shit luck so I wouldn't be surprised if he got kicked out by now. His name is Anthony, Anthony Benson. He's dressed like a hungover, hipster waiter."

The smaller of the two bald men laughed at her accurate description. "Yeah, he's here." His voice was not as deep as his buddies, but still impressive sounding.

"I'll take you to him," the man with the earring said as he turned to lead her down a short hallway.

Jenni's heart raced as she approached her revenge, uncertain what the next part of her plan would be exactly. "Wait." The other man interjected. "Is it your first day? You forgot to check her." The blonde woman felt her muscles tense up from nerves.

The big man with the earring turned back to his friend. "Man, you really think a fine piece like this is going to sneak in a weapon? Look at her, she's got the whole Miss America vibe.

His friend held up his hands. "Fine, then you can be the one to tell King you didn't think it was necessary."

The man with the earring shook his head. "Fine," he gave in and turned towards Jenni. "Arms out, miss."

"Sure thing." Jenni followed, freaking out internally about what she should do. 'Maybe he won't find...'

"The hell?" The deep-voiced man said as he pulled the gun from her waistband. Before Jenni could explain, the other man grabbed her by the shoulder tightly, restricting her movement. "Take her to his office. I'll get King," the man with the diamond earring commanded his fellow guard.

Jenni was taken down the hallway and tossed into a medium-sized office on the left. The man who escorted her stayed in the room after he closed the door behind them, his finger on the trigger of his machine gun as he stood off to the left of the only way in or out. Jenni worked her imaginations on what she should do to escape. She sat on a square black and white rug and there were two black tables with drawers on either side of her. In front of Jenni was a matching black desk. She tried her best to discreetly look at the contents of the wooden furniture. There was a gold letter opener — or at least she hoped it was a possible weapon. Jenni glanced back over her shoulder at the large man watching her. 'Maybe if I'm quick enough, I can get to it before he can stop me,' she thought. Jenni looked back at the desk and was just about to make her move of desperation when the door opened.

The first to enter the room was the big bald man with the diamond earring — his hand in position to fire his gun if needed. He took his place off to the right of the door. Behind him was a man who was smaller in comparison in both height and size. He was a well-defined, muscular six-foot-tall-male with black hair and light brown eyes. He looked like he was in his mid-40's even though he was well into his 50s. Jenni figured this must be King. He was dressed nicely in noticeably expensive clothes and shoes that were worth double the blonde's apartment rent back home in Stargellsburgh. In one hand he had the gun that was confiscated from her. He also carried a cane capped with a silver ornament handle of a globe wearing a crown, but it was a fashion piece, not used for walking assistance. "What shepherds this stunning señorita to my store? And armed of all things," King asked as he strolled around his desk and sat in his black leather chair. He placed the pistol in front of him on the desk. Jenni remained quiet. She just stared at him with anger in her eyes. "Time to talk. My service is sidelined unless you speak."

“Why would I want help from a gambling addict?” She snarled at him.

King laughed softly. “I am no bettor. I am a businessman; one who is wiser than to waste wealth on wagers.” He swayed his cane back and forth, not looking at Jenni. “With such bitterness towards betting men, I can’t help but believe bad intentions brought you here tonight.” King had dealt with the anti-gambling crowd of New Vida before. Ever since he arrived in the city and began to build his empire of underground casinos using the millions he made as the leader of a bank heist crew, he had to handle or bribe those that got in his way. The anti-gambling activist was the most difficult to deal with.

Jenni returned to her silence, but she was answered for by one of the thugs. “She said she was here to see Anthony, sir. Claimed he is her boyfriend,” the large man with the diamond earring responded.

“Anthony? How did a bumbling buffoon like that boy get a beauty like you?” King asked sincerely confused. Jenni’s ex had a reputation at King’s gambling halls. He was a streaky gambler with more bad luck than good and an unwillingness to leave the tables. King often joked his clubs were to give Anthony free drinks when he was on cold streaks to keep him thinking his luck was about to turn.

“Ex.” Jenni replied through gritted teeth, no longer caring to keep up her previous charade.

King could hear the hatred in her voice. So much anger packed into a one-word response. "I See. I know he's a dud, but does he deserve death?"

Jenni could hold back no more. Her fury fueled her response. "He ruined my life! He traded my body to some gambling house to pay off his stupid gambling debt and I want him to pay for the disgusting things they made me do the last two weeks." She replied as she unsuccessfully fought back sobs. As the blonde cried, the makeup that hid her bruises began to fail and revealed evidence of her story.

A veil of seriousness fell over the face of the man with brown eyes. "Where?"

His question caught Jenni off guard. "I-in the swamp. Anthony called it The Rising Sun."

King was disappointed to hear this. He had no issue with prostitution. In fact, he encouraged it in his clubs, but demanded the women and men who performed the acts of carnal pleasure were willing, received more than their fair share, and that they were safe while working. To hear that one of his organizations under his empire was using sex slaves disgusted him. Especially since King considered the man who ran the club's day-to-day for him a close, personal friend. He looked up from Jenni towards the smaller of the two thugs. "Paul, please go pick up Mr. Benson. Last I saw he was two tequilas deep at table three." The bodyguard nodded and left the room. King stood from his desk and walked around to the front of the desk so there was nothing between him and Jenni. He reached back and grabbed the pistol, never breaking eye contact. "That idiot had been indebted to me before and I couldn't be indemnified," he began as he took out the clip from the pistol, "I perceive myself as practical." King removed the bullets — one-by-one — from the magazine with his thumb, placing them in a perfect row on his desk. "When his dough ran dry, I would delegate to him duties I deemed as fair compensation. Manageable missions that I wouldn't mind that moron messing up." He removed the last bullet from the chamber and reloaded it into the clip. King placed the magazine back in the gun and pulled the slide back. Ten bullets on the desk; one in the firearm. "I suspected he would seek similar ways to settle scores with the other holders who run my gambling halls, but this is a serious sin I do not support. You can stand." He said to Jenni, his tone soft and unthreatening.

Jenni rose to her feet, slowly as she was unsure of what was happening. The door opened again and she turned to watch her ex-boyfriend get shoved inside by the bodyguard. "Okay, okay, I'm going. No need to shove," he said to Paul before turning his head to see why he was summoned. He saw King holding a gun and then he saw the one woman he figured he would never see again. "Jen? Oh my god, what are..what are you doing here?" he asked as he stepped towards her. Jenni instinctively stepped back at the same time. Panic set in and the blue-eyed man began to lie. "I've been looking for you everywhere, all over the city. I thought you ran off on me — just split town — when you never came back to our hotel room."

The blonde woman's face turned bright red and veins could be seen on her forehead as she became increasingly more enraged with each falsehood. She could not speak so King called Anthony on his bullshit. "Cut the charade."

"What? I..I don't..." The blue-eyed man stammered, unsure of how to talk himself out of the situation.

"Jen..." King started before turning his head to the pissed-off woman. "Is it Jen or Jennifer, dear?" he asked.

"Jenni," she responded without taking her hateful glare off of Anthony.

"Thank you," King replied before returning to the blue-eyed man before him. "Jenni here told me all about you tarnishing her good nature to take care of your troubling tab. It is downright disgusting what you did to her. That's why I decided since you took her autonomy into your authority, she should be offered the same opportunity," King explained as he offered the pistol on a flat palm for Jenni to take.

"What? You can't be serious?" Anthony responded as he watched her take the gun. "Baldur made me do it, you gotta believe me."

King shook his head in disappointment. He did not care what excuse Anthony had; he ruined Jenni's life to make up for his own shortcomings. "I will deal with Dennis," he replied. Personally, King never understood why Dennis went by Baldur when Dionysus was not only a more fitting alter ego, but also closer to his actual name.

"How do you know she isn't going to shoot you? She could just shoot you or both of us," Anthony said, changing tactics to try and change King's mind.

"Jenni has one bullet to be dispensed at her digression. She can shoot whoever she selects, but if you want to walk out of the room, I would start with the waterworks towards the woman with the weapon," King smiled.

Finally realizing pleading with the black-haired man was pointless, Anthony turned his attention towards his ex. "You don't really want to kill me do you, babe? Are you really gonna shoot me? I know I was stupid — moronic — but I was desperate. I had no other options and I panicked. You know how I'm shit under pressure." He tried again to walk closer to her. Jenni remained still, her hand wrapped around the gun's handle at her side. "Think of all the good times we had. More great times than I can count. Remember the laughs and the love. I love you," the blue-eyed man said as he was right in front of her.

Jenni snapped. She cracked him with the bottom of the grip in the center of the face. Anthony fell backwards holding his broken, lacerated nose as he cursed in pain. "Love?!" she screamed down at him. "Where was this love when you left me there?! You brought me there to die!" Her loud voice could be faintly heard by the guests gambling in the other room, but not enough to make out what she was saying so people continued on with their fun. Jenni pointed the gun at the man who was now on his knees.

He looked up at her in anger, blood gushing from his face. "You're going to shoot me now, bitch? Huh? Pull the fucking trigger? Do you really think you — little miss can't kill a fucking spider— has what it takes to kill me? I know you can't do it. It's not in you, so put the gun down and come to your senses." Jenni considered his words, her weapon still trained on him. She had already taken three lives, but they were strangers and she was acting in a state of desperate survival. This was personal, someone she had known for years and once loved more than she thought was humanly possible. Jenni feared that here and now, at the final step of her quest, she could not follow through with the act of revenge. She began to lower the pistol. Then Anthony loudly uttered under his breath the words that all but signed his death certificate. "That's what I thought you dumb, fucking slut."

Jenni raised the gun again. "I think we should see other people." His eyes went wide as she pulled the trigger. The blonde woman flinched at the sound of the gun firing; it seemed louder now than when she fired it in the swamp. The bullet tore into Anthony's throat. Blood gushed and spewed from the hole in his neck as he began choking on the blood. He collapsed to the ground and bled out on the rug. It was a painful death, yet more merciful than he truly deserved.

The guests who gambled in another part of the toy store heard the gunshot, but ignored it out of fear of King and retaliation. Everyone just shrugged and went on with their day. The few that saw Anthony escorted away figured he had done something dumb. He was not well-liked amongst this crowd.

Jenni stared down at her dead ex-boyfriend. The lifeless look in his eyes gave her hope that maybe, *maybe* the world was going to become a better place now. She was pulled from her thoughts by King's voice. "Are you alright, Jenni?"

The blonde looked over to him, a blank, emotionless expression on her face. "I will be when I get home."

King smiled innocently at her. "Then home is where you're heading."

*****

In a whirlwind of events, Jenni was on a train home. King's bodyguards took care of Anthony's body — promising it would never be found and would never be traced back to her. King gave her the $2,100 her ex had won that night and reimbursed for the hotel room that Anthony had charged to her card. He even had her keep the gun and the remaining ten bullets as a reminder of her strength. Jenni was worried about getting it past security, but King put her in his private service car and the man with the diamond earring showed her how to hide it in her suitcase so it would not be found. As an added measure of insurance, he paid off the right people to let her through checkpoints with minimal resistance.

The first train took her to the American high speed rail hub in Brett City. From there, the private car she was on was transferred to a train that would take her to the main station just outside of Stargellsburgh. She found it difficult to sleep on the train and instead watched the countryside race past the window as she played with the mistletoe she picked off the tree in the New Vida swamp. Jenni hoped that in the coming days she would finally start to find the peace that she desired and put this behind her forever. However, Jenni would soon learn that there was still work to be done.

*****

Jenni stood at the base of her steps, staring up at the apartment she shared with her mother and younger sister. The blonde woman thought it would feel like a dream come true to finally ascend the stairs, but the nervous knot in her gut made it more of a nightmare. Jenni took a step and then another. With each passing concrete stair she climbed, it felt easier to conquer the next. She reached the water-blue door and knocked. Jenni felt as if an eternity passed as she waited on the front porch. The door opened as she saw her mother's welcoming blonde hair and soft green eyes for the first time since the airport on the day she left for New Vida. Immediately, tears began to flow and the two women embraced each other. After a few moments. Jenni's younger sister, Abby, came to investigate why her mother had left the front door open. "JENNI!" She screamed in excitement as the 13-year-old girl joined the hug. They spoke no words, but in the arms of her family, Jenni was reminded she was loved and no matter the distance, her mother and sister would always be there for her.

Over the next five days, Jenni did her best to return to her normal life, but she struggled to leave the past in New Vida. The blonde-woman spent her days in the apartment staring at mementos of who she used to be. She had lost her job after she missed too many shifts while she was trapped in The Rising Sun. Old activities that used to bring her joy, like walking around the park, now failed to cast away the shadow of the trauma she suffered.

Her family tried to be supportive in the face of wanting to know what happened to the girl who used to light up any room she was in with her laugh. Her mother was better at this than Abby, who pressed with questions that Jenni found impossible to answer.

It was two in the morning. Another night that Jenni could not sleep. She was wearing black cotton pajama pants and a large, oversized blue sweatshirt that she stole from a friend in highschool. Jenni sat in the small kitchen, watching the soft rain fall onto the windows as she drank a cup of tea under the yellow glow of the overhead light. The green-eyed woman tried focusing on the water droplets as they raised down the glass to keep her mind from thinking about things she would rather never think of. "Can't sleep, shake?" Her mother's soft voice broke the inconsistent patter of rain. Shake was a silly nickname her mom gave Jenni when she was younger because she was always dancing and shaking.

"No." Jenni responded flatly, her eyes still on the dark window.

Her mom followed her daughter's gaze to the rain. "They say April showers bring May flowers, but what do May showers bring?"

"June beetles?" Jenni joked, causing both of them to laugh at her response.

When the laughter faded, there was a silence as both wondered what to say next. Jenni hoped one day to share with her mom what happened, but not tonight. Her mother wanted to know what happened to her daughter, but was afraid to push her away with inquiries about a sensitive subject. "Oh, you'll never believe who I saw at the store yesterday."

Jenni looked over at her mom — dressed in a mismatch of flannel pajama pants and an oversized hot pink t-shirt with bleach stains. "Who?"

"Your old friend, Emily. The one who would always call me Mrs. Clarkson, even when I told her she can just call me Carly. Such a sweet girl. She really bloomed into her own," Jenni's mom shared. She stared into her daughter's eyes, focusing on the specs of gold in her emerald eyes. Carly used to always joke the bright color was to share with everyone how Jenni had a heart of gold.

Emily used to be one of her best friends throughout elementary and majority of middle school until life separated the neighborhood's notorious duo. "Really? Is she still living in New Jersey?"

"I wish you had been there because I had to embarrassingly ask again where she moved to, but yes, her family still lives out there."

"What's she doing back in Stargellsburgh?" Jenni asked before taking a sip of her tea, now cooled to the perfect temperature.

"She transferred to the University. She wants to be an architect."

Jenni nodded as she recalled her friend always building things with plastic block toys. She always figured Emily would find a career that allowed her to utilize that love of creating. "Good for her." Jenni's reply was one of genuine pride.

"She asked about you," Carly continued.

"She did?"

Her mom nodded. "Yeah, asked how you were doing. She told me how much she missed the sleepovers you two used to have."

A small smile emerged on Jenni's face as an unexpected memory of her younger self and her friend running around playing princess space pirates in Emily's backyard popped into her head. "I miss them too," she whispered as she rubbed her thumb along the lip of her mug.

Carly smiled as she noticed the small hint of contentment on her daughter. "Oh!" She said as she threw her hands up as she remembered a detail of the other conversation. "I can't believe I forgot." The older woman added as she stood up from the table and walked over to her large mom purse on the counter.

"What?" Jenni asked.

"She asked for your number, but I didn't want to give it out without your permission," Carly began as she rifled through the loose receipts and papers, looking for a small sticky note. "So she gave her number...Ah, here it is!" She cheered triumphantly as she returned to the table and handed the yellow paper to Jenni.

"Oh, I'll have to reach out to her. Thank you," the younger woman replied as she stared at the number, playing with the corners of the note with her right thumb.

From there, the conversation shifted to other things. They spent the better part of an hour talking about things that were inconsequential, yet felt substantial. Jenni felt the most at home at that moment than she had all week.

The clock crept towards 3:30am. Carly yawned. "I think I'm going to go back to bed now, Shake. Try to get some sleep too if you can. I love you, Jenni," she said as she stood up from the table.

"I love you too, mom," Jenni replied, fighting back tears. As she watched her mother walk out of the kitchen, Jenni was again alone with the soft tapping of rain against the kitchen window. She pulled out the mistletoe berries from her sweatshirt pocket and set it next to the yellow note with Emily's phone number on it. Jenni stared at both as she was presented with a choice: to continue on with what happened behind her, knowing it still exists and will continue to destroy others as it had done to her or return to New Vida and burn The Rising Sun to the ground.

Jenni was at the train station by eight in the morning. She slipped out of the apartment before any of her family had woken up. Jenni could not handle the conversation that would have come with saying goodbye in person. Their begging her to stay would have been enough to keep her there. Jenni left behind two notes on the kitchen table that she wrote before she left for her journey. One apologizing to her mother for leaving again and ending with a hope of returning home soon. The other to her little sister. In that letter, Jenni shared with her sister the mistakes she made in trusting the wrong people and not the ones that had her best interest in heart. She warned not to do what she had done or else she would end up living a life of disappointment and misery. The note ended with her reminding Abby that she was smart and to listen to her brain not her heart when all else fails. "ALL ABOARD!" the conductor yelled as the blonde approached with her bag in hand.

With one foot on the platform, she looked back towards the morning sun. "Goodbye," she whispered in the direction of her home. She took the dying mistletoe from her pocket and dropped it onto the platform before fully boarding the train. The locomotive would take her to Brett City first where she would pick up the train that would take her back to New Vida.

*****

Including her layover, it took Jenni half a day to arrive in the city of New Vida. The sun was starting to set, but the green-eyed woman wanted to wait until night fell to make her move. Jenni decided to rent a motel room by the hour to act as her staging area before her assault on the Rising Sun. She changed into an all-black outfit complete with a black sweatshirt. She removed the gun — still loaded with ten bullets — from its hiding spot in her suitcase and checked to make sure the safety was still on. With that assurance, she placed the gun in the waistband of her dark-colored pants and used her hoodie to hide the weapon's existence. With one final deep breath, Jenni left the rundown hotel room to embark on her mission.

While she did not know the exact location of The Rising Sun, Jenni had an idea on how to find it. The night she lost her freedom, Anthony took her to a cab depot where her ex told the dispatcher that he was looking for a house where the moon never takes the sky. Jenni had been told it was an off-the-beaten-path kind of club where she could experience true local culture with an unforgettable night of revelry. Before she knew it, they were in a cab and on their way to the trap Anthony had set for Jenni so he could pay off his debt.

Now, she was following the same step, returning to the dispatcher to give him the same code word to take her back to the place she called hell for two weeks. Jenni was once again traveling down the dirt road through the swamp towards The Rising Sun. Only this time, she knew what awaited her.

The blonde woman had the cab stop just before the final turn onto the driveway that led to the front of the mansion. There were armed guards and "hospitality experts" whose job was to inspire and encourage guests to drink, screw, and ultimately spend more. While Jenni was not certain that someone at the main entrance would recognize her, she did not want to take that risk.

Besides, she learned from her mistake at King's Toy Store and did not think she would get lucky a second time if her gun was discovered again.

Jenni pulled her hood over her blonde pony-tail and snuck through the woods towards the back of the house of gambling. Because of the casino's location in the deep swamp, fewer guards were patrolling the sides and back of the building. Off in the distance — diagonal to The Rising Sun — was a small parking lot for employees and valet. Directly behind the mansion was a decently large shed that was used for extra storage. On the building itself, there were two doors — one regular and one medium sized garage door for deliveries. Jenni hid in the foliage of the swamp amongst the trees on semi-solid ground and waited for her opportunity.

There were a few times over the two weeks she was held captive that she was in the same room as some of the women who could come and go as they please — though most were unaware Jenni was trapped there. One day she was brought to a dining area to be given her once daily meal of stale food scraps and she overheard two professionals gossiping. An auburn-haired woman revealed to her friend that she had an ongoing fling with one of the chefs that worked in the kitchen above and would often — almost daily — sneak to the storage shed for a secret rendezvous. That's how Jenni learned the back door could only be unlocked from inside. Luckily for her, they propped the door open with a rock so they could get back inside without anyone being the wiser.

The woman with auburn hair worked there every night, same with the chef she was smitten with. Jenni waited for the two lovers to sneak off. Thirty minutes after she arrived, the door opened but it was just a busboy sneaking a cigarette. He hung too close to the door for Jenni to make a move. After over an hour-and-a-half of additional hiding behind a tree, she finally saw her opening. The door opened again. Out of the mansion walked the auburn-haired woman and her tall chef. Jenni watched as he bent down and placed a rock in the doorway to keep it from closing.

Once the two were out of sight behind the shed, Jenni emerged from hiding and rushed through the warm night air towards the propped entrance. She looked back towards the shed as she kicked the rock away, locking the two out as she snuck inside, preventing them from experiencing what was about to come. They were not their target.

Jenni calmly walked through the chaotic scene of the kitchen with ease. There was too much to do for the chefs and prep cooks to notice or question why she was walking around. The ones who did see her just figured she was a willing professional looking for something to please a client with. Jenni was able to sneak to a backroom and find a natural gas line. She grabbed a pan from a nearby shelf and busted the line open, the sounds were quiet compared to the symphony from the main gambling hall and kitchen. Jenni dropped the cookware and plugged in a hotplate across the room, turning it on to the highest temperature. The blonde pulled the fire alarms as she left the room, causing the kitchen staff and the sex workers in the basement to exit to the backyard. They were not her target either.

*****

Dennis "Baldur" Vandale sat in his office listening to an indebted gambler begging on his knees for extra time to pay back his substantial losses. "Please, if you could just give me one more week, I can get you most of your money back, Baldur." The bruised man pleading for his life had been in this situation before and knew playing to the black-haired man's ego could only help his cause.

"I noticed you accidentally said most and not all. Unless, it wasn't a mistake." Baldur sighed as he looked down upon the gambler with a gaze of pompous pity, his head resting on his right wrist as his elbow was on his desk.

"I...it's just... I'm down so much this time...I-I just..." The man began to stammer as he tried to think of the words that would keep a bullet out of his skull. "I promise I can get what I owe you...soon?" The question was to see if that was okay with the man with the god-complex.

Baldur rolled his eyes. "You are dangerously close to being out of time, permanently. I need more promises and pleading. Maybe someone can work the debt off for you until you pat the rest off in full. Maybe a girlfriend or cute female family member would be willing to help you?" He used the word "willing", but in reality, he did not care if the victims had objections.

The man on the ground stuttered for a response, but before he could speak, the fire alarm screamed overhead. Baldur grabbed his ears with his hands. "What the fuck is that noise?" he screamed to his hired muscle guarding the door.

"I think it's the fire alarm, Baldur, sir." The muscular, blonde man with a buzz cut responded as Baldur stood up from his desk and walked towards the door, ignoring the pleading man on the ground.

"We have a fucking fire alarm?" he asked with genuine shock to learn this information. His employee was unsure how to respond to the question. "It doesn't matter," Baldur cut in realizing he was not going to get a reply. "It was probably one of the idiots in the kitchen. Get this turned off, find me the person who fucked up, and bring them here," he screamed over the alarm condescendingly.

The muscular man nodded and exited the room, followed out by Baldur who took his standard place on the railing of his third floor office balcony. The bruised gambler snuck down the stairs past Baldur and followed the armed employee — who had more pressing matters to attend to in order to keep his boss happy — down the stairs.

People were beginning to leave the mansion in droves. All Baldur saw was money leaving his pocket. "Ladies and gentlemen," he began, screaming as loud as he could to be heard over the deafening beeping, "I can assure you there is no fire. Simply an accident. Please, return to your fun. The alarm will be off soon. Everything is under control and I guarantee that everything is fine." Then the black-haired man locked eyes with Jenni, who stood in the center of the gambling hall with her hood down. Bladur's face turned to anger. "How is she still alive and what the fuck is she doing here?" he said to himself. After his two men never returned, he sent a small search party to find them which came up empty. Baldur assumed all three had sunk into the swamp.

His rhetorical question was answered in the form of an obscene explosion that ripped through the vacated kitchen and engulfed the wall of alcohol bottles behind the bar. Glass and fire rained down like confetti into the main room, causing more of a panic. There was a pipe that carried natural gas from the kitchen to the grill in Baldur's office that he made his personal chef use to make sure the food would not get cold during its short walk from the kitchen to his desk. The flame followed that pipe, tearing up the wall that the hired muscle was walking along until it reached its destination on the third floor. Baldur followed the explosion with his eyes and realized it was heading for him. He climbed on top of the railing to try and get away but was not even halfway up when his office erupted into fire. The force of the explosion sent him flying outward. The flame charred his collared shirt and jeans and burned his skin. A piece of debris penetrated his shoulder. Baldur screamed in pain as he plummeted to the ground before crashing into a craps table, breaking two ribs.

Jenni pulled the gun from her waistband and raised it towards Baldur as he sat up across the room. He was her target. "KILL HER!" Dennis yelled to the members of the security force that stuck around to weather the raging fire.

Men rushed at Jenni. The blonde woman turned and fired one shot into the chest of the first armed guard. Nine shots left. Two projectiles soared past her from the right, causing Jenni to duck for cover behind an overturned roulette table. She returned fire, killing her attacker with only one shot. Eight left. She took out a third guard who was trying to get into position with two bullets, leaving her with six. Jenni attributed her marksmanship to years of archery at the summer camp.

A spray of machine gun fire fell upon her from behind. Luckily for Jenni the burning house took out this guard when part of the second floor fell onto the shooter shortly after the attack began.

Jenni got up from her cover and continued her match towards her target. Another shot and another guard that got into her way was taken care of. Five left. One of Baldur's goons jumped out from behind a wall of flame and wrapped his arms around Jenni. She struggled and realized she could not break free from the man's grasp, so she shot him in the foot. Four left. The man pushed her away, allowing her to quickly fire dead center into the chest of the injured man as he hopped on one foot. Three bullets remained.

Two of her remaining bullets she wasted firing at another guard who shot at her as he fled from the fire. Jenni turned towards the direction she last saw Baldur, ready to use her last bullet on her foe. The blonde woman was caught by surprise by the black-haired man knocking the gun away, the last bullet firing into the ground. Baldur punched Jenni in the face, pushing her back but he did not hit her hard enough to force her off her feet. "You want to kill me? I'll fucking kill you, bitch!" He screamed as he charged again, ready to throw another fist at her.

Dennis "Baldur" Vandale was not a fighter. He preferred to have others take care of his dirty work, but his ego would never let him believe that he could not care of any situation that required him to fight for his life. His inexperience, anger, and broken ribs left him no match for Jenni, who had four years of Muay Thai in high school. The blonde stepped to the side and delivered a quick strike to his side. Baldur yelled in pain and turned just in time for Jenni to catch him directly into his Adam's apple. The blue-eyed man coughed in pain as he grabbed his injured windpipe, leaving his midsection exposed for a punch to the gut. Baldur winced and bent forward, but his suffering only just began as Jenni quickly delivered a swift kick to his balls with the full force of her strength behind the attack. He fell to his knees in agony.

He stared up at Jenni in anger. "I bet you're pretty happy with yourself?" he snarled through gritted teeth, spit flying off his lips. "And for what?"

Jenni stared back at him blankly, his words repeating in her head. He genuinely had no idea why she was angry, why she wanted him dead. Jenni knew that even if she explained it to him, he would never understand. "I guess you'll never know," the green-eyed woman said as she reached back to deliver a knockout blow to his nose.

Baldur flinched in preparation for another painful hit, but when he did so, he noticed the handle of the katana sword that used to hang in his office. Baldur quickly grabbed it and swung at Jenni in desperation. The blonde woman screamed in pain as the flaming scabbard hit her in the side of the face, just behind her eye. Jenni fell back onto the ground for a moment before quickly jumping back to her feet, fighting through the burning agony to prevent giving her opponent the upperhand in this fight to the death. Baldur removed the charred cover to reveal the shiny, pristine 300-year-old blade. "What now, bitch?" His question went unanswered. They both stood there gasping for air as the oxygen became scarce because of the surrounding fire.

The armed man charged at Jenni. She did her best to dodge his inexperienced attacks. For the most part, the blonde woman did well at avoiding the sharp blade. The only thing Baldur hit other than the hot air was Jenni's upper left arm. Jenni grimaced as she felt the heated steel slice into the muscle, cauterizing the wound as it cut her.

Luckily for Jenni, Baldur was more incompetent with a sword in a fight than he was with his own fists. His balance was too far forward after his most recent swing-and-a-miss, allowing the green-eyed women to knock him off his feet while simultaneously disarming him in one swift motion. The man with a god complex flew back-first into a pile of flaming debris. Baldur screamed as he desperately ripped off the melting clothes that scorched his skin.

Jenni did not hesitate. While Baldur was preoccupied with his burned flesh, the blonde woman ended the fight with one slash through the man's abdomen. His blood sprayed onto the floor. He grabbed his opened stomach as a dark realization set in. Baldur collapsed to his knees and looked up to Jenni. Anger, fear, and pain covered his face as blood leaked from the corners of his mouth. "I bet you're pretty fucking happy now."

Baldur coughed and gasped before falling forward. He was dead. Jenni stared at his lifeless body as the flames grew more violent. For the first time since the fire started, the woman felt the heat coming off the orange inferno. The warm sensation was a welcomed change to what she had been feeling: pain. This warmth that wrapped around her body caused tears to swell in her eyes as she was relieved she could feel anything other than suffering, something she feared she would never be able to do. Jenni loosened her grip on her sword, allowing it to clatter onto the floor below. Pieces of the above floors began to crash and fall around her. Water rolled down from her emerald eyes over her soot-covered cheeks. Jenni looked towards the ceiling as ash drifted down like dark snow and she released loud sobs that harmonized with the raging fire as wave after wave hit her. Her biggest sorrow came from the realization that she will never see her mother or sister again. Jenni dropped to her knees, giving into the fire.

As the last of the oxygen burned, a calming white light overcame her.

*****

A long back limousine pulled up to the charred, smoldering remains of The Rising Sun as fire trucks drenched the former mansions with water from tanks. The door opened and out stepped the well-dressed gentleman crime boss, King. He wore expensive satin-black, monkstrap dress shoes with a gold buckle, and a sharp, black suit accented with a bright magenta tie and matching pocket square. His short black hair was freshly cut with pristine edges and his light-brown eyes were hidden behind a pair of stylish, thick, black-framed sunglasses. King leaned to his right side on his cane with the silver ornament handle of a globe wearing a crown. Under his left arm were two ledgers that he had been studying the last two days. One was the falsified finances that Dennis Vandale had given to him at their last check in and the other was the real book with the actual values that one of King's more loyal employees had stolen from Dennis' office earlier in the week. "I believe somebody has beaten me to the blow," King said to his associate and bodyguard, Paul, who joined him by his side after getting out of the opposite side of the vehicle. "Albeit, a more aggressive approach than I would have agreed with."

"Do you want me to ask around to find out who did this, sir?" the large man asked in his deep voice.

"Not necessary," King replied. In his heart, he knew exactly who had done this. Part of him was proud of the woman for what she had accomplished. "Deed is done and that is that." He smiled confidently. King surveyed the wreckage, noting the only people leaving the building were in body bags being carried out from the debris with one exception: two emergency medical technicians hurriedly wheeled a gurney out past the once great mahogany doors that now laid on the muddy ground next to their ambulance. "Curious...go call upon those caregivers to take their convalescent patient to St. Cobb's," King asked Paul as he motioned towards the emergency vehicle with his cane. St. Cobb's Hospital was the crime boss' go-to hospital as he found the doctors and staff delightful, knowledgeable, and willing to turn a blind eye if it meant saving a life.

Paul rushed over to catch the driver and alert him of the change in destination. The EMT was confused at first as that was not the closest hospital, but then he looked over and saw King standing calmly by his limo. The first responder nodded in understanding and hurried to take the patient away.

The large bodyguard returned to his boss. "They agreed after I told them we would be covering her hospital bills."

King smiled with pride. "Good." he said as he watched the ambulance drive off down the bumpy back road with their emergency lights on. "Let's hope she still has some fight in her soul." With that, King concluded that his business here was done. He climbed back into the limousine with Paul joining him. King did not care about the cleanup because nothing would ever be rebuilt there. The Rising Sun had fallen for good in the swamps of New Vida.

Revenge of the Giant Slayer

The past cannot be outrun. It is relentless and neverending in its pursuit. No matter how hard one tries, no matter how hard one wishes it would go and be forgotten, the past will always come back. It will always win in the end.

*****

"So that's it, right? We're in the clear?" Aaron Samuel asked his two companions in the room. His button-up shirt was untucked and his tie was removed and placed haphazardly in the middle of the table. The brown-eyed man's left sleeve was still rolled up, but his right sleeve had begun to roll back down towards his wrist. "There's no way to trace this back to us?" Aaron asked as he ran his right hand through his blonde hair. This time he was directly asking the man sitting next to him after not getting the enthusiastic response he had hoped for after his first round of inquiries.

Gary Augustine was silent as he stared at the pile of papers, documents, and used fast food containers and cups that were scattered across the table. It was late and he was exhausted, so the black-haired man was being very cautious to make sure he missed no detail. His tie was still on, his shirt still tucked in, and the only sign of his long night was his messed up hair and blood-shot eyes. "Well, Gary?" asked the third man, Andy Constantine, who was standing by the window of the conference room, his back to the Los Guerrero skyline. Andy was a lanky man and looked the most stressed of the three as his button up shirt was fully open and his tie hung around his neck untied.

"Will you two shut up for a goddamn second? I need to make sure there are no more loose ends," he barked, causing Aaron and Andy to become uneasy. Aaron tapped his foot and Andy stared out the window as the men waited for Gary to give them either good news or a new task to take care of.

Gary, Andy, and Aaron worked together for a company called Dalton Industries. They specifically worked in the aviation division. A few months ago, a quality control report came across Gary's desk outlining a glitch in the coding of one of the altitude instruments made by their company. This tiny flaw had a chance of malfunctioning and reporting the wrong altitude which could lead to serious problems during a plane's flight and landing. It would have cost the company a little over 30 million dollars to recall the part and fix the glitch. This is why Gary, Andy, and Aaron decided to ignore the problem. Then planes started crashing. Only a few at first, but soon that small glitch began to deteriorate and was causing more problems than they had expected. As a result, six commercial airplanes had crashed and thousands of people were injured or dead because of their decision. When talks of an investigation into the software began to flutter around the industry, the three men knew they had to act quickly to destroy and cover up any evidence that showed that they had known about the flaw. That is why the three men were locked inside the conference room on the 103rd floor at five in the morning with two private security guards standing outside the door to prevent any unexpected drop ins.

After 20 minutes of tense silence, Gary spoke. "Did you take care of the factory report?" he asked Andy without looking up.

Andy rushed over from the window to look for a paper, "Um... yes!" he excitedly proclaimed. "The plant manager was paid through a now disbanded shell-company to erase the report from the system's history and the employee that reported the problem has been, um...well, um...taken care of," he said, getting squeamish about the details.

Gary shook his head slowly as he began to laugh, he clapped his hands once and looked up to the ceiling with a relieved smile on his face, "we are officially in the clear, boys," he cheered, causing the other two men to clap and cheer along. "Once we take care of this stuff, there will be no proof anywhere that shows the company or us knew anything about that stupid glitch." Gary chuckled through his exhaustion, now that the night's work was complete, the late hour was finally hitting him.

Andy pulled out a couple bottles of chilled champagne from a cooler and began to pop them to celebrate their destruction of the truth. The three men began to cheer and joke about their success. Gary, Andy, and Aaron were so boisterous in their celebration that the men guarding the conference room door did not hear the determined footsteps coming down the hall.

He emerged from the darkness in an instant, covered head-to-toe in black and silver armor. Without hesitation, he pulled out two taser guns, firing one at each guard, incapacitating them before they could defend themselves or raise any alarms. Andy watched the two muscular guards collapse to the ground like ragdolls through the glass double doors of the conference room. "What the fuck?" he said softly, more confused than alarmed as the dangerous visitor was still hidden under darkness. His statement caused Aaron and Gary to look over towards the doors as the armored man stepped into the light that leaked from the conference room. Then the mystery man threw open the doors and entered the room with swift authority. The mystery man was wearing heavy-duty military grade armor that included a helmet and mask that hid his face. On the right side of his chest, just below his collarbone, was a crack in the armor that had been repaired.

"Who the fuck are y..." Gary began, but before he could finish his question, the masked man pulled out a black pistol with a silencer and fired one shot into Gary's heart. He fell forward onto the conference table dead.

The mystery man then turned to Andy who had just thrown his glass in the air as he covered his face in a desperate attempt to protect himself. One shot later, he was dead on the conference room floor with a hole in his chest.

Aaron collapsed on the ground in fear, curling up in a ball as he huddled against the window. He was sobbing, begging for his life. "Please, I'll give you anything. Do anything.." He pleaded as tears and snot poured from his face.

"You already had your chance," the man responded before firing a bullet into the forehead of his final victim. With all three men dead and the guards still unconscious, the mystery man holstered his weapon and removed three manilla folders from a small backpack. He carefully placed specific ones next to each man. All the folders had the names of the men that had just been killed along with a logo that said AP Genetics.

The mystery men then removed a burner phone and proceeded to call 911. "Hello? I think there has been a shooting on the 103rd floor of the 107 Clear Street Building. I heard gunshots from across the street. Come quickly," he said in a voice that sounded panicked and scared. Before the person on the other side of the phone could respond, he hung up and placed the burner phone on the center of the table and left the conference room, disappearing back into the pitch black hallway.

*****

The police arrived at the scene of the two unconscious bodyguards and three dead businessmen surrounded by incriminating papers. By 5:30 am, homicide detective Will Halle entered the room to investigate the shooting. The dark-haired man with green eyes initially thought that a vengeful victim of the plane crashes had taken matters in their own hands, but then he noticed the folders on the ground. Will bent down and opened one of the folders that said AP Genetics with his gloved hands. Inside was evidence that connected the men to a scandal that had happened three years ago. Evidence that showed they participated and made quite a good amount of money from it. It was a scandal that the detective had heard of, but had no clue as to what actually happened. He was about to ask a uniformed officer a question when an Irish man in a trenchcoat, light blue button up, and a yellow tie came walking into the room. "Be that the AP Genetics connection?" the brown-haired man with brown-eyes asked in a soft Irish accent.

"Who are you?" Detective Halle asked as he stood up. At first he thought this strange man at his crime scene was a reporter looking for a quick and dirty exclusive.

The Irish man rolled his brown eyes at the fact that he once again had to remove his badge from his pocket. "Sorry, Agent Theo Beck, Interpol. Now tell me, be that the AP Genetics connection?" he asked as he stepped closer to Detective Halle.

"What's interpol doing here?" Halle responded as he handed Beck the folder.

"The scene matches me perp's MO. And this," he said, referring to the file. "Confirms that this is the guy I've been chasin' for the last three months. He always gets away clean and we have no leads as to who he is or where he'll go next. He last struck up north in New Morneau and I took a lucky guess that he'd come to a big city like Los Guerrero," Theo Beck explained.

"So what does any of this have to do with AP Genetics?" Detective Halle asked, hoping to be filled in on this man's obsession with this particular piece of evidence.

"Sorry, someone leaked all this information and exposed all the illegal activities that Advanced Phenotype Genetics was doin'. They were genetically modifyin' kidnapped people and turned 'em into monsters or giants, if ya will. They would then send out fighters who thought they were saving the world to face the Giants. AP Genetics offered those with enough cash a chance to place bets on who they think will win the battles between giant and giant slayer in unpopulated areas like dense forests and such. After the information was leaked, many of those who wagered on these matches faced no charges because they used their money and recourse to hide their names from the list that ended up online. We think the killer has a copy of the original list. That's why he leaves behind all this evidence that connects his victims to the AP Genetics gladiatorial ring," Agent Beck explained.

Detective Halle just stared at him as he processed what he was told. Beck continued, "Personally, I think the fool doin' the killin' is the same fool who released the list. He thinks these men and women got away with it, so he's makin' sure they pay for it with their lives."

The green-eyed detective was unsure of what to do with the theory presented to him, so he ignored it. "Okay, since you know the guy so well: How did he do this? What's his next move?"

Agent Beck smiled confidently. "He'd have entered and left usin' the door that had the least amount of cameras, like a service entrance. Where be the buildin' manager?" he asked as he walked past Halle to find the person he wanted to talk to. The detective followed after him after taking a moment for himself.

The building manager informed Agent Beck and Detective Halle that the service elevator and entrance, which exited into the alley, both had broken cameras for months. Not only that but the cameras on the 103rd-floor had been disconnected hours earlier by the three men who were trying to hide proof of their cover-up. That's when Detective Halle had an idea. "Well, this building's cameras are of no use, but maybe a building in the area caught him entering or leaving the alley."

Agent Beck smiled and patted the detective on the shoulder in excitement. "Brilliant!" he cheered as he charged off to trace the steps of the shooter. Halle once again took a moment to collect himself before following the Interpol agent to the service elevator. He could tell this was going to feel like a long day.

Halle, Beck, and a handful of uniformed officers reached the alley that the service entrance exited into. The alley had openings on both sides. "Detective Halle, you take that end and check the cameras on that side," he said pointing towards the north end of the alley, which was narrow and flooded with deep puddles of water. "I'll check along this road." He said pointing towards the major road behind him with his thumb.

Detective Halle sighed. "Alright, take some units with you," he responded as he grabbed half the officers and walked off through to the flooded alley.

Agent Beck began to direct the units towards the different buildings that he saw external cameras on. "You two, check the corner mart. You two, check that bank across the street." He was about to go check the diner across the street with the two remaining officers when he heard an unexpected melody. He looked to his left at an overflowing dumpster. The Irishman walked closer and as he approached the noise, he recognized the melody as "God Save the Queen" the National Anthem of England. Agent Beck rolled his eyes as he moved a box and found a ringing, disposable flip phone in a plastic sandwich bag. The interpol agent picked up the phone, removed it from the bag, and answered the phone. "Hello?" he began, cautiously.

"Hello Agent Beck, it's nice to finally speak to you." A stern, strong voice spoke calmly over the phone. "You're very good at your job, Agent."

Agent Beck knew exactly who he was talking to, but he needed confirmation. "Ya know who I am, but I don't know who I have the pleasure of conversin' with," he replied.

The voice on the other side of the phone remained quiet for a moment. "You can call me what I am: Hunter. I was tricked into fighting giants. I thought I was doing the right thing, protecting the world from them and their destruction, but I was a fool who was risking my life to entertain those who do not value life. Then I learned the truth and now I will hunt down all those who made money from these twisted games."

Agent Beck smiled, "well, isn't that poetic. So why the call then? Are you trying to gloat?" he asked while looking around.

"No. It's just that I need to stay in town for a while longer to finish some personal business. I figured I would get to know the man who's been chasing me. Try to determine how quickly I need to wrap up my business," Hunter explained.

"So if you want to get to know me, why just a phone call? Why not meet in person?" Agent Beck asked.

The other end of the line went silent for a moment, "we could have met for breakfast, but you were running late. I hope you don't mind, I went ahead and ordered for you."

At that moment, Agent Beck looked across the street, his eyes falling upon a 24-hour diner. "HE'S IN THE DINER!!" He yelled as he hung up the phone and raced towards the restaurant. "HURRY, LET'S GO!" he shouted to the other officers as he dodged traffic while he raced across the street. Agent Beck threw open the diner door and ran inside with his weapon and badge drawn. He frantically looked around for anyone suspicious and then he noticed a booth in the back corner that faced the front window and looked down the alley. Half the booth was hidden from the front door, preventing him from seeing if anyone was seated at the booth. He slowly made his way through the sparsely filled diner to the booth. "HANDS ON THE TABLE!" Agent Beck yelled at the empty booth that had one eaten off plate and a used glass of water on the table. The Interpol agent grunted in disappointment as he re-holstered his weapon. On his left, he noticed a frightened brown-haired waitress who was holding a plate of food. "Sorry ma'am, Agent Beck,

Interpol. What can you tell me about the man who was sitting here?" he asked her as he looked at her name tag. "Any detail would help me out, Becky."

"Interpol?" she asked. "Like the art theft police? Your friend mentioned you were late because of a case, but he didn't say you worked for Interpol," Becky explained.

"He said he was a friend of mine?" Agent Beck asked.

She shifted nervously. "Yeah, he talked a lot about you. He even ordered for you. An English breakfast, he said it was your favorite." Becky lifted up the plate of food and showed it to the agent.

Agent Beck looked at the food with an annoyed expression. He was getting tired of these jokes Hunter was making at his expense. "Did you happen to see where he went?"

Becky looked around the diner to see if she could see the man who she had served at the booth. "I don't see him, but I didn't see if he left. Maybe he went to the bathroom?" she suggested.

Agent Beck motioned for the two cops to check the bathroom. "And check the kitchen too. Maybe he snuck back there." Unfortunately for the Interpol agent, the officers found the bathroom empty and only kitchen staff in the kitchen. Theo Beck turned back to the waitress. "Did he give you a name? Pay with a credit card?"

"He said his name was Hunter and he paid in cash," she answered.

Agent Beck looked at the young waitress with disappointment. "Can you tell me what he looked like?"

Becky thought for a moment, "He had light brown hair, he was tall-ish. I don't remember his eye color. He was cute looking. Square-jawed and very muscly," she described, doing her best to remember as many details as she could. "I'm sorry I don't remember more. He was supposed to be my last table of my shift," Becky informed the Agent.

"It's okay, dear," Agent Theo Beck sighed. He looked over to the door as it chimed and watched Detective Will Halle walk into the diner. Agent walked over to let him in on how their killer got away.

*****

Oliver McNeill's life was the definition of excess and luxury. He was the rich CEO of the company Heathands, a fortune 500 company that had a hand in many different specialties. McNeill woke up in a bed made with expensive silk sheets. He showered in his 500-square-foot bathroom before dressing himself in the finest Italian-made suits that money can buy. When the balding man arrives downstairs, he greets his supermodel wife, covered head-to-toe in diamonds and designer accessories, and enjoys his version of a modest breakfast of lobster, scrambled eggs, with a side of toast with caviar butter. Once full, he exits his lavish house through his garage, passing numerous expensive one-of-kind cars that are rarely driven until he reaches his helicopter pad. The helicopter, which had been running for the last half-hour so the AC could get to the perfect temperature that Oliver McNeill enjoys, takes off and carries the blue-eyed man to his company's large skyscraper where his work day begins. The helicopter ride only saved him 20 minutes than if he were to drive.

"Stacy, my mail better be on my desk by now or you're going to go flying out that window, down a 100 stories," Oliver McNeill angrily barked at his frazzled assistant as he walked past her desk to his office. He usually threatened her three to four times a day.

Stacy could barely look up from her small desk at the large angry man. "I already took care of it, sir," the brown-haired girl fearfully responded. "And here's your coffee, sir." Stacy handed her boss his piping hot coffee, doing her best to keep her hand from shaking. She learned the hard way that Oliver wanted his mail waiting for him on his desk and his coffee to be handed to him as he walked in. If it was done any other way or if his coffee was not hot enough, he would go on a tantrum and throw the beverage at Stacy.

Oliver took the mug and looked at the near broken girl, "competence is a good look for you. Even if it is the bare minimum," he scoffed as he walked into his spacious office.

McNeill's office was a shrine to his vanity. Wall-to-wall with riches, trophies, and objects that made him feel strong and intimidating. He sat behind his large oak desk and took a sip of his coffee. "This isn't hazelnut!" he shouted as he looked down in disgust at his hot coffee. Oliver was about to call his secretary Stacy into his office so he could belittle and scream at her for not knowing that he wanted hazelnut today despite never requesting it before when he heard a phone ring. Oliver stopped for a moment and listened to the sound. It was not the ringtone for any of his phones. "Is that that helicopter song?" he asked himself as he moved papers and objects around his desk as he looked for the phone that played "Flight of the Valkyries". Then he realized the mysterious ringing phone was in his top desk drawer. The balding man pulled a burner phone out of his desk and stared at it for a moment before answering it. "Who the fuck is this?" he asked angrily.

"Hello, Mr. McNeill. You can call me Hunter," said a calm, deep voice on the other side of the phone.

Oliver scoffed, "Oh yeah? I don't know a Hunter so you can fuck off."

The blue-eyed man was about to hang up the phone when Hunter spoke again. "I wouldn't hang up just yet."

This angered McNeill even more. "And why not, asshole?"

Just then a red dot appeared on the black screen of his computer. "That would be why, and as long as you stay on the phone, the dot stays where it is."

Fear flooded over Oliver McNeill. A man known for being a bully now sat in his chair, scared for his life as he knew a gunman was threatening his life. "Please, just tell me what you want," he said into the phone, his voice cracking as he held back tears.

"Right now you are receiving an email." Oliver McNeill's computer chimed as the screen turned on to the lock screen. "In the email is the banking information for two accounts. In the first account, you are going to put 87,500,306 U.S. dollars. In the second account, you are going to put in 35,020,891 U.S. dollars. Those numbers should sound familiar to you. You have one week to put the money in the accounts or you will die," Hunter explained to the CEO.

Those numbers were immediately recognized by the large CEO. Those numbers were the two largest winnings Oliver had made betting on the AP Genetics gladiatorial matches. "Oh," he said into the phone, his anger beginning to return. "That's what this is about? Well. Let me tell you, buddy. YOU CAN FUCK OFF BECAUSE YOU ARE NOT GETTING A DIME OUT OF ME!" McNeill screamed into the phone.

"One week," Hunter calmly responded back to the shouting. "Paying is the only way to stop me."

The balding man scoffed. "Yeah, well fuck you asshole. You are going to regret trying to strong-arm my money out of me. Do you know who the fuck I am? Do you know how connected I am?" he rhetorically asked Hunter.

"I see. Well, we could always just end it here," Hunter responded before the red light turned off. Oliver's eyes went wide in fear as he lost sign of the dot. He immediately dropped the burner phone and dove under his desk and prepared for a shower of bullets to fly into his office. "One week, Mr. McNeill," Hunter responded through the phone on the floor before disconnecting the call.

*****

"So what do we know?" Detective Will Halle asked the interpol agent. They were in a conference room in the police station going over all the evidence and witness statements from the diner patrons. Detective Halle was sitting down while Agent Beck paced back and forth on the other side of the table.

Agent Theo Beck smiled at his colleague. "We have a general description of what he looks like, we know he's stayin' in the city presumably to attack someone else, and we know he used to be a giant slayer for AP Genetics."

"That's not much," Will responded, confused as to why Theo Beck was so happy.

The Irish Interpol agent smiled and shook his index finger up and down at the detective. "True, but we've learned more today than I have over the last six months. He's getting cocky. He's makin' mistakes. Small ones, but they will start to add and then we got him," Agent Beck cheered.

"Maybe the best way to find out who he is is to figure out who his next victim is?" Detective Halle suggested.

"That is bloody brilliant. The pond of possible victims is smaller than the pond of possible suspects. So, you know this city, anyone who you think our gut is going to target?" Theo asked Will. "You know, rich, bored, morally questionable character. I'm sure in the great city of Los Guerrero there has to be a few."

Will Halle just looked at the Interpol agent. "I suppose there are a handful," Detective Halle answered.

Agent Beck smiled, a twinkle in his eye. "Are you a bettin' man, Detective?"

Detective Halle rubbed his eyes with his right hand as he processed the question. "Not really."

"Oh, come on. Give me your best guy. Who is Hunter going to go after? I know you got one. Roll the dice, as they say," Agent Beck said as he walked around the table and sat next to Detective Halle.

The detective looked at Beck with an annoyed glare. "Okay, my best guess... Oliver McNeill."

"That's my man, why?" Agent Beck interrupted with excitement.

Halle sighed, "Because he was wealthy during the AP Genetics timeline. He has has countless allegations of damn near every vile thing under the sun,

"Perfect! Let's go have a talk with him," Agent Beck cheered as he shot up out of the chair.

"Well hold on," Detective Halle said as he stood as well. "McNeill is extremely connected. It's why the accusations are always withdrawn. He makes insane donations to both the Mayor and Governor's reelection campaigns. They consider him a friend. He's not a guy you just drop in on and interrogate," the detective explained.

Agent Beck smiled at the detective with mischief in his eyes. "We aren't going to interrogate him. We are gonna check in on him to make sure he's safe. We are just concerned for his safety and are doing our jobs," Beck joked as he left the conference room. "You drivin' or am I?" he called back to the detective.

Detective Halle threw his hands up and followed the interpol agent. He hated the idea, but his protests were being ignored.

The two agents of the law arrived at the Heathlands skyscraper. As usual, when the police showed up to see Oliver McNeill, they were quickly sent upstairs to the penthouse to meet with him within minutes of arriving. Oliver found it better to keep the authorities happy and not allow them the opportunity to snoop around the building while they waited to meet with the CEO. Other CEOs would have lawyers stand in, but the blue-eyed man's ego is the reason he always met face-to-face with the police. Agent Beck led the way into the office. "Ah, Mr. McNeill, it's a pleasure to meet you. I am Agent Beck of Interpol and this is my American companion, Detective Will Halle." He motioned to the slouching detective who was standing on his right.

Oliver McNeill remained seated behind his large desk, his large fingers locked together in front of him. "Ah, it's wonderful to meet you as well, Agent Beck," He said ignoring the Detective that clung to the wall. "To what do I owe the pleasure of a visit from an Interpol agent? Is there an art thief in town I should be worried about?"

Agent Beck laughed despite being confused as to why people keep bringing up art. "Not to my knowledge sir, no, we are here because I'm chasin' a murderer who likes to hurt those who live a well-off and luxurious life. So, this is just a well-bein' check. Have you received any threats to your safety lately?"

McNeill laughed as he sat back in his chair. "Gentlemen, a man in my position receives death threats with surprising regularity. I rarely take them seriously and I would by no means ask the fine officers of this city to waste precious time and resources chasing wild geese when there are more important things this city needs. A self-made man like myself is often seen as a target by those who look to make a quick buck," the blading CEO said with a cocky smile. In reality, Oliver McNeill was not a self-made man. His father built a successful company from scratch, allowing Oliver to live a life of pampered luxury. When he turned 19, his father gave him a sizable amount of money to start his own company. That company went bankrupt within a year and Oliver returned to work as a generously compensated employee of his father's company. When his father retired, Oliver took over as the CEO. Once again, poor financial decisions caused the company to fail. The only profitable thing he did was approve the sale of the company to Heathlands. Oliver was then appointed as a board member of Heathlands and when the CEO position opened up, he used bribes, blackmails, and backhanded deals to make sure he got to sit on the golden throne. Now the large, bald CEO does nothing but spend his lavish paycheck as the board handles all the important decisions. All the glory with none of the hard work.

"Oh, of course," Detective Halle responded with sarcasm that McNeill did not pick up on. "But this one is a little more serious. Of course, you don't have anything to worry about if you never had associations with AP Genetics. He's only gone after people who participated in their illegal gladiatorial ring," he said with animosity in his voice.

The smile faded from the balding man's face for a moment as AP Genetics was mentioned. It then returned in an instant, but with less arrogance. "Gentlemen, I will be honest. I was approached, years ago, by a representative of AP Genetics who wanted me to invest in their company. Immediately, I could tell that they were making money through immoral activity. So, I politely declined the invitation and had no involvement with that company whatsoever," he lied. "I am an honest man who believes in morals and good old-fashioned hard work above all else," he lied again.

Agent Beck smiled, "I can tell that you are no doubt an upstandin' member of this city. We just want to get this guy before he hurts more people, so we are leaving no stone unturned."

"Well, consider this stone turned and tossed gentlemen. I thank you again for your concern with my safety," he said before looking over to Detective Halle. "It was a pleasure to see you again, Detective." McNeill smirked egotistically at the green-eyed detective.

Detective Halle did not respond. He just turned and left the shrine to the CEO's ego. Agent Beck noted the strange interaction before he followed his new friend into the hall.

Agent Beck caught up to Detective Halle as he waited for the elevator doors to open. "So, what was that all about, friend?" Agent Beck asked the annoyed Detective who would have preferred to wait in silence.

The elevator doors opened and Detective Halle stepped inside. Once the doors closed, he shared his past unfortunate interactions he had with the obnoxious Oliver McNeill: "It was just a couple months after I became a detective. This girl came into the precinct sobbing. She was scared. Her name was Taylor and she spent the next three hours telling me through a river of tears all the horrible things that her asshole-of-a-boss did to her. McNeill tortured her, assaulted her, abused her. That dick put her through hell and she couldn't take it anymore. I promised her that I would make sure he pays for how he treated her. I spent months collecting evidence to build a case against McNeill, even after my captain, the police chief, and the mayor told me to drop the case. The DA told me if I was going to continue with the case I needed a strong witness. I told them that Taylor had finally caught the son-of-a-bitch assaulting her on camera and that she would be willing to take the stand. Then all of a sudden, Taylor just disappeared along with the tape. The one person who brings credit to everything I've put together just gone without a trace until she was found dead a week later. I lost it, man. I stormed into his office and I screamed at him. I wanted him to know that I was going to make him pay for hurting her. Within an hour of leaving his office, I was suspended for a month. When I returned from my suspension, I realized there was no point anymore. It was just a job. So I keep my head down, do the job, and collect my check," Detective Halle explained to the Interpol agent as he fought back tears.

Agent Beck nodded, feeling the pain of the Detective's past. "Sounds like this is definitely Hunter's next target." Beck responded as the two excited the elevator and walked towards the exit.

*****

Meanwhile, Oliver McNeill's arrogant mask he put on for the detectives vanished from his face. He threw open his top left desk drawer and removed a spare phone that he used to conduct his unsavory business. The blue-eyed man redialed the last number he had called before his visit with Agent Beck and Detective Halle. "It's McNeill. Are you certain you can stop this lunatic?"

"Of course." A smooth voice reassured the CEO, "You know I'm the best." The arrogant man on the other end of the phone was Manny Ratti, a bloodthirsty mercenary that Oliver McNeill had dealt with before when he had other problems that had gotten out of hand. Manny had considerable skill and resources he planned to use to spoil McNeill's death sentence. The only complaint the stingy CEO had now was with the mercenary's price. He had increased his cost because he was well aware of the hunter of the rich that was going after rich men around the world.

"Fine. Then I'll pay what you want, but you're only getting half now, the other half is your incentive to make sure that asshat is dead at my feet," McNeill grunted into the phone, angry about having to spend money on something that was not shiny and for his own ego, even if he was just going to embezzle the money he needed from the company.

Manny chuckled, "Don't worry Mr. McNeill. This hunter stands no chance against my men and I," he boasted to his client before hanging up.

"Oh god," Oliver cried into his hands after he tossed the phone onto his desk. "I need a drink," he said to the room of meaningless nothings that surrounded him before going to pour himself a glass of an expensive 50-year scotch.

*****

Over the next couple of days, Theo Beck and Will Halle monitored Oliver McNeill closely, hoping to catch Hunter when he made his move. Detective Halle's captain was not happy about him following a man who he has such history with, but Agent Beck backed up the detective, alleviating the doubts of his captain. Doubts which completely disappeared with the increase of muscular security that appeared around the Heathland's building and McNeill's private residences.

"I don't know why we don't just leave for the country and hide," Oliver complained to his hired gun as they sat in traffic. They were en route to Oliver McNeill's office in a five car convoy of black armored SUVs. Ratti would not let the CEO use his helicopter as he believed it would have been too easy for Hunter to track and take down. The customized SUVs were made with reinforced steel and six-inch-thick acrylic windows. McNeill sat in the middle row of three rows of seats, but faced the rear of the car instead of the front. Across from him was the mercenary commander, Manny Ratti, with four of his strongest and finest soldiers on either side of the two men.

Manny Ratti laughed. "Because we want to show him that you're not scared. Draw him into a sense of over confidence so we can kill him when he makes his move," the dirty blonde-haired Italian man with brown eyes explained to his client.

"Wait? You're using me as bait?" McNeill responded, shocked as he coughed up the expensive Scotch he was drinking.

"You already are bait," Manny responded in a cavalier tone. He then reached to his hip and unholstered a gold, Desert Eagle pistol. "No mouse trap is effective without the cheese. If you want me to put a bullet in his head, I need to know who he is," the mercenary explained as he waved his gun in the air before he placed it back in its holster.

McNeill sat in a stunted silence as he watched the muscular man wave his gun around inside the armored car. "That... that makes sense," Oliver stuttered. He had never spent time with Manny before. Usually their interactions were over the phone when he gave him a new problem to take care of or Manny was collecting payment. In this moment, the balding man learned how intense and intimidating Ratti really was.

Just then, Oliver McNeill heard a familiar ringtone. It was the same song that had played the last time Hunter called him. "What the fuck is that noise?" Manny asked the CEO. He had told him to lock all electronic devices in a safe in the truck for security reasons.

McNeill began to frantically search his pockets for the source of the noise. "I don't know. I put my phone in the safe and got rid of the burner like you said," he responded before pulling out an orange burner phone.

"Then what is that?" Manny asked, now more annoyed.

"The other one was silver. Oh god. He was in my house this morning," McNeill cried with fear filling his voice.

Manny snatched the phone from the frightened CEO. "Give me that," he barked before answering the phone. "Is this the man I'm going to kill?" There was no response from the other side. "Hello? I'm talking to you. Can you not hear me or are you just stupider than I've been led to believe."

"I see Mr. McNeill spared no expense when it came to his own protection. You have quite the reputation, Mr. Ratti. I knew I would have to deal with you eventually," Hunter responded. "I should warn you, Mr. Ratti, I'm not a village of helpless women and children, so you will struggle to kill me." Hunter was referring too Manny Ratti's history of whipping out innocent native villagers for companies that wanted the land.

Hunter's comments angered Manny. "I am the deadliest soldier this world has ever known. A half-assed assassin like you will be no problem for me. I am the man who killed the fucking devil himself and I'll fucking kill you too," he shouted into the phone, his ego damaged.

Hunter was unphased by the threats of the mercenary. "Tell Mr. McNeill he has three days left and the only way to stop me is to pay up, or else this is the fate that awaits him." Just then a loud crack was heard as a high-impact round pierced the bulletproof window and hit the leg of the mercenary sitting next to Oliver McNeill. The soldier began to scream in agonizing pain as blood gushed from his wound onto the petrified CEO. Hunter hung up the phone.

"HOLY FUCK!" Oliver screamed over the cries of the wounded man as blood sprayed onto his 5,000 dollar suit. "I thought you said the car was bulletproof!" He was terrified that another bullet was about to come through the compromised window.

"It is. That asshole must have some serious firepower and armor piercing rounds," he calmly replied to McNeill. "Will you shut up!" Manny screamed at the soldier to Oliver's left before he pulled out his pistol and shot the man in the head to get him to stop screaming at the pain. Oliver McNeill went into shock. He was covered in blood, his ears were ringing from the bang of the pistol going off in such a small confined space, and he was sitting next to a man he just watched lose his brains. "There. I could barely hear myself think," Manny griped to himself. "Hunter is better than I anticipated. I think a change of plan is needed. Time to barricade you in the safe house," Ratti said as he grabbed his radio. "New order of business. Head to safe house alpha." He said into the radio to alert the drivers of the other SUVs to the change of plans. "I'm gonna make sure this bastard dies slowly." His anger and frustration were apparent as the SUVs began to change direction. He felt embarrassed by this unknown advisory and he did not like feeling embarrassed by those he's sworn to kill.

*****

As the deadline approached, Oliver McNeill fell apart. As the hours ticked away, the CEO feared for his life more and more. He flinched with every movement from his peripheral vision, cowered with each loud sound, and even struggled to eat as he feared being poisoned by his enemy. He spent the last day locked inside a safe room in the middle of the large secluded house in the middle of a forest just outside the upper city limits of Los Guerrero. The only other person in the room with McNeill was Manny Ratti. He sat on the couch reading the day's paper as the balding man paced back and forth in the small room. "Maybe I should just pay the money." Oliver panicked as he noticed the time. "I'll still pay you for your trouble, of course."

Manny folded the paper and glared at his client in disgust. "You pay that fucking ransom and I'll kill you myself. This isn't about your stupid money or your pathetic life anymore. This is about my reputation. If it gets out that you paid that fucker after hiring me, I'm ruined. This ends with him dead on the floor," the mercenary captain responded before going back to his reading. Oliver McNeill took this as a sign to panic in silence.

Outside, a silhouette moved amongst the trees, hidden from the moonlight. It approached the forest line that surrounded the house and studied the 15-foot-tall fence from the dense forest. There were small, open-platform guard towers with flood lights every 10 yards. Hunter stood watching the two guards in the tower as their rifles scanned the tree line, illuminated by the flood light, as he waited for Oliver's deadline to officially expire.

Hunter was relieved that the greedy CEO had hired this group of mercenaries to protect him instead of going to the police. If he had sought out protection from the police, Hunter would have been forced to change his method of attack and be more careful to not kill someone who he felt was innocent. The armor-clad man checked his burner phone. The deadline had officially passed and the accounts were empty. It was time to begin. He texted the burner phone he left in the care of Agent Theo Beck, sending the location of the safe house that was about to face his one-man siege. After the message was sent, he dropped the phone and crushed it beneath his boot. Hunter then detached the collapsible bow from his lower back. With one push of a button, the compound bow extended to full length. He attached the string and loaded the first arrow. He pulled back and fired, striking the mercenary on the left of the tower directly in the chest. As he fell from the tower, Hunter fired a second arrow into the final guard of the tower.

Hunter then sprinted into the light and tossed his bow over the fence before he scaled the 15-foot fence with ease. He reached its peak and dropped to the other side as he heard yelling and alarms. "He's over there!"

That was his cue to set off his diversions. He clicked a button on his belt twice and triggered a chain reaction of timed explosive devices that he had hidden in different areas along the perimeter over the last couple of days. Various explosions of different sizes began to erupt along the fence and woods to create some confusion. The explosions could be faintly heard from the room where Manny Ratti and Oliver McNeill locked themselves inside. "Oh god. He's here," the blue-eyed man whined.

Hunter sprinted towards the house. He rearmed his bow and fired at the soldier that stood in the window of the second floor before he could fire at him. As he reached the side door, two more soldiers came around the side of the safe house, but Hunter fired two more arrows, killing them before they could shoot or alert others of what door he was entering. He collapsed his bow, returning it to behind his back, and then pulled out a short stock custom machine gun that fired three round bursts. He broke down the door and continued with his one-man assault into the house. Manny's radio sounded-off like crazy as his men tried to figure out where Hunter was as the house filled with gunfire and smoke from smoke grenades. Through the static shouting one phrase scared the color from Oliver McNeill's face, shaking him to his core. "He's in the house. I repeat the target has breached the house."

Hunter calmly moved through the halls, changing directions to create confusion and prevent them from blocking his path to his target. He would head in one direction, take out any mercenaries he found along his route with near unnatural accuracy before changing his course without hesitation. He wanted them to think he was lost within the smoke-filled, maze-like halls of the safe house, but Hunter knew exactly where he needed to be and used his movements to lure his enemies away from the room that Oliver McNeill was locked in. Hunter knew the layout of the safehouse from breaking into Manny Ratti's computer when he left it unattended in Oliver's Office. He knew where his target was hiding and where the guards were supposed to be stationed throughout the building.

He worked quickly, taking out his enemies by alternating quickly between his machine gun and a 9 mm pistol. Between his quick reaction time and the smoke, many of the mercenaries were dead before they knew he was there. Even the few lucky shots that did get fired off, his state-of-the-art and near-impenetrable black and silver armor deflected the rounds that hit him.

Hunter finally reached the center of the maze where his prey lay in wait behind a locked door. He peered around the final corner and noticed two mercenaries armed with two M-16 rifles guarding the vault-like door. While Hunter's diversions and misdirections caused many of the soldiers to wind up deceased or chasing nothing, these two were under orders from Manny Ratti to stay in front of the door no matter what happened. Hunter's machine gun was out of ammunition and he had only a few rounds remaining in his last pistol clip. He waited for the closest guard to turn his head slightly and then swiftly made his approach with a custom-forged combat knife drawn.

He quickly plunged the knife into the back of the closest mercenary while simultaneously pulling out his enemy's 9 mm pistol. As the dead mercenary fell off to the side, Hunter fired one shot into the forehead of the second mercenary before he could raise his weapon. While the rest of Ratti's soldiers searched for Hunter as he retrieved the key from one of the dead guards and unlocked the vault door to begin his final attack.

Manny was sitting unfazed by the commotion on his radio as his men fought against the invader. He had confidence his small army could defeat one man and he could easily replace any soldier that died in the process. Then he heard the large door of the room begin to unlock. "Oh my god! He's here!" Oliver McNeill cried hysterically.

"Shut up!" Manny barked, as he got up he drew his large golden pistol as he got between his client and the unlocking door. He was going to fire as soon as he saw Hunter enter the room. The door opened and Manny fired five times. As the door opened, the dead body of one of his soldiers came flying at him, all five shots hit the dead soldier before the body hit the mercenary captain and knocked him back. By the time Manny got back onto his feet, Hunter had entered the room and threw the large door shut, locking it once again. Manny Ratti, Oliver McNeill, and Hunter were now locked in the room together. Hunter rushed the mercenary leader, grabbed his weapon, and disarmed him as he punched him in the face before tossing the pistol off to the side. Manny stumbled backwards, but Hunter waited for Manny to collect himself. Hunter wanted to do more than just beat Manny Ratti, he wanted to embarrass him.

Hunter motioned for Manny to attack with left hand. Manny drew a large bowie knife from his belt and charged at the armored attacker with a guttural scream. Hunter dodged the initial two of Manny's attacks and then delivered a gut punch to Manny and followed it up with a quick left hook to Manny's jaw.

Manny stepped back and spit blood onto the ground. He gave Hunter a bloody smile. "Oh, you fuck," Manny grunted before starting another attack. This time Hunter did not dodge, he caught Manny's wrists, turned, and elbowed him in the face while removing the knife from his grip. He sent the mercenary flying over his shoulders and into a support column that stood in the middle of the room. Manny let out a painful scream as he felt one of his ribs break on impact.

As Hunter watched the leader of the mercenaries climb back to his feet, he plucked at Manny's ego. "I told you that a real opponent would be no match for you. You stand no chance against someone who can hit back."

These comments drove Manny wild. "I'll fucking kill you!" he grunted through the pain. He charged once again at Hunter, this time armed with only his fists. Manny swung blindly at Hunter, who easily dodged all the attacks. Manny then made his final mistake. He sold out on a haymaker and Hunter took advantage of Manny's momentum. Hunter grabbed his arm, pulled towards him, and then quickly moved to get the mercenary into a headlock with his right arm. Hunter delivered the final blow to Manny's face with his left fist. The mercenary fell to the ground bloody and unconscious. The armored man stood above his beaten opponent and stared with indifference. His mission had nothing to do with this vile man, so he would leave the defenseless mercenary captain for the police to find and do with as they saw fit. With Manny out of the equation, nothing stood between Hunter and his target: Oliver McNeill.

Hunter heard the sound of a pistol being grabbed off the floor. He turned to see the terrified CEO pointing Manny's large, golden Desert Eagle pistol at him. "Mr. McNeill, we finally meet in person." He calmly spoke to the man as he stared down the barrel of the gun.

"Stay back," McNeill barked, his voice shaking almost as much as his body was. "I will fucking kill you," he said, more so to convince himself than Hunter.

"I have to confess. Of all the gamblers I have threatened over the last year, you were the one I hoped more than anything would not pay the ransom," he admitted as he took a small step towards the CEO.

McNeill wanted to pull the trigger, but the nerves overwhelmed him. "I said stay the fuck back," he blurted out.

"This is personal to me. You are more than just a name on a list to me. You are someone I hate more than anyone," Hunter said, his calm voice being forced out by a more angry tone. "And I want you to know why."

Oliver lowered the pistol just a little as he collected what Hunter said and that's when Hunter struck. He quickly pulled a small throwing knife from his belt and tossed it at Oliver McNeill. The blade caught him in the shoulder and the CEO let out a scream. The feeling of the knife piercing his skin caused Oliver's trigger finger to clench, firing Manny Ratti's pistol. A loud bang filled the room as the bullet glanced off Hunter's armor as he charged forward, leaving just a small scratch on his right shoulder. Hunter knocked the pistol away and pushed McNeill hard in the chest, sending him crashing into the wall behind him. The scared, defenseless CEO crumbled to the ground and stared up at his attacker. "Please, I didn't know. Please.," he pleaded for his life.

"Ah, but you did know," Hunter said before crouching down so he was face-to-helmet with McNeill. "You just did not care. Why should you get mercy for not caring as you made millions on the death of my parents?" Hunter said as he removed his helmet so Oliver McNeill could look into his blue eyes.

McNeill could not believe who he saw. "It can't be. You're dead."

*****

Hunter had not always been his name. He grew up in a heavily wooded area outside a small town of 100 people in the American northwest and went by the name his parents had given him when he was born. That name died the same day the world thought he died. He lost everything in the name of protecting the world from monstrous giants. His mother, his father, and his uncle were all killed by the same giant. A giant known as Loudmouth.

Years ago, he stood on top of a small hill surrounded by fallen leaves and crisp cool air. He waited in his armor, ready for revenge against the giant that killed his family and many other giant slayers who met the same grim fate. A giant is a nearly unbeatable beast and the only of its kind. Hunter watched as the lumbering beast walked into the valley below. It was time.

Loudmouth was large and intimidating. Beyond his reputation, he stood at nine feet tall, with large hands folded into fists, a jaw that hung low and swayed as he moved, bright, toxic green eyes, and tattered and torn cloth that hung loosely around his waist. The giant looked the part of a destructive monster that struck fear into the hearts of those who laid eyes on him.

The size of giants has been exaggerated over time. Most giants ranged between six and 13 feet tall; the misconception about their size came from the devastation they left behind. Humans would come across destroyed villages void of survivors, those who discovered the smashed community assumed the beasts responsible must have towered over the Earth like mountains. Eventually, some people learned the truth and figured out how to catch and kill giants. Those who became especially skilled made it their occupation. They were the first giant slayers. Various companies formed that employed giant slayers. They ranked the giants on a scale of one to 100 based on how strong they were to keep track of reward money for those that killed them. Those same companies kept track of how good a giant slayer was by giving them the one level higher than the giant they just beat. In death, the giant slayers were given one level lower than the giant they were killed by. In the case of a rare draw, the slayer was given the same level.

Over time, the giants became stronger and more destructive. Not wanting the giant slayers to become unmatched, the head scientist at AP Genetics partnered with the giant slayer companies to give the slayers pill-based enhancements to bring them back to near-equal playing field. The pills improved reaction time, strength, eyesight, hearing, and various other aspects of their physiology.

Hunter stared down at the level 100 giant. He had just been labeled as level 92 giant slayer and had climbed to that ranking from 0 in a single summer, faster than anyone before him. That was because Hunter had an advantage that few giant slayers had. Hunter was the son of two giant slayers who had been taking the treatments since before his parents got married. Hunter was born with natural abilities greater than the average human. When he began taking the pills, just as every other giant slayer of the modern era, it increased his speed, strength, constitution, and reaction time greater than any other giant slayer.

Loudmouth walked into the middle of Hunter's trap, setting off two small explosive charges on either side of the beast to confuse it. Hunter emerged from behind a bush and raced down the hill. He pulled out a remote trigger, pressing the first button. A high-powered rifle with heat-tracking sights that Hunter set up in the valley on a tree came to life and focused on Loudmouth. He was unsure if the projectile would be able to puncture enough layers of skin and fat to hit any vital arteries, but he hoped a few shots could slow the beast down to make it easier. The first bullet never got close to its target.

The rifle clicked as it loaded its round into the chamber; it was a sound that Loudmouth recognized. The giant turned towards the direction of the metallic click, breathed in the smoke around him, expanding its chest, and let out a fearsome, low bellow. The air-based attack was what made Loudmouth so formidable. The bullet stopped midair and was sent back the way it came. The force of the scream pushed the tree that the rifle was attached to out of the ground and sent it crashing.

With the smoke gone, Loudmouth could now see Hunter rushing towards him with a four-foot sword that he had brandished quickly after the rifle attack failed. The giant breathed in again for another attack, but struggled to fully fill its lungs. The smoke he had to breathe in to stop the gun had damaged its lungs and made it harder for Loudmouth to put all his power into his attacks. The giant coughed and unleashed a weaker version of the scream just as Hunter reached the bottom of the hill. Hunter was able to jump off to the side at the last second as the air crashed into the hill, sending dirt, grass, and rocks flying into the air.

In one swift motion, Hunter rolled from his back to his feet and swung his blade at Loudmouth. His blade caught the back of the giant's hand, slicing it open enough to draw blood. Before Hunter could get another swing in, Loudmouth began to punch angrily at his armored attacker. Hunter shifted his focus to dodging the powerful fists. A direct hit from Loudmouth at this range would break more than a few bones. He maneuvered from side-to-side as the giant struck the air and ground. Hunter jumped to the left to avoid the most recent attack and slipped on the newly loosened dirt, falling to the ground. The giant slayer panicked and quickly jumped to his feet, only to be immediately struck by Loudmouth's forearm. Hunter was sent flying off to the side. He crashed hard onto the ground and felt his breath violently leave his chest. He was in pain, but thanks to his armor holding up, he was alive. Despite the pain, Hunter had to continue. It was the giant's life or his. He rushed to his feet, fighting through the pain of minor breaks and bruising, but before he was fully upright, Loudmouth was standing in front of him, its chest puffed out about half its max size.

Hunter's life flashed before his eyes. Memories of his father teaching him how to shave and track, his mother teaching how to cook and shoot, his uncle raising him as his own after he lost his parents to Loudmouth. Then the scream hit him. Even at half-strength, it was an extremely powerful attack. Hunter crashed into the forest edge of the valley, bouncing off the ground until he finally stopped against a tree.

His head pounded, his ears rang, and almost every inch of his body burned with pain. He watched a blurry Loudmouth lumber towards him. He feared this was the end. Then he set his hand on a familiar weapon. It was one of his uncle's signature weapons: a crossbow. Hunter had taken a few of them and set them up in the area with a remote trigger just as he did the rifle. This one came free when the tree it was attached to was pulled from the ground during the most recent gush of air. Hunter grabbed it and rose to his feet, slowly. The arrow that had been loaded into the weapon was gone, but Hunter had four spares tied to his right thigh. Luckily, one was unbroken. His uncle always swore that these arrows were special, designed specifically to fight Loudmouth. He loaded the bolt as he watched the giant stop. This was it. One final attack. Life or death. He raised the crossbow, aimed true, and pulled the latch. The arrow went flying. Loudmouth took a quick breath in and unleashed a small low-decibel scream. Hunter watched as the arrow stopped midair before it came flying back towards him. The air rushed past him, back against the tree. It was like life was going in slow motion as he watched the projectile rush back towards him. He stood frozen as his last ditch effort pierced his armor, splitting it apart. He felt the cold metallic tip on his skin and the pain of the arrow as it drove itself into the left side of chest, just above his heart. The bolt of the arrow broke away, leaving the arrowhead behind. Hunter collapsed to the ground, the air now still around him. He sat there and waited for everything to fade to black, for death to claim him, for him to join his family in the next life.

But he did not die.

Loudmouth stopped. The giant stood there, staring at the fallen giant slayer, breathing heavily with nothing behind his bright green eyes. Hunter slowly reached for the bowie knife that was attached to his belt. His bones and muscles burned as he moved his left arm. His eyes stayed on the beast. He snapped open the holster and wrapped his hand around the handle the best he could with a broken pinky and ring finger. It took every ounce of will not to shout in pain. Hunter held the knife in his hand, keeping it in the holster, waiting for Loudmouth to approach him. Once he was close enough, Hunter was going to sell out for one final desperate act.

The monster just stood there. Loudmouth breathed slowly as he stared at Hunter. Then, he turned and walked away. Hunter could not believe it. 'Did he not see me moving?' he thought to himself. Anger filled his mind as he watched the thing he hated most in this world leaving the fight. "Hey," he called out weakly, his lungs aching. "HEY!" Hunter called out louder before wincing. The wounded giant slayer attempted to stand up, but collapsed back to the ground. Despite the noise, Loudmouth kept walking away.

Hunter tried once more, screaming in pain as he got onto his feet. Still the giant continued on his way as if he did not care that his opponent was still alive.

Hunter did his best to keep up with the slow moving Loudmouth, but with all his injuries, the beast was quickly disappearing. He watched as the giant vanished down a large hill. The giant slayer began to panic as Loudmouth was approaching the small town that sat on the edge of the forest. Hunter stumbled his way to the top of the hill and crashed against a tree, using it to remain upright. He was prepared to see the worst, to see a small town reduced to ruble. Instead, the giant slayer watched as Loudmouth calmly approached a large gate in a fence that surrounded a nondescript warehouse and stopped. The giant stood there and waited until the gate opened, it then slowly lumbered towards the building and disappeared inside a loading dock bay. Hunter wondered if he was hallucinating from the pain. He slowly slid down the tree till he laid on the ground. The pain was becoming too much for him and he passed out.

When he woke up it was dark and a light rain was falling. Hunter was still in immense pain, but found it a little easier to breathe now. He got back onto his feet and carefully made his way down the hill to investigate the warehouse that the giant had entered. He took out his knife and cut through the fence. If he had not been as injured, he would have just scaled the barrier.

Once Hunter was inside the building, he was stunned to a standstill. He looked upon rows of cells, all containing giants. They stood there still, only moving to breathe. It was like there was some sort of trance. Hunter limped his way through the building, looking over the various giants. They looked like statues in a wax museum with tubes connected to them. He had to find a control room to figure out what was really going on. He found the door he was looking for and went inside.

After his parents passed, Hunter's uncle had him attend high school since he did not have time to homeschool the boy anymore. It's there where he learned how to code and use computers. Hunter hacked into the computer system and found evidence of what AP Genetics was doing. Naturally occurring giants quickly fell into extinction with giant slayers being too effective at killing the animal-like beasts. A forgotten sorcerer saw an opportunity to make money. He created new giants by turning men into mind-controlled monsters, first with magic and then with more stable genetic modifications. The giants would be sent out on rampages and then the giant slayers sent to save the innocents from these new monsters for money. Eventually, a group of individuals who made the giants realized they could make more money by allowing lords and kings to bet on the battles than with just ransoms and threats. They recruited the giant slayers under the guise of being heroes protecting the world when in reality the giant slayers were pawns in a game for entertainment. Soon, AP Genetics was created to create giants and set up gladiatorial rings.

The giants he had passed in the hall were all once men and women who had been altered and enhanced to become powerful giants. The company then sent these mind-controlled victims out to fight giant slayers in high-stakes gladiatorial combat for people to bet on. There was a list of who had been turned into giants, of giant slayers with their records, and even the names of the people who had placed bets with how much they won or owed the company. Hunter copied everything he could find onto a hard drive. While he waited for the data to finish downloading, he opened the file with his name on it. DECEASED was written across the file in bright red letters. He reached up and felt the crack in his armor as he read the words. "Heart rate monitor chip stopped. Body not found. Killed in battle with Loudmouth." It all made sense to Hunter now. When that arrow pierced his chest, it only went in far enough to destroy the monitor chip, but not kill him. The computer program that runs everything thought he was dead, so it halted Loudmouth rampage and told the giant to return for stasis.

Hunter held the hard drive in his hands after the last of the data finished transferring over. It had all the evidence he needed to end this sick gladiatorial game. He knew he had to release it, he just did not know that many of those people would avoid being punished despite the lives they destroyed.

*****

"How is this possible?" Oliver McNeill asked in shock before the monetary aspect of the reveal dawned on the greedy CEO. "I lost millions because you lost to that big jawed jackass or whatever he was called. You came after me because I won a few bets? What about the money you cost by losing?" McNeill screamed at Hunter.

Hunter stood and stared down at Oliver. Money won or lost does not matter. What mattered was how the money was won and lost. He had wagered on innocent lives in a cruel game. What matters is Oliver McNeill using his wealth and power to avoid the law for numerous crimes. All that mattered was the CEO's belief that he was above all. Now Hunter was going to bring him down to Earth. "You play with lives with no regard for the true value they hold," Hunter talked sternly as he delivered kicks to the gut and head of the CEO.

Hunter picked him up and threw him against the wall before sending his right knee into McNeill's groin. He then grabbed the knife that was embedded into his victim's shoulder and twisted it, causing Oliver to scream out in horrific pain. He pulled the knife and used that same hand to punch the CEO in the nose, breaking it. Hunter took a knife and plunged it into Oliver's gut. He stared into the eyes of his enemy and watched them tear up in fear and pain. Hunter removed the knife before tossing the balding man across the room onto the floor. The CEO groaned in pain as he rolled on the ground. Oliver McNeil coughed as blood dripped from his numerous wounds. "Please, I'm sorry," he begged one final time as Hunter slowly walked over to Manny Ratti's Desert Eagle pistol.

Hunter picked up the gun and pointed it at the man who looked up at him from the floor. "No, you're not. That's the point," he spoke calmly as he fired two shots dead center into the heart of the heartless Oliver McNeil. Hunter had killed other high ranking members of the now disbanded AP Genetics and other millionaires and billionaires who made money on the gladiatorial games, but this kill felt different. This man made more than anyone on the deaths of his mother, father, and uncle. This was personal and it only reassured him of his mission to keep crossing names of his list of gamblers.

*****

By the time the police arrived at the safe house, the surviving, conscious mercenaries had fled the grounds to avoid persecution. Agent Theo Beck watched as uniformed officers walked the battered mercenary captain, Manny Ratti, out of the room in handcuffs. He was a man that Interpol had been chasing for years and was happy to see the war criminal in handcuffs. The agent then looked over to his new friend, Detective Will Halle, who stood above the dead body of Oliver McNeil and the manila file full of AP Genetics connections. He was silent. Agent Beck walked over to the detective. "Looks like you finally got justice for Taylor," Beck spoke softly as he stood next to Halle.

"This isn't justice." That was all Detective Will Halle said before exiting the room.

*****

Hunter sat in the airport watching the planes fly away from the Los Guerrero airport as he waited for his flight to board. The brown haired man scrolled through his laptop reading news articles for national and local media outlets. They all talked about the death of CEO Oliver McNeil and the arrest of one of Interpol's most wanted: Manny Ratti. Then an article caught his eye. It was a small online news source from a coastal city just south of him sharing a story about how a nearly 100-year-old church was purchased and torn down in one night. It intrigued Hunter. He began to dig deeper, scouring other media sites and online city records for information. Hunter was finally able to find the companies that purchased and destroyed the house of worship. Kap Securities purchased the land and hired Raze Construction to begin demolition and construction on a new office building. They were hired to build security systems and buildings that AP Genetics owned. Both companies claimed they had no idea what was actually going on and were used so little that no one asked any further questions. The two being used again made Hunter suspicious. "Looks like I need to take a trip to San Gywnn," He spoke to himself before closing his laptop and putting it away in his bag so he could go to customer service and ask if they could change his flight for him.

From the Past Came Vengeance

A vendetta is all-consuming, an endless quest that will bring no closure, resolution, or peace of mind. In the end, those who walk this inescapable path of vengeance are destined to lose themselves amongst the violence they create.

*****

She raced around the corner of the abandoned Vernon Hale High School building of the city of Ryanton in the middle of a hot night, looking behind her for the assailant that chased her. The blonde girl could not tell if she was still being chased because of the lack of moon on that dark night, but she was sure it was still back there. She ran for her life, until her foot went into a divot and she went flying forward, scraping up her face and arms. The blonde rolled over onto her back and looked around for any sign of danger. She rose slowly to her feet as the hope that she was finally safe began to set in. She was so focused on the darkness around her that she did not hear the hum of the wood chipper behind her as it started up.

From the warm night grew the ominous shadow that was chasing her. It reached out, grabbed her by the throat, and lifted her up high above the ground. "Bethany. You and your friends have ignored my warnings and have not confessed to your atrocities. It was your voice that convinced the rest of your demon worshiping friends to not turn yourselves into the authorities. I hope that this little show of force will convince you and your vile friends that my threats are not to be taken lightly," the black cloud of smoke with eyes that shined like freshly polished rubies bellowed in a deep intimidating voice.

"Fuck you!" Bethany screamed out while struggling to free herself from its grip. "We aren't scared of you! Dark Lord Eldisey will bring upon the new age of man. All but the faithful will suffer." She choked slightly as more pressure was applied around her neck. She spat at the faceless smoke monster that held her above the ground, her spit went right through the smoke without any resistance.

"Very well. It is obvious that your soul cannot be saved," it boomed with a very matter-of-fact tone. "Maybe your friends will be wiser than you and disavow that demon Eldisey. Maybe they will not take Vengeance lightly." Bethany's eyes went wide at the ominous threat from the thing that held her. The smoke released her, causing her to fall towards the ground. Her feet hit the ground and she lost her balance. The smoke monster watched as the demon worshiper fell backwards towards the running woodchipper.

*****

Detective Neal Barnes of the Ryanton Police Department hated mornings. The detective with short black hair pulled up to the abandoned Vernon Halle High School, parked his car, and took a moment to enjoy his cheap cup of coffee before he got out to investigate the crime scene. He was about to take his first sip when a hand knocked on his car window. He rolled his brown eyes and lowered his window. "Hey, Detective Barnes," a beat cop addressed the detective. "Rice and Heldenburg are waiting for you up the hill behind the school," he said as he pointed in that general direction.

Detective Barnes set down his coffee and got out of his car to head over to meet his fellow detectives. This was not the first time that he had been to this school. He used to make regular trips to this place back when it was still open. Vernon Hale High School held low level drug dealers, bullies that love to rough up weaker kids, and worst of all bratty, spoiled rich kids that think the world was made for them. After they shut down this place of despair, they built its replacement down the street and Detective Barnes had hoped that meant the last of his visits here. Unfortunately for him, he was wrong.

He walked around the side of the school and approached the mass of detectives and uniformed officers. Detective Barnes worked his way through the crowd to his fellow detectives. The seasoned detective was about to inquire as to what crime had brought him out here when he noticed the grotesque scene for himself. The side of the school was covered in flesh and blood and in that gorey paint was a note that read 'A show of force was needed to warn the quality that Vengeance is coming.'

"Jesus Christ..." he mumbled as he stared upon the horror before him. "Is-is that a person?" Detective Barnes asked as it was the only thought in his head.

"No idea," Detective Rice said as he looked over at Detective Barnes. "Lab techs sent a sample back to the precinct to run it against the database. There's an abandoned car belonging to a miss Bethany Rizzo. Heldenberg and I have bets on whether she's the person sprayed on the wall or the person who pushed the victim into the woodchipper," he explained in an uncaring voice.

Detective Barnes glossed over his colleagues' disregard for the victim. "Bethany Rizzo? As in the daughter of Granton Rizzo? The hedge fund manager?"

Detective Carl Heldenburg nodded. "The very same. That's why the chief called you in on this with us, this is a priority case now. Mr. Rizzo is a very important man," he began. "You are going to head over to the new Vernon Hale High School and talk to some of her friends to see if they know what happened last night." Heldenburg flashed a con man's smile at Detective Barnes. Everyone in the precinct knew of the distinguished Detective's distaste of highschool kids.

"Of course..." Detective Barnes mumbled to himself as he walked over to get a closer look at the wall.

Detective Rice and Detective Heldenburg shared joking glances and grins. "Let us know if you find anything out over there," Rice called out as he and Heldenburh left down the hill to go talk to Mr. Rizzo. Barnes decided to stay at the crime scene for a few more minutes before leaving for the high school to start his interrogations.

*****

Detective Barnes arrived at the school and immediately noticed the foul smell of despair, body spray, and puberty that filled the halls of the school. He called ahead and informed the school that he needed to speak to Bethany's friends. The school placed him in an empty room in the office and brought him the students that were friends with Bethany Rizzo. The first was a young woman named Amanda Burfict. She was a short girl with longish blonde hair and pale blue eyes. Like Bethany, her parents were also wealthy and powerful in the community. Both Amanda's parents worked in finance just like Bethany's father.

Amanda entered the room with the school's guidance counselor Gianna Ventress. Both women sat down across from Detective Barnes. "Hello Ms. Burfict, my name is Detective Neal Barnes. Can you tell me the last time you heard from your friend Bethany?"

Amanda took a moment before answering the detective's quotations. It was obvious she was nervous about something. "Last night. I talked to her on the phone. She thought she heard someone break into her house. I told her to get into her car and leave. The phone got disconnected and she didn't pick up when I tried to call her back. I haven't heard from her since. Is she okay?"

Detective Barnes looked at the concerned face of the young girl. That's what we are trying to find out. Do you know if she contacted anyone else?"

"She might have called Brad. At least that's what Allison implied." Amanda paused for a moment. Detective Barnes could tell she had more to say, so he waited to ask his next question. He let the silence of the room pressure her into continuing. "Allison was afraid that Bethany was calling Brad in an attempt to steal him from her. They were hanging out last night and Brad left her house after a phone call. She swore she saw Bethany's name pop up on his phone."

"Can I have Brad's and Allison's last names?" Detective Barnes asked without looking up from his notepad.

Amanda nodded. "Brad Gruden and Allison Bound."

Detective Barnes wrote down the names and smiled, "thank you. I have only one more question and then you are free to return to class. Do you know anyone who would try to hurt Bethany?"

Amanda took a nervous gulp, "there is one kid, Dominic Gunner, who has been harassing Bethany...well all of us really."

"All of you?" Detective Barnes asked as a point of clarification.

The blonde nodded. "Our friend group: Allison, Bethany, Brad, Douglas Lester, Ryan Smith and I," She explained. "Dominic has been harassing and threatening us for months. His friend died last year and he thinks we had something to do with it when we didn't. He's just constantly bothering us about it."

"What was this friend's name?" Detective Barnes asked.

"Tim Shoto," Amanda responded and Detective Barnes wrote down the name. He remembers hearing that name, but does not know much about the case since it was not assigned to him.

The Detective nodded as he set down his pen. "Thank you, Ms. Burfict, you are free to go back to class. Mrs. Ventress can you get Mr. Brad Gruden, please?" Mrs. Ventress nodded as she escorted Amanda out of the room.

Around 10 minutes later, Mrs. Ventress returned with a tall, muscular blonde haired boy. The boy sat down across from Detective Barnes and Mrs. Ventress sat next to him. "Mr. Gruden, it's nice to meet you, I'm Detective Neal Barnes. I have a few questions I would like to ask you about your friend Bethany Rizzo."

"Ask away, but you should know that my father is a lawyer," Brad replied in an annoyed, yet cocky tone. Detective Barnes had met his father, Albert Gruden. He was a very wealthy defense attorney with a client list that was well known around the precinct. Detective Barnes realized the son had inherited his father's arrogance.

"Don't worry, you're not in trouble. I just want to know when was the last time you talked to Bethany?"

"Last night. She called me and said she was being chased and that she was driving over for protection. Then she hung up. I haven't heard from her since," Brad told the detective, being very deliberate in what details he shared.

Detective Barnes looked at the young man who sat across from him, "did you attempt to contact the police about this?" he asked.

Brad scoffed, "of course not. I figured it was a lame excuse for a booty call. Bethany and I had history, but let's just say...I already conquered that continent." Brad winked with an obnoxious smile.

Detective Barnes ignored his comment and moved on. "Do you know anyone who would want to hurt Bethany?"

"Yeah, that crazy nerd, Dominic Gunner. He's been threatening us like crazy, especially Bethany," the blonde boy explained with an angry demeanor.

"Why?" the detective asked the upset boy.

Brad flashed a vile, cocky grin as if it was an involuntary reaction. "Because his lame, virgin friend killed himself and he blames us for that. I barely even knew the kid and Dominic goes around accusing us of bullying his friend, of being the reason his friend is dead. I am no bully. I am the president of the anti-bullying initiative, I would never bully someone in my life." He explained. His grin became a smile as he thought of what else he was gonna say. "It's not my fault that loser Dominic couldn't see his own friend was depressed and suicidal. Tim was always sitting by himself at lunch. Me and a couple other guys would try to be nice to him, but it was obvious the nerd was antisocial." Brad was a notorious bully and could not resist mocking the dead he thought so little of.

Detective Barnes was taken aback by Brad's candid and sadistic reaction. "I see," he said softly. He found Brad annoying and wanted to move on. "Well, that's all the questions I have for you. You are free to go back to class. If you hear from Bethany, please let me know." Detective Barnes handed Brad his card as the blonde stood up from the table.

Brad mumbles something as he left the room with the guidance counselor. Detective Barnes did not hear him clearly, but it sounded like he said, "I doubt she's still alive."

Detective Neal Barnes spent the next couple of hours questioning the remainder of Bethany's friends and they all said the same thing. Bethany was being chased and the only people she talked to were Brad and Amanda. All three of them also pointed the finger at Dominic Gunner as their best guess for Bethany's unknown pursuer. The older detective decided it was time to talk to Dominic.

Mrs. Ventress walked him into the room just as she did with the other students that Detective Barnes talked to. Immediately, Detective Barnes noticed that Dominic was vastly different from the other students he had talked to. Dominic was a scrawny kid with black matted hair, cheap, well-worn clothing, and shoes that were at least three years old. The other students he had interviewed had wealth and wore it without pause. It was obvious Dominic was not so fortunate. "Hello, Mr. Gunner, I'm Detective Neal Barnes. Do you mind if I ask you a few quotations about Bethany Rizzo?" he asked the boy.

Dominic rolled his green eyes, "let me guess, Brad and all his dumbass friends said I was some kind of monster who has been threatening them. Well, look at me, detective. Do I look like I could hurt them?" The detective saw what he meant. Brad and the other kids were all-star athletes at the school and would have no trouble defending themselves against someone who looked too weak to lift a dumbbell.

"Tell me about your friend, Tim Shoto." Detective Barnes' request caused tears to swell in Dominic's eyes.

"He's dead because of them. They killed him and tossed his body in the park to make it look like he killed himself. Tim wouldn't do that, he would never do something like that. They are the reason Tim is dead because they sl..."

"ENOUGH OF THAT SLANDEROUS TALK YOUNG MAN," Mrs. Ventress interrupted Dominic before he could finish what he was saying. Detective Barnes was caught off-guard as it was the first thing she had said since introducing herself to the detective.

"Mrs. Ventress, please allow Dominic to finish what he was saying." Mrs. Ventress, whose face was red with anger, acknowledged the detective's command. Detective Barnes motioned for Dominic to continue, but he seemed hesitant to do so.

"Answer me this detective, how many people kill themselves by cutting their own throats?" Dominic asked as he wiped tears from his green eyes.

Detective Barnes sat quietly for a moment to ponder the boy's question and to give Dominic a moment to collect himself. "Where were you last night between 10pm and 3 am?"

"I was home."

"Is there anyone who can confirm that?"

Dominic looked down at the table. "My mom was asleep by then and my dad was at work. So, no." Mrs. Ventress scoffed at the boy's alibi as if to say she knew he was guilty. "But you can check my GPS on my phone. It will show that I was home all night," Dominic said in response to the guidance counselor's reaction.

"I will. Thank you for your time, you're free to return to class." Dominic stood up and left the room, but Mrs. Ventress did not escort him out like she had the others. Detective Barnes took her hesitation as an opportunity to ask her a favor. "Mrs. Ventress, can you make sure none of the students go around implying that Mr. Gunner did something to Ms. Rizzo? We aren't sure what happened so it would be in everyone's best interest if no conclusions are jumped to yet." Mrs. Ventress nodded and left the detective alone in the room to pack up his belongings.

As Detective Barnes reached his car, he received a phone call from Detective Rice. "Barnes speaking," he answered the phone as he got into his car.

"Barnes, figured you should know that the lab called...it was Bethany on that wall. Meet us back at the station. Her parents were unhelpful, so we're hoping that you had better luck at the school." Rice hung up before Detective Barnes could respond. Detective Neal Barnes just sighed as he turned on his car and began his journey back to the police station.

*****

Detective Barnes returned to the Ryanton Police Station before Rice and Heldenburg, so he decided to pull the case file for

Tim Shoto. He poured over every little detail that was in that file. Tim's throat had been cut and the knife that had cut it laid by his side. The report said that the knife has no fingerprints on it, only Tim's blood. The coroner's report in the file said there was alcohol in Tim's system. What Detective Barnes found to be strange was the lack of photos in the file. None of the crime scene, none of Tim's body. Detective Barnes checked to see who the detective in charge of the case was and it was a name he did not recognize. Numerous questions flew through the detective's head but before he could answer any of them, Heldenburg and Rice returned to the station. "Whatcha reading?" Rice asked as he walked past Detective Barnes' desk.

"Just something pertaining to another case," Detective Barnes lied as he closed the file and threw it into his top desk drawer.

"Any luck with the friends?" Heldenburg asked as he took a sip from the coffee that Rice and he had stopped for while on the way back from talking to Behtany's parents.

Detective Barnes rubbed his eyes and then leaned back in his desk chair. "Her friend's said someone was chasing her last night. My guess... the person chasing her is our killer. Did the parents notice anyone trying to break in last night?" Detective Barnes asked Rice who had just sat down at his desk.

"Nah. Parents were on a trip upstate. They got in early this morning. They had no idea anything was wrong until we showed up," Detective Rice answered as he turned on his desk computer and began to play a game of solitaire.

"Did her friend's give you any suspects?" Heldenburg asked as he sat on his desk.

Detective Barnes hesitated for a moment, “One, but I’m not sure he’s our guy. He just doesn’t look physically capable of throwing someone into a woodchipper.”

“Maybe he drugged her before he threw her in. What was his name?” Rice asked without looking up from his computer.

“Dominic Gunner.”

Heldenburg and Rice exchanged looks. “Dominic Gunner? I’ve heard of him, why have I heard of him?” Heldenburg asked his partner.

“Yeah, he’s that kid who came in telling us his friend was killed by a demonic cult at his school. We looked into it, but there was no evidence to his claim. You think he decided to take justice into his own hands?” Rice asked the room.

Detective Barnes was about to disagree with Rice’s theory when Heldenburg jumped in. “No doubt in my mind. He's just a crazy nut job who can't accept what happened. I say we pick him up for questioning," Heldenburg said as he stood up.

"I don't think we should. We don't have anything tying him to the crime scene," Detective Barnes interjected, forcing Heldenburg to sit back onto his desk. Rice had not moved at all as he was in the middle of his game of solitaire.

"Very well," Heldenburg began, staring down Detective Barnes,"but more evidence could be more bodies."

*****

Allison arrived at Amanda’s place after school and noticed there were no lights on in the house. The brown-haired girl had gotten a text from her friend asking her to come by since her parents worked late and she did not want to be home alone with everything that has happened lately. She walked up to the door and knocked, but there was no answer. She tried the door and found it unlocked. Allison walked inside and noticed the foul smell. It smelled like gasoline and it got stronger as she walked further into the dark house. "Amanda?" she called out. No response. Then the front door slammed shut. "This isn't funny Amanda, you need to..." Allison stopped dead in her tracks after she entered the living room. She found her friend Amanda tied up and sitting in the middle of the room. Even in the darkened room, Allison could see the tears streaming out of her friend's pale blue eyes.

The girl's attention soon shifted from her captured friend to the cloud of dark smoke that began to form behind her. The smoke shifted from a cloud to the shape of a man. "Well hello Allison." The smoke bellowed in a deep ominous voice. "Bethany made it clear that my first attempt to convince you and your friends to come clean about what you have done failed. Hopefully you now see how serious I am."

Allison began to back away slowly, "be careful. You may knock over a candle." Vengeance bellowed as numerous candles around the house seemed to light themselves simultaneously. Allison freaked out and made a break for the sliding glass door in the back of the house. Just as she reached the sliding glass door, she slipped on a puddle of gasoline that covered the floor and bumped into a table that held three candles. All three candles fell to the floor, causing the puddle to ignite. Allison ran into the backyard and watched in horror as Amanda's house was engulfed by flames. Tears of fear poured from Allison's eyes as she listened to her friend's screams of agony and terror pour out with the escaping smoke.

In the midst of the horror, Vengeance exited the house using the door that Allison had just fled from. "How many of you must die before you give up this silly charade and finally admit what you did? Your friend is burning alive because of your stubborn cowardness. Vengeance is unavoidable and I will come for you if you do not admit your quilt," the dark cloud of Vengeance boomed before dissipating into thin air leaving the frightened girl alone in the backyard of the burning house.

*****

Detective Barnes pulled up to the smoldering remains of Amanda Burfict's house. There was a large group of firefighters, police officers, reporters, and spectators from the neighboring houses. The detective parked his car and weaved his way through the crowd until he reached Detectives Heldenburg and Rice. "Still think it was smart to not bring that son-of-a-bitch in?" Rice asked rhetorically.

"You found evidence connecting this to Dominic?" Barnes asked.

Heldenburg handed Detective Barnes an evidence bag that held a note, 'Amanda's death was unavoidable. I gave her and dear Allison a chance to admit to their crimes. Yet they continue to play games. Vengeance is unavoidable and it comes for the guilty.'

"We found it in the mailbox," Heldenburg explained. "Same crazy message of revenge. Not a big leap to connect this crime to the other one. The good news is we have a witness who can place Dominic at the scene. Dominic is taking the law into his own twisted hands."

"Who was the witness?" Detective Banres asked.

"Allison Bound. Says she showed up and found Amanda up in the living room, but before she could free her, a man in all black showed up and attacked her. She grabbed his hood and saw Dominic's face. Allison was lucky enough to get out alive before the fire started, but the poor girl was forced to watch her friend die," Rice explained. Heldenburg mumbled to himself and then walked away from the detective he blamed for Amanda's death.

Detective Barnes looked around and took in the surroundings. "Do you mind if I talk to Allison?" he asked Rice. Rice just shrugged and pointed towards the ambulance that was checking on Allison for injuries.

Detective Barnes walked over to Allison. "Hello again, Ms. Bonds. I'm sorry for your loss. I was hoping you could tell me what happened."

Allison looked up at the detective with tears in her eyes, "I already told the other detectives it was Dominic. He thinks we killed that loser and now he's attacking us." She cried, relaying the story Brad told her to say to the police when she called him before the cops arrived. "I saw him in the house. He killed my friends. How many more of us have to die before you idiots arrest him?" Detective Barnes tried to change the subject and ask more questions but Allison would not answer them. "I have nothing more to say to you," Allison said through gritted teeth and tears. Detective Barnes nodded his head and walked away.

*****

Detective Barnes sat at his desk and contemplated the events of the day. Then Detective Heldenburg walked into the room, "we brought Dominic in for questioning, but he says he will only talk to you. Interrogation room four." Heldenburg left the rooms without another word. Detective Barnes got up and walked to the interrogation room.

On his way to the interrogation room, Detective Barnes was stopped by a man in a three thousand dollar suit. "Excuse me detective? I'm Albert Gruden," he began as he held out his right hand to Detective Barnes. The veteran detective shook Mr. Gruden's hand. "I would like to officially offer my services to you and the DA's office."

"Not very common for a defense attorney of your caliber and reputation to offer to help the police," Detective Barnes said to the well-groomed lawyer.

Albert Gruden just flashed a sly grin, "well it's not very often a murderer threatens my son. I feel it's my obligation as a father to help in any way I can to ensure this monster gets the chair."

"I see. I'll keep that in mind, Mr. Gruden," Detective Barnes said as he walked past the lawyer towards the interrogation room that held Dominic. Mr. Gruden watched the detective as he walked away.

Detective Barnes walked into the drab concrete room where Dominic and his lawyer, Andrew Wood, were waiting. He sat down at the metallic table across from the two men. "Hello again Dominic," the detective spoke softly.

"Detective, my client has instructed me that he only wishes to talk to you, but he is not going to answer any questions until after you hear what he has to say. Agreed?" Andrew Wood asked.

Barnes leaned back and fixed his suit coat, "Very well."

Dominic looked the detective in the eyes. "They killed my friend. They slit his throat and then dumped his body in the park. I know they did and I have the evidence to prove it." Dominic paused for a moment as tears filled his eyes and he began to choke on the sentences that he had been trying to share for so long. Detective Barnes just sat silently and waited for the young man to collect himself. "That semester, Tim and I got placed in separate lunch hours. It sucked and it forced both of us to sit alone. Then one day after school, Tim was telling me that some of the rich, cool kids approached him at lunch and sat with him. He claimed they had bonded and were going to hang out after school one day. I thought they were fucking with him, but Tim... Tim always saw the best in people. Even if those people don't have anything good in them. He believed everyone was capable of good," he said as he paused to hold back tears. "Then one Saturday, Tim tells me he got invited to hang out with them at Bethany's place. He was so excited. He told me his plan to talk me up the whole night so I could get invited with him next time. I wanted to tell him not to go, to try and convince him that it was a trap to humiliate him, but I didn't. I didn't want to ruin his excitement. I figured the worst that would happen is they pick on him all night. He was texting me updates all night. Telling me how much fun he was having and how Ryan had brought booze and that they were all drinking together. Then just before midnight the texts stop. The last text I got from him was about how happy he was and that he can't wait for me to come next time." Once again the words got caught in his throat and tears rolled down his cheeks.

"Do you still have these texts?" Detective Barnes asked softly.

Dominic shook his head and pushed his phone across the table to the detective. "I even have screenshots saved on my computer and another hard drive."

The detective looked through the text conversation. It matched up with what Dominic said. The texts added to Detective Barne's growing uneasy feelings regarding the truth of this cause. These texts and the fatal injury should have been enough to spark an investigation. "Why didn't you bring these to us sooner?"

"I did, I gave an officer copies of the screenshots and they said they would look into it. Two days later these two detectives came to my house and told me my friend was sick and that these texts were lies he sent me to keep me from stopping his plan to take his life in the park. Do you know how angry that made me? I watched his parents cry at his funeral because they thought they had failed him, but they didn't. I know they didn't. He was happy and he loved them. I had proof he didn't kill himself and no one would listen," Dominic said through gritted teeth. "So I decided to look into it myself. I owed him that. Someone had to investigate. I started looking for proof that would show Tim was at Bethany's house that night. Then one day I had to grab something from my gym locker after school and I overheard Brad, Ryan, and Douglas talking about that night. Ryan and Douglas were upset, claiming

Brad lied to them. Talking about how they followed his instructions and still nothing. I even heard them say Tim's name. That's when Brad shushed them and told them to be patient. Then they all praised someone named Eldisey and left the locker room. I looked up that name. It's a demon. Those goddamn assholes sacrificed my friend to a fucking demon as a virgin sacrifice. But Tim got the last laugh, he wasn't a virgin like everyone thought. They didn't know that the summer prior, Tim hooked up with a girl at his summer camp. Their demon's never gonna show up because their sacrifice wasn't a virgin like they thought," Dominic laughed at the absurdity of the situation he had described. He believed it and it still sounded insane to him, he could only imagine what Detective Barnes would think.

Detective Barnes sat silently as he processed what he had been told. He was by no means a religious man as years of seeing the worst of humanity had chipped away at his beliefs in God, but he was all too aware of what a person was capable of. "Are you trying to get revenge for Tim against the people you think killed him?" Detective Barnes asked.

Frustration filled Dominic's face, "Think?" he sneered. "My friend was killed by these pompous, arrogant assholes."

"Are you seeking revenge by attacking them?"

"No, but whoever is attacking them is doing the world a favor. Those demon worshipers deserve to die for what they did. I'm just not the one doing it," Dominic said. Detective Barnes sensed the boy telling some semblance of truth. He was not attacking them, but he definitely knew who was.

"Where were you today after school?" the Detective asked his suspect.

Dominic's lawyer jumped back in and answered for Dominic. "My client was home and has a neighbor who can confirm that. He was all the way across town when the fire started."

Detective Barnes nodded his head at Dominic's alibi. He tried asking Dominic a few more questions but he struggled to get any more information from him. "Very well," Detective Barnes said as he stood up from the table. "Don't leave town," is all he said before leaving the interrogation room.

*****

Detective Barnes sat at his desk reflecting on the past couple of days. Something was amiss, but there was still more to this story than had been revealed. His thoughts were interrupted by the emergence of two frustrated detectives. "He's our guy. I know he is," Rice said as he began to pace the room.

"We walked in after you left and let him know that we have a witness that places him at the scene. You should have seen the look on his face. He was razzled." Heldenburg filled in Detective Barnes as the two men watched Rice pace and think.

"What about his alibi?" Barnes asked.

Heldenburg scoffed. "It's a weak alibi. A neighbor? Come on. The victim is placing him at the scene. It's not like she would lie to send an innocent kid to jail."

"I still don't think he killed anyone," Barnes commented. "I think he's involved, but I don't think he's working alone."

"You think he hired a professional?" Rice asked as he stopped dead in his tracks. "Heldenburg and I can go downtown and ask around. I have an informant who keeps his ear to the ground on the hired gun racket. Let's go," he said to his partner as he walked out of the room. Heldenburg gave Barnes a slight nod before joining his partner in leaving. Detective Barnes was once again alone to think. He was in for a long night.

*****

It was the dead of night. Allison was driving back to Vernon Hale High School to meet up with her friends. Brad said he had a plan to take care of Vengeance and make sure Dominic gets blamed for Bethany and Amanda. He asked Allison, Douglas, and Ryan to meet him at the school's gym parking lot. The brown-haired girl was freaked out beyond belief and raced down the dimly lit back road. Tears streamed from her eyes as the screams of her friend continued to play in her head. She was so distracted by the sounds that haunted her, that she never saw the figure who appeared on the road in front of her.

Allison's eyes went wide as her headlights illuminated the figure on the road. She slammed on the breaks, but it was too late. Her car collided with the person, sending the body over the top of the car and back onto the pavement behind her. Her car came to a stop and Allison jumped out of her car to check who it was she hit. The red light from her tail lights shined onto the face of her victim. Allison let out a terrified shriek as she looked into the eyes of her dying friend Ryan.

Blood dribbled from his mouth as he wearily reached up to his friend with a scraped and bloody arm. "h-help me..." The brown-haired boy groaned softly through the pain.

Allison began to shake as a dark cloud of smoke formed behind Ryan. "He was running from me and he saw your car. He was so confident you would stop to help him that he walked into the middle of the road," Vengeance explained to the sobbing girl. "Another friend dying right in front of you. Another opportunity to save them." Vengeance boomed.

The blonde took a step back. "Fuck you," she cried as she turned and ran to her car. The tires screeched as she sped off into the night, leaving her dying friend alone with the smoke monster.

"It looks like you chose the wrong friends," Vengeance mocked as he faded back into the night. Ryan looked out into the distance, hoping to see his friend's car turn around. She did not. His life now depended on another car driving down the road.

Allison raced at full speed. She swerved all over the road as her emotional state removed all concerns of personal safety. Allison's car climbed up the winding hill that led to her school. She was almost there when she heard her phone ring. It was Brad calling her. Feelings of relief and hope entered her chest as she tried to answer her phone, but her actions were not steady and she dropped the phone. She tried to get it without taking her eyes off the road, but she was unsuccessful. Allison looked down, grabbed the phone and looked back up at the road just as her car hit the metal guard rail. Allison screamed as her car flew off the hill. It crashed hard, rolling multiple times and stopped at the base of the hill.

Vengeance laughed at the sight of Allison flying off the road to her death before he vanished in the night, leaving Ryan to die. As he laid dying in a pool of his own blood, Ryan heard footsteps approaching him. "He...help," he cried out.

The Stranger stood over the dying man. "I bet you wish you could Vengeance for what he did to you? Allow me to assist you with that," The Stranger said with a smile. He knew Vengeance was going to be someone he would have to deal with sooner or later.

Ryan looked up at The Stranger. Even in the dark of night, he could see the storm-like-nature of the Stanger's blue eyes. "Deal."

*****

"I can't reach Ryan," Douglas said with frustration as once again his call went to voicemail. "What about Allison? Is she almost here?" the black-haired boy asked his friend.

"No," he said as he put his phone back in his pocket. Douglas and Brad stood alone in the school parking lot by their cars.

Douglas looked at him. "Then what do we do?"

"Nothing," Brad said as he kicked a rock.

"What do you mean nothing?" Douglas asked.

Brad rolled his eyes in frustration, "As in we don't have to do anything because they were weak. They're dead because they were not strong enough to survive. Vengeance isn't an enemy, he's a test from Eldisey. I'm sure of it. Only the strong can receive his blessing."

Douglas stared at his friend, "Those are our friends you're talking about. You don't even know if they are dead."

"They aren't here, are they?" Brad scoffed as he held his arms out to his side.

"This is getting to be too serious, man," Douglas responded with fear in his voice. He looked at the ground and took a nervous swallow as he worked the courage to speak his mind to the narcissistic leader of the group. "I've been thinking that maybe we should turn ourselves in."

Brad froze and glared at his friend. "What?" he snarled.

"Look, I don't think this is a test from Eldisey. I think it's something else. Whatever is chasing us is strong. He killed Behtany and Amanda and...and now Ryan and Allison. We can't beat him, so we need to do what we have to do to survive," Douglas pleaded to Brad.

Brad walked closer to his friend. "I didn't realize you were weak too," the high school quarterback sneered. "I finally see why the Dark Lord Eldisey hasn't come yet. I was surrounded by the weak and unworthy."

Douglas looked up, "Brad..." He was interrupted by a fist to his jaw. Brad struck his friend with a powerful right hook that sent Douglas to the ground. Brad proceeded to kick his friend in the gut multiple times. After numerous kicks to his defenseless friend's body, Brad stopped to collect himself. He looked down upon Douglas who was coughing up blood.

Brad noticed Douglas's keys had fallen out of his pockets during the barrage of kicks. The blonde grabbed the keys and used them to open the trunk of Douglas' car. "You think I'm scared of that thing?" he asked rhetorically as he picked his bleeding friend up off the ground by the back of his shirt and threw him towards the open trunk. "I am not weak. I will not let anyone ruin everything I have worked for. I have a future of glory waiting for me and I will not let the death of some meaningless virgin stop me from taking my place next to the Dark Lord Eldisey," He screamed hysterically as he grabbed the trunk hood and closed it on Douglas' neck multiple times. Brad took a step back and watched in anger as Douglas' lifeless body fell to the ground. "Pathetic," he mumbled as he wiped blood from his face. Brad turned and got into his car. He drove off towards his father's office where he knew he would be undisturbed.

*****

Coach Jonathan Huff was putting away equipment that he had been using for his after school workout. He found it a good way to save money instead of paying for a gym membership. "Hello. Mr. Huff," a voice boomed and scared the middle aged man, causing him to turn in fright. He laid eyes upon a dark cloud of smoke that blocked the only exit of the equipment storage room. "I know what you did."

The coach laughed arrogantly at the thing that hovered before him. "And what is that?"

"You are the one who told Brad about the demon you worship. You offered him power in exchange for a sacrifice. Brad and his gullible friends fell for you lies and false promises. The life they took is on your hands too," Vengeance said. "You either confess to the authorities or you will regret it."

"I'm not scared of some smoke cloud. What are you gonna do? Give me lung cancer?" The coach laughed to himself and broke into a laughing fit.

"I'm growing tired of giving you demon worshipers second chances." Vengeance picked up a 15-pound medicine ball off of a rack by the door and threw it at the coach with impressive speed. The ball slammed into the coaches chest with great force, knocking the wind out of the middle aged man and sending him flying into the back wall of the equipment room. The coach crumbled to the ground coughing and wheezing as he cursed at the dark entity.

Vengeance picked up another medicine ball and threw it again at the back wall. The ball crashed into the wall with a loud bang, causing all the weights and equipment that hung on the wall to shake free. The coach fell silent as two 50-pound weights slipped off their pegs and fell onto his head.

Vengeance began to fade from the room. "With the head of the snake removed, only one remains."

*****

Brad entered his father's large office on the 75th floor of a large downtown skyscraper and flipped on the lights. No one saw the blood covered boy enter the building as he knew all the back entrances and camera blind spots. He rushed to the bathroom in his father's office and grabbed a few clothes that he had stashed there a few months back. Brad washed the blood off his hands and face and put on the clean set of clothes. He walked out of the bathroom and noticed the figure over by the floor-to-ceiling window behind his father's desk. "You," he sneered.

"This is your final warning. Turn yourself in." Vengeance warned.

Brad clenched his fists and walked towards the shadowy figure. "You think you can intimidate me? I am not weak like the rest of those pathetic losers. Once I kill you, I will have shown Eldisey that I have conquered his trial and belong by his side."

"You overestimate your strength. You underestimate me. Doing so will not end well for you. It did not for your coach," Vengeance's comment caused Brad's eye to twitch in anger.

"You're lying."

Vengeance laughed at Brad, "He's currently lying dead on the floor of the equipment room. His skull split in two."

"Fuck you!" Brad screamed as he picked up a chair and threw it at the smoke monster. The chair went right through the smoke monster and hit the window, cracking it. Brad continued screaming as he grabbed the other chair and threw it at Vengeance. This chair passed through the monster just as the first, but this one shattered the large office window. Vengeance responded by grabbing the desk in front of him and swiftly pushing it away, sending it flying across the room with ease.

With nothing between him and Vengeance, Brad decided to charge at the monster that had caused the death of his mentor. "I'll kill you!" Brad cried out as he sprinted at the cloud of smoke. Brad's eyes went wide as the cloud of smoke moved just before Brad reached Vengeance leaving nothing between the angry blonde and the broken window. "Oh fuck!" Brad screamed as he unsuccessfully tried to stop himself from falling to his death.

*****

It had been five days since Brad's death. Everyone at the high school had been treating Dominic differently as rumors of his role in the death of the popular friend group grew. Detective Rice and Heldenburg wanted so badly to find the proof that tied Dominic to the murders that they would visit his house daily at various hours of the day in hopes of catching him off guard or with his co-conspirator. They never did.

Dominic stood alone on the third floor of the abandoned building that was Vernon Hale High School. He looked over the balcony and saw a pile of old desks and chairs that were stacked by the entrance but never picked up. He had been waiting for 30 minutes and was just about to leave when he heard a thunderous boom behind him. "Hello, Dominic."

The black-haired boy turned and watched as a cloud of black smoke poured from the vents and formed a human-esque figure before him. "I'm surprised you wanted to meet again. I thought you said once it was done, I would never see you again," Dominic asked the creature as he took a few steps toward it.

Vengeance began to circle Dominic while still remaining a good distance away. "That was before."

"Before what?" Dominic asked. A sense of fear emerged in his voice.

"Your obsession with your revenge caused the death of six others. Their deaths were caused by you, but your obsession comes with a price. It is time to pay for your revenge," Vengeance said ominously.

Dominic was caught off guard. "I'm not the one who killed them. You killed them." He responded, becoming more scared.

A deep, booming laugh bellowed from the dark cloud. "Each of those kids who you had disdain for died in unfortunate accidents. I have not killed a soul. It was you that sent them to their deaths when you freed me from my lantern and tasked me with making them pay for what they did to you and your friend. Your obsession killed them. I learned long before I was trapped in that perpetual hell you found me in, that committing a sin such as murder destroys my physical form, making me less human. I am no longer a flesh and blood human because of my quest to punish the guilty. My form has not faded. I am not guilty for their deaths which means the universe believes that you are."

"You're human?" Dominic asked. He had come across the legend of Vengeance while he was studying the dark arts that Brad and his friend group had been linked to. The legend portrayed Vengeance as a monster of moral purity that punished those who have avoided justice. The legend claimed the monster could see the sins that people had committed when it looked upon them and would make sure they paid for what they did.

After months of searching, Dominic found someone online who claimed to have the lantern that contained Vengeance and sent it to him for 500 dollars. When it arrived, he opened the dark green lantern and freed Vengeance. The black-haired boy pleaded for justice for his friend.

"I was once a proud knight, Sir Victor Mallory. I fought for all that was good in this wretched, vile world, until I failed to bring justice. A young woman came to me, tears in her green eyes. She said her sister had been murdered by the son of a local lord, whose father I considered a dear friend. I denied her claim as I did not see it possible that the boy I had watched grow up could commit such an act. The woman then revealed herself to be a powerful sorceress named Aricane who found my lack of action an insult to the truth. She cursed me to witness all the sins that hide within the memories of men and feel their guilt or lack thereof as if it were my own. I looked up those I once considered colleagues and saw what they had done. I was filled with anger and punished them myself, but I soon learned that my own sins would cloud my site, making it hard to see the sins in others, forcing me to sacrifice my own flesh in order to properly restore my sight. Little by little I became what you see now. I learned that my sight did not become clouded with each person I punished. If they died indirectly of my actions, then I have not committed a sin that would affect my gift. I set out, determined to rid the world of the unpunished, until I was stopped, trapped in that lantern by the very sorceress who gave me my power after she learned she could not control me and make me part of her dark army," Vengeance explained to Dominic. He elaborated further, "Now that you have freed me, I can continue with my life's work. I can punish the one truly responsible for the deaths of those demon worshipers. You see, my vision was unaffected by the death of Bethany Rizzo, Amanda Burfict, Ryan Smith, Douglas Lester, Jonathan Huff, or Brad Gruden. They may have deserved to die, but in your heart, I see sin in you. You will pay for their deaths. One way or another." Vengeance boomed as he began to slowly close in on Dominic while still circling him. "You will admit to your crimes and be punished. Either by the laws of this world or mine. Now choose your fate."

Dominic began to back up until his back hit the railing. “They won’t believe me if I turn myself in,” Dominic responded as the monster of smoke trapped him in that spot by closing off all routes of escape with smokey appendages. Vengeance got within inches of his face. He stared into the glowing red eyes of the monster and could see his own reflection staring back at him.

"Then make them believe, Dominic. You have three days to confess to your crimes or will face the full wrath of Vengeance," his voice thundered. "I thank you for freeing me into this changed world. I am interested to learn why my power feels dampened. I thought it was just from being locked up for so long, but since I have not regained my strength yet, I have to wonder what is causing my weakened state. Much must have changed since I was locked away. I do not want to stay here longer than I have to. Three days Dominic. Three days."

The man-turned-smoke monster was about to dissipate when an unusual object came rolling down the hall. It looked like a flaming tire made entirely of black flame and it was heading for Dominic and Vengeance. The creature of smoke moved quickly to avoid it and Dominic hugged the balcony tightly as the tire zoomed between the two of them. It came to an explosive stop when it crashed into a wall of lockers. Metal churned as they melted to the will of the black flame. It burned everything it touched to pure, dark ash.

"Vengeance! You will pay for killing my friends!" A pain-filled voice screamed from down the hall. Into the fluorescent light stepped a beaten and bruised boy in makeshift armor that appeared to be fashioned out of car parts and leather. Across his chest was a tire tread and he wore a full motorcycle helmet without a visor. In his right hand was a shiny, all-black Roman gladius that was 25-inches long. The armored threat could have been anyone, but Dominic knew who it was the minute he heard his voice. He looked up and gazed up at Ryan Smith.

"Ah, Ryan," Vengeance boomed as the smoke monster reappeared. "You are looking a lot more alive since the last time I saw you. Who would have thought becoming roadkill would look so good on you." The dark cloud's comments angered Ryan. He let out a battle scream and his eyes sparked into the black fire. Then his black blade ignited into the same black flame as his eyes and the tire he launched just moments ago. Ryan swung his sword back behind him, stepped forward with his left foot, and then brought his weapon forward in a sweeping, underhand motion. As the blade moved forward, the flame formed a ball around the tip of the sword and then the ball collided with the laminate floor as Ryan's motions continued in front of him. The ball of black flame formed a tire shape and raced towards its target, leaving burnt tire marks behind it. Vengeance disbanded to avoid the attack. The tire continued on past him and eventually crashed into another wall, creating another large explosion. "This power?" Vengeance pondered as he reformed again. "It feels familiar to me. Like a long-lost enemy. Where did you get it?" Vengeance asked. But Ryan did not care to answer. He just fired another flaming tire at his enemy. While both powered individuals dueled, Dominic saw his opportunity to slip away from the two people who wanted to see him dead.

While Vengeance was able to easily dodge Ryan's long-range attack, the mass of smoke was not going to take being attacked lightly. Vengeance waited for Ryan to move in closer and then reappeared behind his attacker, thinking that he had caught him off guard. He was going for the lethal blow when Ryan looked back over his shoulder. Ryan quickly turned and swung his flaming blade up to block the attack. Much to Vengeance's disbelief, the blade stopped his attack. He felt the warmth of the steel as he slammed his limb against the side of his attacker's sword. Ryan knocked the limb away and swung his sword at Vengeance, just barely clipping a piece of the smoke monster. Vengeance felt a pain that he had not felt in centuries. He retreated from his failed attack as he finally realized what he was facing. Vengeance reformed across the large open area at the entrance of another hallway directly across from where Ryan stood, a good safe distance away. This sting of his wound was all the proof he needed as to what weapon Ryan possessed. "How did you get that cursed blade?" Vengeance screamed. The dark cloud of smoke originally thought Ryan was using some kind of demonic, divine, or magically enhanced blade, but now he knew he wielded a much more powerful weapon: one lost to time, one of the few weapons on the planet that could deal deadly damage to him. Ryan had the true Black Flame Sword.

Ryan did not answer Vengeance's fear-filled question, he just continued his attack by raising his weapon to the ceiling and charging at Vengeance. The smoke monster considered dissipating again and fully retreating, leaving Dominic to be the new focus of Ryan's revenge, but Vengeance's ego would not let himself run from a fight with someone he looked upon as inferior to him, even if he held such a weapon. To run now would only cause the cloud of smoke to live with the knowledge that he allowed an enemy to hold on to a blade that posed a danger to him. Vengeance also knew that if he took the blade from Ryan after he killed him, he would become nearly unstoppable in his mission to bring vengeance to this world. Vengeance tried to carefully embrace Ryan's attack, wrapping up his right arm and preventing him from using the sword. Vengeance then attacked the back of Ryan's leg, slicing his calf just below his knee. He then formed a sharp point on the end of a newly formed limb and drove it through Ryan's crudely made armor and into his chest. The monster finished his attack by throwing Ryan across the room and into a set of lockers. Vengeance felt triumphant as he watched Ryan crash into the metal lockers with a loud bang and then crumble onto the floor with a solid thud.

Any feeling of victory faded as Vengeance watched his attacker rise back to his feet, his wounds bleeding with black flame. A crooked smile rested on Ryan's face. "My turn," he taunted. Ryan's feet exploded into the black fire as he raced towards Vengeance at near-inhuman speed. The smoke cloud had barely enough time to react to such a quick attack. Vengeance tried to move out of the way but was unable to prevent the blade from slicing across the front of his formless body. Vengeance let out an angry cry of pain. The wound stung as the black flame began to eat away at his smokey form. Vengeance was able to push Ryan away as he tried to regroup, but he noticed he could not dissipate as the flame ate away at his body. Ryan saw his opportunity to finish his enemy. When he landed away from Vengeance, he formed two more tire-shaped fireballs and sent them rolling on either side of the monster to prevent Vengeance from dodging his killing blow. Ryan sprinted towards his enemy at full speed, staying behind the two fireballs. Vengeance was trapped. Still weakened from the previous attack, Vengeance was unable to dodge the impending attack. He had no chance to escape. The two flaming tires roared past Vengeance and then Ryan plunged the Black Flame Sword into the center of the smoke monster. Vengeance let out a final bellow of pain as the black flame engulfed him. The fight ended as Vengeance was consumed by and destroyed in a giant fireball of pure dark fire. The two tire-shaped fireballs rolled into open classroom doors and exploded inside those classrooms. Ryan then turned and looked for Dominic. He peered through smoke, fire, and debris that surrounded the victor, but there was no sight of his next victim. He figured Dominic ran off as he and Vengeance squared off. Ryan took a deep breath and then ran down the hallway that Vengeance was guarding, trying to run down Dominic before he could leave the abandoned high school.

Dominic ran for his life. He raced down the stairs to the ground floor. Dominic reached the final hallway and was approaching one of the school's side doors that exited to the parking lot where Dominic's beat-up used car waited for him. He approached the doors when they suddenly flew open. Dominic slammed to a halt, his momentum pushing him to the ground. Dominic stared in terrified shock as he watched a figure emerge from the sun ray that flooded the school when the door slammed open. Then a moment of calm crashed over him as he realized it was not Ryan, but Detective Neal Barnes. He entered the school, his weapon drawn and ready for almost anything.

Detective Barnes entered the school and found Dominic on the ground. He was relieved to see him alive after the frantic voicemail he received from the boy just moments ago. Then he saw a strange object come racing down the stairs and roll towards Dominic with great speed. "WATCH OUT!" he screamed at Dominic.

Dominic turned and made eye contact with the impending flaming tire. "Oh fuck!" Dominic panicked as he began to scramble out of the way of the tire. He frantically kicked his way to safety, knocking off one of his shoes. The tire raced over the shoe, leaving behind a pile of smoldering ash in its place. With Dominic no longer in danger, the detective realized that he was now standing in the path of the flaming attack. Detective Barnes jumped to safety and covered his head as the tire crashed into the doorway and exploded into a giant fireball, sending bits of the metal door and stone wall everywhere.

Detective Barnes then looked up, back towards Dominic and the stairs that the flaming tire descended from, and saw the perpetrator of the attack. He was covered in strange car-themed armor and wielding a black, flaming sword in his right hand, but Detective Barnes did not recognize who this attacker was.

Dominic shot to his feet and back peddled away from Ryan. "You're not going anywhere, Dominic," he screamed before his feet burst into black flame. "I know you released Vengeance on us!" Ryan was on Dominic before he could even react and could have easily plunged his sword into Dominic there, but Ryan wanted revenge. He wanted Dominic to suffer through broken bones and fatal wounds just as he had to after he was left to die after being struck by that car. He struck Dominic hard in the face with his left hand, sending his prey flying onto his back. "It's time we end this." Ryan grinned as he slowly walked towards Dominic, who was dazed and bleeding from being struck so hard.

The detective did not hesitate to act. He knew if he did nothing, Dominic was a dead man. Barnes drew his weapon and fired two shots at Ryan's chest. The first bullet hit Ryan in the right shoulder, the second dead center in his chest. Ryan stepped back from the sudden impacts, but he did not fall. The holes that the bullets made leaked melted metal and black flame. Ryan looked over to the detective whose eyes went wide with shock. "That wasn't very smart, detective. I was gonna let you live." Ryan laughed as he charged another fire tire. Detective Neal Barnes was frozen as he watched the flame take shape. His only hope was to dodge the attack.

The attack was charged, but just as he was about to unleash it onto Detective Barnes, Ryan was hit over the head with a broken piece of a 2x4. The sudden force caused Ryan to launch his attack in the wrong direction. The flame tire raced towards the wall and exploded sending debris everywhere. Ryan recollected himself and looked back to who hit him. It was Dominic, standing there with the broken 2x4 in his hands. "You leave him out of this. This is between you and me, Ryan," Dominic said with anger in his voice.

Ryan's eyes glowed with the same black flame that his blade burned with. "Oh, I'm going to enjoy killing you. You are the reason my friends are dead. And for what?" Ryan screamed out as he rushed Dominic, grabbed him, and threw him into the wall with great force.

Dominic coughed up blood as he readied himself for that final blow. "I wanted justice!" he screamed, expecting those to be his final words, but Ryan froze. "But I couldn't have justice so I took my revenge! You and your fucking friends murdered my best friend for some dipshit demon legend. You killed my friend. Why do you deserve to live? Deserve to get what you want?" Tears of pain and sorrow rolled from Dominic's eyes. "Well, I got my revenge and all it did was cause you to get yours. You are doing exactly what I did. The only difference is you were a murderer then and you are a murderer now. So do it! DO IT! Get it over with and kill me, roadkill!" Dominic cried at Ryan who stood there, staring at him.

Ryan hesitated as Dominic's words rang in his head. He began to question his mission, doubt his actions and second guess his role in the story. His black flame slowly faded from his eyes and his blade stopped burning as it rested by his side.

Then Ryan felt a terrible pain. It started in his chest and then moved the rest of his body, becoming more intense as it spread. It was a pain he had never felt before. The black flame that he once commanded was now burning his soul and body. He doubted his actions and the blade was punishing him for that. Fear filled Ryan's eyes, unsure of what was happening. He screamed and tried throwing the flame off his body, throwing it into the walls of the school. He cried for help, but there was no one to help.

That's when Detective Barnes saw an opening. He ran over, helped Dominic to his feet, and ran towards the exit as Ryan continued to be destroyed by his own power. The two escaped and collapsed in the parking lot as Ryan ignited his black flame again in hopes of making a speedy escape to find The Stranger who had given him the cursed weapon.

The school began to burn with the uncontrollable black flame. Dominic Gunner and Detective Neal Barnes watched as the school burned and smoke filled the air. Detective Barnes stood up to talk to the police and firefighters that arrived on the scene, but Dominic stayed on the black asphalt, watching the school burn with fright in his eyes. He breathed in the smoke and coughed. His nightmare was far from over. Vengeance was still with him.

*****

Off in the dense forest, stood a well-groomed man in an expensive black suit with a silver tie. His long black hair was slicked back as he waited for his experiment to return from his mission. Out of the thick of the forest came Ryan, the black flame now burning and consuming his body. "Help me! It hurts, you gotta put it out! You have to save me!" Ryan sobbed as he fell to the feet of The Stranger that had given him the blade. He looked and stared at the piercing crystal blue eyes of The Stranger.

"I'm afraid it's too late for that. The black flame cannot be extinguished. Once it has found a victim, it will not stop until there is nothing left to burn," The Stranger said in a calm, matter-of-factly manner. "I had high hopes for you Ryan. I saved your life because I believed you were the one. I was wrong."

The grimm words that The Stranger spoke were the last Ryan ever heard. He let out a final scream of pure pain as the flame engulfed his head and burned the boy into ash that blew away with the wind. The Black Flame Sword fell to the ground, its flame extinguished with its master-turned-victim dead. The Stranger pulled out an old red cloth and used it to pick up the dark blade. "Thank you for taking care of the pompous cloud of smoke for me. I hoped you had been the one I was looking for, but I was wrong. You are not the one I need and with each failure I fear the answer to my searching has already slipped through my fingers. Rest easy now, young lad," The Stranger said to the ashes of Ryan as they floated away. The Stranger walked off, his mind focusing on all the things he still had to do before his plan could reach its climax.

*****

Detective Barnes sat at his desk, trying to find sense in the events of the past couple of days. Dominic had been arrested in the parking lot after police and fire arrived to put out the burning abandoned school. As soon as Dominic was back at the station, he confessed to detective Barnes to the deaths of Ryan, Allison, Amanda, Douglas, Brad, and Bethany. The veteran detective did not want to take his confession, because he knew it was a lie. He knew it was not Dominic who was really at fault for all that transpired. His fellow detectives and chief took the boy's confession and ran with it, booking Dominic and charging him with the deaths of the six friends. Detective Barnes was left to sit alone to ponder how he shared the truth of what was really happening without sounding insane to his coworkers. He was lost in thought when detective Rice and Heldenburg walked into the room. "We got him. I told you he did it." Rice clapped as he sat at his desk.

Heldenburg chimed in next, "And if we arrested him on day one, well, their deaths are on your hands," he said pointing at Barnes, who just rolled his eyes.

"Well at least Mr. Gruden is on our side and he's gonna do everything in his power to make sure that monster fries," Rice added.

Detective Barnes stood from his desk and grabbed his suit coat. "Where you going?" Heldenburg asked with disgust.

"Home," he responded. "I'm tired of listening to you two talk like parrots," Barnes jabbed as he left the room.

*****

Dominic confessed to the deaths that Vengeance caused out of fear that the man of smoke would return if he did not. He told no one about Vengeance. Dominic wondered if Detective Barnes would object and share the truth of Vengeance, but the truth was too crazy to be believed.

He told everyone that he acted on his own and the police never questioned it. He pleaded guilty at his trial and was sentenced to be executed. The whole thing sat wrong with Detective Neal Barnes.

Today was Dominic's first night in prison. He wanted to keep his head down and avoid trouble, but something happened. Dominic met his roommate and became filled with a sudden anger. Dominic charged his roommate and beat him to an inch of his life. He seemed to know everything his roommate had done to people, saw the fear and pain of his victims, and it sent him over the edge.

After a few days in solitary, Dominic met his new roommate in cell 0-7-1-1. His name was Daniel. He was quiet, reserved, and content. More importantly, when Dominic looked at him, he did not feel anger. It was as if he was guilty of nothing other than the contraband business that he ran out of his cell. Daniel was respected and left alone which, in turn, meant that Dominic was left alone as long as he avoided more altercations. Nobody wanted to be banned from Daniel's contraband convenience store.

Dominic's days were filled with anger and pain, but his nights were worse. Every night, Dominic had the same strange dream. In the dream, Vengeance was there. The monster slowly changed from black smoke to a man with flowing blonde hair. He only ever said one thing to Dominic: "Now, it's your turn." Then

Vengeance would laugh as he transformed again, but this time into a mirror image of Dominic only with bright, glowing red eyes. Dominic stared into his copy's red eyes and saw something familiar, something terrifyingly real as the copy joined him and became one with Dominic. Then he would wake with fright, dripping in sweat on even the coldest days of the year. "It's just a dream," Dominic would reassure himself, unaware that his pupils glowed red in the darkness for a moment before returning to normal. Everytime he woke from the nightmare, Dominic felt as if a new power was growing inside of him: a power waiting to be awakened, a power he would use to bring all those who go unpunished for their crimes to damnation.

86

The actions of man are not independent. One's misdeeds and dastardly dealings can create misery for those who would much rather be left alone. No human lives in true isolation and they will always be caught up in messes they did not make.

*****

"So, this is the target?" Norman Lucius asked his brothers as they sat in the back room of The Concord Bar that was located in downtown Erniego, a large metropolis that sat on the banks of a large, grand lake. He, the youngest of the triplet hitmen, had long brown hair and brown eyes.

Raymond Lucius checked the file on his phone. "Yes, that's the hit, Eric Silver, a former Giant Slayer. Command Central verified it," the older brother with short brown hair confirmed. They were staring at a bouncer near the bar entrance that was in a three-piece, light blue suit made of a kevlar-cotton blend.

"So now what? We had to leave our swords in the alley because of that stupid metal detector. Do you want to run at him with a steak knife?" the last brother, Harrison Lucius, asked as he waved the steak knife he got with his burger in the air. He had dyed his hair blonde to feel more original than his siblings. He was also the most violent of the triplets.

"Don't be dumb," Raymond barked sternly at Harrison. He had taken the role of leader of the assassin trio since he was the oldest. "He's worth 8.6 million dollars dead. A former giant slayer won't be easy to kill. Besides, look at his coat. He's armed with two pistols. We need to get him outside somehow so we can catch him off guard," he said as he tried to think of a plan.

Just then an intoxicated girl in a green dress bumped into their table. "Sorry," The brown-haired girl with brown eyes slurred. The Lucius triplets watched as the women stumbled towards the front of the bar.

Harrison sported a cocky grin as he stood from the table. "I know how to get him outside."

"Go with him to make sure he doesn't do anything too stupid," Raymond commanded Norman. "I'll be right behind you." He finished as Norman stood up and joined Harrison in following the drunk girl out of The Concord Bar.

As his brother left the bar with the girl, Raymond threw a large wad of cash on the table and went over to get the attention of Eric Silver. "Sir, you have to come with me. I saw two guys follow a drunk girl out of the bar and I think they are going to hurt her," he said with a convincing panic in his voice.

Eric Silver rushed outside, but as he exited the building and rounded the corner into the neighboring alley, he realized something. The men he had seen follow the poor girl outside looked like the man who had warned him. Just then he heard a *shingk* noise that sounded like someone unsheathing a sword. He looked back just as metal flew through the air towards him. Eric dropped his head, allowing the short sword to swing wide over his black hair, and then in one swift motion delivered a kick to the chest of Raymond Lucius, sending him backwards towards the street. Before Eric could draw one of his pistols, Norman came running at him with a sword identical to the one wielded by his brother. He swung it hastily at his target.

It took all of Eric's skill to keep dodging the fast attacks of the middle brother of Lucius triplets. Eric Silver was finally able to catch his second attacker off balance; he grabbed Norman's left shoulder and tossed him to the ground, but by then, Raymond had recovered from the kick and returned to the fight. The man in the light-blue suit knew he would have to take out one of the brothers quickly as his strategy of defense would only last for so long. He dodged two more of Raymond's slashes before he saw his opening. Raymond had left his head exposed on his last downward swing, allowing Eric to leap into the air and catch him in the jaw with a quick strike from his left foot. After landing, Eric positioned himself to deliver the knockout blow to Raymond. He struck him right in the mouth, sending the unconscious, eldest Lucius brother onto his back.

Norman watched as his older brother fell to the ground. He let out a primal scream as he charged once again, but Eric Silver was prepared for his attack. He quickly dived under the moving blade and rolled from his shoulder to his feet. As he rose upright, he removed the pistol from his left side armpit holster. Norman turned around to find himself staring down the barrel of the all-silver pistol. "Don't do it," Eric spoke calmly, trying to convince his attacker to surrender.

Norman just gritted his teeth and began to slowly lower his blade. Eric saw him giving in and pointed the weapon over towards Harrison Lucius who was struggling to hold their captive with just his left arm as his sword was in his right hand. After seeing Eric turn, Norman thought he saw an opportunity to finish the job. Norman tightened the grip on his sword and lunged at Eric, but he was not caught off guard. The black-haired man fired two shots into the chest of Norman Lucius, killing him instantly. Eric then turned to face the last standing Lucius triplet. Harrison quickly pulled the girl in front of him, using her as a human shield. "You killed my brother. You fucking asshole," the blonde-haired brother said with fear and anger in his voice as he held his sword to his hostage's throat.

"Just let her go and I'll let you walk away with your surviving brother; he's just unconscious. No one else needs to die," Eric spoke calmly. By now, a few of the bouncers and a couple of curious customers had emerged from the bar to investigate the gunshots. Upon seeing the scene, many people began to call the authorities.

Harrison began to panic. The impulsive, youngest triplet's eyes shifted across the large crowd of people watching, blocking the only exit of the alley. His anger began to overtake all reason. "That's where you're fucking wrong. You need to die. So drop your gun and she won't be harmed. It's easy, her life for yours."

Eric stared at him. His serious and emotionless face remained unchanged as he watched for an opening. He considered taking the deal to save this stranger's life. Eric had always looked for a way to make up for the mistakes of his life. Maybe this is how he paid penance.

The woman who was being held captive by Harrison Lucius watched Eric's face. She saw him contemplating, considering the deal, but she could not allow him to do that. She quickly and subtly drove her right elbow into the gut of the man hiding behind her, causing his sword to vacate its spot in front of her throat. The woman then dropped to the ground, giving Eric Silver a wide-open shot that he did not miss. Harrison Lucius fell to the ground dead just as the police arrived.

Over the next couple of hours, the police took statements from all who had witnessed the events. When they learned that Eric was attacked after trying to save the woman's life, they decided not to arrest Eric since he was defending himself with a licensed weapon. "Look, just don't make it a habit to shoot everyone who attacks you," an officer spoke as he uncuffed Eric.

"Yes, sir," he responded without emotion. "May I ask, were you able to find anything about these men?"

The officer shook his head as he put the cuffs back on his belt. "No. They had no identification on them. No credit cards either, just cash and swords. They don't look familiar at all?"

Eric looked again at the remaining Lucius triplet as he was loaded into an ambulance. "Never seen them before today," he spoke honestly.

The officer sighed, "That's what the lady said too. If you think of anything, let us know." He handed Eric a business card with his number before he walked off.

With the office done with Eric, Parker Owen walked over to his employee. "You okay, son?" he asked with genuine concern. Parker was a well-respected member of the community. The Concord Bar had been in his family for generations. The gray-haired man was affectionately referred to as 'Pa' by many because he called everyone son and had a fatherly aura about him, even if the brown-eyed man had no children of his own.

"I'm good, Pa. I'm just confused," Eric responded softly.

"They look professional," he responded as he stroked his bearded chin in thought. "I have a few friends that might be able to get me some information. I just feel terrible for that young lady. Wrong place, wrong time. The chaos of it all has to be frightening,"

Parker said as Eric looked over to the woman who was still sitting with the paramedics.

Eric looked back at Parker. "Anything you can do to help Pa, I appreciate. I always do," he spoke as he patted his friend on his left shoulder. Parker Owen just smiled and walked back towards the bar. Eric stood there looking around the scene, playing the events over in his head as the red and blue lights illuminated the night. He was lost in such deep thought that he was caught off guard by the woman he had saved. He was surprised by how quiet she was, he did not hear her walking up to him. Eric was unsure how to greet a person he had put in harm's way, so he just went simple: "Hello."

The woman smiled at him. "I wanted to thank you for saving my life," she said in a sweet voice that floated in the air like a melody. "I would be dead now if it wasn't for your bravery. I just wanted to know, what's your name?" she asked, staring into the piercing blue eyes of the man with black hair.

He smiled at her. "My name is Eric," he responded. "May I ask your name?"

The brown-haired woman returned his smile. "Dominique."

Well, Dominique, I'm glad you're okay," he said sincerely.

"I wish I could thank you somehow. Maybe I could buy you a drink? I would like to know more about the man who saved my life." She looked up at him with big, brown, doe-like eyes.

Eric smiled, "Could you come by the bar tomorrow around seven, that's when my shift ends? Just tell the bouncer up front you're here to see me. Or we could meet somewhere else. I understand if you don't want to come back here," he suggested, trying to be considerate of the woman's feelings.

Dominique flashed him one last big smile. "I'll be here at seven." With that, the two parted ways for the night.

*****

Eric finished his shift the next day a little early so he could meet with Pa before his date. He was up in Parker Owen's third-floor office wearing a light blue suit nearly identical to the one he had on yesterday. In fact, 90% of his closet contained copies of the one suit. He always joked that it saved time when getting ready each morning.

The third floor of the bar was for employees and private events. There was Parker's office on one end and the employee break room on the other, with a full-size bar between the two rooms. "So any news?" Eric asked the older man who sat across from him at the old, worn-down desk.

"Yeah, I was able to cash in a favor to find out what was going on. He's supposed to send a messenger with some information," Parker finished saying just before a walkie-talkie on his desk crackled to life.

"Pa? You there?" the current bouncer asked.

Parker Owen picked up the radio and clicked the button. "Yeah son, go ahead." He responded.

"You have a visitor for you. A man that says he is expected by you," the walkie informed the room.

"Send him up to the third, son," Parker responded. Eric and Parker stood up and left the office to wait for the man in the top-floor bar.

“Who is this guy you cashed a favor in with?” Eric asked Parker as the gray-haired man struggled to get the radio to stay on his belt.

“Um, oh, yeah,” He responded, distracted by the walkie-talkie. Once he got it, he refocused on the conversation. “He works for Carson Franklin. I figured he would know something. That control freak makes it a priority to know everything happening in this city,” Parker informed Eric.

There were three knocks at the door before it opened. In walked Andrew Aaron Anderson, a tall lanky man with a particularly generic face. He had green eyes and short, spiky blonde hair. He carried a large briefcase and an even bigger smile that had just the right amount of confidence. “Hello there gents, I’m Andrew,” he said casually as he walked over to the bar and sat on one of the red and gold stools.

“Eric,” the black-haired man responded as he joined him on a neighboring bar stool.

“And that must make you Parker,” Andrew said as he pointed at the older man as he took a standing position behind the bar, “a man I’ve heard only good things about.”

“Well thank you, son,” Parker responded, “would you care for a drink?”

The blonde man smiled, “I would love a triple of whisky with three ice cubes,” Andrew responded as he cracked open the case and removed a file from it. He set the file in front of Eric and then pushed the luggage down the bar. “Well, I got bad news Eric.

There is a hit on your head," he said casually. "A very large one actually. If I wasn't taking a break from the business, I would have taken my shot at you," he shared with the other two men in the room who stared back at him with blank expressions. "But I'm here as a friend, not a hitman. My boss doesn't want you dead," he assured them as Parker set down Andrew's drink. "Ah, perfect, thank you," he smiled as he took a sip of his drink.

"Why would there be a hit on my head?" Eric asked calmly as he opened the file.

Andrew finished his sip. "Mmm, that's a damn good whisky," he said before answering Eric's question. "It seems someone has been killing some very rich and powerful people. Those that haven't been killed yet are getting nervous for their lives," he started to explain.

"But that doesn't explain why me. I'm not out there killing billionaires." Frustration entered his words.

"Well, an Interpol investigation revealed that the killer is a former giant slayer, so the list of all known and surviving giant slayers was made and hits were placed in their heads. 100,000 dollars for each level. You know, since a higher level means they should be harder to kill and all." Andrew took another sip of his drink.

Eric sighed in frustration. "So I got a target on my back because of some other asshole's actions." He slammed the file onto the bartop in anger.

"Life's shit. Good news for you, like I said my boss doesn't want you dead and he definitely doesn't want a bunch of hitmen and assassins running around the city trying to kill you. So he's gonna get your name off the list," Andrew informed Eric and Parker as he finished his drink. "He knows you're not the one killing those men."

"How does he know?" Eric asked Andrew.

Parker chimed in with the answer, "Like I told you earlier, he's a control freak that makes everything his business."

Andrew smiled at Pa. "I like that. A perfect name," he joked with a big smile. "The important part is, you're gonna get off the list. You just have to stay alive long enough for it to matter."

That's when the three men heard a knock at the door. They looked over to the open door to find the brown-haired woman, Dominique. "Sorry, am I interrupting?" she asked. Her hair was straightened and she was wearing a light pink sweater and black slacks.

"Not at all, dear. We are just wrapping up," Parker said as he checked his walkie to see if he had accidentally turned it off while attaching it to his belt earlier to figure out why he was not warned of her approach. "I'll walk you out, Mr. Anderson," Parker said to the blonde man as he grabbed his now empty briefcase.

"I'll let you know when your problem is solved. Till them keep your eyes open. That much money goes a long way. Make sure you're keeping good company," Andrew said to Eric with a wink as he stood up. He walked with Parker to the stairs. "You are quite lovely," Andrew said to Dominique with a smile as he walked past her. He turned back to Eric and gave him a thumbs-up with a wink before descending down the stairs.

Parker shook his head at Andrew's antics. "I'll leave you two alone. I have to talk to Bailey about him slacking at the door again," the older man said as he closed the door of the third floor and descended the stairs, leaving Dominique and Eric by themselves.

Eric gave the woman a kind smile, putting the news he had just learned in the back of his mind. "Where would you like to sit?" he asked motioning to the numerous empty seats around them.

"Could we sit at one of the booths?" she asked, pointing at the row of red booths on the other side of the room.

Eric stood from the stool. "Of course. Would you care for a drink? On the house."

"I was supposed to be buying you a drink ... to thank you," Dominique responded as she walked further into the private bar.

The black-haired man chucked a little. "Not necessary. What would you like?"

Dominique smiled, "A red wine." She sat in a booth.

"Coming right up," Eric said with a small smile. He walked behind the bar to a small wine chiller and pulled out a bottle of red wine from 1979. Eric poured two glasses and joined the woman in the booth. Normally, Eric did not drink alcohol, but he did not want to make his guest feel uncomfortable.

The two sat there in the booth for a better part of two glasses of wine each with only the occasional interruption as employees went to and from the breakroom. They talked about everything unimportant: small talk that meant nothing and shared very little for neither wanted to share their past. However, despite the simplicity of the conversation, both were becoming enthralled with each other. "Have you lived in Erniego your whole life?" Eric asked with hope in his words.

Dominique just smiled, "For a couple of years. How about you?"

Eric played with his wine glass, spinning it between his index and middle fingers. He searched for the words he wanted without making himself vulnerable. "I moved here a couple of years ago as well. I lived up north before this."

The woman finished her drink and smiled at the man who sat across from her. "Why the change?" she followed up.

"It was just..." He paused. "Just the right move for me. No special reason at all," he lied.

Dominique smiled, not pushing more. She looked down at her slim, gold watch on her right wrist. "It's almost midnight," she said casually, prompting Eric to look at his watch. "I should get going," the brown-eyed girl said before lingering in the booth. "I've had a wonderful evening."

"It was entirely my pleasure." He grinned. "I enjoyed every moment," Eric added.

"I would like to see you again," Dominique said.

Eric's heart began racing. "I would like to see you again too." Then he remembered the reality that forced her into his life. "But it's not a good time right now. I have some issues I need to take care of. I promise as soon as it's safe..."

"I'll hold you to that," Dominique interrupted.

The two wrapped up their night by walking Dominique home. Neither lived that far away from the bar with her apartment being on the route that Eric would normally take home. From the moment they said goodnight, Eric's mind was only on the woman he spent the evening with.

He reached his front door, put his key into the lock, and opened the door to a dark apartment. Eric's thoughts were far from that room until he flipped on the light switch by his front door and the wrong light turned on. He stopped in the doorway and wondered why the kitchen light had turned on. He reached for the light switch again and then everything went black after a deafening explosion.

Eric woke up in a shock against the hallway wall as dark smoke bellowed into the corridor from his apartment. He coughed as he climbed to his feet and made his way to the stairs. He reached the street and looked up at his building. Fire and ash spilled from his apartment with the fire located where his kitchen used to be. There was a new person trying to collect the 8.6 million.

*****

"I heard you have a problem, Mr. Baez." A man with short black hair spoke in a low and calm voice. The owner of the words was wearing a clean patternless black suit with a matte red tie and was seated in a standard desk chair behind an empty black desk. The room itself was a minimalistic design, using the wall's pristine solid hush-gray paint to act as decoration.

The two men standing across the room were dressed casually, with loose-fitting clothing hanging off their bodies. Their sleeves were rolled up to show their numerous tattoos. "No problem on my end. I'm expanding my territory. If you don't like that, that's your problem," Johan Baez, the leader of the Reyes Rojos, angrily replied. His associate and second-in-command Ricardo Velazquez stood behind him shaking his head in agreement.

The seated man's eye twitched once from being opposed. "I have no problem with that, per say," he began, methodically choosing his words, "though someone else might. The more land you gain, the more others lose. It puts stress on the agreement, but I am sure I could find a deal to get you more land if you believe you need more. I could help you negotiate with the Murphy family to the north or..."

"I think you misunderstand me." Johan's interruption caused the man in the suit to clench his fists as he attempted to control his anger. "I'm not asking permission. I'm takin' what I am owed. We are tired of playing by your rules. You got everyone convinced you're just a middle man, but I see. I see what you really are. You got them fooled into thinking you're nothing, but you have all the power. You're a control freak," he said with pride in himself for revealing the grand conspiracy.

Carson Franklin had been called a control freak his entire life. He always kept his fingernails neat, his clothes without wrinkles, his teeth straight and white, and his hair kept short without a hair out of place. He used to struggle with why potential peers hated that he wanted control. A sense of peace and tranquility came with being in command. Where others let chaos control their lives, he let rules and order control his. Yet, the people in Carson's life always fought for the control they had no idea how to properly use. It was not until he realized that the best way to be in control was to make them think he was not. Carson Franklin sighed, "Therein lies the problem. People just never see the benefit of me being in charge." He spoke softly, more talking to himself than the other men in the room. "There has not been any fighting in the streets in years. There are rules in place to ensure that everyone is happy." His calm demeanor started to slip as frustration entered his tone. "I cannot have the greedy disrupting what I have built."

Johan Baez laughed, "Oh yeah? And what are you going to do about it?" he asked as he raised his shirt slightly to show Carson the pistol tucked inside his waistband.

Carson sighed and made a small motion with his right hand. That's when Johan heard a familiar noise behind him. He looked over his shoulder and gazed down the barrel of a pistol. "Ricky? What are you doin'?" he asked, looking his friend in the eyes and raising his hands.

Ricky was too emotional to respond, so Carson Franklin spoke for him. "Your betrayal was expected, Mr. Baez. You are just not the team-player-type. Mr. Velazquez here understands the benefit of what I bring to the table. A territory war would destroy your community and cost many people their lives for minor gains," he spoke matter of factly. "I would say it has been a pleasure Mr. Baez, but it has not."

With that, he nodded and Ricky fired twice into the back of his friend and former leader. Carson stared at the blood as it pooled on the floor. He hated the sight of blood. It was messy, chaotic, and uncontrolled. It was everything he hated, but he knew better than to trust others to get their deeds done. Carson pulled himself from the red puddle with a deep breath. "Mr. Velazquez, you may go now. I will take care of the few remaining details. You shall inform your compatriots that Mr. Baez was the victim of personal gambling disagreement with a lieutenant of the 3rd Street Wild Hogs, caught cheating again." Johan Baez was a notorious gambler and expected cheater, something that had caused him problems in the past. "You can pick up the compensation tag at the reception desk." The compensation tag was something Carson had implemented shortly after his takeover of Erniego. He created a monetary value for every member of the city's gangs, mobs, and biker clubs. He created this to reduce retaliation killings. Of course, it took strategic action to get it to be accepted and used properly. Carson even had to use some of his own millions that he acquired by being the brains behind an elaborate bank heist group. Ricky just nodded and left the room, not looking back at the friend he had slain.

Once Ricky left, Carson Franklin got up from his chair, walked to the wall on his left, and opened a hidden door that led to a much nicer, brightly lit room. It was decorated with bright colors and works of art. Sitting across the room on a small two-seater couch reading a newspaper was Andrew Aaron Anderson. He looked up at his boss, who was visibly distressed from the events that happened in the other room. "Did Johan enjoy his retirement party?" the blonde joked with an arrogant smile.

Carson did not respond. He sat down in a large ornate chair that looked like it belonged in a king's castle. He reached down to the lowest drawer on his left which was actually a fridge. He opened it and pulled out a chilled glass bottle of ginger ale to settle his nerves. Carson never drank as alcohol would cause him to become inebriated. Being inebriated meant not being in control. He took a sip with his eyes closed and sighed. "He nor the Reyes Rojos will be a problem," Carson said before opening his eyes. "Have the cleanup crew take care of the mess."

"Sounds good," Andrew replied. "Eric Silver is here to see you."

"Let him in," Carson said as he hid his ginger ale in a secret cup holder out of sight.

Andrew got up and opened the door, bringing Eric Silver in from the waiting room. He was wearing the same blue suit he usually wears. Luckily, he kept a few clean ones at work because his entire wardrobe at his apartment fell to the street as ash the night prior. "Eric Silver, Carson Franklin," Andrew said as he walked back to the couch. Eric chose to stand instead of taking a seat in one of the two chairs across from Carson.

Carson smiled and began to speak, "Please to meet you, Mr. Silver. I have good news and some unfortunate news. The good news: I have cleared up your little problem with the powers that put the hit on your head. The catch, however, is that the price on your namesake does not end until the stroke of midnight on Wednesday morning. Now..."

"I have to deal with madmen trying to kill me for five more days?" Eric interrupted.

Carson Franklin closed his eyes and stretched his neck to the right as he paused to keep his composure. He really hated being interrupted. "As I was saying, I understand it may be frustrating, but things of such nature take time," he lied. In reality, the bounty could be removed immediately and dismiss notices sent out to the management organizations with due haste. Carson, however, had them keep the bounty open for a few more days. He was curious to see how skilled of a survivor Eric Silver was. If he proved himself strong enough, Carson Franklin would be gaining a powerful pawn that owed him a debt.

"Usually the person's death is what resolves the bounty, so it doesn't matter," Andrew jumped in, lying for his boss. He had received dismiss notices in the field before; even had targets in his sights about to pull the trigger when the machine he carries prints off the red paper. The blonde man was not certain why his boss was lying, but he found it best to play along than to question.

Eric was annoyed and had a problem showing that. "So that's it?"

Carson did not appreciate his tone. "A thanks would be appreciated, but I am nothing if not understanding of your frustration. Which is why I am willing to assist you more if I can. I have a few leads to determine who has accepted the task of collecting your price. Not many are up to the task of taking you on and even fewer of those utilize explosives as their choice of means. Until then, as you said, that is it," he spoke sternly, ending the meeting.

Eric did not care to stay any longer. He greatly disliked Carson Franklin, something Pa guaranteed would happen. He turned and left the room. Andrew followed him out. "Eric," Andrew called after him, following him out of the waiting room and into the hall.

"Your boss is something else," Eric turned to face Andrew.

Andrew shook his head to the right in agreement. "You're not wrong, but there's something else you should know. No one knew where you were until recently. The bounty has been open for nearly four months and you were listed missing, location uncertain, lost amongst the masses, etcetera, etcetera, etcetera."

"What is your point?" Eric interrupted.

"Someone told them where you are. called an agency and told them where you live, work, and party on the weekends." His joke did not land so he returned to his more serious nature. "I just think you should watch your back," Andrew continued, "Could be nothing. Could be something. Just lay low for the next couple of days and try not to die." He patted Eric on the left shoulder.

"Thanks for the advice." The sarcasm was not lost on Andrew as he watched Eric Silver head to the elevator.

Eric walked outside of the building and turned towards his car. It was an old-school metallic gray square-body car from 1960 that was parked about a block down the street. His mind was fogged from the events of the previous night and the meeting he had just exited. Then a voice cut through his clouded thoughts like a light. "Eric?" softly called to him from behind.

He turned to face her. "Dominique?" he asked with genuine surprise, "What are you doing here?"

"I was coming back from meeting a friend," she replied. "The bus stop is just over there," she said, pointing in the same direction as Eric's car. He turned and noted the blue bus stop sign that was just a stone's throw away from his vehicle.

Eric turned back to face her. She was wearing a black cardigan with brown buttons despite the weather being on the warmer side. "Would you like a ride home instead? It would be no trouble."

Dominique smiled. "I would appreciate that." Eric turned to walk to his car, but she stopped him. "Are you okay?" she blurted out, causing him to face her again. "I heard about your building on the news. I wanted to make sure you were okay."

Eric forced a smile. He appreciated her concern. "I'm fine. It was just an unfortunate accident." He lied, not wanting her to worry about him. Eric was surprised she knew it was his building. He figured he must have mentioned to her where he lived the other night and forgotten he had.

"I just," she started before pausing, "I really enjoyed the time we spent together and when I thought something had happened to you..." She let her voice trail off as if she could not even speak the unfortunate thoughts she was fearing.

"You don't have to worry about anything like that. Everything is fine," he reassured her as she made it obvious she was holding back tears. "Why don't we.." Eric stopped mid-sentence when he heard his car alarm going off behind him. He spun around and watched as a masked man climbed into his car and began to hotwire it. "HEY!" he screamed out as he broke into a full sprint.

The masked man looked over his shoulder and saw Eric running towards him. The car thief just sped up his actions, knowing once he had the car started he could make a clean getaway. He tapped the ignition wire together and the car began to turn over. Finally, it roared to life. Then it exploded.

A bright orange fireball lit up the night sky, causing him to flinch and cover his head with his forearms. He watched as the car burned in front of him. Dominique ran up behind him, a phone in her hands to call the police. "Are you okay?" she asked, her voice filled with fear.

"Fine." Sirens rang out in the distance as Eric just stood there watching the chaos before him. Once again luck intervened, but he knew better than to invest much in pure luck.

*****

After hours of talking to the authorities, Eric returned to The Concord. With his apartment and car destroyed, he spent all day and night on the third floor of the bar, sleeping in a secret room that Parker Owen built into the side of his office for the nights when he was too tired to head home after closing up.

Eric spent the next five days hidden away from the world which marked him for death. Being isolated had nearly driven him mad. Parker would not let Eric work, fearing it would leave him too exposed. All the meals Eric ate were prepared by Parker himself. He did his best to mix it up from time to time, but the meals were still predominantly bar food.

It was six in the afternoon on Tuesday, the last day his hit was open. Eric sat at the bar in his blue slacks and a white t-shirt. He stopped shaving after the second day. His facial area was past the five o'clock shadow but not quite a full beard. He rested on the stool, a bored look in his eyes.

"Food's up," Parker Owen said as he walked onto the third level with two plates of fried chicken sandwiches and fries. He placed one of the dishes in front of Eric and sat in the seat next to him.

"Thanks, Pa." Eric replied as he stared at the greasy food before him. This was the worst he had ever eaten in his life, but he appreciated all the effort the gray-haired man was putting in to keep him alive. Even if it meant clogging his arteries.

Parker Owen could see the distress on the face of the man who sat next to him. "Cheer up, son. It's almost over," he said before taking a large bite of his sandwich.

Eric picked up a fry. "I just hate feeling helpless," he admitted before eating the fried golden string. "I just wish I could do something to get this maniac off my back sooner."

Parker sighed. He once joked that Eric reminded him of a hammerhead shark because he was hard-headed and always kept moving, to which Eric would correct him that their head is not that hard, despite its shape. Parker kept the analogy the same, mainly because that was his favorite shark. Parker decided to distract his employee by reminiscing. "Do you remember the first day we met?" he asked, setting his food back down.

Eric Silver sat up on his barstool. "Yeah, why?" he asked with genuine confusion.

Parker laughed a little, "Do you remember what I said to you?"

A smile emerged on Eric's face for the first time in weeks. "You said a pretty boy like me can only take a few more beatings before the girls stop calling." Both men laughed and Parker softly pounded his fist on the table as he laughed.

The two men had not met by chance. Parker Owen was in need of a new bouncer, someone tough who could take care of the more drunk and aggressive patrons when they got out of hand. One of the bartenders at the time told Parker about this guy he saw fighting at an underground club called Hell in the Wall, about how this man could take a beating and fight back even harder. Parker knew of the place well and had saved other young men from dying on that cement floor. He was confused by how this kid fought. He looked to be just a hair older than 18 and he would let his opponent land shot after shot, refusing to dodge attacks and leaving himself open. Then once he was bloody and bruised, he would begin to unleash a barrage of attacks that would quickly conquer his adversary. After that fight, Parker offered him a job which Eric accepted after very little convincing. "I've seen you fight since," Parker said once he stopped his chuckle. "You never told me why you would let them get so many hits in. Why take the abuse, son?"

Eric took a bite of his food to delay answering. "It was a way to numb the pain."

Parker and Eric had not talked much about his history as a giant slayer up in the wooded forest in the state to the north. "I see. Real bruises to numb the bruises of the heart," Parker responded, allowing the gaps in the conversation to be filled with the muted noise from the floor below. "You never talk about your family."

"Nothing to talk about. After we learned the truth about giants just being brainwashed humans being sent to slaughter; they couldn't live with themselves. So they didn't," Eric shared, his words chosen carefully as the subject was a rough one for him. Similar thoughts had crossed his mind in the dark days before Parker Owen saved him from himself.

Parker cleared his throat as quietly as he could. "I'm sorry to hear that, son. I am sure that realization was a heavy weight to bear. If you don't mind me asking, how many giants did you kill?"

Eric took a deep breath. "I never killed any giants." Eric confessed, which shocked Parker.

"But I thought you made it to level 86? At least that's what the file that what's-his-face gave us." He pointed towards the door with his left thumb over his left shoulder.

"I did, but without killing. All my encounters were listed as draws, even the ones I captured without killing. When I looked at the giants, I saw wild animals. Man is evil, animals just live, defending themselves and their homes. In my last encounter, just days before we learned what the giants really were, I was hunting a level 86 Leviawolf that was spotted in the area and my dad demanded he come along because this was the same one I had encountered before. Each time we fought, it ended in a draw. I refused to kill it and it couldn't kill me. In this last battle, it fell down a small mountain cliff into a river. It climbed onto the bank and was about to escape again. I felt the job was done because he had been diverted away from the town, but my father tried to kill it before it got away. I pushed up the barrel, he missed, and that night we fought, the whole family did. He called me weak for not being able to kill the Giants. I called him a heartless monster. I called them all monsters for not seeing that these 'beasts' were just scared animals." He paused as he got choked up. "Wh-when the news broke that we learned they were just human, they wouldn't look me in the eye. My face reminded them that everything they believed in was a lie. Their guilt over the innocent lives they took was my fault. I..." He stopped.

Parker put his hand on the shoulder closest to him. "It's okay, son."

"I just wish I could tell them I'm sorry for what I said. I wish I could tell them that they are now monsters." Tears began to roll from his piercing blue eyes.

The phone rang and pulled the men from their conversation. Eric made a motion with his right hand, letting Parker know that he was alright and that he could answer the phone. The older man got up and walked into his office. "Parker speaking," he answered the rotary phone. After the other side responded, Parker looked over towards the door and called back into the bar. "Eric...it's for you."

The black-haired man stood and walked over to the phone. He cleared his throat on the way and took the handset from Parker. "Hello?"

"Hello, Mr. Silver, I am glad to hear you are still alive," the monotone voice of Carson Franklin came through the receiver.

Eric rolled his blue eyes. "You don't come across as a man who worries enough to call just to check in."

A soft, slightly annoyed, fake chuckle responded to his remark. "No, I never call without a reason. I have located the man who attempted to kill you. His name is Mason Nobel. If you would like, I can give you the location of where he is hiding, or you could just wait out the deadline and let this man go on to kill another day."

Eric looked over to Parker, who leaned against the wall of his office, watching him. "What's the address?"

*****

Eric Silver shaved and put on his last clean, light blue suit before he loaded his two pistols into his armpit holsters. He had two extra clips in the inside pockets of his coat, a medium-sized knife attached to his belt, and two weapons on his ankles — a small five-shot revolver on the left and a small knife on the right. The black-haired man wanted to be prepared for any eventuality he might face. Lastly, he picked up a blue bandana with a white paisley pattern and a pair of black sunglasses to disguise his face from any potential security cameras. Eric straightened his suit by grabbing his jacket's lapels and pulling it forward. Then the man with blue eyes walked out of the side room, through Parker's office, and into the third-floor bar. It was 11pm.

Eric stopped and stared. "Dominique? What are you doing here?"

"I called her," Parker said, still sitting on a stool at the bar. "I was hoping she could do what I couldn't."

"Don't go Eric," she said with fragile air.

Eric shook his head and rubbed his eyes with his left hand. "You shouldn't be here."

"And you shouldn't be going," Parker interjected.

Eric's frustration began to show more. "I have to go."

"Why?" Dominique asked. "Why do you have to go? Parker told me it all ends at midnight. Why go?"

The question frustrated Eric. He did not know why he had to go. He just knew he did. Eric Silver felt as if he had been challenged by this unknown bomber and that luck was the only reason this maniac had failed. "I'm going," was all he replied with, ignoring her question.

Dominique moved to the side as Eric walked past her towards the stairwell. "So that's it? You're going to kill him?" she asked the back of his head.

Eric stopped and turned back to her. "Would that be so bad?" he asked rhetorically. "This is a killer that blows people up for money. I haven't killed many worse. I killed two men while saving your life, didn't I?"

"I didn't ask you to save my life," Dominique cried, tears forming in her eyes. Eric was left speechless. "If you want to stop him, then bring him to justice," her voice trembled as she spoke.

Eric took a deep breath. "Okay," he practically whispered, "I won't kill him." Eric intended this to be a lie, but as he stared at her, this girl he had just met, and watched the streams of tears wash down her blushed cheeks, the falsehood felt more like the truth. "No one else will die tonight." With that he walked down the stairs; the image of crying burned into his brain. This sight changed his whole plan and he had no idea that they were crocodile tears.

*****

Since his car was destroyed, Eric borrowed Parker Owen's car, with his reluctant permission. He did not fear that it was sabotaged as it was unregistered with the state. It also sat in a single-car garage that could only be accessed by a door in the kitchen and the door that the car left through could only be opened from the inside. Few people knew Parker even had the vehicle.

Eric parked the car out of sight in an alley two blocks away from the abandoned lakeside warehouse where his assassin was hiding. He put on the bandana and sunglasses before he ventured towards the building, avoiding stepping in any street lights.

The black-haired man reached the building. It was all dark except for some lights on the third floor. Eric investigated the perimeter of the building, looking for a way in. He figured it best not to walk through any of the doors as a bomber of Mason's skill most certainly has the doors rigged. On the side of the building that faced the deep blue lake, Eric found a small window that could be reached by climbing on a rusty, grimy dumpster. He investigated his potential entryway and found it safe to enter, allowing him to enter the building in the middle of a stairwell.

Eric quietly removed his disguise before pulling one of his pistols from the holster under his left arm and beginning his investigation of the warehouse's interior. The first floor was clear, containing only dust and broken pallets. The second was just as empty. Then he approached the third floor, hearing the faint sound of classical music. He slowly opened the door, checking for traps as he moved the door. Eric then cautiously entered the room, walking on the balls of his feet. Stacks of wooden boxes marked with various languages littered the floor in an unorganized pattern. Eric got to the center of the room and saw a man seated on a stool at a desk littered with components to make bombs and a compact record player. He raised his gun. "Turn around slowly," Eric commanded.

The man looked up from his tinkering, raised his hands till they were even with his head, and swiveled around at an easy pace to show he was no threat. "It's you," Mason Nobel spoke in a matter-of-fact tone.

"You don't seem surprised to see me," Eric responded while noticing how frail the man before him looked. He was skinny with little-to-no muscle, as if he were just bones covered in flesh. He wore reading glasses and had multiple watches on his arms, three on his left and four on his right. Each was set to a different time, but ticking in sync.

"I figured you would find me eventually. You were the first one of my targets that needed more effort. Was quite frustrating, but I should have expected as much from a level 86 giant slayer," the short man with thinning blonde hair and dull blue-green eyes said over the sound of the orchestra music. "So, are you going to kill me now?"

Eric was unsure himself what he was going to do. He pulled back the hammer of his pistol in response, not wanting to reveal his internal dilemma.

Mason nodded slowly. "I see. If I'm to die anyway. May I tell you a tale? The reason why I am...this. It's something I wish to share before I die." Mason Nobel paused for a moment. With Eric not firing, the bomber took this as his green light to share his origin. "I never wished to be a hired killer. No, I had dreams of being a famous scientist, to be a great mind of my generation. This childhood fantasy, of course, left me with nary a friend. My only companion was my dear pet rabbit, Nitro. He was my everything. His fur was so perfectly white and soft. Thanks to him, it didn't matter to me my classmates wanted nothing to do with me. As long as I had Nitro by my side, my world was perfect. Until that dark day came. Scott Huff, the school bully, found me in the backyard playing with my dear friend. He ridiculed me for having a bunny as a pet. He killed my poor Nitro in front of me and I could do nothing to stop him. I wanted revenge, but I was weak. To fight him would be to sign my own death certificate. I had one advantage: my intelligence. I put a note in his locker, one with forged handwriting to look like his crush wrote it. It told him to meet her in the boiler room after lunch. I knew the neighboring classrooms would be empty at that time. He walked into the room and I set off my first bomb. Scott was the only one hurt. I thought for sure they would know it was me, but the sheriff chalked it up as a freak accident and that the school was lucky only one student was killed. Ever since then, I made sure only my target died. There is a misconception that explosives are just chaotic and uncontrollable, but in the hands of a master they are finesses, they are perfect. I have never seen a bystander hurt by one of my explosives. That was until you got lucky with that man trying to steal your car." Eric was about to pull the trigger, tired of hearing the ramblings of a maniac, when his muscles froze. "I almost believe a higher power wants you alive. I set the one in your apartment to ignite when your kitchen light turned on, but your wiring was different from the blueprints and the wrong switch set the bomb off. I then rigged an incendiary to your ignition only for someone else to get to the explosives first. Then you hid yourself in a crowded bar. I really believed I had missed my opportunity. Your guardian angel had beaten me. You were going to live," he finished with disappointment in his voice.

Eric did his best to hide his shock. The black-haired man assumed Mason had messed up the wiring when he planted the bomb, but a man as meticulous as the one before him would make no such mistake. Yet the wires changed before he got home. Then there was his car, was it really just luck that intervened to save him once again? Or was there another reason? One name came to the forefront of his mind. The person in the middle of his encounter with the Lucius triplets. The girl who knew he was at work the day his apartment exploded. Dominique, who stopped him from his car, but if she was keeping him alive, the question was why?

Mason Nobel could read the confusion on Eric Silver's face like a children's book and took the opportunity that was presented to him. He slowly lowered his hands to his sides. "I envy people like you. You're strong. You have no weaknesses. I have my brain, but it has limitations. Like now, it would be futile to try and beat you. After today, you're the one who got away. The penalty for killing someone after a dismiss notice is death. This is my last opportunity and I stand no chance." His right hand reached behind him under his desk. While still trying to make sense of all the new details he learned, the normally eagle-eyed Eric did not notice Mason as he hit a small red button under the desk. "Well, I have one chance."

The room erupted into flame. Explosives on either side of Eric went off, causing him to discharge his weapon high over his target. Mason leaped from his stool and ran to the main stairwell exit before it was covered by a wall of fire. Small bombs were scattered around the room and building to kill intruders and leave Mason with time to flee with his life. "I have no doubt you will survive this too, so I will be seeing you again, Eric Silver. You will be killed by me one day; I promise you that Mr. 86," Mason called back to Eric, mocking him as he fled.

Eric holstered his weapon as he stood in the middle of the room looking for a way to escape. The direction Mason Nobel had fled in was now covered in bright orange fire after another bomb covered his exit. He staggered through the hot room as it filled with flame and smoke. Then Eric saw water through a window. A last-ditch effort led to him rushing towards his only exit at full speed. Explosions kept going off as he ran for his life. The blue-eyed man reached the glass and jumped, crashing out of the building. The surge of fresh oxygen ignited around him and charred his suit. Eric hoped he had jumped out far enough before gravity pulled him down. His life hung in the fire as the fire lightly burned his skin. Then he began to fall. Eric quickly raced towards the Earth. He turned as he fell so his back would hit first; the black-haired man felt his back hit the old wooden pier that lined the lakeshore. He smashed through the rotted-out planks and plunged into the cold water.

The frigid water surrounded him and slowed him to a stop. Eric felt as though he was floating there for a small eternity, the sight of the burning warehouse distorted through the lake's disturbed surface. He finally swam back up and emerged from the water with a deep gasp for air. Mason Nobel was long gone. Midnight had passed.

*****

It was well past one in the morning. Eric, still wet from his impromptu dive in the lake, sat at the third-floor bar drinking a bottle of whisky. "You can't honestly think he was tellin' the truth. Can ya, son?" Parker Owen asked Eric as he finished another glass.

"Why would he lie?" Eric asked as he poured himself another drink. "It wasn't like he was saying it to save his life. He was complaining."

Parker sighed. Early in the night, Dominique left shortly after Eric did because she did not want to wait around to find out he got himself killed. Parker did not blame her for feeling that way. "So what now? What are you going to do about her, son?"

Eric stared at the caramel-colored liquor. "I have no idea, Pa, but I don't think she wants me dead."

"You're going to see her again?" Parker was shocked. "Are you sure that's wise?"

Eric knew it was completely irrational to want to see her again, but there was something about her that made him feel safe. Even now, with the knowledge that she was hiding something from him, that feeling remained when he thought of her. Dominique was a mystery and he wanted more even if she turned out to be dangerous. "You know how you always say, 'if you numb the pain, you numb everything'? Well, I think she might bring pain, but she could be everything." He smiled as he thought of her.

Parker's radio clicked to life, "Pa, Eric has a visitor at the door."

Eric laughed to himself and looked at Parker Owen. Parker took the black-haired man's look to mean one thing. "He said send her up," the older man responded to his radio.

Parker was about to walk into his office when Eric called him back. "He called me 86, you know." He took a final sip of his drink. "86, like when you get banned from a bar. I'm who you'll see if you're not welcome anymore. If you get out of line, I'm the one who will take care of you. A man like Mason Nobel doesn't deserve to walk away. The next one won't. I like being 86," Eric laughed a little drunkenly as Dominique opened the door. Eric glanced over at her with a smirk on his face.

Parker chuckled, "I like it too, 86," he joked back as he walked into his office, closing the door behind him.

Dominique sat down next to Eric at the bar. She ignored the end of the previous conversation. "Did you...?" Her voice trailed off.

Eric shook his head. He wondered if this was an act. "No. I hesitated and he got away," he replied before finishing his refill. "He said a guardian angel was the only reason I was alive," Eric laughed softly, glancing over to her with a smirk.

Dominique looked into his blue eyes. He was looking at her differently, no longer viewing her as fragile. He seemed to know she was hiding something from him, yet his eyes invited her into his life anyway. Dominique smiled a unique smile that was both coy and devilish. "Then let's drink to your guardian angel," she said as she took a glass from behind the bar and poured them both a glass of whisky. They clinked the glasses and drank.

They talked until dawn broke, finishing one bottle and then another, once again talking about everything unimportant. One night Eric will solve this riddle disguised as the cute, brown-eyed woman, but he has no interest in doing so quickly, because what would be the fun in that?

He walked her home to her apartment again as before, though this time it was less because he was concerned for her safety and more to keep the night going. When they reached the door to her building after the slow walk home, they stopped and faced each other. "See you soon, angel," he teased with a cocky smile.

Dominique smiled once again with her trademarked, unique grin. Eric found it adorable. He learned in and she kissed him. The brown-haired girl grabbed his face in her hands as he wrapped his around her: a kiss that would last on their lips until they met again. With that, Eric Silver walked back to The Concord and Dominique went inside.

Her apartment was normal: a couch, a TV, a bed. Everything you would expect a modern living space to have, except for the wall full of pictures of Eric Silver. Surveillance photos of him all over the city dating back to his sixth month in the Erniego. There were images of him working at the bar, walking in the city, relaxing in his apartment, and even ones of him fighting at the Hell in the Wall club. The brown-haired woman stared at her wall with a confident smile. Then she heard the floor creak behind her, but before she could react, an arm wrapped around her throat and pulled her head back. "You're a crazy bitch," said Raymond, the last surviving member of the Lucius triplets, "but dropping your bloody, dead body at the front door of that bar will be payment enough to get back at that fucking asshole for killing my brothers," he angrily whispered into her ear through gritted teeth. Raymond's face was still badly bruised from his battle with Eric Silver.

Dominique remained calm. She jabbed her left elbow into her attacker's gut and spun out of his hold. Before he could recover, Dominique kicked him in the back of the knee, dropping him to a kneeling position. She grabbed his head and snapped his neck in one swift motion. Raymond Lucius fell to the floor dead. "Sorry,"

Dominique cooed as she flashed a big smile, "but I don't need to pretend to be a damsel in distress anymore."

Zombre vs. Red Reaper

There is an eternal internal struggle within all. Self-doubt and fear tangle with human emotions, creating monsters within the subconscious. Those who refuse to fight the creatures of the wicked soul are consumed by them.

*****

What do you think the reward is?" Redford asked his older, but shorter brother in an early Germanic language as they walked along a dirt road towards the nearby village on the bright sunny day. Both blonde boys were dressed in simple, neutral color leather garments, stitched by hand by their mother. They lived an uncomplicated life on their small family farm that produced only a little more than they needed to survive.

"I am not sure. Aberlin just said a merchant set up a tent for some contest. He did not say what you get if you win," Wolfgang responded in the same language. Normally, the two brothers would still be working the land, but their father allowed the two eldest brothers, 16 and 15 respectively, to take a few hours off as they had been working so hard, as long as they picked up a few things while they were in town.

The two boys shared their guesses on what potential prize awaits them when they win the strangers game: treasures, royalty, a magical creature to raise as their own, the possibilities were endless for the brothers who often used imagination to escape the monotonous struggles of their daily lives.

When they finally arrived in town, they found a large blue tent, created using a wagon and two wooden posts. There was a line, longer than they expected, leading up to the temporary shelter. "We will not get back by sundown like father asked if we wait in this line." Redford sighed as he stretched his neck to see the front of the line from their position at the end. Even though he was younger, he was more mature than his brash older brother.

"Do not worry about father," Wolfgang scoffed. "Besides, when we return with arms full of treasure, father will dance like the town drunk." The image of the stern and serious patriarch prancing around the room in a ridiculous celebration made both boys laugh.

The line moved at a constant pace. A person would enter and leave shortly after, frustrated and disappointed. "What do you think the game is?" Redford asked.

Wolfgang shrugged. "Who knows, but it seems no one is winning. I should save everyone's time and go to the front now," he laughed.

By the time the two brothers reached the front of the line, they had to decide who would go first. "I'm the oldest, I will go first," Wolfgang commanded as he stepped in front of his brother. It was the rule of their family. The oldest got the most difficult chores and responsibilities, but in return was rewarded accordingly. Redford had no counter, so he just motioned with an open palm toward the opening of the tent.

Wolfgang walked through the opening to find a tall man sitting behind a table with various weapons of different shapes and sizes. Across from the table was another chair. "Welcome. Please have a seat." The tall man spoke in the same language as Wolfgang, but his dialect had a slight accent as it was not his primary tongue. The tall man was also wearing a large fur hat that covered his ears, which Wolfgang thought was strange. The climate of the region was on the colder side, but it was still in the summer months and quite warm for such headgear.

Wolfgang sat down and noticed how short the chair was; it forced him to look up towards the already tall man even more. Feelings of inadequacy began to slip in.

"Let us begin with a simple question. What is your name?" the tall man asked.

"Wolfgang."

The tall man nodded. "Good, good. I am Wayland. Now, which weapon would bring you the most respect?"

Wolfgang shifted his gaze from Wayland to the table of weapons before him. There were swords, maces, axes, spears, and daggers from various parts of the globe. After surveying his choices, Wolfgang finally selected. "This one," he said pointing at a large, shining broadsword. "This one is big enough to bring you respect."

Wayland nodded his head and sighed as another person failed his test. "Thank you, you may go now."

Wolfgang's heart sank as a frown formed on his face. "That's it? What about the reward?"

"There is no prize for failing. You may go now," Wayland said in a matter-of-fact tone. It was not his intention to be rude, but after hours of failed candidates all asking the same question, his patience had worn.

Wolfgang scoffed and got up from his seat. He exited the tent to the waiting eyes of his younger brother. "How did it go?" Redford asked.

"It is just a stupid trick. Let us go home," Wolfgang responded as he began to walk away.

"Wait, I still need to go,." Redford protested, stopping his older brother in his tracks.

The older brother turned back. If his brother wanted to go embarrass himself so badly he would let him. "Fine, go ahead," Wolfgang said. Redford smiled and walked through the opening.

Wolfgang walked around the side of the tent, looking for an opening so he could watch his brother fail. He found a small hole near the bottom of the tent. Wolfgang crouched down and spied into the tent. Wayland and Redford had just finished their introductions. "Now, which weapon will bring you the most respect?" the tall man asked. Even though Redford was around the same height, the short chair still forced him to look up towards Wayland, though not as much as Wolfgang had to.

Redford surveyed the weapons. Wolfgang waited in anticipation for his younger brother to pick the wrong one just as he had. "It does not matter," Redford replied after contemplation.

Wolfgang stifled his laugh. 'How ridiculous,' he thought to himself.

"Interesting." The eldest brother's cheerful mood and smile vanished as he heard Wayland answer. "Even this one?" the tall man asked as he pointed towards the smallest weapon, a short dulled silver bladed dagger with a leather handle that was dyed a dark purple.

Redford stared at the blade. "Yes, it is the skill one poses with the weapon that brings them respect, not the weapon itself."

Wayland nodded his head, finally, he may have found who he was looking for. He took the dagger and presented the sheathed weapon to Redford. "Here, take it." Redford took the weapon and surveyed it. "How do you feel? Any different?" Wayland asked.

Redford looked up at the tall man and shrugged. "I feel the same. Am I supposed to feel different?" he asked.

Wayland smiled and clapped his hands once. He had finally found a worthy user. "Not at all. Thank you my lad, you may go now."

Redford smiled, "You're welcome. Here is your dagger back." He attempted to hand back the weapon, but Wayland held up his hands, palms out towards the boy in refusal.

"No, no my lad, that is yours to keep. That is the prize. Please, take it and go," he congratulated the boy as he stood to escort him out.

Redford smiled and left the tent to find his brother, but Wolfgang was frozen in place. 'A trick? It was all a trick question. This is unfair. Absolutely mad,' he thought to himself. Then he considered the prize. 'A dagger? A tiny, insignificant dagger? No riches, no treasures. A small dagger. Who cares if I did not get a prize as stupid as that one,' he justified to himself as he stood up and went to rejoin his brother.

"Thank you everyone for coming, but the contest is done," Wayland announced to the line, still waiting for their turn to compete in his game. The crowd dispersed with murmurs and curses.

Wolfgang joined his younger brother. "Wolfgang! I won!" Redford exclaimed as he showed off his new dagger.

"Such a small prize?" Wolfgang scoffed. "I would ask for a new prize," he belittled as he began walking away from his younger brother.

The two brothers made a quick stop to grab the new farm tool and bag of feed they were asked to get from the village before they began their journey home. The sun was still up meaning they should be home just before their father would become angry with their tardiness. They soon ran into trouble. The first half of the route they walked home followed along the ridge of the forest. The siblings were not far from the village when three men emerged from the tree line. "So you are the lucky brat who stole our prize?" the man in the middle asked in the same language the two boys speak. He was the oldest of the three, in good shape but his face was worn from the years. The man and his two compatriots were dressed in green and black fabric, representing they had some nobility. They were from the nearby castle where the lord of the land resided; they were nephews and cousins of a lord with many heirs, meaning they would never have a claim to land themselves, but enjoyed the perks that came with being in a wealthy, respected family. They had just arrived in town that day and were walking up to the line when Wayland announced they were too late. "If you are smart, you will hand over the prize and walk away," the man in the middle said before drawing his sword; the other two drew their swords as well.

Wolfgang backed up at the sight of their weapons, he was holding the farm tool, which he held out in a defensive position. "Just give it to them. A stupid dagger is not worth dying," the eldest brother said in fear.

Redford dropped the feed bag and pulled out the dagger, unsheathed. His brother was right, no prize was worth their lives.

He was about to hand it over when the blade began to glow a fuschia purple color and grew to the length of the men's swords. "What the?" Redford astonished to himself.

The three men stepped back in shock. "How did you do that?" the man in the middle asked Redford.

"He possesses magic," the man on the left blurted out.

"If we gave such a weapon to Uncle, he would surely reward us in turn," the final man of the right chimed in.

The man in the middle tightened his grip on his sword. "Get it," he commanded before he charged and swung at Redford, who blocked the attack before stepping to the side to stop another sword strike from the man on the right. The man on the left waited back, allowing his two comrades to do the heavy lifting.

Steel flew through the air, clashing with fury. While Wolfgang and Redford's father had taught them the basics of defending themselves with a pair of rusted swords, compared to men who are formally trained regularly, they should stand no chance. Yet, Redford defended himself like a pro against the two attackers.

The blade was infused with a common Elvish spell known as the "Master's knowledge." It was used by Elves to train their armies quickly. The spell allowed the first person, after the magic-maker, to grip the handle of the unsheathed blade to gain all they needed to know to use the weapon and its powers. The incantation allowed Redford to learn things about his new dagger that would normally take years of intense training.

Redford swung his dagger-turned-sword at the center man, who lifted his sword in defense, but their blades never clashed. Instead, Redford shrank his weapon back down to its normal size in a sudden flash of purple light, passing by the defending sword. Redford then spun the dagger in his right hand so the blade faced his opponent and then the dagger once again returned to the larger size. Redford's sword was now between the man and his weapon. Using the leverage to his advantage, he pulled his arm back, slicing open his opponent's hand, who dropped his sword in pain. As Redford turned his body, he placed his left hand on the back of the center man's head, pushing him to the ground.

As the man fell to the dirt, disarmed and injured, Redford turned to defend himself against the second man. He waited for an opening. The man who started on the right swung his sword and Redford ducked to dodge, he then grew his sword in the purple light to the size and shape of the long, curved farm tool his older brother was holding, using it to trip his opponent by catching the back of his ankle and pulling it towards him. The man rocked back and fell hard onto his back, hitting his head on a small rock.

With two men on the ground, Redford turned to face the third, his dagger back to its traditional size. The final man trembled in fear; he did not want to fight after seeing his friends fall so easily. Luckily, he did not have to. The man who started in the center rose from the ground, holding his bleeding hand. "Forget it. Let us get out of here," he said as he began to run off, the man who started on the right took off behind him, followed shortly by the other man on the ground, who stopped to grab his cousin's weapon from the road.

"What was that?" Wolfgang asked his brother as he sheathed the dagger.

"It was the dagger. It...I do not know how to describe it," the younger brother explained poorly.

"Well give it to me. I want to try," Wolfgang commanded.

A voice in Redford's head warned against that. He knew the dangers of letting the dagger fall into the wrong hands because it was part of the information passed on to him by Wayland. The younger brother knew that jealousy would overpower them and the end result would not be pretty, but it was his brother, he did not want to hurt him. "Maybe later. We should be heading home now."

"Right," Wolfgang responded with a mixture of disappointment and frustration. The younger brother picked up the feed bag and noticed that it had torn open when he tossed it down and ground. "Look what you did!" Wolfgang yelled as he looked on. "Now we have to get another one. We will never make it back in time."

"I am sorry," Redford responded as he tried the bag shut to prevent any more of its contents from falling out.

Wolfgang shook his head in disapproval as he counted the modest amount of coins they had left. If he used some of his personal stash, they would have enough to replace what was lost. "Thanks to your stupid prize, I have to use my coins to go get more." He tossed the farm tool onto the ground at his brother's feet. "Here, take this and explain to father how you made me late," he snarked before turning back towards the village.

Redford picked up the repaired sack and the farm tool. He watched as his older brother walked away angrily back to town, unsure of what to say to his brother or if there was anything he could say.

Wolfgang returned to the village and purchased the second bag of feed. As he walked out of the store, the sun began to set and all the buildings had lanterns out front to provide extra light. Wolfgang found the sight calming, he had never been in the village this late. As he looked around, he noticed Wayland, still wearing his fur hat, packing up his tent into his wagon. Wolfgang decided to speak his mind. "Excuse me?" he said as Wayland tossed up a tied-up section of tent fabric into his wagon. "May I have a word?"

Wayland turned to face the boy holding the feed bag. He did not recognize him. "Sorry, the reward has already been claimed," the tall man in the hat said as he reached down to grab another item to toss into the wagon.

Wolfgang set down the feed bag. "I know. My brother won. I saw the dagger in action and it was wonderful. I want to know why I was not chosen."

Wayland placed the last pack into his wagon, leaving only the two large wooden posts still left to be packed. "Because you failed the test." He remembered the boy now.

The words seemed so wrong to Wolfgang. "Failed? But... but it was a trick question. How can I fail a trick?" Anger began to seep into his words.

Wayland sighed. "It was no trick. It was to expose your jealousy. Jealousy comes from your own self imposed fears of inadequacies. It makes you crave what others have to improve yourself. I have traveled through countless towns looking for one without jealousy in their heart. You, like countless others, failed to recognize what your brother knew. The possessions and views of others do not matter. When he held the Dagger of Envy, he did not give in and allow the feelings of self doubt to poison his mind," the tall man explained as he pulled the first log out of the ground and walked it to the side of his wagon and placed it onto the side. "In your hands, it would drive you mad in an attempt to quench your jealousy."

Rage filled his very being. 'What did this stranger know? He does not know me. He thinks my younger brother is better than me? He is wrong. I will show him that he is wrong.' These words rang through his mind.

"Now if you will excuse me," Wayland interrupted his internal breakdown as he pulled the last pole from the ground and packed it onto the side of his wagon, "I wish to get some supper." He looked at the rage-filled face of the boy, recognizing the pain. "Look, if you want to prove me wrong, be happy for what your brother has earned."

Wolfgang watched as the man left him alone in the darkness. He stood there for a while, unable to move. He did not remember his journey home. It was filled with hate, anger, and jealousy. When he finally reached his family farm, he saw the soft orange glow of a lantern leaking from the barn. He peeked through the door and watched as his younger brother practiced with the dagger on a wooden post. 'A weapon that can turn into any weapon and keeps it as a pathetic dagger?' Wolfgang thought to himself. He entered the wooden structure.

The sound of the door opening turned Redford's attention from his practice to the entrance. "Wolfgang, you are finally home! Are you okay?" he asked, noting the anger on his brother's face.

Wolfgang dropped the feed bag onto the ground carelessly. "I talked to the man."

"Wayland? The one from the tent? What did he say? Redford asked, perplexed by his brother's demeanor.

"That I was not good enough to hold your stupid dagger," Wolfgang said as he walked slowly into the barn. There was a strange look in his eyes that Redford had not seen before. "Give me the dagger," the older brother commanded.

Redford stood still. "Why?"

His brother's resistance angered him, "To prove him wrong," Wolfgang responded as he approached his brother, stopping just in front of him. "To show him that I am worthy."

The younger brother placed his hand on the dagger's hilt. "I am unsure, Wolfgang," Redford hesitated. The Master's knowledge spell included warnings. Redford knew what would happen if the wrong person got a hold of the weapon and a life of watching his older brother made Redford certain Wolfgang had no mastery of his jealousy.

"You agree with him," Wolfgang scoffed at his realization. "I cannot believe it, you are my brother."

"I am sorry, Wolfgang," the taller boy began as he stepped past his brother and left for the door. "I will see you in the morning."

The events that followed were a blur to Wolfgang. He reached down, grabbed a large rock at his feet, and swung it at his brother. Redford collapsed to the ground, blood gushing from his head. With his brother disoriented, Wolfgang reached down and took the contested dagger. "See?! Nothing bad happened. You underestimated me! But you were wrong!" Wolfgang screamed as he stared down at his younger brother who lay on the loose dirt.

Then a voice spoke calmly in the back of Wolfgang's head. 'If you kill him, it is all yours.' Redford looked up at Wolfgang in terror as blood spilled over his eyes. There was a still silence in the orange glow of the lantern light as the brothers watched each other, waiting for someone to make a move. Redford started a desperate crawl for the door and Wolfgang pounced, driving the dagger into the ribcage of his younger brother, piercing his lungs. Redford gasped in pain as Wolfgang repeatedly stabbed him. Wolfgang's anger and jealousy fueled him to destroy the very thing that challenged to take what he wanted.

After numerous strikes, Wolfgang stood slowly and stared down at the bloodied body of his dead brother, Redford. The red liquid dripped from the tip of the dagger and stained his hands and clothes. In that moment, Wolfgang died in essence with his brother and from the blood was born Red Reaper.

In the years that followed, Red Reaper traveled the land looking for Wayland so he could show him he was wrong. As he ventured, he learned of the seven other weapons forged by the tall man. Red Reaper began to collect them by hunting down the men and women who had been deemed worthy to wield such powerful magic weapons. As the years passed and his collection grew to contain all seven weapons of sin, the man clad in crimson armor became obsessed with having every weapon created by Wayland. Eventually, Red Reaper's memory changed as a side effect of possessing such powerful weaponry. His memory lied to him, telling him that his brother surrendered the Dagger of Envy willingly and encouraged Red Reapers on his journey to complete the collection before going on to live a normal and long life until he died of old age.

*****

It had been three weeks since Zachary Ombre's encounter with the Cult of Arios Pearl. The brown-haired man still had a few bruises and sprains from this fight under that warm summer moon. Every night since that event, he stopped by the construction site where the church he defeated Arios Pearl used to stand, but all traces of zealots were gone. It looked like a standard work site, at least as far as Zachary could tell.

The regular checkups on the lot of dirt and rubble were not the only thing that Zachary was doing after his near loss to the egotistical power-hungry leader. He decided to finally learn to fight. He found an instructor who taught adults self-defense at the local community center. Zachary was slowly improving, but not as fast as he would have liked.

It was a cool night in San Gwynn with a full moon high shining down. Zachary Ombre stood on a roof from across the church in his Zombre persona, dressed in a white t-shirt, black nylon, and polyester pants, his curved Roman Sica in his right hand, and the faceplate of Arios Pearl's skull that he had transformed into a mask. It took him a couple of washes, but he was finally able to get rid of the aged smell it had. He stared down at the construction site, waiting for the night guard to finish his inspection and leave. The man dressed in the all-black security uniform exited, driving down the street and out of sight. Zombre descended to investigate.

He walked through the dirt lot, looking for anything out of the ordinary, but, like each search he conducted prior, there was nothing suspicious to find. Zombre was starting to feel he was chasing ghosts after another failed inspection. He returned to his apartment to get some sleep before work.

Zachary took off his mask on his building's roof and climbed down the fire escape. He opened the window, turned on the TV, and turned the lights on. Zachary did a quick check of his living area to make sure there were no intruders before he relaxed for the night. He changed into sleepwear, worn-out blue lounge pants, and a loose-fitting, black t-shirt, and was about to settle into bed when there was a knock at his door. His clock read 5:45 am. The gray-eyed man grabbed his blade and walked to the door. He hoped it was his elderly neighbor, Mr. Harwas. It was not uncommon for him to stop by early in the morning to ask for a favor. Zachary looked through the door lens. A brown-haired man wearing an open black trench coat, dark shirt, and black jeans stood on the other side. "I know you're home. Let me in so we can talk." The man spoke as if they were old friends. Zachary remained silent, continuing to watch through the curved glass. "I'm unarmed," the man continued, holding his coat open to show his lack of weapons.

"O...okay," Zachary finally responded as he unlocked the door and opened it. He kept his sword in his right hand, hidden behind the door. "What do you want?" Zachary asked. He had few social interactions. Most of the people he dealt with were customers at the fast food place he worked and he found bluntness worked the best in those conversations. The only real friend he had was his elderly neighbor, Mr. Harwas.

The brown-haired man with blue eyes flashed a small smile. Zachary looked younger than he was expecting, "Mind if I come in?" he asked, motioning towards the apartment. Zachary noticed something weird about the strange man. The gray-eyed man saw no weaknesses. Ever since his encounter with Arios Pearl and his worshipers, Zachary could see exploitable injuries — things like Hairline fractures and internal bruises — when he held his sword.

Zachary looked over his shoulder quickly and then back to the man in the hall. "I think here is fine." He was hesitant to let his guard down after the last time strangers were in his apartment. The gray-eyed man also did not want the mystery man to see the weapon he was hiding behind the door.

The other man laughed, "If I wanted you dead, you would be dead."

"That's not as reassuring as you thought it was," Zachary responded.

"Fair, but it would also be pointless to try and kill an undead man."

Zachary involuntarily swallowed and tried to act confused instead of surprised. He failed. "What are you talking about?" he stuttered.

"So you're not the man who fights crime in a mask that the tabloids call a zombie?" the man in the hallway rhetorically asked.

Zachary stepped back to allow his visitor to enter. "Come inside."

The man walked into the apartment and Zachary closed the door. He no longer cared if the man saw the weapon in his hand. The mystery man looked around his studio apartment before turning back to Zachary and addressing the sword in his hands. "That's a beautiful blade," he commented as if he did not seem to care that the gray-eyed man was armed, as if he expected it.

"Who are you and what do you want?" Zachary asked, becoming increasingly impatient.

"You can call me Hunter," he said as he held out his right hand for a handshake. Zachary just stared at him. Hunter shrugged and receded the formal greeting. "I want to know how you're connected to Advanced Phenotype Genetics."

Zachary was confused. He had never heard of the company. "I don't know what this is."

"Then why have you been snooping around the construction site downtown the last three nights?" Hunter asked, becoming more interrogative.

"I'm looking for remnants of the cult that tried to kill me there when it was still the church." Zachary replied. The man made it clear he knew a lot about him, so there was no need to be nuanced.

"A cult?" Hunter asked for clarification. "So you have nothing to do with AP Genetics?"

"Nope, just a bunch of crazies that worshiped some giant monster named Arios Pearl," he replied.

Arios Pearl was a name Hunter recognized from the data he had stolen from AP Genetics and from research he had done on the company's founding. Rumors of an ancient king who turned himself into a giant, but Hunter always thought it was a myth to romanticize the atrocities. "Interesting," Hunter said softly, almost under his breath. "So, Arios Pearl is real. Then what happened at the church?" His voice went back to normal volume.

"They tried using my sword to bring him back to life but I stopped them," Zachary bragged, for some reason he wanted to impress the mystery man.

Hunter shrugged, "Well, I'll get out of your hair." He said as he reached for the door and opened it. "I'll be talking to you again soon. I just need to dig a little deeper than I thought." Hunter walked into the hall. "By the way, I would try to blend into a small crowd before heading back here, it's too easy to follow you back." Hunter shared the advice before leaving for the door.

"Thanks," Zachary replied with a single wave of his left hand as he watched Hunter walk down the hall to the stairs. "That's actually a good idea," the gray-eyed man said to himself as he locked his door and went to bed.

*****

Zachary finished his shift at work and changed into his Zombre disguise. He stuck to his usual location on the lower side of San Gwynn, using the even rooftops of the valley's buildings to get around. The brown-haired man decided to avoid the mysterious construction site that night.

It was once again a quiet night. Aside from a few purse thieves, there was not much crime for Zombre to intervene in. Then he saw a strange-shaped balloon from a couple of roofs over. As he got closer, he noticed it was a party balloon of a cartoonish zombie. Zombre rolled his eyes as he inspected the helium-filled plastic. There was a piece of paper attached to the red ribbon of the balloon. "If he wanted to talk, he could leave a note at my door," he griped, assuming this was a ruse from Hunter.

But it was not from the mysterious man he had just met the night prior. The letter only had an address on it and a code to unlock the side door; it was for the Natural History Museum located in the Wharfway borough. There was no hint at who it was from. Even if it was dumb, Zombre went anyway.

*****

Zombre walked through the red side door marked 'security' with his sword drawn; even if he thought Hunter had lured him here, he did not fully trust the man he just met yet. He slowly made his way through the empty and dark building, looking for the person who summoned him there. The gray-eyed man approached a main room that held an exhibit on medieval weapons from holy wars of history; it was the only room illuminated.

Standing in the center of the room, looking at one of the exhibits as he waited, was a man in head-to-toe armor with a cloak and hood, all the color of crimson blood. The man looked up as he heard Zombre approach. "Ah, welcome. I have been expecting you." He spoke in an unrecognizable European accent. He pulled down the hood that covered his head and revealed his helmet. It had many small holes over the eyes and seven vertical slits over the mouth and jaw of the face plate.

"I was not expecting you," Zombre responded. "Who are you?"

The man in armor laughed deeply. "I am a collector who seeks to finally complete their collection, but in terms of names, you can call me Red Reaper." He placed his right fist over his heart in a salute.

Zombre nodded as he looked around the room at all the weapons that surrounded them. He decided to ignore the strange, ominousness of the man's name. "Is this your collection?"

Red Reaper was comically amused by his question. "No, this exhibit is impressive, but not as substantial. My pieces are something to truly behold," he boasted.

"So what does it have to do with me?" the brown-haired man in the skull mask asked. Zombre was hoping the mystery man was not a crazy person who collected people.

"When I read rumors of your escapades of fighting crime and surviving fatal wounds in the tabloids, I thanked the heavens above that the missing piece had finally surfaced: the legendary Sword of Purgatory that I have spent countless years looking for," Red Reaper explained as he pointed to the weapon in Zombre's hand.

The gray-eyed man glanced down at his sword. 'Is that what this is?' Zombre thought to himself. What neither man in the room knew was that this was not the Sword of Purgatory. "Sorry, but it's not for sale."

Red Reaper lowered his hand to his side and clenched his fists, attempting to hide his anger and frustration. "I understand. I figured I would offer my services as someone that can be trusted with such a powerful weapon. There are many dangerous people out there that may come after you to get that sword. If you change your mind or suddenly realize it is not worth the hassle to your life, you can find me here."

"That's it?" Zombre asked, surprised by this outcome.

"That is it," Red Reaper replied. "I am not a villain, simply a collector of fine and unique weaponry. You are free to go if you do not wish to turn over your sword."

Zombre began to back peddle out of the room slowly. "Alright, I'm leaving now then," he said, keeping his eyes on the man in the red armor.

Red Reaper saluted with a single wave. "Remember, if you change your mind. I will be here," he called after Zombre as the gray-eyed man disappeared into the darkness. With Zombre gone, the man in crimson armor stood in anger. "I will have that sword," he remarked to himself through gritted teeth.

*****

Zachary returned to his home. He used Hunter's suggestion and blended in with a large crowd leaving some bars in the Wharfway, hiding his mask and blade in a collapsible duffle he had hidden in his pocket. The brown-haired man had been home watching TV for less than an hour — and still in his Zombre shirt and pants — when there was a knock at his door. Once again, he checked through the door lens while holding his sword. "What does he want?" Zachary asked loud enough that it could be heard before opening the door.

Once Hunter could see Zachary, he responded to the gray-eyed man's rhetorical question. "I want to ask you some more questions. May I come in?" He was wearing khakis and a light blue zipper jacket that was closed.

"Sure," Zachary said while moving so Hunter could enter the apartment. "You a big museum guy?" he asked, suspicious of his new friend.

Hunter laughed and turned back to Zachary. "Are you asking me on a date or if I've been sight seeing while in town?"

Zachary was caught off guard. "What? No, I just meant...I had a strange meeting at a museum earlier in the night with a nut job calling himself Red Reaper or something."

"Was he one of Arios Pearls men?" Hunter asked, ignoring the actual reason he stopped by.

"I don't think so," Zachary responded. "I think he's just a new crazy person that wants to get his hands on the blade. He called it the Sword of Purgatory." The gray-eyed man paused to see if Hunter would react to the name.

Hunter just stared at him. "That means nothing to me. My world travels usually took me to different circles," the blue-eyed man responded.

"Well, regardless, he wanted it for his 'collection' and I said no."

"So what did he do?" Hunter asked.

Zachary moved and sat in a chair in his kitchen, his blade still in his hand. He looked up at the brown-haired man. "Nothing. Let me walk away."

"Weird," Hunter responded before changing the topic. "I just stopped by to give you an update on what I learned."

"What did you learn?" Zachary asked.

"I was able to get into their computers at the construction site," Hunter began as he unzipped his jacket and pulled out a pile of papers that were folded into thirds in an interior pocket and tossed them on the table. Zachary noticed the Glock holstered to his hip. "AP Genetics and Arios Pearl's cult are connected. Now that I knew what I was looking for, I was able to find internal payments between the two. The cult didn't run the company, but both benefited from the other. Same thing with Kap Securities and Raze Construction."

Zachary looked at the papers full of money trials and evidence. "I don't know what this means," he admitted to missing the bigger picture.

Hunter simplified his point. "Basically, there are three companies that are pretending to be independent, but they are run by people who have pledged an oath to Arios Pearl and his cult."

"So this is far from over?" Zachary asked.

The blue-eyed man shook his head. "Most likely."

"Fuck." Zachary sighed. "Well, I don't have time to worry about that right now, I have to deal with this red asshole."

Hunter shook his head. "If you need help with that, let me know."

"Thanks," Zachary responded. "Do you want something to eat or drink?" the gray-eyed man asked, pointing over his shoulder to his fridge. He felt as though he had to be polite and offer something to his guest.

“I’m good, thank you,” Hunter politely declined. “I have to get going.” He walked over to the door, stopping just short before turning back to Zachary one last time. “I was serious. If you need assistance with this reaper guy, I can help.”

Zachary smiled, “Thanks. Hopefully he’s just a fanatic and not actually dangerous.”

Hunter shook his head. “Take care and good luck,” he said as he opened the door.

“Take care,” Zachary responded as Hunter left into the hall, the door closing behind him. The gray-eyed man was left alone in his small kitchen with his thoughts and worries.

*****

The next day, Zachary kept his eyes out for danger as he patrolled the roofs of the borough of Lowerside as Zombre. He hoped the kind words of Red Reaper were genuine. Maybe he was just an unfortunately named collector looking to expand his hoard. Zombre was standing on the ledge of a roof, looking over the city when he heard an angry, vengeful voice call out behind him. “Hey Zombie asshole!” The gray-eyed man had never heard such rage before.

Zombre turned and found a man with long, messy, black hair and a mad look in his eye. He wore black leather armor that looked like he was from the 12th century and had a large sword with a black handle attached to his hip. However, the strangest thing about him was the orange glow that surrounded his body. Unsure if it was the aura around him or not, Zombre saw no exploitable injuries. "Can I help you?" Zombre asked as he unhooked his sword from his belt.

"Give me that blade!" the random man screamed, his anger unceasing. "Or face my wrath!"

Zombre stared at him through his mask. "No, I won't be doing that."

Somehow, his face became angrier from his command being denied. He grabbed his blade and unsheathed the weapon, tossing the cover off to the right. It was no modest blade. In his left hand was a five-and-a-half-foot, two-handed great sword with a silver blade that came to a squared-off, slanted edge. The sword's tip crashed into the floor of the roof. "Fuck you, then." he said with fury as his face involuntarily twitched. Then the sword lit into flame. The orange-glowing stranger yelled as he lifted it over his right shoulder and threw the flame at Zombre by swinging the sword down. The masked hero jumped from the ledge back towards the middle of the room as a wave of fire crashed against the edge of the building.

Zombre quickly got to his feet in time to catch the flaming sword with his blade. He did his best to keep up the attack of the glowing man, but each block brought more anger from his opponent and the greater the rage, the stronger his opponent became. The onslaught increased in speed and power until it was too much for Zombre to handle. The force of the steels colliding on the most recent strike knocked the gray-eyed man off balance, leaving him open for a fatal attack.

The long sword of fire sliced through the gut of Zombre, causing him to scream out in pain. He collapsed to the ground and held his burnt guts in with his left arm as a ghostly green aura leaked from the wound and turned Zombre's eyes from gray to green as his blade healed him.

"Why won't you just die!" The glowing man screamed as he lifted his flaming weapon to the night sky. "Just fucking die!" Zombre was able to dodge the blade, but not the fiery explosion that followed the sword crashing into the roof. The flames burned the left side of his body as he rolled off to the right. Before he could get back into a fighting position, the glowing man rushed at his target, swinging his great sword and slicing off Zombre's left arm. The masked hero yelled as he was grabbed by the strange glowing man and tossed across the burning building like a rag doll.

The sound of sirens rang in the distance as first responders came to put out the fires. Zombre stared down his enemy, his arm slowly bleeding red blood and a green aura. He was no match for this villain, but he had to try something. The hero with glowing eyes went on the offensive, charging at the man who glowed orange. Zombre swung at his attacker, but his blade was stopped by the cross guard of the flaming longsword. With only one arm, Zombre could not get the leverage for the upper hand, allowing the other swordsman to overpower and disarm him.

With his sica clattering onto the ground, the healing green light that surrounded his nearly healed stomach wound and severed arm vanished, leaving only intense agony. Zombre nearly fainted from the sudden shock of pain, his power lessened the feeling of pain from wounds along with repairing the damage.

The glowing man kicked him to the ground and pinned the masked hero to the burning roof with his left boot. He looked down on Zombre — who had started to cough up blood onto his mask — in a fit of crazed anger as he pointed the slanted edge of his greatsword down at the injured Zombre. "Fuck you!" the glowing man screamed as he raised his flaming weapon straight up into the air, ready to skewer Zombre. The gray-eyed man frantically reached for his blade, but it sat just an inch from his fingertips.

The wrathful man let out a primal scream as he prepared to drive his flaming sword through the heart of his target. Then a bullet hit him in the head, knocking him off of his wounded target and allowing Zombre to lunge and grab his weapon, resuming the healing and once again slowing the bleeding of his wounds.

Fire spewed from the hole in the side of his head as he looked up to see who had entered the fight. He stared down at the man in black and silver armor — a repaired crack on his right chest plate — on top of the neighboring building, holding a pistol at the ready. "You fucking assh..." He screamed as Hunter began to fire his entire clip into the chest of the ghostly, orange-glowing man. The barrage of bullets made the wrathful man advance towards the new attacker, his rage making him so one-minded that he forgot about Zombre. He approached the edge of the burning building and prepared to launch another wave of fire at the gunman when Zombre jumped up behind him and ended the fight. The one-armed man used a back-handed attack to sever the head of the glowing stranger from his body. The flaming sword was extinguished and fell to the ground while the head and body of the man turned embers and were carried off by the wind.

Hunter jumped onto the other roof to check on his wounded friend. He walked over to Zombre, who had grabbed his severed arm, and watched as he held the two bloodied ends together. The green light surrounded the wound and fused the two parts. "That's gross," Hunter remarked in mild disgust.

Zombre looked up at the man who assisted in saving his life. "Thanks," he responded sarcastically as he checked the movability of his fingers. They felt numb and not all moved that well, but he knew over time they would return to normal. Zombre grabbed the great sword that the glowing-orange man was wielding; Hunter grabbed its sheath. "Come on. Let's get out of here," the gray-eyed man said to Hunter.

"Good idea," Hunter agreed as the first responders arrived on the scene. "I need to teach you how to fight.." the man in black and silver armor joked as they left under the cover of smoke.

*****

"What is it?" Hunter asked as the two men stared at the large sheathed blade that sat on Zachary's kitchen table.

Zachary shrugged, icing the scars on his arms and stomach. There would be scars there for the next couple of days. "No idea, but the man was almost supernaturally angry."

"Let me look at it," Hunter said as he reached for the black handle of the longsword. This was the first time he held the weapon and it would be the last. As soon as it was in his grasp, a wave of anger washed over the blue-eyed man. An uncontrollable rage towards AP Genetics and the wealthy who wagered on the lives of him and his family was all he could think about as he stood motionless in the apartment.

Zachary stared at Hunter as the blue-eyed man stared at the blade in his hand, tears began to welt in his eyes. "Are you all right, Hunter?" Zachary asked as he touched Hunter's right arm.

The physical contact shocked Hunter and forced him to drop the longsword. A light, white steam emitted from his hands. "Yeah," the blue-eyed man responded as he cleared the tears from his eyes. "I just...that thing is definitely cursed."

Zachary glanced from the emotional man to the sword on the table. "What happened?"

"I don't know," Hunter responded, still trying to collect himself. "I just felt so...angry when I picked it up."

The gray-eyed man looked at the weapon, "Weird. I didn't feel anything when I picked it up." He stood up and set his ice packs on the table, leaning over to get a better look at the weapon.

"Why do you think that is?" Hunter asked.

Zachary shrugged, "Maybe because I'm technically dead. Dead men don't feel anger," he replied. "Well, except for poltergeists I guess," Zachary added as he looked back at Hunter.

"Wait, you're actually undead? Like a real zombie?" Hunter asked. He had assumed the zombie stuff just because of how he dressed and that he could survive lethal strikes while fighting crime.

"Well, I prefer the title Zombre, but I don't have any cravings for brains if that's what you're worried about," he joked before changing the topic of the conversation. "So how do we learn more about this thing?"

Hunter looked at the sword. "I might know a guy."

"I thought you ran in different circles?" Zachary asked.

"Normally." Hunter responded. "I was in Japan for a ... business and I met a man who specialized in unusual weaponry, specifically cursed weapons, as he put it."

"What business requires a cursed weapons specialist?" Zachary asked while raising one of his eyebrows.

"I'll tell you when you're older," Hunter joked, referencing Zachary's young appearance. Hunter had been in Japan hunting one of his billionaire targets when he heard rumors the man had a mystical item protecting him. Even if Hunter had his doubts about magic's existence, he wanted to do his due diligence and found a man who went by Nikkō who could shed some light on magical protection items and curses. Nikkō helped Hunter learn that the protection item was fake. "For now, I'll make some calls." He said as he grabbed his jacket and headed for the door.

"Let me know what you learn." Zachary requested as he watched Hunter leave his apartment.

*****

"So what can you tell me about this longsword?" Hunter asked in English as the video feed connected. He can speak some Japanese, but Nikkō is better at speaking in English than Hunter is at Japanese.

"We haven't spoken in what? Almost a year? You don't have any time for greetings?" Nikkō replied in a Japanese accent with a smile. He had light brown eyes, a shaved head, and a goatee.

Hunter rolled his eyes and sighed, "Hello Nikkō, how are you? What can you tell me about the sword I sent you pictures of?"

Hunter's response was humorous to Nikkō. After he stopped laughing, he asked: "You said it made you feel angry when you touched it?"

"Yeah, it was weird as soon as I picked it up, I was filled with this sudden and intense rage," Hunter paused as he recalled that sensation. He shook himself free from the memory. "Then it dissipated as soon as I dropped it."

Nikkō nodded for a moment as he ran through his internal knowledge of weaponry. "I see. Then I do believe I know what this is," he replied as he stood and walked across the room to a bookshelf offscreen. He returned shortly after with an old, worn, black, leather book with yellowed pages opened to about halfway. "I think this is it. The drawing looks similar...some slight differences, but these drawings are rarely completely accurate. I think what you found is The Greatsword of Wrath, one of seven weapons forged by the legendary Elvish bladesmith Wayland to use the power of the seven deadly sins. The Greatsword of Wrath gives the user the ability to control the emotional elements of water, air and fire. It says here they were assumed lost to time after their original owners were defeated. How did you get a hold of it?" Nikkō asked.

Hunter smiled, impressed with the other man's impressive knowledge and resources. "I'm in San Gwynn looking for information on," he paused, not wanting to overshare, "a new lead. I found someone who I thought might be able to help. Anyway, he was attacked by this weird glowing man, but he only controlled fire."

Nikkō thought for a moment. "Only fire," he began as he read the page and flipped through a few others. "Hm, must not have been a true user. Seems all the weapons have serious side effects if not wielded by those who have control over the sin of the weapon. I guess not having control of your anger will cause you to be consumed by it. Wait, did you say he was glowing?" Nikkō asked, circling back to a plot point he glossed over initially.

"Yeah, it was weird. He was glowing orange... and wearing this weird old school amour. The weirder part was when we killed him, he disappeared into embers," Hunter explained.

"Interesting," Nikkō responded as he flipped through the pages of the book again, looking for an answer. "Here we are. I think you fought a ghost."

"A ghost?" Hunter asked, unsure if he heard him right. 'Ghosts and Zombies, what did I get myself into?' he asked himself.

Nikkō nodded. "Yes, it looks like The Dagger of Envy can create mirages like replicants of past victims, but they shouldn't be that powerful, no more than apparitions. Envy can replicate powers, but only one at a time and only if that person is in front of them. I don't know how they're doing it exactly, but I would guess whoever sent the ghost after you is using the Dagger of Envy."

"I see, I wonder if that Red Reaper guy is behind this," Hunter pondered out loud.

"Who?" asked Nikkō.

"The guy I'm helping out, his name is Zachary, said a weird man named Red Reaper approached him about adding his sword to his collection."

"Does your friend have one of the seven weapons of sin?" Nikkō interrupted.

Hunter felt 'friend' was an incorrect word, but felt there were more pressing matters to address. "He doesn't know what he has. It keeps him from dying by healing his injuries, the Red Reaper guy called it the Blade of Purgatory."

Nikkō paged through the book again, taking more time to respond. "There is a Blade of Purgatory, but not much is known about it, not even what it looks like. Legend has it that Wayland forged it as well. I suppose if Red Reaper has all seven weapons of sin, then next would be to collect any other weapons forged by Wayland." He correctly theorized Red Reaper's intent.

"If he sent one ghost with the wrath sword, then there's a good chance he will send more ghosts with the other weapons, right?" Hunter asked.

Nikkō looked up and off to the side as he considered possibilities. "I wouldn't be surprised if he did. I'm not sure why he's sent the ghost, but if he sent one, he may send more."

"Well in that case, it's probably best if we know what to look out for. What are the other sin weapons and powers?"

"Good point. Here are the weapons, excluding The Dagger of Envy and The Greatsword of Wrath," Nikkō said as he flipped back a couple pages. "First, the Golden Sword of Pride: emits a blinding light that can intimidate opponents. Second, Gluttony's Trident: allows the user to absorb an opponent's energy, creating a sense of starvation. It also says the energy stolen can be amplified once absorbed. Third, Sloth's Warhammer: allows the user to slow their opponents when they are in their sight while doubling the damage dealt. Fourth, Lacerator of Lust: the opponent is tricked into seeing what they love most, usually their ideal mate. This often voids the opponent's will to fight and places the opponent under the control of Lust. Lastly, the Halberd of Greed can steal opponents' powers, similar to Envy, but Greed can store the stolen powers to be reused later." Nikkō stopped speaking for a moment and pondered an idea. "You know, if someone were to combine The Dagger of Envy's ability to make ghosts with the Halberd of Greed's power of power collection then that would explain why the apparition you fought were able to use the weapon's powers."

"Is that what you think happened?" Hunter asked.

"Most likely, but I'm not sure if anyone can even use two powerful weapons at the same time. I also doubt the ghosts would be able to use the weapon's full strength," Nikkō added.

Hunter looked at him quizzically. "What do you mean?"

"Well, the weapons of sin are extremely powerful and in the wrong hands have serious side effects. Even if this Red Reaper guy killed the ideal users, the ones who would be able to use the sin weapons without the negative side effects, that would not mean their ghosts would be true users. They would be bastardized versions of who they once were," Nikkō explained. "It was why the ghost of Wrath was unable to control his anger, meaning he could only control fire. Pride's negative side effect is extreme narcissism which prevents the user from taking opponents severely. Gluttony's trident makes the user lose their self-control and increases their appetite for food. The user of Sloth's Warhammer is slowed by their own weapon's effects, decreasing their speed and their opponents. Lust loses control of their lust, both romantic and blood. Greed becomes a kleptomaniac with no sense of personal property; they often feel compelled to steal whatever they can get their hands off. The Dagger of Envy makes the user obsessive with things others have, creating an unceasing obsession to claim what they feel should be rightfully theirs."

Hunter was writing down info as fast as Nikkō shared it so he could relay as much as possible to Zachary. He clicked his pen and looked back up to the man on the screen. "I'll make sure to share all of this to Zachary. Thanks Nikkō, you've been a lot of help."

Nikkō smiled, "No worries, and Hunter, one more thing," he called back to Hunter as he was about to log off the call.

"What's up?"

"I'm glad you're finally making new friends. I was getting worried since I was your only one," Nikkō laughed softly.

Hunter just rolled his eyes. "Bye, Nikkō," he replied before hanging up on the man with the goatee.

*****

Over the next two days, Hunter and Zombre patrolled Lowerside together. Hunter felt like a major leaguer playing high school ball while he helped take out street muggers and low-level crime, but it allowed him to show the inexperienced hero the fighting techniques Hunter wanted Zombre to learn. It was just after midnight, they had just stopped a couple of robbers who broke into a house and were sitting on a building overlooking a park. "I can't believe you didn't know how to fight," Hunter said. "How did you fight crime before? Or beat Arios Pearl on your own?"

"Not really sure. I just relied on my power to win fights and tried my best to not kill people when I used my sword. Then when I went up against Arios Pearls and his nutjobs...I guess I had taken so much damage that I fell into a trace. It was like I was on autopilot. I only remember parts of the actual fighting, but when I came too, I was surrounded by people that I had hurt." He paused as he began to get choked up. "It's a sight I can't forget and I won't try to. I don't like hurting people." Zombre closed his eyes and took a deep breath. "Anyway, I got a new power that night."

"A new power?" Hunter replied, going with the sudden change of subject, not wanting to push the other.

Zombre shook his head. "Yeah, I can see people's physical weaknesses when I look at them now. It happened for the first time during my fight with Arios Pearl."

Hunter was impressed. "That's pretty cool. What do you see when you look at me?"

Without looking, Zombre responded. "I don't see one. It's usually like bad joints, bruises, or weak spots in bones. Neither you or that Wrath ghost had any."

Hunter smirked under his helmet. "Interesting. So what do..." His voice trailed off as he got distracted by something down in the park. "What was that?" he said as he got to his feet.

"What?" Zombre asked as joined his armored friend in standing.

"There's something down there. Come on, let's check it out." Hunter said as he walked over to the fire escape.

The two men — Zombre had his sword drawn, but Hunter had his pistol holstered — walked into the park, following the trail of lamp posts until they reached a clearing in the park, where they found a glowing pink woman in dark pink armor with only her head uncovered. "Hello, boys," she cooed in a playful tone. "Do not worry, there is enough of me to go around." She giggled crazily. In her hand was Lust's Lacerator. A double-sided S-curved sword with the handle in the middle. The blades were purple in color and sharpened on both edges. The woman was the ghost of the original user of the weapon. When she was alive, she was beautiful in her own right, but had complete control over her desires of lust: both sexual and blood. The blade gave her the advantage of controlling the emotions of her opponents and actions with her words. Their eyes would deceive them, making them see her as the most beautiful woman of their wildest dreams, leaving them powerless in her presence. Even other women would fall to the power of her blade. Only those without lust in their hearts were not affected. However, this bastardized ghostly version of her was not the weapon's true user meaning this echo of the past could not control her own bloodlust. This was the negative side effect of Lust's Lacerator.

To Zombre, there was nothing special about this strange woman, but to Hunter, she was beyond gorgeous. Her smile was contagious and her voice hypnotized him. "What do you want?" Zombre asked. Like the man of Wrath, she had no physical weakness.

She laughed. "I want that blade and the other one you stole. Will you give them to me, pretty please?" Her tone was playful with overtones of danger.

"The swords stay with me," Zombre responded as Hunter stood still next to him.

The glowing pink ghost of Lust mockingly frowned, "He will be so disappointed if I return empty handed. How about your friend gets them for me?" Her words floated through the air and filled his mind with one goal, to deliver her what she wanted.

"What are you..." The masked man with gray eyes stared before Hunter pulled the pistol from his left side and fired it into the side of Zombre's head without looking away from the glowing pink beauty. The force of the projectile forced Zombre to step to the side to keep himself from collapsing. His eyes turned ghostly green as his sword began healing the hole in his head. Zombre turned and stared at the man who had just shot him; he found it hard to think with part of his brain on the grass. Before Zombre's mind fog could fade, Hunter turned and fired four more shots into the chest of the masked hero.

The pink-armored woman laughed sadistically as she walked behind Hunter before stopping on his left side. She leaned up against him, her smile wide and menacing. "Oooh, he's durable. I like when a toy is hard to break, but I always find a way to break 'em." The glowing woman giggled demonically as she put her hand on Hunter's pistol and pushed it down, forcing him to lower his weapon. The sight of Zombre's blood was erotic to the ghostly gal as it intensified her bloodlust. "Guns are grand, but everyone knows knives make a girl go crazy."

On cue, Hunter holstered his pistol and brandished his large six-inch serrated hunting utility knife that was on his left thigh. The armored man charged at Zombre, forcing him to block the strikes. "What is wrong with you?" The glowing green-eyed man pleaded as he struggled to keep up with the speedy onslaught. He winced in pain as Hunter sliced open his thigh on the most recent attack. The woman consumed by lust watched on in delight.

"Oh, he cannot hear you," the woman explained in a sing-song voice. "He is my special friend now and he is going to do everything I want." Hunter was completely under the trances of the ghostly wielder of Lust's Lacerator. Spellbound by her hypnotic looks and siren-esque voice. In his eyes, she was a beauty worth destroying worlds for.

Zombre continued being defensive as he did not want to hurt Hunter, though it may not have mattered if he did wish to do him harm. Zombre did not believe Hunter was working with Red Reaper and his ghosts. Zombre figured if Hunter was, he had easier opportunities to take the undead hero's blade. "Snap out of it will ya?" he pleaded as he took more and more damage from Hunter's attacks.

The onlooking woman snuck in behind the occupied Zombre and made small cuts to the back of his legs. She would laugh and then quickly retreat back to safety. The masked hero with green glowing eyes figured he had to stop her to snap Hunter out of the trance, but as long as the armored man kept up this pace, Zombre would have no opportunity to attack her without leaving himself exposed to a more dangerous opponent.

Then fate forced his hand. "Oh, just take it already..." The impatient glowing woman cried out. "I want to have my fun before we bring master his blade," she giggled. Hunter moved in close to get more leverage, he broke Zombre's arm and ripped the weapon from the hands of the wounded hero.

"Fuck," Zombre screamed in pain as his magical healing ability ceased. He stumbled back from Hunter, who stood motionless as he waited for his next command. Zombre's eyes turned from glowing green back to dull gray as he turned to face the charging woman who wore a deranged smile.

The pink-armored woman drove her sword into the gut of Zombre. She looked him in the eyes as blood began to drip from the corner of his mouth. "What is wrong, little toy? Do you not want to play anymore?" she teased as she licked her lips at the sight of blood dripping from the bottom of his mask.

Zombre felt the end coming. He had one last chance. The gray-eyed man grabbed her shoulders, pushed her away a little before pulling her back towards him. Zombre wrapped his arms around her and forced the other half of the two-sided blade into the woman who had impaled him. She cocked her head to the side. "A toy that plays back? I think I'm in love." Her voice echoed into nothing as her pink aura faded and disappeared into a pile of pink petals carried away by a soft gust of wind.

Zombre dropped to his knees and looked over at the blade that could save his life before the world faded to black and he collapsed to the side.

"What the...?" Hunter stumbled back as he came out of the trance. His actions from when he was under Lust's trance seemed like a faded memory fogged by time. Hunter saw Zombre lying on the ground, his blood pooling under him. "Zachary?" he asked as he rushed over to him after putting his blade away, but keeping the curved Sica in his right hand. Hunter knelt to check on Zachary. As he knelt beside his fallen friend, the armored man set the blade down, and its ornate handle came in contact with the dead man's upper thigh.

Zombre's eyes shot open, filled with a ghostly green light. He gasped for air as he frantically reached for the blade until it was fully in his grasp. The masked man sat up with the help of Hunter. "Here, let me help," Hunter said as he reached for the blood-stained, double-sided blade's handle.

"Wait!" Zombre shouted in heavy breath before Hunter made contact with the weapon. "The swords have a bad effect on you. I already saw you under her spell, I don't want to see you acting like her," he said before pulling the purple blade out of his stomach. His green aura filled his wound.

Hunter helped him to his feet. "So, what now?"

"I think it's time to take the fight to Red Reaper.." Zombre replied.

"Are you in good enough shape to go now?" Hunter asked, noting the damage the blood-covered man was still recovering from.

"No," Zombre responded honestly as the two men walked away from the bloody mess.

*****

A plan rose with the morning sun. The two men dawned their street clothes and headed over to the Wharfway to investigate the museum where Zachary first met the mysterious man who called himself "Red Reaper." They rented a room at a hotel that was a couple of streets away and had an unobstructed view of the front entrance of the building that sat on the harbor. Since they could not bring their weapons or the confiscated ones in the hall of history, they decided to leave them the room. They were afraid Zachary's apartment may have been compromised. "So this is where you met him?" Hunter asked as he made notes of the room's layout in one of the trifold maps and information brochures that he had picked up on the way in.

"Yeah, right here in the center of the room." Zachary pointed at a glass display case full of different-shaped daggers.

The two meandered around the room, inspecting the weapons for clues, but found none. "Is all this his?" Hunter asked.

Zachary shook his head while he looked around the room. "No, he boasted how his collection was more selective or something like that. I would assume it's just the sin weapons."

Hunter acknowledged the response with a slow nod. "Hopefully his collection is just the sin weapons and nothing more. With his sending out two of the seven as those crazy ghosts, the most we would have to fight is five poltergeists," he spoke matter-of-factly as it would be an easily manageable task to take on that many.

"Five feels like a lot. Even for ghosts."

The blue-eyed man turned and stared at his gray-eyed compatriot. "Well, with your healing power it should be no problem. How does that work anyway?"

Zachary sighed as he tried to find the words to explain. "Have you seen the green mist...light...thing that surrounds me when I get hurt?" he asked Hunter, struggling to explain a power when he had no idea how it worked.

"Hard not to notice. You glow like a neon sign," Hunter joked, a soft smile sneaking onto his face as he chuckled.

The gray-eyed man laughed a little to himself. "Fair, but that's only half of it," Zombre began. He was not sure exactly what happens when he delivers a lethal blow, but he knew what the experience was like to him. The times he had taken lives, he felt something when he delivered the fatal wound; it felt like his sword swiped a piece of his victim's soul, but not much, the same amount that his sword spent when reviving him. "When I ... hurt someone badly, there's a purple light that leaks from them, like I'm stealing some of their lifeforce to use later." He did his best to describe what he felt was happening. It was a strange feeling to know without knowing, as if the blade was whispering in the back of his brain, but there were no words. The blade was alive in some capacity, but only Zachary could tell.

"I see, and despite that, you don't have an urge to kill?" Hunter asked.

"Not as long as I stay in control," Zachary replied. "So we have to kill ghosts," he said, wishing to change the subject.

"Yeah, I'm still a little unclear on how," Hunter confessed.

Zachary shrugged, unsure himself how to tackle the task that lay ahead. "No idea. Bullets seem ineffective. Swords seem to work."

Hunter ran through a mental list of what arms he had with him in the city. Most of his armory was stashed in another city, the location he was planning on heading to before he decided to make this detour. "I'll have to pack more generally for tonight," Hunter said more to himself than Zachary. He wrote down on his map a list of what he felt would be the most useful to bring.

The two men finished up their recon of the museum, talking strategy for their potential encounter. They left as the building closed for the night. On the way back to the hotel, Hunter and Zachary stopped and grabbed some dinner. They ate on the balcony of their third-floor room and watched the entrance for their potential villain.

After they finished eating, the men got ready. Hunter sat on the porch with his helmet off, watching the sunset over the water behind the museum while Zombre got changed. In his life, Hunter rarely took moments to observe the small, beautiful things the world had to offer. The fluorescent sky painted orange, red, and purple was calming. In the moment that he sat there alone, he forgot his past, he ignored the reality of his potential future, and all that was left was the moment in the warm evening air.

His thoughts were pulled away from the picturesque sky when Zachary joined him on the balcony, he was in an unblooded version of his costume and left his mask on the bed closest to the bathroom. Zachary sat down in the metal chair on the right side of the balcony. "I've lived here for some time now and the sun set still leaves me in awe. It makes life worth ... undeading," he laughed to himself.

Hunter nodded and softly chuckled. "I always enjoyed looking at the stars. Though, I don't get too much anymore."

"Why not?" Zachary asked as he looked over to the man whose eyes were still fixed forward towards the watercolor heavens.

"I spend most of my time these days in large cities. You can't see the stars that well," he responded before a moment of vulnerability slipped past his lips. "Not like when I lived up North on the border." Memories flooded his mind as he remembered the nights he spent learning the constellations and their myths with his parents, something he had forgotten to miss when he began his vendetta. Wanting to avoid a rabbit hole he had been evading, Hunter changed the subject. "We should take shifts," he began, looking over to meet the gaze of the gray-eyed man. "That way we can rest and still keep an eye on the museum.

Zachary nodded in agreement. "Sounds good. You can take the first rest shift. I don't need that much sleep to function."

Hunter took a detachable clock from his belt and made a note of the time before setting it next to a pair of compact binoculars on the small glass and metal table that stood between them. "I can keep watch with you for the next three hours and then we can start shifts."

Nothing occurred as the sun fell into the ocean. The two men watched the well-lit entrance in silence as they waited to see if the rare pedestrian would stop or keep moving. Occasionally, one of them would get up to get a drink of water, a quick snack, or use the bathroom. When Hunter's clock read 10:30, he set a timer and left the balcony without a word to try and sleep in the bed closest to the sliding glass window because the other bed was covered in his excess arsenal and the two sin weapons that they had confiscated. For the next three hours, though, he struggled to doze off. His brain just would not let him trust Zachary enough to fall asleep entirely.

Zachary sat there with a brain full of thoughts that he wished he could drown out. The gray-eyed man hated silence. It was why he would often turn on his TV as soon as he got home and would leave it on until he left or was about to fall asleep. He found his self-reflections undesirable and struggled to turn them off. He was relieved when Hunter's timer went off at 1:30 in the morning, signaling them to switch their roles. However, his relief was short-lived as she struggled to sleep, allowing his mind to continue its torment of him.

*****

Hunter struggled less with silence. Growing up a giant slayer, he often found days where he would be stationed in the woods for hours in wait and a single noise could scare off the giant, wasting all that time. The quiet that came with downtime was nothing new to him. He stared forward, hyper-focused on the museum until Zachary rejoined him on the balcony. "You can rest for a little longer, you still have some time," Hunter said to the man who was ending his rest period a half-hour early.

"It's fine," Zachary responded. "It's not like I slept much anyway. Might as well keep you company as we wait."

Hunter shrugged in acceptance. He understood the inability to sleep while on the hunt. The nerves of anticipation that keep you in a tense state were all too familiar.

It was a little after five when Hunter asked something he had been wondering about ever since their encounter with the glowing ghost of lust. "Do you mind if I ask you something? Something... personal?"

Zachary shrugged. "Sure."

"Your healing power, how didn't it work earlier?"

"What do you mean?" Zachary questioned back to buy himself time to consider if he wanted to share everything,

Well, when you fought that first swordsman, your power seemed to work without hesitation, but when I woke up from that... spell, you were just lying there and you looked dead. Like actually dead, like your power wasn't working, and then all of sudden you sprang back to life. I was just wondering why it seemed to stop working."

The sounds of an approaching storm thundered off the coast as Zachary contemplated his answer. There was no one in his life he could talk to. He had not seen or talked to his parents since he fled home for the city. Even those in his life that he did interact with regularly — his neighbor Mr. Harwas and his coworkers — he usually just exchanged pleasantries with, nothing substantial. Even a potential love interest was out of the question. It would be difficult enough to find someone who would be okay with his crime-fighting, but he had lost all sense of intimacy the night he first died. The dead do not need to reproduce. It is the same reason why Lust's power had no effect on him when it seduced Hunter's mind. The gray-eyed man lived a life of isolation. Everything in his mind told him to hide his secrets from the man he had just met days prior, but his heart was desperate for a friend to confide in. "It's the sword. I have to be touching it in order to use its power."

"So when you were laying there, you were actually dead? What was it like?" Hunter could not help but ask.

The thunder rumbled again as it got closer to the shore. "It's just darkness. Black emptiness until I touch the sword again."

Hunter nodded, "Next time I'll get your blade to you sooner."

Tears began to form in Zachary's gray eyes. "I wish you wouldn't. I wish you would leave me dead," he spoke candidly.

The blue-eyed man looked at him with a confused look at what he had just heard. "What?"

Zachary swallowed the lump in his throat and signed. "I hate what I am. I wish it would end. I don't dream anymore. I don't feel love. I don't feel anything but emptiness and sorrow."

"Why continue then? Why not throw the sword into the ocean and walk away?"

"I can't," the gray-eyed man began, tears now streaming down his face. "When I get too far from it, my whole body begins to itch. It's like an addiction. I can't walk away, no matter how hard I wish I could. I can't even take my own life. Whenever the thoughts enter my head, the sword calls to me, like it knows what I'm thinking and won't let me escape. I feel like an imposter wandering through the world. I ran away from my own parents without saying goodbye because I no longer felt human. But as much as I miss them, I don't want to be around them like this."

The summer storm sounded as the sorrow of Zachary Ombre left the two men in silence. It was at this moment that Hunter felt the reality of his isolation. "I know what it's like to feel alone. I've been running from that feeling ever since I lost my family." He struggled to stop the tears that came with this realization. "I miss them every day, but I do everything not to think about them. I don't have time to mourn," he admitted to his new friend, feeling guilty over his confession. "Hunter isn't my real name. I changed it when I started going after the people who killed my family. I needed to become someone else, or so I thought. In reality, it reminded me of them. The name they gave me. I can't imagine what they would think of what I was doing. I changed my name because... I didn't want to think of them...because it was too hard."

Zachary wiped away the signs of his crying from his cheeks. He cleared his throat. He was not sure what to say, so he offered what he would want to hear. "They loved you. No matter what you call yourself. They loved you."

Hunter cleaned his right eye with his left hand. "Thank you.," he said through a cracked voice.

"I understand if you don't want to tell me..." Zachary began before being interrupted.

"Christopher... They named me Christopher."

Over the next couple of minutes, the two men looked out towards the dark sky, the occasional flash of lightning in the distance as it moved closer. "Can I ask you a favor?" Zachary asked, finally interrupting the thunder's solo.

"Sure."

Zachary took a deep breath and closed his eyes as if it would make it easier to speak. "If you ever find me dead again...let me be. Free me from my curse." Once again the tears flowed.

Hunter contemplated the request he had been asked. "I will if you do me a favor first." He paused to see if Zachary would look at him, but the gray-eyed man continued to stare forward in an unsuccessful attempt to hide his sobbing. Hunter resumed. "Talk to your parents. It's the only thing in this world I wish I could do one more time... and I think it's what you want, too." Zachary did not say yes or no, he just nodded to accept.

The two remained quiet in sorrowed self-reflection as the sounds of the city awakening began to harmonize with the approaching thunder. "Well, it's getting early and I don't think he's coming," Zachary said through a raspy voice as he stood up from the balcony chair.

Hunter then noticed a man ascending the front stairs of the museum. "Hold up, we have someone." He grabbed the binoculars that sat next to the clock to try and get a look at his face, but the man had his back to the hotel. The figure walked past the main entrance and entered through a smaller door with a red sign that read 'security'.

Zachary leaned over the railing, though he had no sight assistance. "He's probably just a manager or security guard opening up the museum or something."

The blue-eyed man in black armor set down his binoculars and picked up the building's map that he had written notes on. He had been studying it during his solo moment of the steak out. "I doubt it. Museum's closed today," he said as he looked over to Zachary, holding up the glossy paper with the hours of the operation.

Zachary looked on in realization before both men rushed back into the room to ready themselves to investigate the museum again. The rain had just started to fall as they approached the door their target entered. Zombre stopped at the door and looked back at the helmeted Hunter, who had a modified multi-shot rifle in his hands. They gave each other a nod to signal they were ready and Zombre opened the door for them to enter.

They cautiously walked through the vacant halls of the museum, looking around for Red Reaper. They entered the illuminated main exhibit room that they had investigated earlier, the same room Zombre first met his crimson-clad foe. The room appeared clear, so the two men moved along the north wall and were heading towards a side exit when Zombre got a sudden uneasy feeling, he looked back at his friend who had been following him. Hunter was a good distance behind him and looked as if he was moving in slow motion. Zombre looked around the room and found the cause. Standing across the room, perpendicular to Hunter was the ghost of Sloth in bronze armor, blending in with the vacant metal suits behind him. Neither man had noticed him because he moved just as fast as the stationary mannequins. He had a dull, ghostly, brownish-yellow aura that was mundane below the shine of the fluorescent lights above. In his hands was a yellow, five-foot Warhammer that had a head with a flat end on one side and a downward curved spike on the other side. The hammer was swinging forward, but it defied gravity with its descent, moving just as slow as Hunter as it approached the ground. This was the Hammer of Sloth.

Zombre raced towards his friend and attempted to pull him forward out of the way of the slow-downed field. Zombre did not know what would happen when the hammer struck the ground across the room, but the gray-eyed man knew it would not be good. As he attempted to pull his friend to safety, he found Hunter's weight had doubled. With it just a few feet from impact with the floor, Zombre was becoming more desperate to move Hunter. Right before the flat side of Sloth's hammer made impact, Zombre pulled with all his might and was finally able to throw his friend to safety. A violent wave of air, concrete, and flooring came flying toward Zombre. He caught the full force of the attack and was blown back into the hallway. Two of the ceiling's support beams came crashing down after him, separating Hunter and Zombre.

Hunter — back to his normal speed — jumped and looked toward the rubble that separated the allies. "Are you okay?" he called out to Zombre as Sloth slowly began to reset his hammer to a rest position parallel to the floor.

"I'm fine," Zombre coughed as his green surrounded him. He was lucky that he was able to hold onto his sword. "I'll find another way around."

Hunter turned and looked at the yellow, glowing ghost. "You go find Red Reaper. I'll take care of this one." There was a determination in his voice. He wanted redemption after being so easily manipulated in their fight with Lust's ghost.

"Are you s..."

"Just go!" Hunter interrupted, and go Zombre did. Following a trail of lights until he reached a door at the top of a stairwell that led onto a lower roof of the museum.

*****

Thunder crashed outside as Hunter quickly glanced between his foe and his rifle that had been tossed some 20-feet away and his opponent stood a good distance across the room. He could attempt to quickly draw and fire his pistol, but his pistol had less firepower than his preferred weapon and he was unsure it would be enough to stop the foe which would leave him a sitting duck when the sloth power activated once more.

Hunter needed to be strategic in his attack until he found a way to stop Sloth's ghost.

Hunter sprinted at full speed towards his rifle, but when he was just five feet away he felt the world slow once again. His brain felt like it was pulled back by a seatbelt as his whole body came to a sudden halt. The hero in full armor could still think normally, his eyes still moved at full speed, and he could still breathe, even if it was more difficult. Hunter could see from the corner of his eye that the hammer was just about to reach the apex of its swing above the glowing man's head. Confirming his theory that the power is activated when the Sloth begins another long range attack.

It was agonizing as he willed in vain for his feet to move faster. The slowed movements almost drove him mad, but his determination to redeem himself would not let him give in, 'Come on!' He screamed in his head. His left foot which was slowed midair had finally touched the ground and his right was beginning to push off.

Hunter tried to keep his thoughts on running, but had to refocus each time the violent summer storm roared outside. It was the only way to keep himself going forward at his slowed-down version of full speed. It was like he was running through a wall of gelatin. As the attack reached its final moments, Hunter's front toes were fully planted and his back foot was off the ground. It was time for the blue-eyed man to switch his strategy. With every ounce of willpower he could muster, he forced his leg to push down into the ground. His muscles burned with red-hot pain as he fought against the power of Sloth's Warhammer as it crawled towards the completion of the attack.

Hunter's effort paid off. Just before the head of the hammer hit the floor, Hunter felt himself be released. He jumped forward as a wave of debris and air rushed behind him. The attack almost completely missed him; only his back left foot got up with the edge of the chaos, spinning the man in black armor off balance. Hunter slammed into the ground on his upper right shoulder just a few feet from his rifle. He winced in pain at the moment of impact but quickly recovered to his feet. He grabbed his gun as a Sloth came back to his resting position. Hunter aimed and fired.

The gunshots echoed the thunder that raged outside as the blue-eyed man hit his target dead center in the chest. Sloth did not fall. The bullets ricocheted off the glowing yellow ghost's slanted chest armor, hitting the empty suits behind Hunter's target. The force of the impact knocked the specter of Sloth back, but right into his next attack. The blue-eyed hero was now a sitting duck.

When the feeling of being slowed washed over him again, Hunter feared defeat was imminent. 'Damn it,' he thought as he realized he had made the foolish mistake of selling out for a big attack, a mistake someone of his skill level should not make. Then he noticed a key detail that would help him defeat his sluggish enemy: a suit of armor behind the dull-yellow ghost had been hit by one of the bullets that ricocheted off Sloth's bronze chestplate, causing it to collapse to the ground at full speed behind the glowing figure despite Hunter moving at a speed that would make a tortoise blush. This gave Hunter a new plan. If could get behind the ghost of Sloth, then he could use his enemy's power against him, but first, he would have to survive a direct attack.

When he was alive, the man who would become this glowing abomination had mastery over his Warhammer and its powers without the negative side effect. Beyond slowing down enemies caught in his gaze, the alive Sloth could control his entire surroundings and pick the speed at which everything moved, even speeding himself or others up if he so chose. In the hands of a true wielder, the user was unaffected and still could still move at full speed. This bastardized version of the master of Sloth could only slow down what was in front of him, slowing his opponent and himself down as slow as his power could allow.

As the hammer finally reached its apex above the head of the yellow ghost, Hunter began to move his body into a pose to take the full Sloth's attack. He let go of the rifle and started to curl his body into position. The gun hung in the air, unaffected by the pull of gravity, just a few inches from the hand that just released it. His superior reflexes and agility allowed him to move faster than the average person would under the circumstances. Hunter turned his shoulder and folded over to protect himself as much as possible. By the time the hammer finally connected with the ground, Hunter had readied himself for the worst. The violent wave of debris flew towards him, crashing into his side. The blue-eyed man trusted his battle-tested armor. If a giant could not break it, then nothing could, though this attack came close.

There was no time to feel pain. If he took too long to recover, he would die. As the rain pounded on the large glass windows on the ceiling above, Hunter busted free from the wreckage — the adrenaline of the fight dulling the pain. The animalistic need to best his opponent sent him charging at his opponent, the knowledge that he had to get behind Sloth's ghost before the glowing man activated his power pushed Hunter to give his max effort. The blue-eyed man was running just towards the left shoulder of the brownish-yellow ghost.

As Hunter charged across the room, Sloth began his next strike, raising his Warhammer. Once again, Hunter was slowed to a crawl by the glowing ghost's gaze. Hunter pushed himself even harder, each step he was able to complete brought him closer to vanquishing his rival. The hammer inched closer to completing its attack, but there was a difference in this strike than the others. The previous times Sloth raised his weapon it came straight down to the ground to deliver a long-distance offensive. This time, however, the attack was angled parallel to the floor to hit the charging Hunter dead on.

Hunter watched the face of Warhammer's head as it crawled through the air towards him. If he messed up the timing, it would end poorly for him. Hunter had seen the holes the hammer made when it struck the ground. He knew his armor, strong as it may be, would not survive a direct collision with such a powerful weapon.

It was agony. Hunter kept his focus on his movements to keep himself moving at full speed against the strain of Sloth's power, but the hammer teased him with the threat of painful death. It was time for the next part of his charge. Hunter slowly pulled his left foot up, putting it behind his right leg as he gradually collapsed to the floor in a sliding position.

The hammer continued its steady, slow approach as Hunter attempted to dodge the attack. His head was level with the head of the weapon as it crawled towards him. That moment lasted forever, Hunter feared he had mistimed his slide. He feared that at any moment the Warhammer would speed up and strike him in his head. Hunter's heart pounded in his ears, all he could do was wait to either clear the weapon's path or for his painful death to come.

Hunter's head dropped below the hammer, allowing it to gradually pass harmlessly over him. The armored man slowly slid on the floor until he left the gaze of the slow-moving yellow ghost of Sloth. It caught him off guard when he suddenly crashed up to full speed. He hastily stopped his slide with a spin into a crouched position on his feet, now facing the back of his lethargic moving target still mid-attack. Hunter had no desire to take it slow anymore. He quickly pulled his six-inch serrated hunting knife from its holster on his left thigh and rushed at the back of Sloth. He plunged the blade into the upper back of the glowing yellow man, separating the spinal cord from the head.

Sloth's ghost let out a primal scream as he was pulled from his weapon's trance. The ghost faded into a cloud of dull yellow mist as his hammer flew from his hands and crashed into a wall display of shields. The display exploded, sending metal, glass, and wood out in all directions. Hunter fell to the ground to protect himself from the rubble. As the last pieces clattered to the floor, the blue-eyed man stood up and looked around. All traces of the ghostly yellow figure were gone, and the Warhammer lay peaceful amongst the wreckage. Hunter was victorious, but there was no time to celebrate.

He was surprised he had to face only one ghost of sin, but he was unaware that the crimson villain they were chasing could only manifest one ghost at a time with the current state of the world.

As the storm raged outside, the man in silver and black armor grabbed his rifle and ran to find his fellow hero as he battled against Red Reaper.

*****

Zombre opened the door at the top of the stairs and emerged onto the roof — slanted on each side of a level row — as rain droplets began to fall inconsistently. Standing at the end of a long pathway that was only wide enough for one person, was the man dressed in blood-colored armor, Red Reaper. "I was starting to think I was going to have to keep sending my pets after you. Have you finally come to your senses to give me all that is rightfully mine? I cannot help but notice you seem to be missing the other weapons you stole from me." Red Reaper asked in his unrecognizable European accent, annoyed frustration apparent in his voice.

The rain fell harder as Zombre stared down the man across from him, loosening and tightening his grip on his blade. He considered giving up what he wished to be rid of, freeing himself from his pain, but then he remembered the last time the weapon fell into someone else's hands. Even without the addiction that ruled his mind, Zombre knew better than to give such power to this obvious madman. "I'm afraid you lost your magical weapon privileges," the masked hero called out. "I'm here to make you leave me alone."

Rage filled the mind of Red Reaper; years of possessing the Greatsword of Wrath and obsessing over his quest to own the blades of sin and all the weapons forged by Wayland had poisoned his mind with the instability of his emotions. "How dare you keep my collection from me!" the man in blood armor yelled. "The only way I'll leave you is if you give me my blades." He pulled out a small dagger, with a dull blade of only five inches long. "And if you won't give me them willingly, you'll surrender them with your dying breath."

Zombre watched while thunder crashed above the rampaging waters of the seas as the dagger began to glow a fuchsia purple color. It then started to grow in size until Red Reaper's blade looked identical to the sword wielded by the masked hero. The only difference between the two curved Roman Sicas was Red Reaper's had grown an inch longer than Zombre's. The weapon the angry villain had brandished was the Dagger of Envy.

The rain fell with a fury. Zombre could hear loud crashes around him but was unable to distinguish if it was thunder or the sounds of Hunter battling his sluggish yellow phantom in the museum below. "Last chance," Red Reaper screamed out. "Give me what is mine and save yourself from death."

"You're not getting this sword." Zombre's final response of defiance was too much for the crimson villain to resist any longer. He let out a primordial cry as lightning lit the sky around them. Red Reaper charged and swung his mimic blade at Zombre.

The masked man caught his opponent's weapon with his own and then recovered to block the next strike from the man in blood-colored armor. The onslaught of frustration-filled strikes pushed Zombre back on the platform soaked from the storm. The gray-eyed man lost his footing and slipped down to a knee, leaving his chest exposed. Red Reaper saw his opening and took it, slicing upward through the rib cage of Zombre, who grunted in pain as his blood splattered onto the slanted roof. His wound began to glow green as the healing began. He knew he could not stay on defense forever. With Red Reaper distracted by the ghostly aura that leaked from Zombre, the man whose eyes glowed green leaped back onto his feet and started his barrage. He swiped and sliced at the man in red armor who did his best to block Zombre's strikes as rain fell all around them.

The act of being attacked annoyed Red Reaper. Each swing from Zombre enraged him even more. The two clashed blades and stared each other down as Zombre's eyes turned back to gray, each pushing to maintain their ground until they finally broke away and reset themselves.

The waves crashed along the side of the building as the two stood still. "You are no match for me. This game of resistance you play is one of ignorance, not heroics." As Red Reaper spoke, his copy of Zombre's weapon glowed purple, growing in size once more until it was six inches larger than the sica he was trying to seize.

"I will die before I give you this sword," Zombre responded.

"It will be my pleasure," Red Reaper screamed out before raising his weapon to the storm.

Zombre needed something to turn the tide of the skirmish. That is when he recalled a lesson Hunter had given him earlier while showing him ways to fight and defend himself. 'Your ability gives you an insane advantage. An average person would have to protect themselves from fatal blows, but you can use them to your advantage. Leave yourself open so you can deliver a fight-changing strike of your own.' Zombre heeded the advice, moving his sword up and out of the way, allowing Red Reaper's weapon to cut into his gut. The masked hero winced through the stinging pain, but the agony was worth it. His opponent was completely exposed. Zombre's eyes turned their ghostly green once more as he swung at the left side of his attacker's helmet, hoping to clip his head in a way that would incapacitate him without killing him. Red Reaper was unable to block the attack, his only hope was to dodge.

Red Reaper attempted to jump back as Zombre swung his sword, but he was not able to fully evade the attack. The blade of the masked hero caught the helmet of Red Reaper, breaking off a large piece of the crimson faceplate. The injured villain stumbled back, holding his injured face with his left hand and his weapon in his right. Zombre hoped he had won when he saw blood leak between Red Reaper's fingers, but an all too familiar green glow replaced the viscous crimson liquid. An ominous laugh echoed into Zombre's ears. "You can not beat me with that little trick of yours if I use it too." Red Reaper pulled his hand away. The injury healed in a similar, but different way than Zombre's did. The masked hero's power worked by speeding up his own natural healing process, healing the wounds from the inside to the upper layer of skin. This looked more like a zipper as it erased the cut. It was the work of the Dagger of Envy. It allowed the user to mimic not only the weapon of their opponent but also any powers they had. The ability stealing aspect was not exact though, instead, it was the perceived power that was robbed. That was why Red Reaper's looked different from Zombre's, it's what the villain thought the healing power worked.

The soft yellow light that leaked from the museum below gave Zombre his first look at Red Reaper's true face through the broken helmet. It was weathered and wrinkled by time. His goatee and eyebrows were white. There were large bags under his left eye, which were bloodshot and filled with a look of pure intensity and obsession. Red Reaper had survived long beyond humanly possible because The Dagger of Envy and Halberd of Greed fueled his obsession so much that he refused to die until his goal was complete. Until the day he felt satisfied, death could not take him.

Using his free hand, Red Reaper pulled off his damaged helmet to reveal his balding head covered with intermittent patches of mangy white hairs. He tossed the broken headwear behind him, letting it crash off the slanted roof and into the raging coast below. "You have no chance to win, but I am tired of offering mercy," Red Reaper snarled through clenched teeth as his Dagger-turned-Sica grew once more, now the blade was 28-inches long and a full foot longer than the one wielded by Zombre. As the storm raged on, Red Reaper screamed in harmony with the thunder and charged across the roof. He put all his rage and power behind the attack — each one more powerful than the last. With neither the rain nor Red Reaper letting up, Zombre could find no opening, not that he was worried about that at the moment. All of his attention was on keeping his footing with each clash of their blades. "Why!" Red Reaper screamed as he struck from the side, his blade growing three more inches. "Won't!" Followed by a swing from the left from the enlarging sword. "You!" Another powerful strike from the right as his weapon reached three-and-a-half feet long. "Die!" Red Reaper yelled at the top of his lungs as he swung downwards the four-foot blade, Zombre raised his blade to dodge the attack. After the swords clashed, Red Reaper kicked him in the chest, knocking the masked hero back.

The gray-eyed man looked up at the deranged man as rain fell. Red Reaper had no poetic line to deliver as he raised his weapon in a final strike. He let out a scream composed of all his frustration, obsession, and anger at being denied what he believed without doubt was rightfully his. He drove his sword down at his exposed opponent.

*****

Lighting lit the skies as Red Reaper's blade came down with the rain. It collided with the raised defenses of Zombre, but the increased weight of the enhanced weapon of his opponent forced the hero's sword down causing Red Reaper to strike the bone mask. The old school hockey mask that Zombre used to wear would have shattered on impact and his opponent's blade would have sliced through his brain — disorienting him long enough for Red Reaper to take his sword and leave him dead on that rainy roof. However, the face plate of Arios Pearl was much stronger and denser than normal human bone. Red Reaper's blade hit the mask and bounced off, chipping just a tiny sliver away.

The recoil gave Zombre an opening. He kicked up into the gut of his blood-colored armored rival, knocking Red Reaper onto the wet walkway, almost falling off the side and down the sloped roof. Zombre jumped to his feet, "Enough. Just give up," the masked hero pleaded in vain.

Red Reaper slowly rose to his feet. The deranged look in his eyes intensified. He was too angry to speak coherently; instead, he just let out a primal scream towards the dark clouds above. His four-foot sword glowed its ghostly purple once more as the blade grew until it was six feet in length. He rushed towards Zombre.

Once again the swords clashed in the storm. While Zombre struggled against the weight of the attacking sword before, he had an even harder time standing his ground now. The only advantage the gray-eyed man had was Red Reaper's anger made the villain's movement sloppy and erratic. Red Reaper swung high and Zombre ducked down to dodge the attack. The masked hero then swiped at an upward diagonal angle, slicing into the chest of Red Reaper.

The villain screamed in pain and instinctively stepped back a foot as the stolen healing power went to work. Both men labored to breathe, their clothes and armor drenched from the storm. They were evenly matched, but the man in crimson thought he could change the tide.

With his mind clouded by his rage and jealousy, Red Reaper grew his copy of Zombre's blade to ten feet long. A wicked smile grew over his face as he stared down the man he was trying to kill. He screamed as thunder and lightning danced above them; Red Reaper raised his blade high into the air in preparation for a final assault, but the sword did not stop. The extra weight of his enhanced weapon made it too front-heavy. Inertia took over and the blade kept moving, pulling Red Reaper back with it.

The look of obsession in his eyes changed to fear as he lost his balance. "Oh fuck!" Red Reaper screamed as he fell off the walkway. His body crashed into the wet, sloped roof, the sword clashing next to him. Zombre watched as Red Reaper struggled to stop his descent, grasping drastically for something on the slippery surface to save him. He screamed in terror as he lost contact with the building. Red Reaper's head smashed into the concrete sidewalk and flipped into the raging water. Waves crashed onto the sidewalk; washing away the blood stain. All traces of Red Reaper had disappeared into the sea.

Zombre stood there for a moment, allowing the rain to drench him even more. He stared into the angry surf below, waiting and fearing the sight of Red Reaper breaking free from the surface, but only water came onto the sidewalk.

The door behind Zombre opened with a loud crash. The masked man turned to see a battle-tested Hunter standing there in the doorway, his rifle drawn and ready. "Did you stop him?" Hunter yelled over the storm.

Zombre did not answer because he was unsure himself if Red Reaper was actually dead.

*****

In the next couple of days, Zombre and Hunter returned to their investigation of the site where Kap Securities and Raze Construction were working, all while keeping an eye out for Red Reaper and his sinful ghosts, but there were no signs of the man who fell into the stormy sea. Eventually, the two heroes uncovered an old, supposedly abandoned building in Worley, England that used Kap Securities.

"I'll stop in Japan and drop these off with Nikkō before heading out to Worley," Hunter said as he clicked the final padlock on the second latch of the case that held Sloth's Warhammer. Also on the table were the locked crates that held the Greatsword of Wrath and Lust's Lacerator. They used containers that Hunter stored some of his armory in. The Dagger of Envy had followed Red Reaper into the sea and they had no idea where the other weapons — Gluttony, Pride, and Greed — were hidden or what they looked like. "It will take me a couple of days because I'll be traveling by boat to Japan, but I'll let you know when they have been handed off."

"You trust your friend?" Zachary Ombre asked as he looked over the black cases stacked on his small kitchen table. He was in jeans and a gray v-neck.

Hunter, who was wearing jeans and an army green zipper jacket, shrugged. "Yeah. He'll know how to properly store them."

"Maybe it's better if they are destroyed." The image of the intensity in Red Reaper's eyes haunted Zachary's memories. He feared what would happen if they ended in worse hands than the maniac he already encountered.

"I agree," Hunter began, "but I would think weapons of such power will need to be destroyed safely. If they can be dismantled, Nikkō will be able to do it," the blue-eyed man reassured his new friend.

Their conversation was interrupted by one of Hunter's burner phones ringing. "Hello?" he answered before pausing to let the other side respond. "All right, I'll be right down. Thank you," Hunter spoke into the phone before hanging up. He looked into Zachary's gray eyes, "My taxi to the dock is here."

Hunter grabbed two of the cases and Zachary grabbed the last one. The gray-eyed man struggled with carrying his one case downstairs whereas Hunter had no trouble. They loaded the cases into the yellow taxi. Hunter opened the back seat door and turned back to his new friend. "Stay safe."

"You too," Zachary responded.

Hunter reached into his pocket and pulled out a business card, the only thing on it was a nondescript email address. "If you ever need me, reach out." He used email because he went through burner phones too fast to hand out those numbers. Email allowed him to log in from any device, anywhere in the world.

Zachary took the card. "I will and thank you." The last couple of days had been a whirlwind of emotions; the two men came out the other side with a bond that neither of them would have thought possible after choosing the lives they did.

"No, thank you," Hunter responded in reference to their night on the balcony, his voice a hair softer than before as he felt the same emotions his new friend was feeling. The blue-eyed man sat in the taxi and closed the door.

Zachary stayed on the sidewalk as he watched the taxi pull away and drive off down the road. He wondered if he would ever see his friend again. Even if their paths never crossed again, Zachary was glad to have met Hunter. More importantly, he was glad the Red Reaper drama was behind him. The gray-eyed man with brown hair was happy to get back to more simple crime fighting, dealing primarily with muggings and carjackings. Zachary was looking forward to being left alone.

*****

Zachary stared at his phone and took a deep breath before picking it up. He dialed the number and waited as the other line rang until a soft click was heard. "Hello?" a soft female voice answered.

A lump formed in the throat of the gray-eyed man. He figured this was going to be hard, but he had no idea how difficult until he heard her voice. "Hello?" the woman asked again when no one responded.

Zachary finally found himself able to respond. "Hi, mom."

The Abduction of Zachary Ombre

Life is often out of one's own control. The actions of others will always play just as important a role as one's own actions. Strangers playing with lives they have never met until the world as we know it is changed forever.

*****

It was created to hide the Earth, an oasis in the middle of a vast desert of space. It protected not just humans, but various powerful objects and weaponry that ended their galactic journey on the blue marble. It worked as intended, keeping the power auras from leaking out beyond the stars and being discovered by unsavory and rather dangerous characters. However, there was an unintended consequence. The shield did not just hide the magic and power of Earth, but it also slowly weakened its inhabitants. Many magically inclined races that took up residence on the planet fled to avoid growing weaker.

There was something unique about the human race. They are a species with an unstable soul containing uneven amounts of the eight celestial base elements: Fire, Water, Stone, Air, Life, Death, Innovation, and Imagination — the latter two often referred to as Technology and Magic. The instability caused a peculiar, albeit rare, phenomenon at the moment of their untimely demise. If everything aligns, a human could evolve to survive and overcome their death, often gaining new abilities as a result.

This is what led to the formation of the Reaper corps. The first ruler of the Kingdom of the Dead, Osiris, disliked when humans evolved to master their deaths, seeing it as a violation of natural laws. He may have ignored it altogether if it were not for the newly powered humans abusing the powers they gained. Osiris disliked seeing those who should have entered his Kingdom walking on Earth and reaching havoc. He called upon one of his fellow gods, Anubis, to create an army whose purpose would be to go onto the land of the living to collect the souls that would not pass on. Anubis created the Reapers, one for each possible death that could cause an evolution moment. It was not a perfect solution and occasionally Evo-humans were able to escape the grasps of the Reapers.

When Hades took over as the third ruler of the Kingdom of the Dead, he began to worry, not just about Evo-humans but also the magical weaponry that ended up on Earth and were created by humans. It was the guidance of the Elemental Council and a visiting Archwarrior named Orion that suggested the power shield around the Earth to conceal its location. The shield was created and the magic in the world slowly began to fade. Many of the Gods and various magical races left once they felt their power fading. The humans, however, adjusted their lifestyles from magic dependent to technological advancements as fewer people were able to perform the difficult tasks of sorcery. It was not just magic that declined. Evo moments became even rarer. The world changed without the vast majority of humans ever realizing it.

*****

On the Southeast coast of Italy, along the Adriatic Sea, was the small town of Cervelli. It only had a population of a couple hundred people, but this town had a secret. In the center of the town was a large, ornate, square building, made of pale yellow and white bricks. There was a circular bell tower on the ocean side. This was the headquarters for the governing body of the Dark Arts Collective and Depository.

The interior was deceptively larger than the exterior would suggest. The biggest room in the building was mostly empty. Full suits of armor, from different eras and countries around the world, lined the walls. A long, red and black carpet ran down the center. There was a large wooden double door with a rounded peak at the south and an elevated stage at the north end of the room with two more smaller matching doors on either side.

On the stage, there were two large, wooden chairs covered in silk robes and luxury pillows. The larger of the two chairs was front and center while the other was pushed back and off to the left. A row of armored guards with swords and crossbows stood at the back of the stage. "I am not sure about this brother," the woman in the smaller chair spoke in Italian. Her name was Vittoria Sapienti and unlike her brother, she carried no title. The 26-year-old woman had medium-length brown hair and soft blue eyes. Vittoria was wearing a long, pale blue dress with white silk trim. The dress was large, fluffy, and excessive, not at all her style.

Standing on her right side was her personal servant and bodyguard, Guerino. The green-eyed man with short black hair had no last name. He was found as a child and trained to serve and protect Vittoria. His clothing matched in color, but was more form fitting, designed to protect him in battle. Geurino had a small sword and hatchet attached on opposite sides on his hips.

"It's not your decision to make," the brown-haired 30-year-old man in the large chair responded in the same language, keeping his blue eyes forward towards the large wooden door. "And you are to refer to me by my title. Do not forget your place, Vittoria," he snapped at his sister. He was dressed in dark olive drab clothes with silver accent buttons and epaulets, along with a slew of unearned medals on his chest. His wardrobe matched his personality: a childish wanna-be dictator.

"My apologies, Duke," Vittoria corrected herself, lowering her head slightly. Guerino had to bite his tongue, he disliked it when her brother disrespected her, but he had no authority to stop him.

"I know what I am doing." The man in the larger chair was Enzo Sapienti who went by the self-given title the Duke of the Dark Arts.

The Sapienti Family had been in control of the Dark Arts Collective for the last five generations. With each new leader, a new title is chosen. Their parents ruled as the King and Queen before they passed away and the responsibility of leadership was passed to Enzo.

The Dark Arts Collective and Depository was like a magical bank. Originally created as a way to use a cursed items' magical abilities without the consequences that followed thereafter because the room filtered away the negative. Eventually, those looking to access the spell fuel to increase their magical power set wanted in but without any cursed items to give up, they offered either their natural abilities first or monetary wealth instead. There was a room next to the main vault room where sorcerers, wizards, and magicians could transfer their intrinsic power into the room and in return they were given a talisman that allowed them to access the magic inside the vault. Since then, a near thousand magic users would surrender their intrinsic magical ability along with all magical and cursed items to the Collective in exchange for unlimited use of the power deposits. It was a technique that the less magically inclined used to advance their power. The Dark Arts, and other similar groups, grew in popularity as naturally magic abilities began to fade over the years from the magical barrier that surrounded the Earth.

A bald man entered the room from the door on the right side of the stage. Quinto Bonomo was the head assistant to the Duke of the Dark Arts. The brown-eyed man had served at the end of the King and Queen's reign and continued his servitude once the new regime took over. The Bonomo Family had served the Sapientis ever since the first leader of the collective. "My lord, our guests have arrived," he said softly into Enzo's ear. Quinto was wearing a dark olive drab high-color overcoat that stopped around the knees of his matching pants.

"Please, brother. Think of the potential consequences," Vittoria desperately pleaded once more.

Quinto glared back at her for her burst of insubordination. Enzo exhaled in annoyed disdain. "If you are going to continue in this manner, I will have you dismissed," her brother responded. The only reason his younger sister sat on the stage was because of a request by their parents to have her lead beside him, simply because they did not trust his maturity level. Of course, he held all the power and rarely listened or confided in her. "Let them in," he commanded his assistant.

Quinto nodded in response before taking a small bronze-colored bell from his waist. The bald man rang it and a soft golden light surrounded it. The sound triggered the large door on the south end to open on its own. Three people entered. Leading the way was Melanie Kane, dressed in a stylish white blouse, black pencil skirt, and top-of-the-line black heels with crimson colored outsoles. Her bright red hair was pulled back into a tight bun, her hazel blue eyes were behind a pair of black cat-eye style glasses, and a touch screen tablet was in her left hand. Melanie walked with purpose and confidence.

Following behind her was a man in a black leather jacket with dark blue jeans and a black goatee. He was a hired gun Melanie used to help her transport her boss, or more accurately, her boss' vessel.

Lastly, there was a man strapped to a wooden chair with wheels and a burlap sack over his head. He was a well-dressed man in a black and green suit named Maxwell, although Melanie could not care less who he was. He pleaded weakly under his breath for mercy in Greek; he wished to be freed from the torturous hell he was enduring. His palms faced upwards and the left arm sleeve was rolled up to just before his elbow. The serious looking redhead and her entourage stopped 20 feet from the stage. "Good evening, Duke," Melanie spoke in Italian. She spoke 45 languages fluently and could understand or read another 15. "It is an honor to be in your presence," she lied in the name of diplomacy. "I am Melanie Kane, liaison for Mr. Bogman."

"Ms. Kane, I was under the impression your boss would be present," Enzo responded.

The redheaded woman flashed a fake smile. "He will be with us momentarily." She turned her attention to the man in the black jacket. "Prepare for arrival."

With that, the mercenary grabbed a sedative from a pouch on his belt. He uncapped the syringe and moved Maxwell's rolled up sleeve past the elbow, giving him access to his vein. Unfortunately, the captive man knew what was coming next. Adrenaline from fear kicked in as felt the needle pierce his skin. "No, please stop, don't. NO! NO! NO!" Maxwell begged in his native language as he fought against the restraints in vain. His pleading became quieter and weaker as the strong sedative caused him to drift off to a forced sleep.

Everyone in the room watched the sleeping man in the chair as they waited. Then, his head went from slouched to upright, menacing, frightening, dark green eyes glowed through the tan burlap sack. He was awake, but it was no longer Maxwell; he had been possessed. Normally, possession is easily tracked. Magical safeguards and spells had been set up to make it difficult to hide the unholy act and allow those who specialize in exorcisms to find the victims. When a person is possessed, Reapers are alerted and able to track the perpetrator and send them back to the afterlife. However, it is much harder to detect if a sleepwalker is possessed. Their body's ability to function via subconscious thought made them ideal hosts for those looking to complete a full take over which is why Melanie's boss had multiple abducted sleepwalker vessels that he had stashed all over the world in various major cities. "Mel, dear, do you mind releasing me?" the possessed Maxwell said in Italian with a calm confidence.

"Yes, Mr. Bogman," Melanie responded as she unlocked the restraints with the tablet.

This spector was no ordinary ghost. His name was Mancellous Bogman, a man feared just as much dead as when he was alive. When he walked the Earth in his own body, he was renowned for his expertise in fear magic. The metal locks clicked and the restraints opened. Mancellous stood slowly. He removed his sack from his head, presenting a wide, sinister smile that matched the intensity of his glowing dark green eyes. He ran his fingers through his vessels long-black hair while staring down Enzo. "Why if it isn't the Duke of the Dark Arts. To what do I owe this pleasure?" he asked sarcastically in Italian. Before Enzo could respond, Mancellous held up a finger. "Well hello there beautiful, apologize that you have to stare upon this ugly mug. I can leave the sack on if you prefer." His offer to Vittoria was genuine. Despite Maxwell being an objectively attractive man with a square jaw and piercing blue eyes, it was not the face Mancellous fell in love with when he looked in the lake he grew up next too. Guerino took an instinctive step forward to protect Vittoria. Mancellous' grin shifted from deviant to condescending arrogance. "Calm down, tough guy, I don't bite...too hard," he said to the armed man before winking at Vittoria. Guerino took a step back but kept a hand on his hatchet.

"Mr. Bogman," Enzo interrupted, annoyed that he was losing control of the room. "If we could get to business."

Mancellous tilted his head to the Duke of the Dark Arts. "And what business would that be?" The fear sorcerer had no respect for the organization that sought his help. He saw it as a futile attempt for weaker magic users to increase their power.

Enzo cleared his throat. "We need you to bring someone back from the Kingdom of the Dead."

"Interesting. You want to break a cardinal rule? Not enough juice in the safe to do it yourself?"

"It's not a matter of power. We need it done without Reapers showing once the deed is done," Enzo explained.

"So you were hoping I knew how to schedule a breakout without alerting the guards?" Mancellous interrupted with a smile. "I may have a few tricks and ideas. All depends, who are we bringing back?"

"I cannot say," Enzo responded.

The grin turned from cocky to annoyed. "And why not? Don't tell me it's that arrogant asshole Arios Pearl. I heard rumors you struck a deal with his war dogs. I will not help bring that ego maniac wanna-be-god back."

While the Duke of Dark Arts had made a deal with the Knights of Arios Peal for protection, Enzo had no interest in resurrecting him. It was strictly a deal for protection. The leader of the Knights of Arios Pearl was also in no hurry to revive his boss and surrender the power he had become adjusted to. "No, I assure, on my honor, this has nothing to do with Arios Pearl."

Mancellous had little stock in Enzo's honor. "Then why the secrecy?"

"It's because 'the who' does not matter," the blue-eyed man in the chair responded, trying to assert power.

The possessed man with glowing dark green eyes laughed condescendingly. "If I don't know who, then how am I supposed to find them? Guide them to their vessel? Am I just to guess and hope for the best?"

"A vessel will not be necessary. We do not want a possession, but a full resurrection in the original body," Enzo explained.

"And you have the original body?" Mancellous asked condescendingly, as if he did not believe the Duke had it in his possession.

"Yes, we have the original body of the person we wish revived," the Duke of Dark Arts replied, annoyed with Mancellous and his tone.

"I see. A corpse definitely changes some plans. See what happens when you share?" the fear sorcerer teased with a toothy smile as he began to confidently pace in front of the stage.

"Not a corpse, exactly," The Duke of the Dark Arts interrupted, causing Mancellous to stop and stare at the seated man. "It's a skeleton."

The possessed man raised an eyebrow. "A skeleton? Now that is an interesting challenge. I'll do it. Now let us talk about compensation. I'm thinking ... because of the delicate nature of the task ... and of course I'll have to add a fee for withholding information ... an even ten million Euros should be fair."

The large price tag was such a surprise to Quinto Bonomo that he broke his training. "That is ridiculous," he interjected.

The Duke of the Dark Arts jerked his head towards his servant and glared at him. Enzo then turned back to Mancellous. "Mr. Bogman, I'm afraid that much money is not feasible." Vittoria was relieved and hopeful that their dealing with the sorcerer was near complete. If they could not pay the dangerous fear sorcery what he wanted, then that would be the end of this cursed business proposition.

Mancellous shrugged. "Oh well, it's been fun," he said as he turned back to his chair. He stopped just short and looked over his shoulder. "Of course, we could always work something else out."

"Like what?" Enzo asked, his left eyebrow raised.

The fear sorcerer turned around. "Oh, I don't know... maybe a little fun?" he said with a wink directed towards the disgusted Vittoria. Her bodyguard took a step forward towards the unthreatened Mancellous, who just raised his eyebrows to Guerino while maintaining his grinning. "Then again, fun only goes so far to excite. How about a wager?"

His words scared Vittoria "Brother, I..." she began before being interrupted by the Duke raising his right hand with his index finger raised to stop her.

"And what would the wager be, Mr. Bogman?"

Mancellous laughed, "I heard you claim that little chair makes you invulnerable: a stew of spells and hexes to protect you from any magic attack, completely unbeatable. Put your life on the line and let me test that declaration."

Enzo glanced down at his chair without moving his head, his hands tightly gripping the armrests. The possessed man was not wrong. He had put lots of time and energy into creating a chair that could not be bested by other forms of magic. Various runes, hexes, and precious metals covered the chair made of a composite of various woods that have notorious magical backgrounds. He even had it blessed by countless religious figures. It was his passion project and he had tested it on various attacks before, but Mancellous Bogman was well known for being a trickster with a ruse up his sleeves. "You want to test it?"

“Why of course. If you’re going to claim a ship is unsinkable, I want to be the iceberg that tests that claim. Unless your keeper says no?” Mancellous added as he motioned his head towards Vittoria in a successful attempt to goad Enzo’s ego.

“I can make my own decisions,” he retorted with a mix of annoyance and anger. “You want to test what I have created. Fine. In exchange for your help, you will get one chance to best my spellwork.”

His mischievous grin widened as he watched his prey wander into his trap. “One chance is all I require.” He then clapped his hands once. “I’ll be in touch.” Mancellous sat back into the chair, the metal restraints locking him into place. “See you soon,” was the last thing he said before the dark green glow faded from his eyes and Maxwell’s head slumped back as he returned to his deep slumber. Mancellous’ spirit was gone from the room.

*****

Zombre leaned over the room as he looked out of the city of San Gwynn. He had just stopped a car thief, leaving him unconscious for the police to find. He had gotten much better at fighting since his impromptu team-up with Hunter two weeks prior. That was not the only thing that Zombre owed to his new friend. The undead hero had also reached out to his parents. They talked for hours on the phone. He told them he was safe and living in the city before promising to return home for a visit soon. Zombre emailed Hunter all about the progress he made, thanking him for the push in the right direction, and finally pledging to send him an update on the reunion: good or bad.

The air was still as Zombre listened to the subtle symphony of the city below. Embracing the silence was something he challenged himself to do more often after his chat with the man in silver and black armor. The man in the bone mask stood up straight and took a deep breath. Then he felt an ominous cold chill. "What the?" the gray-eyed man said out loud as he experienced the frigid air covering him. Zombre turned around to investigate.

Zombre was staring down a muscular red-haired man with evil glowing green eyes and a wide, devilish smile. The color was a darker, muddier green than Zombre's aura. "Well hello there kid," Mancellous Bogman said through the possessed man.

"Um, hi," Zombre responded.

"You and your sword are coming with me." He pointed with his left hand to the weapon the masked hero was holding.

Zombre sighed, he was tired of these crazies coming after him. "I'm good." He was confident he could handle this new enemy after his last two encounters.

Mancellous laughed with genuine amusement. "I'm not asking." With his arm by his side, he opened his hand so his palm was facing his opponent. A dark-green gas-like aura leaked from his fingertips, forming a ghostly translucent dark green two-headed Labrys ax. Mancellous reached back and laughed the magic weapon at his victim.

Zombre's gray eyes went wide as he watched the supernatural ax fly towards him. The masked hero rolled forward to allow the Labrys to soar over his head. Once he was back on his feet, Zombre prepared for an attack from a charging opponent, but there was no blitzing villain in his face. Instead, two glowing green spikes pierced his chest. Zombre screamed as he felt an excruciating pain in his lungs, but his healing power did not activate. The phantom spikes did no fatal damage, only caused immense agony. Attached to the stakes were chains that shined with the same eerie translucent color that led to the left hand of the sleepwalker Mancellous was possessing.

Mancellous yanked the chain back pulling Zombre off his feet towards him. He reached up and caught the masked hero by the throat with his right hand, squeezing tightly around his neck. The situation was made worse as the Labrys ax returned and slammed into the back of Zombre. He struggled to let out another intense scream as it felt as though the weapon separated his spine in two, but once again it was all pain without a wound for his power to heal. Zombre looked down at the arrogant smile of his possessed attacker. Mancellous' hand squeezed too tightly around his throat for Zombre to speak.

"Nighty night," Bogman laughed as he brought his empty left hand up to his mouth and blew air over the open palm. A dark green dust covered Zombre's mask. His vision began to blur and his mind fell to darkness.

*****

Enzo sat in his chair, his elbows on his armrest, his fingers forming a triangle in front of his mouth. He wore his usual green militant outfit. In less than a week, Mancellous Bogman had claimed to find exactly what they needed even if they did not know what that would be. Once again, Vittoria and her servant and bodyguard, Guerino, were stationed behind the Duke of the Dark Arts. "Brother," the woman with soft-blue eyes and light blue and white puffy dress began in Italian before correcting herself. "My Grace, perhaps we can convince him of another arrangement." Since her brother made the wager with the fear sorcerer, Vittoria had been trying to convince him to reconsider. Quinto would scold her whenever she tried to change Enxo's mind, but with the servant gone, she tried one last time.

Enzo did not want to hear it. He let out an exasperated exhale and looked towards the vaulted ceiling. He was tired of being badgered about endangering his life in lieu of traditional payment. "I am done discussing this."

Vittoria was going to try one last time to plead with her brother to change his mind, but before she could, Quinto opened the side door on the right side of the stage. He walked up onto the stage and took his place next to his master. "They are here, my Grace, when you are ready, of course." The bald man also believed Enzo was making a mistake by wagering his life with a madman like Mancellous, but he would never show doubt in the decisions of his ruler.

The Duke of the Dark Arts nodded as he pulled his hands apart and repositioned himself in his chair so he was sitting up straighter, hoping to give the perception of confidence and poise. "Bring them in," he spoke sternly.

Quinto moved his gaze from Enzo to the large door at the end of the room. The bald man took out his bell and rang it. The golden light returned and the wooden door creaked as it opened on its own.

As before, the redhead with the bun — Melissa Kane — led the way, followed by the mercenary who pushed the restrained, sedated Maxwell into the room. Maxwell was once again dressed formally, but this time his sleeves were all the way down. They stopped short of the stage. "Enzo, Duke of the Dark Arts, my boss will be here shortly," the woman in glasses shared in Italian. She was wearing a blue button-up blouse and black pencil skirt, identical to the one she had worn previously.

"Very good," Enzo responded.

The next moment, a dark laugh filled the large room. It was an ominous and evil noise filled with twisted joy. The green eyes emerged through the burlap sack that covered Maxwell's face. "It's good to see you again ... my grace." The last part had an added level of mockery. Melanie looked down at her tablet and unlocked the metal restraints before she was asked. The possessed man stood and removed the sack from his head and shook his black hair.

Enzo ignored his tone. "Do you have an update on your search?"

Mancellous smiled wider, "I am pleased to report that I have found exactly the item needed to bring back the desired soul into the original body."

The Duke of the Dark Arts looked around at the feet of the three guests for a chest or baggage of some kind. "And that item would be?" he asked, bothered at the feeling he was being messed with.

“In San Gwynn, of course,” he laughed as if it was a stupid question with an obvious answer.

Enzo breathed out aggressively from his nostrils. “America? Why would it be there?”

Mancellous laughed in the same way again. “Because he’s still alive. Much easier to move a corpse than a living, breathing, pissed off person.” In reality, it was to maintain stake in the situation he was intrigued by.

The Duke of the Dark Arts lets out an irate chuckle as it all became apparent. “And harder to take control if you bring it here.”

The possessed soul in Maxwell flashed a cocky smile as if to pass off the accusation as preposterous. “Please, would I do something that...dishonest and deceitful?” he asked rhetorically, for in reality, he was very dishonest and deceitful. Breaking a rule with such a heavy penalty was too much of a risk for a low-level player like Enzo, there had to be someone else pulling the strings, someone powerful enough to not fear the wrath of the King of the Dead and that person made the risk worthwhile for Mancellous. He wanted a larger stake in the plan and if that meant hijacking control, then so be it.

The man with short brown hair in the large chair shook his head from the left to right in defeat. There was no point in arguing with the arrogant ghost before him. “Fine, so how do we proceed?”

“Well, I think the most logical next step would be for me to take your mystery cadaver to sunny San Gwynn. If your employer wishes to join, I would make accommodations.” His smile was that victory.

“My employer?” Enzo tried to act shocked.

"Please kid, you are playing above your weight class on this one. I don't need to read dreams when it is so obvious you work for another." Mancellous laughed. He was referring to one of his more well-known spells where he would slip into the dreams of those with information he wanted and use nightmares to ascertain what he desired to know.

The blue-eyed man was unsure of what his next move should be. He sat there in silence for so long that Quinto interjected to break the silence. "Sir?"

Enzo took a swallow of spit and turned his head to his assistant. "Please inform our other guest that he is needed," he whispered to his aid. The feeling of complete defeat setting in.

Vittoria wanted to interrupt again, but she knew nothing she would say would stop what had been set in motion. All she could do was watch in fear as Quinto nodded his head. "Yes, My Grace," he replied before walking across the stage behind his master and towards the door on the left of the stage to fetch the mystery employer.

Once the door closed behind the bald servant, Mancellous began his next scheme. "While we wait, why don't we settle our debt?"

"Now?" Enzo asked. "You have yet to fulfill your end of the deal and still you seek payment?"

"Actually, I have, I was only asked to find the means to revive your mystery skeleton, which I think I have done rather outstandingly. Helping your...well, soon-to-be former employer, consider that *pro bono*." He laughed.

The Duke of the Dark arts took a deep breath in preparation. "Alright, take your one shot."

"First, I want assurances that your army of Arios Pearl goons behind you won't attack me, or either of my associates, if I find fault in your mystical seat." While the fear sorcerer could not be killed — for he was already dead — he did not want to have to deal with the hassle of locating a new assistant that could track down vessels and manage his day-to-day dealings.

Enzo scowled, his brow lowered in anger at the arrogance of Mancellous. "Fine. No matter what happens, you are to be allowed to leave unharmed. Barring you only take one attempt."

"Excellent," Mancellous responded as he began to pace back-and-forth like an actor commanding center stage. "Just to be perfectly clear, as long as you are seated in that chair, you are immune to all attacks, or at least so you claim?" He stopped and glared at Enzo so his last jab hit home as intended.

The blue-eyed man took the bait. His nostrils flared in anger at being ridiculed. "Exactly, your fear magic will fail you. It is inferior to what I have created."

Mancellous chuckled as he rolled his head around, his grin never fading. Unlike Enzo, he was not easily provoked as his narcissistic ego was too strong to listen to the opinions of others. "Yes, I'm sure that's what you believe, but my fear magic is not how I will best you." Mancellous' magical expertise was the creation of magic based on the fears of others. He used what others were scared of the most to create magical spells or used nightmares to extract information from his target without them realizing it.

He turned so his back was facing the Duke of the Dark Arts. The ghost with the glowing green eyes reached up his left sleeve and removed a small throwing knife that was tapped to his wrist. Mancellos palmed the blade and turned back towards the man with short black hair. "But that won't matter to you because you are unkillable in that chair. Unless of course, you missed something."

Enzo shifted awkwardly in his throne as the anger faded. Something was wrong. Mancellous knew something that the Duke did not and it was apparent in his voice. Sweat dripped down his forehead as he watched the possessed man continue his monologue. "The one thing the magically inclined always seem to forget. Something I realized long ago. There are more dangers on Earth than just spells, hexes, and curses."

It happened quickly. A flash in midair as light reflected off flying metal. Enzo's blue eyes went wide as he stared at the large, arrogant smile of Mancellous. The man with short brown hair slowly reached up with his trembling right hand and felt cold steel and warm liquid. He confirmed his fear. Enzo heard the laughter of the maniac, but Mancellous' mouth did not move. The sinister sounds filled the dying Duke's brain as if to tease him in final moments. The laughter drowned out all other noise. Enzo did not hear Vittoria's scream nor did he notice her rush to his sides with tears falling from her soft blue eyes. All he could focus on was the possessed man who threw a knife into the center of his chest.

"As I suspected: a frivolous claim by a frivolous man," Mancellos teased.

Vittoria glared over to her brother's killer, rivers of tears causing her makeup to run. "Fuck you, you devil," she screamed.

"In due time, my dear, but first I have business with whoever hired you amateurs." Then the side door opened. Mancellous' nostrils flared just a little as he smelled formidable power walk into the room. Standing behind Quinto, who was frozen in shock at the sight of his master bleeding to death, was a tall man in a three-piece black suit, blood red tie, and slicked-back midnight black hair. Mancellous turned his head towards The Stranger, "Ah, if it isn't my new partner."

"What happened here?" the crystal blue-eyed Stranger asked as he calmly stepped past Quinto and walked up to the possessed Maxwell. When he spoke, Mancellous could see flashes of the man's silver tongue. Mancellous noticed how The Stranger's eyes seemed to swirl like clouds of a storm around his pupil. It was subtle, only noticeable up close.

"Just a wager's debt being settled is all. Standard stuff, save this time the house lost," the man with glowing green eyes said over the loud sobbing from Vittoria. "Mancellous Bogman, a man of fear quite feared." He held out his right hand in greeting.

Instead of introducing himself or accepting the handshake from the sorcerer, The Stranger looked over at Enzo, whose labored breathing worsened with each gasp for life. The Stranger had to remind himself that the ends would justify the means, to not become entwined with the troubles of man.

Mancellous put down his hand. Normally, he would retaliate for such an embarrassment, but this man who reeked of power was given a pass. "I think it's time to move on. So, you're the one who wants to wake the dead? I will be taking care of all your needs from here on out. How many are we bringing back again?" he asked, even though he did forget the task he seized control of.

The Stranger held his head high. He was not intimidated by Mancellous' presence or reputation. The only reason The Stranger sought the help of the Duke of the Dark Arts instead of Mancellous was because of the fear sorcerer's reputation of being a wild card. It appears working with him was inevitable. "Just one."

"Good," his creepy smile impossibly grew larger. "I've been told you have a skeleton to work with, is that correct?"

"Correct," The Stranger replied.

The Stranger's short response felt like a game to Mancellous. A challenge to see if he could get him to break this stoic demeanor. "Care to share who?" he asked.

"No," The Stranger replied in a monotone voice.

Mancellous chuckled softly. "It will be a surprise then. You're going to have to bring it to San Gwynn if you want this dead man to walk amongst the living again. I trust you can move this skeleton to San Gywnn without assistance?"

"Will not be an issue."

"Wonderful." Mancellous said to The Stranger before turning his back to the dying Duke of the Dark Arts. "Pleasure doing business with you, Dukey," the fear sorcerer mocked. That was the last thing Enzo heard before his world went dark forever. The man with glowing green eyes began to walk away towards the doors. He wanted to pass the threshold in a physical form to let all those who serve the former leader of the Collective know that

Mancellous had won. Melanie Kane, The Stranger, and the hired mercenary pushing an empty chair followed him out. Mancellous looked back over his shoulder with his vile grin aimed at Vittoria. "Oh and congratulations on your promotion sweetheart." He laughed as he exited the great hall.

Vittoria was furious beyond even her own comprehension. The brown-haired woman was forced to watch her brother die in front of her for none listened to her fears and warnings. Vittoria sobbed one final time over her clenched fists. Mancellous had made a mistake that day: one that a man as arrogant as him would never consider a possibility. The sorcerer of fear had awoken a sleeping giant far more dangerous than Enzo, the former Duke of the Dark Arts, could have ever been.

*****

A sudden wave of chilling water splashed onto the face of the passed out Zachary Ombre. The cold rush caused the shocked hero to sit up suddenly as he gasped for breath but stopped before he could fully sit upright. Two sets of iron chains — one around his wrists and one around his ankles — stretched back to the red brick wall behind him. "What the?" he asked himself as he tested the chain's strength. The gray-eyed man then slowly looked up at the figure who had doused him with water.

Standing above Zachary was the same muscular red-haired man who had taken him. The glowing dark green eyes and wide devious smile made the unmasked hero uncomfortable and exposed. Mancellous tossed the empty metal bucket off to the right. He bent down to a squat so his face was inches from the chained man's. The possessed man slowly reached for the bone mask that lay on the ground next to Zachary. "I have to say. I am rightly confused." He spoke in a soft, intense whisper as he examined the faceplate of Arios Pearl. "When I heard rumors that those nutjobs tried and failed to bring back that wannabe god, I was under the impression that the person who stopped them was this grand, formidable hero of legend." Mancellous had gotten this notion from the nightmares of the few zealots who witnessed and survived the battle between Zombre and Arios Pearl. In their minds, the undead hero was a force like no other. "So I searched for you, keeping tabs here and there. Then when the opportunity arose to test your skills myself, I was looking forward to the challenge. Least to say, you disappointed." The muddy green glow from his eyes reached out like tentacles touching Zachary's face. The gray-eyed man shuddered in disgust. "The good news is you can now make it up to me. You helped me once by preventing that obnoxious maniac and once again you are graced with the opportunity to assist me."

"Fuck off. I'm not helping you," Zachary responded with gritted teeth. His skin was beginning to feel itchy as he was away from his Sica.

Mancellous began to laugh. He found it genuinely humorous that Zachary thought he had a choice. The possessed man tossed the mask down onto the ground, stood, and walked across from his chained captive to The Stranger. Zachary looked out to the rest of the room. On the right side of the room was an old, rusted hospital bed with a torn-up, faded pale green mattress positioned at 60° angle. On the mattress was a human skeleton placed in anatomical order. The bones had a yellow color to them because of their age. In front of the mattress was a cheap folding table with a dark brown top. Zachary's curved Sica sat on the table with a large wooden box designed with a gold latch and polynesian pattern on one end of the blade and a black cloth robe on the other side.

The Stranger, who stood behind the table, shifted his gaze from Zachary to Mancellous. He did not trust the ghost within the possessed man. "Is there a reason you have him here?"

"A crucial ingredient if you want it done right," Mancellous explained. "Now, care to share who it is we are returning to the land of the living? Or what's in here?" he asked as he reached for the wooden box."

The man with slicked back hair placed his hand on the chest, stopping the fear sorcerer's hand from approaching any farther. The Stranger changed the subject, not wanting to share the information Mancellous desired. "How about we begin instead?"

"Straight to business, I can appreciate that." Mancellous replied as he walked around it and the old mattress. "To accomplish your desires, we will use the magic of a former acquaintance of mine. While I found her magic archaic and chaotic, I must begrudgingly admit this is adequate work. Though it was created when someone destroyed her monster," the fear sorcerer mused to himself, feeding his natural need to command attention. He noticed that The Stranger had no care for his lore. "But I digress, the sword struggles when it must resurrect from bare bones. It can, but it's more effective when repairing flesh and blood. Keeping the user from dying from their injuries, hence why it's called the Sword of the Undead. That's why we need some special ingredients." Mancellous pointed with two fingers towards the chained-up

Zachary Ombre. A dark green tube-shaped aura emerged from his hands and snaked mid-air towards the gray-eyed hero.

Zachary desperately crawled backwards until he felt his back hit the coarse brick wall behind him. He began to panic as he watched it work its way towards him. It seemed to stop a foot away from him, bobbing midair as if it was looking for the most painful place to pierce him, then stuck quickly like a snake into the gut of Zachary. "Ow fuck!" he screamed. The gray-eyed man looked down at his gut and watched as his blood traveled up the tube with decent speed.

Mancellous walked over to the hospital bed, continuing to create the magical pipe, setting it to end with three exits: two above the skeleton's shoulders and one above the aged skull. Zachary desperately reached for the blood siphon, but the chains restricted his reach, keeping his outstretched fingers just short of being able to touch the tub that pierced his gut.

The liquid red life poured onto the mattress and worked its way down the bones, covering every inch. The blood began to drip from the bed and onto the floor below. Mancellous picked up Zachary's Sica — the Sword of the Undead — and his grin turned from devious to excited. The possessed man placed the sword onto the blood-covered ribcage. Instantly, a green aura leaked from the blade and began to wrap itself around the body. The bones began to shift and shake as they moved closer to one another. The blood stopped cascading down onto the floor as veins, nerves, and muscles began forming around the aged bones. Darkness began to take over

Zachary as he became dizzy from the loss of blood. His head nodded forward and he could no longer keep his shoulders off the ground. Zachary gave in and collapsed to the ground, dead.

Neither of the other two men in the room noticed the passing of the gray-eyed hero. Mancellous and The Stranger watched as the green aura mixed with the bright red blood and muscle. "That should be plenty of starting material," the possessed man said as he stopped the flow from Zachary's body. He waved his hand in the air and the dark green pipe moved away from the mattress and disbanded over Zachary, the blood that was trapped inside splashing onto the concrete.

Skin and black hair formed around the muscles revealing the identity of the skeleton. The one that got away, the one The Stranger hand-picked for his mission, a man no other than JD Brooks.

While they never crossed paths in the afterlife, Mancellous recognized him from New Marris media coverage. It was a hobby of his to follow macabre news. The possessed man was curious why The Stranger would bring back a normal human serial killer. Mancellous walked back around the table and watched. His job was done, now he was going to let the answers to his questions reveal themselves.

For the first time in decades, breath filled the lungs of JD Brooks. The naked man with black hair looked around the room in panic as he tried to piece together what was going on. Then he laid his green eyes onto the man he despised almost as much as he hated his own father: The Stranger. "You?" JD grabbed the Sword of the Undead off of his chest and stepped off the titled mattress into the puddle of Zachary's blood. It was then he noticed the bleeding deceased man chained to the brick wall.

"Hey kid. Long time," The Stranger responded, bringing JD's attention back to the men behind the table.

JD looked over towards the redhead with the glowing green eyes. "And who is this? Another fool you've tricked?"

Mancellous laughed once. "I am no man's fool but my own," he began as he picked up the black robe and tossed it towards the armed, naked man. "Just the one with the means to bring you back properly, Mancellous Bogman." He held out his hand for a hand shake.

JD put on the robe, switching the sword from hand-to-hand so he did not have to let go of the weapon. "So why bring me back?" he asked The Stranger as he tied the garment belt and ignored the fear sorcerer's outstretched hand.

The Stranger shifted his weight and glanced over at Mancellous — who had put his hand down by now. He wished this conversation could happen in the absence of prying ears. "To help you realize your potential."

"My potential?" JD interrupted with a scoff. "Was I not enough of a monster for you? Cause believe me, everyone else would disagree. Do you know what I've been through?" he asked rhetorically. "I was forced into isolation because everyone I had ever known despised what I had become, what I had done. My love, my sister, even the people who tortured me in life looked down upon me in death. What potential is there left to gain?"

The Stranger took a step forward, placing his hand onto the large brown box with red patterns. "I had to prepare you for this. Trials like no other to remove doubt and uncertainty from your mind and show you how to act without hesitation." The stormy blue-eyed man unlocked the golden latch and opened the box.

Mancellous' nose and eyes twitched as he smelled the power that was just unlocked. It carried the same scent as the Sword of the Undead, as the same magic was used to create it. Inside the box was an old red cloth wrapped around the object. The Stranger began to reveal what the fabric was hiding: a Roman Gladius with a 25-inch, black blade and black leather handle. The possessed man recognized it as the Black Flame Sword. Another weapon his former colleague and betrayer indirectly created. "All this for a stupid sword?" JD asked.

"Not just any sword. A weapon that will make you unstoppable in all that you do. My gift to you now that you are ready," The Stranger explained as he held the sword out on the cloth for the black-haired man in the robe to take.

JD began to scowl as anger filled his mind. "What makes you think I want anything from you?" he screamed as he slammed the Sica into the table, sticking the blade into the wooden top.

"Because it will help you achieve everything you want," The Stranger added. He spoke more of himself than the man he offered the power too.

JD looked down at the black sword contemplating if the man with the blue eyes was speaking the truth or if it was all another trick. "Do you want to know what I want?" he asked, not taking his eyes off the dark metal of the sword.

"What do you want?" The Stranger asked, hoping he was finally getting JD to at least partially trust him again.

"I want to destroy everything that made me the monster I am. I want to rid the world of the curse that is weakening humans and stopping them from evolving. I want to destroy the shield around Earth." He looked up with fiery intensity into the crystal blue storm eyes of The Stranger. Ever since JD learned of the energy barrier surrounding Earth, he became convinced that if it did not exist then Lily, his older sister, would have survived that dark day by the river bank. That she would have evolved to conquer death.

Mancellous' ears perked up at the reference to the shield. If it was destroyed, then his power would return to the level it was before the creation of the planetary defense. He held his excitement and watched patiently. "The Black Flame Sword can help you achieve that goal. As can I," The Stranger responded.

JD looked for signs of deceit on The Stranger's face and while he saw none, he still was hesitant to fully accept the blue-eyed man for his word. After a moment of consideration, he was certain as to what he wanted to do. JD reached for the Black Flame Sword. As soon as he wrapped his right hand around the hilt, he felt a wave of sensational energy run up his spine. It was exhilarating and like nothing he had ever felt before. JD felt its weight in his right hand and smiled. It felt as if he had been reunited with a long-lost limb that he never knew he was missing until it was returned to him. The sword lit into black flame that then crawled its way up JD's sleeve, but there was no pain. It did not burn, on the contrary, it felt inviting. It covered his entire body and then dissipated into gray smoke, leaving behind black leather-like armor. JD felt like the blade was speaking to him, as if it was alive and it happily shared with him all its secrets. JD looked back to The Stranger. "Yes, you will help destroy the things that made me, but not in the way you expect."

Before the man with blue eyes could inquire about what he meant, JD reached up with his left hand and a small fireball of black flame shot out from his palm. The Stranger reacted quickly, dashing down to his left to avoid the dark fire. It crashed into the wall, sending small pieces of brick everywhere. It was not a max effort attack so the damage was minimal.

The Stranger rolled onto his back and prepared for another attack, his left leg bent and his right knee an inch above the floor. JD rushed over to attack with a strike from above. He swung downward with his blade, but he did not meet flesh. A nearly silent *shingk* sound was succeeded by the clashing of two pieces of well-forged steel. A previously-hidden, 10-inch blade attached to The Stranger's right forearm stopped the Black Flame Sword. The Stranger did not wait, he proceeded to spin on the ground and caught the front foot of JD Brooks, knocking him off balance and allowing the man with the blue-eyes to get back onto his feet. Mancellous stood back. He decided to wait back and see who won before deciding which side to take.

JD quickly got off the ground and stared down his former master. "I should have expected hidden weapons from a man such as you. You may be no devil, but you are just as evil."

The words hurt The Stranger. If only JD knew the truth; he was not evil, he was just desperate. The blue-eyed man just took a deep breath. If he fought at full strength, he could beat JD Brooks even with the assistance of the Black Flame Sword, but he did not want to kill the key to his plan's success. However, as he looked up the intensity of JD's green eyes, he was unsure if they both could walk away. "There is a lot you don't know or understand yet," The Stranger responded. "If you just calm down, I can explain your purpose in everything."

"I am through listening to your lies," JD screamed as he reignited the black flame of his weapon, his eyes lit with matching fire. In preparation for another round of fight, The Stranger revealed the rest of his weapons. Two curved blades tore free from his suit sleeves; all three connected to an elaborate mechanism on his wrist. A matching set on his left arm emerged at the same time. He could control the blades with his thoughts like extra limbs thanks to a cybernetic implant at the base of his skull that was far more advanced than anything that could be found on Earth.

JD charged at The Stranger, swinging from left and right, but every attack was blocked. JD was skilled with a blade, but he was trained by the man he was attacking. Luckily for JD, The Stranger was taking it easy, focusing more on disarming than killing. The blue-eyed man got into position and used one of the curved blades on his left arm to catch the guard of the dark Gladius, separating it from JD's right hand. The Stranger collapsed the blades on his right wrist and swung a sucker punch at the exposed jaw of his attacker. What happened next completely shocked The Stranger.

Based on all the research and stories The Stranger had read and heard, once the Black Flame Sword was removed from one's possession, they could no longer access the power. Except that did not happen. JD's entire body turned to black flame, allowing him to travel like fluid away from The Stranger's clenched hand and blades. JD reformed safely and grabbed the weapon mid-air with his offhand. Continuing his motion, he punched The Stranger in the chest with a flaming fist. The force of the blow sent the blue-eyed man onto his back. JD smiled down at his former master. He felt a rush of excitement. The feeling of becoming pure fire was nothing like he had ever felt before. Mancellous was taken aback by what he saw. A move like that with the sword out of his grasp can only be achieved by someone who was chosen by the magical weapon as its true wielder and JD had embraced that title.

The Stranger was not dead, much to the disappointment of JD Brooks. The dark flame charred his suit in a perfect circle around his chest, the now exposed skin bright red from the sudden temperature change. The blue-eyed man jumped onto his feet and once again released all the blades on his wrists. He had to change strategies now. His next best option was to kill JD and use Zachary's blade once again to bring him back, just with more precautions taken.

The two charged at each other, their weapons colliding in the air with ferocity. In his rage, JD made a tactical mistake. He swung high on the backhand and The Stranger was able to duck below the weapon and thrust one of his straight blades into the stomach of JD Brooks, but there was no blood. The man with eyes of black flame had altered the matter of his gut, replacing flesh with fire. JD elbowed The Stranger hard in the back of the head, knocking him back far enough for the black-haired man to grab him and toss him off towards the wooden table. The collision broke the table. Sending the empty box and Sica crashing off towards the deceased Zachary and stopping just a half foot short from his hand.

Before The Stranger could fully recover, JD once more turned his entire body into black flame and rushed towards the disoriented man with blue eyes. In a flash, he reached the partially standing Stranger and plunged the Black Flame Sword into his gut.

The Stranger let out a soft gasp as he felt the warm blade pierce his abdomen. He turned his head slowly and looked into the flaming black eyes of JD Brooks. "I'm sorry," The Stranger spoke softly, a small trail of blood starting to leak from the corner of his mouth. "There was no other way. It was the only way, but I guess that does not matter now." The realization that all the atrocities he had committed since he arrived on Earth were for naught. His legs became weak, no longer able to sustain his body weight because of the blood loss. When he collapsed, JD pulled the black blade from The Stranger's stomach. The man with storm-esque crystal blue eyes stared at the tip of the weapon, watching his blood drip off of it. "I am sorry." This apology — unlike the previous — was not directed towards JD. His final words of regret were for a man who could not hear them. It was for the man The Stranger was traveling the universe searching for, making unsavory deals just for a potential clue that could help The Stranger find him. His final words were for his father.

JD watched The Stranger finish his descent to the ground and turned his eyes towards Mancellous Bogman, whose smile remained steadfast. Light smoke began to waft off the black blade from boiled blood as JD heated up his weapon for another attack. Mancellous held up his left hand. "Calm down there, kid. I think we can help each other."

"I have no interest in making deals with aspiring devils," JD responded.

The possessed man laughed. "Please, the devil wishes he could be me. Besides, our interests align and I am willing to take a wager on you." JD ignited his eyes and the Black Flame Sword. "Fine, I guess you weren't actually interested in destroying the shield."

The dark fire extinguished as Mancellous' response caught JD off guard. "What do you mean?"

"To destroy the shield, you have to destroy the generator, that's located in the Kingdom of the Dead. Easier to do if you can get there alive and I know how to get you there without a death certificate," Bogman answered.

"And why would you help me?"

The smile of the possessed man seemed to grow to an impossible length. "I hate that shield almost as much as you. I know how to get rid of it, but I don't have the means." Since Mancellous was possessing people, if he tried to go to the Kingdom of the Dead with a vessel, his soul would separate from the sleepwalker he was controlling and return to its spot in the afterlife. "That's where you would come in."

JD considered it for a moment, hesitant to jump into a deal with another mysterious man he had just met. One thing he learned in death was there was always another choice and with his new life, he was eager to be more wise with his decisions. "And what do you desire in return? Servitude? Loyalty?"

Mancellous laughed deeply, his vile roar echoing off the red brick walls. "A kindred spirit who refuses to trust blindly is grand to see. No, I don't require you to serve me. As long as you follow through, we are right as rain in my book."

"Very well," JD replied, content with the answers the man with the glowing dark green eyes gave him. "So what now? How do we get to the shield?"

"Well, little known fact, Reapers are held in the same facility as the shield." Mancellous paused to judge JD's reaction, testing to see how much he actually knew of the workings of the afterlife. When he did not react, the fear sorcerer decided to keep his explanation on the simpler side. "Anyway, all you have to do is hit me with one of those fireballs and wait for a Reaper to show up. Once you see the gateway appear, do not hesitate and do not miss it. Simple!" Mancellous said as held his palms out as if he was physically presenting the idea to the man with black hair.

JD moved the sword from his right hand to his left and held up right hand with his fingers curved towards the possessed man. A small, dark fireball began to form in the center of his palm and drastically grew in size. Mancellous grinned at the man with eyes of black flame as JD reached back in preparation to throw. "See ya around, kid," Mancellous said before the dark fire raced towards him and struck him in the chest, igniting his body in a storm of black flame. His grin remained. Mancellous felt no pain. "And remember, no hesitation," he sing-songingly reminded JD one last time as his flesh began to melt away. The dark green glowing eyes disappeared, replaced with the normal brown eyes of the possessed sleepwalker. While Mancellous would have preferred to not waste his San Gwynn vessel, he saw it as the ante for his wager on JD.

The now free man's face was that of pain and horror. He mouthed screams but was unable to make noise because Mancellous had taken away his voice. All the redheaded man named Douglas could do was scream silently as he was magically locked out of his motor functions. The fear sorcerer who had been possessing him could have also taken away his ability to feel pain but left it as a cruel joke for no reason other than he could. Douglas was tortured, unable to die because of a spell that prolonged his death. JD watched in confusion as he could not tell if what he saw was genuine or a trick by a sketchy man he had just encountered.

He was about to speak to the abused soul when a sudden red glow emerged, floating in midair. The light turned to a traditional flame and spiraled as it grew larger, forming a doorway. Stepping out of the portal was a man-like creature made of glowing embers. A metal soot-covered boot hit the floor, sending ash everywhere. He was a mix of charred bone and burnt armor. The metal that was not covered in the dark residue glowed red hot. The last thing to emerge from the portal was his broken helmet that revealed his bone jaw, but still fully intact on the top of his head. Bright red glowing eyes stared into the room. A heat vapor poured off his body since it was warmer than the surrounding air. This was the Reaper of burning to death.

JD saw his opportunity. He turned his entire body into black flame and zipped past the Reaper into the portal behind him. The creature swiped at JD's fire form with his gauntlet covered right hand but missed. JD escaped into the Kingdom of the Dead. The Reaper's movements were reactionary. JD was not his target. Reapers, by intention, were one-minded; their goal was to collect souls that did not pass over naturally. They could not be bribed, could not be bargained with, and they had no sympathy for who they were sent for because they could not remember what they were before they became Reapers. All they had to do was touch a person to collect their soul and send it to the afterlife. If someone desired to stay on Earth beyond their death, they would have to survive an encounter with a Reaper by either beating it in combat or running away fast enough.

The Reaper of burning turned back to Douglas, who silently begged for his suffering to end. He walked over and reached out slowly for his burning shoulder with his left hand. As soon as its bony fingertip touched the torched flesh, Douglas was freed. His still flaming body fell to the ground and his soul passed on to the Kingdom of Dead. With his job done, the Reaper turned back and walked towards his portal to return, unaware of the role he had just played in changing the world forever.

*****

It only took a few moments for Douglas' body to burn to ash. Even though the building was abandoned and the neighboring buildings were empty on Saturday, the smell still traveled far enough for someone to call the authorities; the faint trail of smoke alerted them as to where to go. Sirens wailed in the distance as Guerino broke into the room. He followed them to San Gwynn and was tracking them down ever since he arrived. One of the skills he was taught after being found as a small child was how to track people and animals in numerous surroundings, including major cities.

He was taken aback by the high temperature of the room and the smell of burnt flesh. There were only two bodies. The ash that used to be Douglas and Zachary Ombre. The man with short black hair walked across the room and knelt down next to the man chained to the wall. He looked over the body and then the Roman Sica that lay next to him. Guerino pulled out a burner phone and hit the first speed dial. He was severely limited on how much access he had to the magic reserves because of his status as a found servant. The phone rang twice before the other side answered. "What did you find?" Vittoria asked.

"There is a sword, a weird bone mask, and two bodies: one burnt to a crisp and the other sliced open. The burnt body has remnants of Mancellous' power signature: it must have been a vessel. No sign of Bogman or our former employer." Neither Vittoria nor Guerino knew The Stranger's real name; he shared it with Enzo but the late Duke refused to pass it on, concluding it as need-to-know information. "The other body and the sword have a connected aura," he relayed into the phone. Years of training and a spell placed on his eyes by Vittoria's parents gave Guerino the ability to recognize magical signatures.

"Bring me back the sword and its connected body, along with the mask as well. Leave the vessel," Vittoria commanded over the phone.

"Yes, Your Majesty," he replied before hanging up. The green-eyed man picked up the Sword of the Undead and the bone mask of Arios Pearl and placed both into the satchel wrapped around his waist. Guerino took out his hatchet and chopped at the chain. Once Zachary was freed, Guerino picked up his dead body. He looked out the window and saw a sudden flash of pale purple light appearing in the night sky. 'Strange,' Guerino thought before he escaped the room as the first wave of the authorities arrived on the scene to investigate.

The Wrath of Black Flame

What happens when someone is in the presence of something they obsessed over for decades? Finally able to follow through with their dream? When the time comes for the final act, can they complete the mission to bring about the new world they envisioned?

*****

JD Brooks stood in the room that held the shield's power source. The technology was far more advanced than anything on Earth. He stood before the grand machine and listened to it hum as its center spun. A pale purple light shined from the core towards a hole in the ceiling. The black-haired man knew very little about the machine's origins. While many mysteries of the world were revealed to him when he crossed over; the shield was kept a secret. It took countless hours of covert research to uncover the little information he did know. However, now that he was finally in the presence of the machine that he blamed for sending him down the wrong path, it did not matter to him how it worked or what it was meant to do. He saw it as a monstrosity to mankind and he would free them by destroying it.

JD was surprised there was no security. He had wandered the empty white halls passing closed doors, each labeled for a different Reaper. Now he was in the room with the shield's generator, he could not help but wonder if it was all really going to be this easy: an afterlife of fantasies all about to be realized.

Just then, a figure entered from a side room where the controls were monitored. "What the?" the figure in silver armor with green and burgundy painted accents on his legs and arms said in a robotic voice. He was the guardian of the shield, half-man and half-machine who spent his days maintaining and repairing the impressive instrument. He went by the name Cy-turion — for Cybernetic Senturion — or Cy for short. "Who are you? You're not supposed to be here." With his chrome-reflective visor, he was able to scan JD and noticed his heartbeat. There were only a handful that had a pulse in the Kingdom of the Dead and Cy-turion knew all of them. He did not know JD.

"I am exactly where I am supposed to be," the man in black armor responded before launching an attack of dark fire at the guardian of the shield.

Cy-turion's left forearm opened and from it formed a round, burgundy forcefield to block the fire attack. JD charged by turning himself into black flame. He thought for a moment he had the upper hand on his half-robot foe, but was shocked to learn the contrary. Cy-turion guarded himself against a blade attack from JD and then removed a high-energy blaster that blended in with his upper leg and hip armor so well that the black-haired man did not notice the weapon until it was revealed. Cy fired twice at JD, but failed to hit the fast-moving target.

JD tried another long-distance attack by jumping back for a moment. He threw two more fireballs at the metal man before rushing in again. Cy blocked the dark projectiles with his shield and was still able to catch JD's sword with his defenses, allowing him to fire point blank into the gut of his attacker. The energy beam passed through the fire torso and exploded against the wall. JD pushed Cy-turion off and swung his sword and flame, but each attack was blocked by powerful defenses.

The man with flaming black eyes had to figure out a way to get around the guardian's forcefield. He turned back into flame and raced through the legs of the man of multi-colored armor and quickly reformed behind him. JD thrusted his weapon at the Cy's back, but his steel did not hit the metal armor. The forcefield hummed as it absorbed the tip of the blade. Cy-turion had spun his entire upper body around to face JD and defend himself.

Cy pushed JD's hands up and jumped into the air, allowing him to right his legs while attempting a flying kick to the head of the dark-haired man. JD moved back to avoid the strike. With space between them and JD on his heels, Cy-turion shot a rope-like projectile from his upper wrist on his right arm. It wrapped around the Black Flame Sword and the hand of its wielder before delivering a high-powered energy shock. JD screamed in pain as he felt the electricity course through his body, which flickered like a dying candle's flame. Cy took the opportunity to pull the sword away from JD's grip, sending the weapon flying behind the half-robot man.

Thinking quickly to prevent his opponent from taking the upper hand, JD expelled fire from his left hand. A continuous stream of dark black rushed towards Cy who raised his shield in defense. Cy-turion could feel the intense heat through his insulated armor; his sensors were partially affected by the increased temperature. It was now a battle of endurance: Cy's force field strength versus JD Brook's ability to maintain the flame's intensity. The man of metal was confident his technology would hold out and outlast his competition. He would have been correct if not for the Black Flame Sword plunging into his upper back.

Cy could not see around the flame that crashed into his defenses; if he had been able to, he would have seen JD moving his right hand. This would have warned him that his attacker was manipulating his weapon, that the Black Flame Sword was flying towards his undefended backside. While it would have been difficult to defend himself from attacks, it would have been possible.

With the blade in his opponent's back, JD stopped the barrage of fire, turned into black fire, and reemerged behind Cy-turion. The black-haired man grabbed his sword and pulled the blade down the length of the metal spine. A combination of metal, blood, and oil fell to the floor with Cy following shortly after.

With the guardian defeated, JD turned back to the machine. He would delay his revenge no longer. The man with black hair took a deep breath and prepared his mind and body for what would follow. He let out an anguished scream and fired two streams of dark fire from his hands. The flames crashed against the generator's force field, making a loud sizzling sound as the internal cooling system was overloaded. The power barrier sputtered and shut off, allowing the powerful attack of continuous flame to hit the shield's generator at its core.

Alarms sounded as the core began to overheat. Soft white smoke wafted off of JD Brooks as he pushed himself to his physical limit and beyond. He did not care if he died as long as he completed what he set out to accomplish. JD screamed as a bright, pale purple light filled the room, engulfing the black haired man and his dark flame before a deafening explosion rocked the Kingdom of the Dead. The shield that surrounded Earth was destroyed. A new age of humanity would begin as the world began its metamorphosis.

*****

JD awoke on the ground surrounded by tall green grass. The sudden failure of the generator created a vacuum-like effect, pulling JD and the fatally wounded Cy into the portal in the ceiling and dispensed them back on Earth. The black-haired man landed in southern Nebraska while Cy-turion crashed into a mountain range in southeastern Canada near the city of Marcheur.

*****

Pitch-black smoke bellowed up into the evening sky. JD's unforgiving green eyes stared upon the dark cloud he created as small figures below struggled to put out the burning house. It was once where JD grew up. The place where happy memories were soiled by bruises and blood. His childhood home had been vacant when he returned to his unholy ground. After his parents passed away, there were no heirs to inherit the house. Members of the community decided to purchase the house with the intention to preserve it as a monument to Winston and Elizebeth Brooks and their role as pillars of the small-town community. However, they struggled with how best to honor the myth without acknowledging their horrid acts their son, JD, committed. After a few generations of town council elections, the house just became a place for additional storage, gradually falling into disrepair.

JD had started in his old room which was now full of well-used folding chairs. The off-white paint chipped off the water-damaged walls. He had no anger or animosity in his heart. This was not about revenge, it was closure. With JD's weapon holstered on his hip, his eyes and hands ignited into black flame. He gently touched a section of unsoiled walls. In no time, the room was consumed with living paint made of fire. JD calmly walked out, his hand still in contact with the wall.

The black-haired man strolled through the upstairs hall, allowing his fire to transfer from his hand to the house. He stopped at the closed door of Lilian's former room. He placed his hand against the splintering wood and allowed the flame to build as it burned away the door and began to engulf the room. A single tear emerged from his fire-filled eyes.

He continued on, once again tracing the hallway walls with his flaming hands. JD reached the final room and stopped to stare at the partially open door: the master bedroom where his parents slept. This room did not deserve his flame. JD moved on; covering the banister with fire as he walked down the stairs. The lower half of the house was already filled with ravenous black flame. As he heard the sirens of a fire truck approaching, JD snuck out the back door to escape to the neighboring mountain that he now stands on to watch the show.

Originally, JD considered cleansing the entire town of Loveland with dark fire, but this was no longer the community that turned against him in his hour of need. The old shops were replaced with national chains and fresh new businesses. The schoolhouse was torn down and rebuilt to hold more students. The only remnants of the town he used to utter vile curses towards was burning to the ground.

"Having a little bonfire?" a deep voice belly laughed behind him. JD looked back over his shoulder at the grinning man with medium-length blonde hair and ghostly dark green glowing eyes: Mancellous Bogman.

"What do you want?" JD asked as he returned his gaze back to the burning house as the fear sorcerer walked over and stood on his right.

"You impressed me. You destroyed that stupid shield and the results..." Mancellous took an exaggerated deep breath to emphasize the point he was making. "...are wonderful. There is nothing more rewarding than when a longshot pays off."

JD rolled his green eyes. "Is that all? Come to deliver congratulations? Well if that's all, I ask you to leave me be now."

Mancellous laughed again, more obnoxious than before. "I could leave now, sure. Then again... you and I have common questions that we desired answered."

"And what question would that be?"

"Why you? What made you so special that a man from beyond the stars would make you an integral part of his plan? I think together we can uncover the explanation." Bogman held out his right hand for a handshake. "What do you say, kid, partners?"

JD turned his head and glanced down at the outstretched offering of partnership. He would be lying if he said he had not wondered why The Stranger chose him. The black-haired man even wondered if his former master entered his life without him knowing, if he was there that horrid day at God's point. Once again a mystery man with power offered him help with a promise of things JD wanted. This time, however, he would not be so naive as to blindly trust. He shook the hand of the possessed man as dark smoke took its plan in the heavens. "To the beginning of a most fruitful partnership." Mancellous grinned.

Awaken

Earth embarks on a new age of man: one unlike any that had come previously. It will not take long for the laws of nature to change as new things that were never thought possible now become more than probable. A return of old magic to combine with the technological advancements that filled its place. Soon there will be heroes, gods, and villains that once fell under the guise of mythology intertwined into the lives of every human. The trials of Earth and its inhabitants have begun.

*****

His eyes opened and yet it was still dark. The air was stale. He felt groggy as if he had just woken up from a long slumber. He laid on his back and reached out with his hands, immediately hitting a coarse granite ceiling that was just inches above him. He pushed up on the cover in an attempt to free himself from the unknown enclosure. A deafening scratching noise as stone rubbed against stone burned his ears, but he continued to force the ceiling up until a blinding light leaked through the opening he created. With one final shove to the right, he pushed away the granite cover, causing it to loudly crash to the ground and break into multiple large pieces. If anyone had been there to watch him free himself, they would have been in awe of his ability to easily push away the 500-pound slab of granite. He sat up slowly as his eyes adjusted to the sudden change in brightness.

When his sight returned, he found himself in the middle of a small one-floored tomb. The stone coffin he was laying in was in the center of the room with numerous other graves belonging to forgotten family members embedded into the walls to his right and left, but their plaques were unreadable from years of erosion from the elements that leaked in through a crack in the ceiling. In front of him was a large stone door that had not been opened in decades. He had no idea who he was or why he was there. His memories were blurred and incoherent. His thoughts were filled with only confusion and questions that intensified when he looked down at his hands.

Covering his entire body was a strange two-colored material. The primary color was a dark black color like that of coal. The accent color — that covered his palms, innerarms, ran along his side, and covered parts of his face — was a bright golden yellow color. He found the material weird. It looked like he was wearing a wetsuit, but it felt indistinguishable from his own skin. When he felt the granite lid while he was enclosed in the coffin, he would have sworn he was touching it with his bare hands. He pulled at the material, watching it stretch before he let go and it slowly snapped back to its resting state. He then reached up to his face and found the same material covering his entire head, like a ski-mask without holes. It covered his mouth, but he could still easily breathe. It covered his eyes, yet he could see with no obstruction to his sight. It was as if he was buried in a full-body suit. He looked around for clues.

Nature had ravaged the inside of the stone room, destroying the writing that would have shared with him his identity. Moss, vines, and grass covered the stone walls and floor. Dust danced in the rays of light that poured in through the broken ceiling. He got out of the coffin slowly. His muscles felt sluggish like he had been laying there dormant for a long time, however, he had no idea just how long he had been in the tomb. He steadied himself while his legs got used to standing again. Once he felt confident in his lower limbs, he finally looked up at the wall that his back had been facing since he sat up.

On the walls was a message from his parents — who themselves had long since passed —that they had etched into the stone when he was laid to rest in the coffin. Words of love that he never got to read because of the rain storms that had worn away most of the letters. The original message was:

Dear God,

please guide, protect,

and love our

Archangel

But now, the message he laid his eyes upon through the material that covered his head was:

please protect,

Archangel

In the note left to him from a previous time by people who loved him — ones it pains him that he does not remember — he found purpose. A mission given to him that will guide his hand as he reemerged to walk on Earth that had been forever changed because of the actions of a planetary intruder. He shall embark on a journey not knowing it would end with him being called a hero. That did not matter to him. All he knew — and he knew it true in the deepest parts of his very being and soul — was that he was Archangel and his job was to protect those who could not defend themselves. A new dawn had emerged and the Earth had begun to activate its failsafes.

With his mission clear, he turned to free himself from the worn down tomb. Archangel put his hands on the stone door and pushed it forward until a space large enough for his hands formed. He then pushed the door out of the way and stepped into the bright light, entering the cemetery in the southeast district of the city of Erniego. Archangel was awake and he was not the only one.

The Uncertain Fate of Zachary Ombre

No one knows what lies ahead, what secrets their future holds. Many sleepless nights can be lost to the ponders of what tomorrow brings. Left alone with nothing but time and forced to focus on nothing but what fate you have been dealt can drive even the most sure-minded person down the bumpy road of insanity.

*****

Zachary Ombre opened his gray eyes. He laid on a large king-sized bed — which was equal parts stiff and comfortable — above the soft maroon and gold covers. He was dressed in the clothes he would wear as Zombre, which was the last thing he remembered wearing. The only thing that was missing was the bone mask he wore, which brought him some concern. He slowly sat up — the bed springs squeaking as he rose — and looked around the large strange room. The walls were the same deep maroon with golden accents of crown molding and wall sconces. There was a similar colored couch five feet from the end of the bed that faced a large ornate gold marble fireplace equipped with a low burning fire. 'I guess they felt the tacky intense painting over the fireplace would have been too tacky,' Zachary thought to himself, mocking the vibe the room was portraying.

He got to his feet. He felt like he was dreaming, but he knew that was impossible as he had not dreamed since the day he first died. Zachary cautiously walked around the room, trying to find clues as to where he was in the decorations. Yet the same questions kept racing through his head: 'where am I?', 'what is this place?', and 'where is my sword?'.

The door latch clicked while Zachary was by the couch. The large white wooden door creaked and moaned as it slowly opened. Zachary Ombre spun around quickly to face the person entering the room while grabbing the closest knick-knack on the table next to him — a golden, dove-shaped paperweight — in case he needed to defend himself. A bald man dressed in a black butler's suit entered. His face was bland and serious. "Now that you are awake, the King has requested your presence," he spoke in a soft, monotone voice. His eyes drifted to the weapon Zachary had chosen. "Leave the dove," he said before stepping back in a half-turn so his body was perpendicular to Zachary and lifted his right hand out to direct the gray-eyed man to leave the room and enter the hall.

Zachary cautiously followed the bald butler down the long hallway with tall ceilings that were 20 feet high. The walls were painted a forest green with black acting as an accent color. The hall was also noticeably void of windows that could have shed light on where Zachary was. They passed multiple large wooden doors, each one painted a different color. "Where am I?" Zachary asked the bald man he followed down the hall, but his question was ignored. "Not much for conversation or is it a surprise?" he joked in an attempt to get a response, but the butler strolled on in silence. Zachary rolled his gray eyes and gave up on trying to learn more about where he was, at least for the time being.

The two reached the end of the hall which concluded with two large, soft pink, tandem doors. The butler opened both simultaneously as he led Zachary into a humongous room with soft pink walls and white molding. In the dead center of the room was a medium-sized table set for two people at opposite ends. Against the walls were a series of large vases filled with colorful flowers on white marble columns. The butler stepped aside. "Take a seat. The King shall be joining you shortly," he commanded before exiting the room, closing the doors as he backpedaled into the hallway.

"Does it matter which seat I choose?" Zachary called back at the last second the doors were open as a joke before sitting in the closest chair to him.

The gray-eyed man sat there for what felt like an eternity, but was in reality just a couple of minutes, though the lack of clocks in the room prevented him from tracking how long he waited. He played with the silver cutlery, tapping them against the bright white tablecloth. Then the wall directly in front of him clicked and began to move. It was a secret door that was indistinguishable from the rest of the walls in the room. A tall man walked into the room, he wore a black pinstripe suit with a white undershirt and silver buttons and cufflinks. The thud of his shoes echoed across the room with each step he took towards the table. He looked Zachary dead in the eyes and smiled, "Mr. Zachary Ombre, it is a pleasure to finally meet you," the black-haired man with blue eyes said in a soft English accent.

"And it's nice to meet... whoever you are," Zachary replied, his tone a mix of confusion and caution.

The other man let out a soft chuckle as he arrived at the table and joined Zachary in sitting though he did not pull his seat closer instead keeping his chair three feet away. "My apologies for not introducing myself properly. I am the current ruler and King that oversees the Kingdom of the Dead. You, of course, can just call me Jack."

Zachary nodded as the other man's introduction only increased the questions in his head. "So, I'm finally dead? Like dead-dead?" he asked as he raised his left eyebrow.

The King of the Dead sighed softly as visible discomfort covered his face. "I am afraid... afraid that requires a complicated answer," he paused and watched as Zachary loaded his next question in his throat, but interrupted him before he could fire off anything. "Perhaps it is best if I offer some explanation before you ask questions freely. You are currently dead, but as long as The Sword of the Undead exists neither you nor the others who have wielded the weapon may enter my Kingdom. I considered leaving you in the void of darkness that exists between the world of the living and deceased, but instead decided to bring you here to wait out your time until you are either freed from your blade or are brought back to Earth."

"Is here... the Kingdom of the Dead?" Zachary interrupted. "Is that where I am now?"

"Yes. You are within the walls of my castle, but that hall is where you must remain until your fate is decided. I cannot have you learning of what awaits mankind in the beyond and then returning to Earth, which is why if I catch you trying to escape my castle, I will be forced to return you to the darkness."

"Is the afterlife really that bad?" Zachary asked as his mind wandered to the worst-case scenarios. "Like endless hours of dealing with stupid and irritating customers? Please tell me it's not that."

The King of the Dead let out another chuckle. He found Zachary's humor fascinating. He returned to his more serious demeanor. "Good or bad is not for me to say, but that is not why I desire to keep his secrets of death hidden from the living. I do not want this knowledge to influence their decisions in life. I do not want vile acts done in the name of my Kingdom."

After dealing with the zealots that worshiped Arios Pearl, he understood how deadset someone could be in their beliefs. Then a thought occurred to Zacahry as he remembered something the King said previously. "Wait, are the other people that used the...," he paused as he tried to recall the official name of his sword, "...undead blade...?" The King of the Dead nodded as if he was confirming Zachary was close enough to correct. "...are they here too?"

"No," Jack spoke calmly, "you are the only one I saved from the void."

"But why?"

"Of those that wielded the Sword of the Undead before you — .beyond the first — you were the only one who did not know beforehand what awaited you. The rest sought out the power of the blade that you were chosen for," the King of the Dead explained.

For a moment, a wave of relief washed over Zachary Ombre. The knowledge that maybe it was more than just bad luck that placed the blade in his hands, but instead a destiny entailing grand things made the pain and mental suffering he endured a little easier to swallow. "I was chosen," he said softly to himself. It was less of a question and more of a confirmation of what he heard. That sense of relief dissipated with the next question he asked. "Why was I chosen?"

The King of the Dead sat there for a moment as he realized his word choice was misleading. He considered allowing Zachary to continue with the misunderstanding, but it was against his beliefs to do so. In death, the truth was meant to be revealed and while not all secrets can be unveiled to Zachary, Jack decided it best to share what he can. "The Sword of the Undead — just as the other items created in the same event — was unleashed unto the world after their original users perished. It did not take long for the power and danger it possessed to become known. Eventually, it landed in the possession of a wizard named Enq. He feared what would become of the world if The Sword of the Undead was allowed to wander from master to master. He first attempted to destroy it, but found he was not powerful enough to overcome its raw magic. So instead, he used his magic to put the weapon into a dormant state and then gazed into the many possible futures of the blade until he found the perfect person to leave it with. He found you. Unfortunately, it was not because you were destined for great things, but instead you were the one it was supposed to be lost to time with. Once it was in your possession, it was never supposed to reactivate. You were chosen because of what you would not do with the Sword of the Undead."

Disappointment slowly crept over the face of the gray-eyed man. He felt a vast array of emotions filling his chest as he processed the change in reality. Sorrow, rage, and shock swirled within him until only anger fueled his inquiries. "If I was supposed to be nothing, then why did the sword 'activate'," he said with a mocking tone around the last word to ridicule Jack's nonchalant explanation of the destruction of Zachary's life. The King of the Dead hesitated with his answer which only angered Zachary more. The gray-eyed man slammed his fist into the table and screamed, "Tell me why my life was ruined!" The cutlery nearest his hand jumped into the air and clattered to the marble ground below.

"I cannot say with any certainty and I will not supply a wild guess," the King of the Dead replied with a voice that remained calm but spoke with more intensity and gusto than before to match Zachary's elevated fire. In reality, Jack was more sure than he let on about why the Sword of the Undead did not remain dormant. The arrival of The Stranger on Earth provided the spark needed to wake the weapon from its deep sleep. His actions changed the ecosystem.

Zachary broke his rage-filled stare down with the King of the Dead as tears began to form in his eyes and stream down his cheeks. He did his best to hold back sobs. Jack patiently waited for Zachary to collect himself once he had fully dealt with his emotions. After many minutes, Zachary cleared his throat and looked back up toward the King of the Dead while wiping away the tears from his face. "So now what? I just sit around here and wait for others to decide my fate?"

"It is an unfortunate situation," Jack lamented. "While you are here you will have access to a library which is full of books and media that existed before you were killed, along with the sleeping room that you woke up in and the ones you passed, and finally this hall where you collect any food or drink that you desire."

"The dead still have to eat?" Zombre interrupted with skepticalness. "Do I still have to use the bathroom too?"

A small smile returned to the face of the King of the Dead in response to Zacahry's question. "No to the latter. As for the former, it is not for survival, purely for enjoyment or to pass the time. Just request what you want from Burton, the gentleman who collected you previously. I should warn, however, that he has been instructed not to speak to you on any matters that could reveal what is happening outside these walls or on Earth." The King of the Dead sighed and began to stand. "Now, if that will be all, I will bid you goodbye for the remainder of your stay here."

"I do have one more question, if you don't mind," Zachary replied with stone-like calmness. "You said the sword was created at the same time as others. What else was created?"

The King of the Dead nodded slowly and returned to his seat. He did not fear Zachary searching out the other items if he was revived because of the Sword of the Undead's addictive nature. "I know you've already met Arios Pearl. Before he was more monster than man, he enlisted one of his soldiers to take on the task of destroying the enemy that took his kingdom from him: the Roman Empire. He had his Royal Sorcerers turn the soldier into a mindless monster designed after giants: a Beast to Destroy Rome. It was created with raw and uncontrolled magic, but it was deadly and it was sent on its way with the single goal to destroy and cripple the empire Arios Pearl hated. However, it never reached its intended target. It was stopped short when it encountered a Roman legion camp of 5,500 men strong. The Beast to Destroy Rome fell and only six soldiers survived. When their weapons came in contact with its blood, they absorbed the raw and unstable power that leaked from the man-turned-giant. One sword sliced through its liver and when that Roman soldier suffered lethal wounds, the raw power absorbed by his sword kept him alive, thus the Sword of the Undead was forever created. An arrow hit the monster's eye and became the Arrows of True Sight. The Unbreakable Shield was scratched by the beast's claws and covered with its blood. A javelin hit the lungs and could henceforth create strong winds. After one of the soldier's daggers pierced the giant's stomach the wounds from the dagger would burn like acid. The last weapon — the one that penetrated the dark heart and killed the Beast to Destroy Rome — was the Black Flame Sword. Within six months, the six soldiers all passed from the injuries they sustained and all six weapons were unleashed onto the world."

Zachary sat there in silence as he absorbed the information he was given. It was a lot to take in, but he wanted to know all of it. "So then how did Arios Pearl become the monster I met?"

"When he heard news that the Beast to Destroy Rome had failed in its mission, Arios Pearl assumed it was because the soldier was of inferior strength and intelligence. He had his sorcerers turn him into a giant next, but after his transformation he was betrayed by one of the sorcerers and destroyed before he could unleash himself onto the world. His kingdom fell, but factions formed in its wake, one of which you already dealt with: the Church of Arios Pearl," the King of the Dead added.

"Yeah, they were a lot of fun," Zachary said sarcastically.

Jack cracked a small smile. "Yes, I'm sure they were," he joked in turn. "Are all your curiosities satisfied now?"

Zachary nodded. "Thank you," he replied.

"Good, because I just remembered one last thing," the King of the Dead's voice was deeper and serious again.

"What is it?" Zachary asked, a little nervous about the sudden tone shift.

The King cleared his throat. "If you are returned to the land of the living, you will be expected to track down a man who was recently taken from my kingdom using your blade, a man named Jamie Dean Brooks. I have resources searching for him now, but if you are returned to Earth before they find him, you will be expected to do the same, to clean up your mess," he said in a dead serious tone.

"I didn't bring anyone back from the dead," Zachary replied.

"It was still your blade that was used. The one that you were supposed to keep track of," the King of the Dead responded in a cold tone.

Zachary was reminded of his encounter with the two men and the skeleton and took an uncomfortable swallow, "You know you seem pretty powerful in your own right. Why don't you go get him?"

The small smile returned to the face of the King of the Dead, "Because I am actually eight-feet tall with a flaming pumpkin for a head. What you see before you is a mirage to keep you from becoming unsettled."

"That makes sense. You wouldn't really be able to walk down the street in a subtle manner," Zachary replied.

"Precisely. If I do, however, have to come onto Earth to collect Mr. Brooks myself, I will be bringing you back as well, sword be damned," Jack threatened as his serious demeanor intensified further.

Zachary did not reply, he just nodded in confirmation. "I am glad that I am fully understood. Now, I do apologize, Mr. Ombre, but there are other matters I must attend to," the King of the Dead said as he stood and turned to exit the room. "Enjoy your stay, Mr. Ombre. I hope your fate is decided before long." Those were the last words the King of the Dead spoke to Zachary Ombre before he exited from the same hidden door entered from.

Now alone in the room, Zachary Ombre sat in silence as he contemplated what he learned from the conversation that had just concluded. The one thing he thought about more than anything else was his parents, about how he did not get to reconcile with them before he found himself in this forced state of limbo. The final thing that entered his brain before he left the grand hall to explore his new dwellings was a wish: a hope that if he ever returned to Earth, it was while his parents were still alive, even if that meant an undead Zombre once again walking amongst the living.

Made in the USA
Monee, IL
19 November 2024

70575446R00215